I0633610

The Fret Master
Fourth of the
Wallowa Lake Thrillers
By James Dobie
Published March 31, 2025

The Fret Master

James Dobie

Published by James Dobie, 2025.

THE FRET MASTER

First edition. March 31, 2025.

Copyright © 2025 James Dobie.

ISBN: 979-8987133859

Written by James Dobie.

Also by James Dobie

Watch for more at www.jamesdobiethrillers.com.

This novel is dedicated to Barbara Rowton, whose love, music, and moral support over the many years has nurtured and sustained me through both good times and bad.

James Dobie, March 30, 2025

Published Wallowa Lake Thrillers*:

The Fret Master
Angel of Oregon
The Wood Sprite
The Wailing (First of the Series)

*As of March 2025

ACCOLADES FROM REVIEWERS:

"Dobie's storytelling approach focuses on a slow, clever progression leading up to the big reveal, ensuring readers stay glued to the novel." **Readers Favorite Reviews**

"Dobie blend[s] the action with slow-burning tension ..." **Readers Favorite Reviews**

"Dobie's blend of suspense, emotional depth, and vivid setting makes this book a gripping addition to the Wallowa Lake Thrillers, offering a stark yet hopeful look at the possibility of second chances." **Readers Favorite Reviews**

Cover Art by Robert Briones

This is a work of fiction. Names, characters, places, and incidents either are the product of the author's imagination or are used fictitiously, and any resemblance to actual persons, living or dead, business establishments, events, or locales is entirely coincidental.

COVER ART BY ROBERT Briones

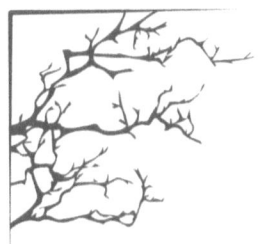

PART ONE
Chapter One

Austin, Texas

Mason Rivers woke up with the worst hangover of his entire life. For the past week, he'd partied like there was no tomorrow, but tomorrow had definitely arrived. At twenty-seven years old, he wore his shoulder-length, raven black hair in a ponytail, and had the chiseled looks of a rock star. His pale blue eyes were blurry from the drinking and drugging, the endless partying that had never seemed to end. Waking on a different couch every night, surrounded by people he didn't know or care about, had grown old fast. For the better part of a year, Mason had been lead guitar player for a popular Austin band called "Stark Naked and The Car Thieves." Then, a week ago, the other three members gave him the boot.

He knew he had no one to blame but himself. That happened when you missed rehearsals and drank yourself stupid onstage. He drank to kill the boredom of playing the same stupid songs at every gig. He considered himself a decent guitarist and had held his own with some of the better players in town. Sadly, over time, the hard partying had eroded his playing skills 'til he was damn near unemployable.

He laid much of the blame and all his frustration on the little finger of his left hand. For a lead guitarist, his pinky was extremely short, making complex chords difficult, if not impossible, to play. His little finger reached only to his ring finger's second joint—too damn short to reach across the neck of a guitar.

Cursing, he groaned and stood up. Stumbling to the bathroom, he unzipped to relieve his bladder. Finished, he zipped up and walked to the kitchen to get a drink from the faucet. He had no idea whose house he was in and didn't care. All he wanted right now was some hair-of-the-dog. Glancing at a cheap clock on the wall, he realized he'd slept past noon.

On his way out the door, he stepped over a woman on the floor. A scorching Texas sun blazed down, causing him to break a sweat. He finally located his crappy car, climbed inside, and discovered he wasn't alone. A redheaded female lay curled up on the back seat, snoring like a bear. *Shit! Another damn groupie?*

"Hey, you in the back, wake the hell up! You're in my freakin' car," he yelled at the woman, shaking her arm.

Waking, she blinked up at him through eyes the color of clover. "Hey, you're Mason Rivera from that, uh ... 'naked band' or something, right?"

"It's *Rivers*, Mason Rivers—and what the hell are you doing in my car?" he barked, irritated at her mispronunciation of his name.

"I—I was late to the party last night and everyone had already crashed. The door of this car was unlocked so ..." she stretched and sat up.

He always left his car unlocked at parties. Hell, there was nothing worth stealing inside, unless someone wanted the pile of fast-food boxes littering the floorboards.

"Well, it's time to wake up and hit the road, I have places to go and people to ... " he paused, realizing she was beautiful, with tousled, loose copper red curls, wide green eyes, a petite nose, and luscious lips. She wore a tight-fitting blue top and tight jeans that displayed her trim, petite figure. Far be it from him to alienate any potential roll in the hay, so he lightened up. "Say, what's your name, anyway?"

"It's April, April Flowers. You know, like 'April showers, bring May flowers.'"

"Well, nice to meetcha,' April. Uh, I need a drink, the keg inside is tapped out. You need a ride, or something?" He was more than ready to find the nearest bar.

"I don't have a car. I caught a ride here with Uber last night. You mind if I tag along? I don't want to be a bother, it's just that I don't have a place to stay right now."

Join the club, he thought miserably. He was between couches now himself and had slept in his car off and on for the past week. "Well, sounds like we're both in the same shitty boat. If you don't mind me asking, just how old are you?" He cocked a brow at her.

"Old enough to know you never ask a lady her age." Her emerald eyes flashed, as she crossed her arms over her breasts in a defensive posture.

Mason had doubts she was of legal drinking age but didn't push it. "Okay, okay, don't get huffy. I just don't need any trouble right now. I had to hock my damn guitar to pay last week's rent and I'm kinda between gigs at the moment, so I expect you to pay for your own booze."

He backed his beat-up Ford Fiesta out of the drive and drove to the nearest bar on Burnet Road, pulling into the parking lot of a cheesy local dive called the "Poodle Dog Lounge." A faded pink poodle holding a martini glass with an olive adorned its outside wall. He pulled up, parked next to a chopped motorcycle, and they got out, strolling inside. It took a few moments for their eyes to adjust to the dark interior.

"They keep this place darker than a well digger's ass," Mason groused, as they stumbled across feet to the crowded bar.

An ancient jukebox in the corner played an old Patsy Cline song. Four cigarette-scarred pool tables were crowded together in the back room, with racks of warped cues and no chalk. A shuffleboard ran the length of one wall, and a couple of older guys were playing. It was busy for the time of day, which spoke volumes about the lives of those who frequented the joint—the unemployed, the lonely, and those whose social lives revolved around alcohol. The barmaid today was called Brandy.

"What can I do ya' for?" She flashed an almost toothless smile. *Smokin' too much crystal,* Mason thought with disgust.

"I'll have a Bud Light myself, not sure about the lady." He took a seat on a bar stool and paid for his beer while April perched beside him.

On his left, a large, older biker sporting a red bandanna and multiple piercings gave Mason the evil eye as he checked out the hot-looking redhead next to him. This place attracted people from all walks of life. Most of the time, Mason ignored the drunk assholes who started trouble—occasionally not. This was one of those rare occasions.

While April was ordering her drink, he turned to the biker. "Is there a problem, mister?" he asked, trying to keep it polite. He wasn't much of a fighter, but he didn't take shit from anyone. Standing six feet, two inches, with a large frame, he worked out—or had, until the last few weeks.

The biker paused, assessing the man next to him, and smiled. "Nope, no problem. Admiring the scenery, is all. Just imaginin' ridin' that sweet, red-haired filly sittin' next to ya.' She looks like she could suck a golf ball through a garden hose," he leered at April.

Mason rolled his eyes at the lewd remark, gearing up for the coming battle. Ready to sucker-punch the asshole, he'd risen halfway from his stool when April interjected.

"Big bad biker dude's got a mouth on him. Ignore him, Mason, let's get out of this shit hole before there's trouble," she took his arm and guided him toward the door. Mason did a slow burn but allowed her to intercede.

"I bet yer pussy tastes sweet as cotton candy," the biker's voice followed them, trying now to provoke him.

Mason's face flushed red, and April knew a brawl was imminent. She marched over to stand in front of the dude.

He crossed his arms, glaring down at her. "What? You gonna give ol' Harley a sample of yer sweet meat?" he sneered.

Smiling seductively at the asshole, without warning, she rammed his balls halfway into his throat with her right knee. A look of surprise turned to agony as he dropped to his knees, cradling his wounded nuts.

"How do your nuts taste, *Harley*?" She cocked a fist and punched him in the nose, breaking it. She turned and strolled over to the front door, where Mason stood with his mouth open, gaping at her.

"Let's book before the cops show up or that asshole recovers." She said.

He shook his head, following her outside. "Jeez, remind me not to piss you off." He dug his keys out of his pocket.

"Guys like him are all the same, big mouth and a little dick," she scoffed.

They got in his car, and he cranked the engine. It sputtered a few times, coughed once, and died. *Shit*! Hell of a time for the crappy starter to quit.

"C'mon, c'mon, you piece of garbage," he tried twice more with the same result. The bar's front door crashed open, and Harley rushed out, blood pouring from his broken nose as he scoured the parking lot for them.

Mason locked the car doors, then realized the windows were halfway down because of the heat. The damn things wouldn't work without the engine running.

"I'd say you'd best hurry, but that would be redundant, I guess." Calmly, she dug something out of her purse.

Harley finally spied them and stalked to her side of the car. With a curse, Mason tried once more to start the car, punching the steering wheel, like that would help. The huge biker reached his left arm through her window and grabbed a handful of April's hair.

"You freakin' bitch, you broke my fuckin' nose! I'm gonna tear your boyfriend a new asshole, then I'm going to have me a taste of your—"

Her right hand whipped out fast as a snake, stabbing his forearm with a switchblade.

Old Harley howled in pain, releasing his grip on her, as he tried to extricate his wounded arm from the window.

C'mon, start, you fucker, Mason cursed silently as he turned the key. When the engine caught at last, he slammed the gearshift into reverse. The big biker toppled to the pavement in a heap. As they heard sirens approaching, Mason turned and sped up, clipping the old dude's bike and knocking it over as they hauled ass out of the parking lot.

"Why the hell'd you have to stab the asshole?" Mason heatedly asked. "All I wanted was a freakin' beer; now I've got a member of the 'Banditos' gunning for me, along with the damn cops!" He was shaking with fear and anger. He stayed on the back roads of the immediate neighborhood, trying to evade any police.

"Seemed like the logical thing to do at the time," she shrugged. Wiping the blood off the blade, she folded it, shoved it back in her purse.

He shook his head at her cavalier attitude and patent disregard for the law. He was no stranger to trouble, but he'd never crossed the line and wounded anyone in a fight. All he wanted from life was the three M's: make music, make friends, and mind his own business.

"Do you have a designation in mind, or are you just cruising around?" she smirked.

"I don't know, I'm trying to think, damn it! I should've tossed you out of my car when I found you. You're nothing but trouble, lady—and stop laughing, it's not fucking funny. I guess you know you committed a felony back there." He slowed to swerve around some dumb-ass kid on a skateboard.

"Lighten up, pal, he was harassing us both," April bit back. "I just took the initiative and taught him some manners. Who are the cops going to believe? Big bad biker dude or little ole me?" Nonchalantly, she pulled a cigarette from her purse and lit it.

Pissed at her, he lowered the windows for a minute. "Somebody could've seen you stab the bastard; he could be tellin' the cops some sob story right now. I don't *need* this shit!" he snapped, turning onto a familiar street, and speeding up.

"Uh-oh, looks like we have company," she ignored his tirade.

Mason glanced in the rearview mirror and scowled. Distracted, he hadn't noticed the police cruiser tailing him. *Crap! Where the hell did he come from?* he thought, reducing his speed.

Too late. The cop's lights came on and the officer inside motioned him to pull over. Sweating in the Ford's feeble A/C, he slowed the car to a stop and parked by the curb. The cop took his sweet time exiting his cruiser. He moseyed over to the car, and Mason lowered his window.

"Afternoon, officer, is there a problem?" he cleared his throat to ask.

Over in the passenger seat, April was giggling, infuriating him. He could've strangled her, but it would only have added to whatever charges he already faced.

"Sir, I need to see your license and registration please," the burly cop said, ignoring Mason's insipid question.

"Yes, sir, just a moment." Mason took his license out of his wallet. When he reached to open the glove compartment and retrieve his registration card, he made an unwelcome discovery. A bag of weed he'd misplaced a few parties back had the audacity to turn up now, at the worst possible moment. *Just my luck,* he thought, gritting his teeth. April glimpsed his illegal stash and in one smooth move, while he handed his license and registration through the window to the cop, she reached in and palmed it, stuffing it in her purse. Mason turned to her and mouthed, *Thanks,* as he waited for the cop to explain why he'd pulled them over.

"Mr. Rivers, I stopped you today because your left taillight is broken," the cop said. Mason let out a quiet sigh. It had nothing to do with the biker, thank God. "I'll let the taillight infraction go if you promise to get it fixed as soon as possible. However, the speed limit here is thirty; I clocked you doing forty-five. I'll have to cite you for that," the cop apprised him, handing his information back. April was doing her best not to laugh out loud. When the cop's radio crackled with a call, he walked away from them to take it.

"You know what? You're turning out to be a tremendous pain in my ass," Mason hissed, while observing the cop in his outside mirror for any change in demeanor.

"Chill out, dude, I saved your bacon twice today, and this is the thanks I get? Honestly?" She narrowed her green eyes at him.

He tore his attention away from the officer long enough to glance over at her—horrified to see her rolling a joint from his stash in plain view, as if a cop was not standing a few feet away. "Are you out of your mind? Put that shit away, now!" He grew more perturbed by the second.

She smiled and calmly finished rolling the joint. His stomach was halfway up his throat as, in his rearview, he watched the cop approach his window with a ticket for him to sign. *Shit!* Mason could only hope the cop wouldn't notice his nutty passenger.

"Please sign this, Mr. Rivers, it's not admitting guilt. You can pay the fine or challenge it in court if you so choose. Now, have a good day and drive safely." The cop handed him the ticket.

At that moment, a pungent, blue cloud of smoke floated past him and out the window into the cop's face. Mason had a panic attack on the spot. *Crazy woman!* The large patrolman slowly leaned forward, staring silently through the window at the attractive redhead toking on a joint and smiling at him. Mason adopted his best shit-eating grin, scrambling to come up with a plausible excuse for her behavior. Instead, the cop shocked him by returning her smile.

"Afternoon, April. You workin' this side of town now or did you just decide to go slumming," he asked her.

Confused, Mason glanced from cop to female. "I don't get it—you two know each other?" he asked her.

"You could say we're 'acquainted," she nodded at Mason, ignored the cop, took another toke.

The cop looked at Mason and shook his head. "Mister, a little free advice, you'd better keep one eye on your wallet and the other on this redheaded wildcat. You turn your back and she'll put a knife in it," he warned. "Speaking of, you wouldn't know anything about an incident over at the 'Dog' a little while ago involving a biker named Harley, would you?" He looked past Mason at April.

"I have no idea what you're talking about," April said. "We've been to a party, and my friend here was generous enough to give me a ride," she replied smoothly.

"Uh-huh. I'll just bet he did. Hope you used a rubber, pal, this gal has more crabs than a Port Aransas pier. I found that out the hard way," he said sourly.

"That's what you get for raping me, asshole!" She finally lost her cool, flipping him off. The big cop shot her a nasty look.

Mason didn't know what to say to any of that. He only wanted the cop to leave so he could get rid of this nut-job next to him. A moment later, he got his wish. The officer's radio crackled with an urgent-sounding incoming call.

"I gotta go. Fix the taillight—and if you're smart, dump that loco bitch before she robs you blind." He got back in his patrol car, raced off with lights flashing and siren wailing.

Mason blew out an enormous sigh of relief. Incensed, he turned to April—if that was her real name—opening his mouth to tell her to get the hell out of his car. Instead, she leaned over and kissed him hard, shoving her tongue halfway down his throat. Surprised, and irked by his lack of self-control, he responded, kissing her back.

Finally, she broke away to smile seductively at him. "You need to get laid, bud, you're wa-ay too uptight." She reached over to unzip his jeans.

Mason started to tell her to stop, that this was insane. He wasn't about to screw in his car, not in broad daylight parked on a busy residential street. Then he realized that was not her intention. Unbuckling her seatbelt, she withdrew his stiffening member from his jeans. Licking her lips, she lowered her head and took him deep in her throat with an erotic moan.

Mason didn't believe he was enjoying this. They could be caught any moment by anyone passing, but it only intensified his passion. A woman strolling by walking a dog didn't seem to notice April's bobbing head as she brought him to a swift climax.

Groaning, he clutched her by her fiery hair and came. As he released his stranglehold on her tangle of red curls, she sat up, licking her bruised red lips, grinning like the cat that ate the proverbial canary.

"Feel better now?" She cocked a brow with a grin.

"Yeah, I do, thanks for the hummer," he tucked his cock back in his pants. "How do you know that cop? He an ex-boyfriend, or something?" He zipped up before someone spotted him.

"One night about a month back he threatened to bust me for hooking. It was a fucking set-up. He knew I wasn't a whore. I was standing alone at a bus stop on South Congress; he walks up outta nowhere and propositions me. When I told him to fuck off, he turned nasty. Gave me a choice, either I screw him, or he'd bust me for prostitution. Some damn choice. With no way out, he drove me to his house nearby and we did the deed. Thankfully, he came fast. Then he drove me back to my bus stop, but he threatened me, said if I reported him, he'd make my life a living hell. It would be my word against a cop's." Fuming, she stopped there, lit another smoke.

Mason didn't know if he should believe the fiery redhead's tale. He knew people, himself included, lied all the time. "Why didn't you just kick him in the balls and run?" he asked skeptically.

She looked at him like he was nuts. "Dude, I'm a homeless person, but I enjoy my freedom, thank you very much. You don't fuck with cops like him, it's like kicking a bear and not expecting to get eaten." She was exasperated by his ignorance.

"Sorry, wasn't thinking. So, if you're homeless, where are you staying now?" he asked, starting the engine.

She glanced over with a sad smile. "Street to street, couch to couch, wherever I can find a spot safe from predators like that asshole cop. It's hard for a girl on her own. Most of the time, I can fend for myself, but it's a lonely existence." She seemed subdued, finishing her smoke, tossing it out the window.

Mason was torn, he sympathized with the young woman, but he didn't need her kind of trouble in his life. They were in similar situations right now, but at least he could crash inside his car.

"Listen, April, I'm kinda between jobs right now, so I've been living outta my damn car for the past week, and it totally sucks. I guess what I'm saying is ..." He was trying to think of a polite way to get rid of her.

"I know, I get it, you want me to go. Sorry to have screwed up your day. I have a knack for attracting assholes. You seem different ... somehow. Nice meeting you, Mason Rivers. I hope you find what you're looking for," she said, leaning over and kissing his cheek.

He felt like a complete dipshit as she smiled, opened the door, and climbed out. Suddenly, he realized she still had his bag of weed in her purse.

"H-hey, wait a minute, you have my stash!" he sputtered while she grinned playfully from the sidewalk.

"'Finders keepers,' dude. Besides, I earned it, that fucking cop would've busted your ass for possession. And for your information, BJ's aren't free, my friend," she smirked. He watched as she strode away, head held high, fine ass twitching in her skintight jeans.

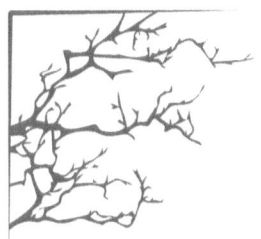

Chapter Two

"**D**amn it!" Mason exclaimed, slamming his hand against the steering wheel. She'd played him like a violin. He should've trusted his gut; he'd known she was trouble when she'd stabbed that asshole biker back at the bar. *Pretty, but dangerous,* he thought, shaking his head at his stupidity. *Well, at least she didn't take my wal—oh, shit*!

He felt in his right back pocket for his wallet, but it was gone. *Sonofabitch*, that prick of a cop had told the truth about her. He felt like the world's biggest sucker. *Well, she won't get away with it*. She'd crossed a line when she'd stolen his stash. He was livid that she had been greedy and stolen his freaking wallet to boot.

He cranked the engine, and it caught on the second try. He did a U-turn and caught up with her a block away. Pulling ahead of her and screeching to a halt, he jumped out to confront her. When he ran over to her, she turned around with a smirk on her face.

"Miss me already? Or are you here to weasel out of our little trade?" her voice was calm, but she kept a tight grip on her purse.

"Hand over my wallet!" he demanded angrily, ignoring what she'd said. "You can keep the weed, you little minx, but my wallet wasn't part of the deal." He got right in her face, with his right palm extended.

She stared at his hand for a long moment before speaking. "Did you just accuse me of stealing your stupid wallet?" She spoke softly, but her face was becoming as red as her hair.

"You and I were the only ones in the car, sweetheart, so hand it over, or so help me, I'll ..."

"You'll *what*? Beat me up? Turn me in to the cops? You're fucking pathetic," she stopped him scornfully.

He was taken aback. Either she was a smooth liar or she didn't have it.

"Here I thought you were a decent dude, but you're just like all the rest," she said with disgust. "Did you ever stop to think your precious wallet might've fallen out while I was giving you the best head of your life? No? I thought not!" With that, she opened her purse for his inspection.

He hesitated, then shot a quick glance at the meager contents. Lip gloss, a couple packages of condoms, his former bag of weed and rolling papers, a small red billfold that had seen better days, a pack of cigarettes and lighter, a small canister of pepper spray and, of course, her switchblade. No wallet. Now he felt like a total jerk.

"Want to search me?" she asked him, turning around slowly for his inspection.

He walked back to his car, rummaging through the interior until he finally found it. Wedged between the driver's seat and the console, it had been sucked into the black hole of lost french fries and loose change. *Shit!*

He crawled out, shoving it in his back pocket, and walked sheepishly back over to her. "I ... I'm so sorry I accused you of stealing it. Any way I can square this with you?" he apologized.

Still simmering, her cheeks red, she relented with a smile. "Well, I haven't had a meal in the past couple days. I could go for a burger and a shake, if you're sure you can afford it," she said, walking back to his car with him.

He grimaced, knowing he was down to his last twenty bucks. "No problem, I could eat something myself. Get in, I know just the place," he climbed into the driver's seat. His crappy car actually started on the first try. "Will miracles never cease," he grumbled.

He drove away, watching his speed, mindful of the busted taillight he'd have to get replaced as soon as possible. He sure as hell didn't need another ticket. Taking back streets again, he turned into the driveway of the "Top Notch Drive-In" on Burnet Road and pulled up next to one of their menus. The long-established burger joint had been a staple in the area for almost fifty years. Their charcoal-grilled burgers were a little taste of heaven. The place harkened back to the days when carhops on roller-skates delivered your order to your car. For safety reasons, now the orders were walked out to the cars.

"I highly recommend the 'Fiesta Burger,' it's a classic," Mason suggested.

"Anything sounds good to me. Oh, they have onion rings, wanna split some?" April had been reading the menu, salivating, as the delicious aroma of charcoal-cooked burgers wafted in through the open windows.

"Sure. What flavor shake would you like?" he asked her.

"Strawberry, of course," she said, as though it should be obvious.

With a chuckle, he placed their order through a speaker on the menu outside his window. He turned the radio on low while they waited for the food to arrive and gazed at her.

"So, want to tell me how you wound up on the street? Or should I mind my own business?"

She shrugged and lit another smoke, staring thoughtfully through the windshield before speaking. "It's a long story. Let's just say, my frickin' mother kicked me outta the house about a month back. We lived in Boulder, Colorado, until the 'Incident.'" Stopping there, she exhaled a cloud of smoke out her window.

"What kind of *incident* would get you booted out of your own house?" his interest was piqued.

She laughed cynically, nodding her head. "My mom's a cop with the Boulder PD. She ruled our house like a freakin' drill sergeant on steroids, dude. Anyway, long story short, my dad passed away about a year ago—a car accident while I was in college. I dropped out and got involved with a bad crowd," she paused. Mason waited for her to continue.

"I started doing drugs, alcohol, anything to dull the pain of losing my dad. So, one thing led to another 'til a couple of us broke into a pharmacy late one night to swipe some 'oxy.' I ended up getting busted ... by my own mother." She flashed him a wry smile.

"Whoa, what are the odds?"

"Evidently, pretty good. She pulled some strings that kept me out of the county lock-up. I received a suspended sentence, performed five hundred hours of community service, and did a stint in rehab. My incarceration began when I moved back home. No friends, no car, no phone, no anything. One day I'd had all I could take. I stole some money from her purse and used it to buy a one-way ticket to Austin. She discovered the cash missing, hit the ceiling, booted my ass out, and the rest is history."

"Wow. Sounds like you've had a rough go of it. Did your mom try to track you down?" he asked, as their food arrived.

"I'm sure she's tried, but so far, I've stayed under her radar. Living off the grid has its advantages." Hungrily, she took a huge bite of her burger.

Mason paid for the food, foregoing a tip and earning a dirty look from the young carhop.

"What about you? What's your story, bud?" she asked between chews.

He gave her a brief recap, saying he'd grown up in Austin in a lower middle-class family. His dad had been a pilot 'til poor health forced him to retire young. His mother had been a homemaker, who'd wanted to study piano but became pregnant and never had the chance. She'd spent many years caring for his ailing father until he died. She had passed several years later.

His older sister was a professional editor for a fashion magazine until she married a rich yuppie and they moved to Tahoe with their two kids. When their mother passed, he'd been shocked to find that she'd left the house and all its contents to his sister.

All he'd received in his mom's will were this crappy car and his guitar, which now hung on some pawn shop wall. His sis had sold the house, giving him a piece of the proceeds, and offered him a place to stay with her family, which he'd declined.

With some musician friends, Mason had formed the band, and things had looked promising for a good while—until last week, anyway. He'd been staying in a nearby older home, splitting the rent and groceries with the other three band members. Waking from a three-day bender, he received the bad news from Jeff, the band's bass player, who owned the house. Since that time, he'd depleted his meager savings and been living out of his car.

"Pretty shitty of them to just kick you out with no warning," she commented between bites, snatching the last delicious onion ring from its greasy container and scarfing it down.

"I guess I deserved it. We had an oral agreement that if one of us started screwing up and causing problems for the others, he'd be kicked. My problem was, I didn't realize I *had* a problem until it was too damn late." He shrugged, frowning.

"Well, at least you have a roof over your head. Try sleeping under a tree during a strong thunderstorm or freezing your ass off in winter with no blanket and a shitty cardboard box for shelter." Noisily, she sucked down the last of her shake.

"Well, this sorry excuse for a car is about to 'nickel and dime' me to death. Now, I've gotta buy a freaking taillight before another cop pulls me over. There's an AutoZone just up the road," he said, changing the subject.

Tossing their trash into a nearby barrel, he drove to the auto parts store. He got out, unaware that Harley's damaged motorcycle sat parked beside a large van, hidden from view. Opening the trunk of his car, he pulled out a screwdriver from his small collection of tools. He removed the screws, freeing the taillight from its plastic cover, and walked into the store to wait in line.

"I need a replacement for this." Mason plopped it down and gave the clerk the make and model.

The guy searched online for the right part. "Um, we should have one of those. Be right back." He'd been here so often lately, the clerks knew him on sight.

A large, tattooed hand seized his shoulder from behind, spinning him around. It was their old friend, Harley, from the bar. "You 'n' me got some unfinished business, asshole!" the big biker barked, dragging him out of the store.

Mason tried to pull away from the man's iron-fisted grip, but that was easier said than done. "Look, Harley, I really don't want any trouble. Sorry about your bike, but it was an accident, okay?" he said, trying to appease the seething gang member.

"You're sorry, alright, but not as sorry as you're gonna be after I kick your fuckin' teeth out the back of your skull. Your redheaded bitch ain't here to protect you this time, shithead!" he snarled, clenching his battle-scarred fist to punch him.

Mason glanced toward his car. Sure enough, April was nowhere in sight. *Shit!* He ducked the first blow, but a roundhouse left caught him on the side of his head, stunning him. He fell against a trash can, knocking its rounded cover off and spilling trash. Scrambling for something to use as a weapon, he snatched up the metal lid, raising it like a shield at the same moment old Harley threw another punch. His hairy fist struck the metal with a resounding *clang.*

The impact hardly dented the metal, but it broke two fingers on Harley's right hand. It took a second for the pain to register; when it did, he screeched like a little girl. With a furious roar, he lunged at Mason, pulling a wicked-looking butterfly knife. As he prepared to strike, a stream of liquid struck him full in the face. Harley screamed, dropping the blade, as he looked for some way to get the burning substance out of his eyes.

April appeared, helping Mason to his feet and half-dragging him toward his car. "Looked like you could use a little help, bud. Sorry I didn't get to him sooner; I was kinda busy," she offered cryptically. "You alright? Can you drive? We need to get the hell out of Dodge," she implored, all but shoving him into the driver's seat. While she slid in on the passenger side, Harley was cursing, wiping at his eyes with a dingy rag.

Mason's head still swam from the punch. Fumbling with his keys, he finally found the keyhole. "What had you so busy that you couldn't spray him *before* he almost took my fucking head off?" he griped, as the old beater roared to life on the second try.

"I was doing a little work on his bike, okay? It'll only slow him down, and that pepper shit doesn't last long, so I strongly advise we depart the premises, post haste." She was watching Harley stumble toward his bike to give chase.

With the infuriated biker in close pursuit, Mason backed up and tore out of the crowded lot, nearly colliding with a cop car. Mason swore loudly. Someone in the store must've called them when the fight broke out. *Shit!* That was all they needed. The cops would be all over them. The only upside was that if they reached him and April first, they might keep the enraged biker from killing them. As they raced toward an intersection with a red light, he saw that Harley was gaining on them.

"Whatever you did to his bike to slow him down didn't work," Mason remarked tersely, braking for the light.

April glanced in her rearview mirror. "I cut his fuel line. It shouldn't take long—there! Bye bye, asshole," she said triumphantly.

In the mirror, they watched as the chopper sputtered to a halt fifty yards back. Hope faded as they watched Harley ditch the crippled bike and race toward them on foot. Mason locked all the doors, cursing the traffic light's untimely hindrance of their escape from him.

Harley had almost reached the driver's side window when the light changed. Two cars sat in front of them; neither moving an inch. Mason laid on the horn just as Harley reached them. With growing horror, Mason saw the bastard had a semiautomatic pistol in his hand and was aiming it straight at him.

"Get down, now!" he shouted to April, ducking. They heard a loud *pop-pop-pop* and his window shattered inward, bullets embedding themselves in the dashboard where his head had been a moment earlier.

With trembling fingers, April dug out the last of her pepper spray. When Harley stooped to finish the job, she blasted him full in the face. "Eat that, you fat bastard!" she screamed, emptying the canister through the broken window, while Mason ducked.

Harley howled and staggered back, swiping at his inflamed eyes. Seeing the crazy biker wielding a gun, the drivers in front of them burned rubber.

"Are you hit?" April yelled at Mason. Saying nothing, he sat up and jammed the gas pedal to the floor.

His beat-up car backfired once and raced forward, leaving the furious biker standing in the road, waving his gun in the air. Mason drove them away from the area while brushing the remains of his busted window glass from his hair. They heard sirens approaching.

"I need someplace to stash the car, they'll have a BOLO out on me, sure as shit!" he advised, through gritted teeth.

"It's not your fault. That asshole biker started this whole mess, damn him!" April replied. She craned her head around in time to watch a sea of cops surround the bellicose biker.

"You didn't help matters by cutting his fuel line. I could have taken him out myself, given a little time," he grumbled, trying to massage his wounded ego.

"Yeah, right after he finished carving you a new asshole, I s'pose," she responded, with a smirk.

He hated to admit it, but she was right. If April hadn't intervened when she had, the outcome would have been questionable, at best. He drove aimlessly for a few miles, trying to come up with a plan.

"I have a friend who lives in this area, he has a huge back yard, lots of parties, blah, blah, blah. Anyway, he might be persuaded to let you hide your car behind his privacy fence," she suggested, while rolling another joint.

Mason frowned at that, but said nothing. Getting busted for a little pot was the least of his troubles right now. "Where does this 'friend' live and how would you persuade him to do that?" he asked, watching for cops in his rearview.

"He's a sucker for redheads, one quick BJ should do the trick," she gave him a small grin.

"So, you what? Turn tricks for favors and spending money?" he asked bluntly, regretting his words even as he spoke. She turned and stared daggers at him.

"I do what I need to, to survive, bud. Don't get all self-righteous on my ass. I use what God gave me to get by in this crappy world. You have no right to judge me, or anyone else, for that matter."

Abashed, he let the matter drop. "What's the address of this friend? We're gonna run outta gas soon."

Still seething, she gave him directions. A couple blocks later, he turned onto Payne Street and, following her instructions, pulled into the driveway of a large, two-story brick condo, and parked behind a shiny red Maserati that looked like it cost a gazillion bucks.

"You sure this is the right place?" An eight-foot-tall, gated security fence surrounded the property, which sat on about a half-acre of land.

"This is it; that's Abby's mid-life crisis parked in front of us. Men and their toys," she rolled her eyes.

"Must be a rich dude, huh?"

"Yeah, I guess. He's a coder, blows most of his money on stupid shit, spends it as fast as he can make it. I should warn you, he has very little in the way of social skills," she said as he followed her to the front entrance. A blood-red sign hung on the door: "*Abandon all hope, ye who enter.*"

Mason didn't like the sound of that. "You sure he's not the devil?" he asked, only half-joking.

"Not sure. You can ask him when you meet him." Avoiding the doorbell, she knocked on the metal door.

They waited while a series of deadbolts were unlocked, and the door opened just enough for conversation. "What's the password?" a deep voice called out from inside.

"Little red riding hood," April was frustrated by having to play this stupid game.

"You may enter," came the response from within. The door opened, and Mason got his first look at Abby. The computer nerd stood at least six-feet, five-inches tall on a lanky frame with black curly hair standing out in a mass of tangles. A pair of Harry Potter glasses sat perched on a long, beaky nose. Mason thought he looked like the human embodiment of Phineas T. Freak, straight out of an old 'Sixties "Fabulous Furry Freak Brothers" comic.

"Hey, Abby, this is my bud, Mason," April introduced them.

Mason gave him an insipid smile as they entered, extending his right hand to shake. Abby stared at his hand, ignored it, ushered them in, and re-locked the door.

"I don't shake hands; she should have warned you," he told Mason brusquely.

With that, Abby turned and walked over to a long, table full of expensive-looking electronics. Three large flat-screen monitors were connected to an array of servers adorning one wall. Sinking down in a soft leather office chair, he began typing rapidly. It looked like a bunch of gobbledygook to Mason, who knew zilch about coding.

"Hey, Abby, I need to ask you for a little favor." April opened the fridge to check what he had to drink.

"What now, April? I don't have time to dicker, I've got a black-hat encryption to break. I'd appreciate it if you would *not* bring unannounced visitors here whenever you decide to drop in out of the blue," he replied snippily, concentrating on the monitor.

Mason looked around for a place to sit. The living area was sparsely furnished with two beanbag chairs and an uncomfortable-looking couch in the middle of a large room. He chose a bean bag and plopped down in it, uneasy about the whole situation. April brought over a beer and handed it to him.

"Mason here needs a place to stash his wheels—only temporarily," she said before Abby could object.

He paused and turned to stare at her. "Is the car hot? I won't have stolen goods on my property, that's out of the question," he scowled, glancing suspiciously at Mason.

Mason started to explain, "It's not exactly 'hot'—there was this altercation with a biker, the guy pulled a gun and—"

Abby stopped him, "Whoa, you can stop right there! I don't wanna know and I don't fucking care. I presume both the cops and said biker are actively searching for you, so get that piece of shit off my property, *now!*"

Mason stood up, looking over at April. She rolled her eyes, but crept up behind the tall geek's chair. Wrapping her arms around his waist, she whispered something to him while stroking his crotch from behind. Mason had no trouble guessing what she was saying.

Abby turned and looked her over before deciding. "Okay. The car can stay, but only for a day. I don't need any heat from the cops or some bowed-up biker. I'll open the gate, you shag ass, and move that bucket of bolts into the back yard," he growled at Mason, flipping a switch on the wall.

Mason hustled out the front door to move his car.

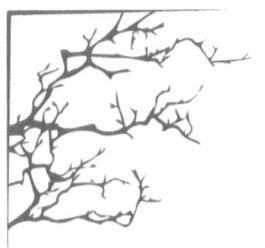

Chapter Three

Austin Police Department

Harley Kilroy, better known as "Tha Killer" to fellow members of his motorcycle club, sat on a hard metal bench inside the Travis County jail, gnashing his teeth and rubbing his stinging eyes. He was waiting for one of his men to come bail him out. The cops had charged him with reckless endangerment and the discharge of a firearm within the city limits. Adding insult to injury, they also ticketed him for a broken fucking taillight. The booking cop told him he was lucky he hadn't killed anybody. *Yeah, lucky for the asshole that got away.* A situation he planned to remedy as soon as he got out of this stinking shit hole.

A burly Hispanic guard with a shaved head entered the holding area and walked over to stand in front of his cell door.

"Okay, Kilroy, let's go. One of your 'boys' paid your bail, move your ass," he growled, opening the door.

"Thanks for nothing, law dog," Harley snapped, stepping out of the cell.

The cop released his handcuffs and gave him a rough shove toward the door. Anywhere else, Harley would have killed the dude for the insult. He let it go and held his temper as he was marched out into the booking area. There, he spotted his fellow club member, Tommy "The Toad" Truman standing by the booking desk, absently studying the "wanted" posters tacked to the wall.

"Hey, Toady, ya' find your picture up there yet?" Harley cackled, getting the young biker's attention.

"Shit, no, not today anyway," Tommy said. "What the hell you done this time, old man?" Tommy chided, as Harley retrieved his valuables from the desk sergeant.

"Some chickenshit copped an attitude over at the 'Dog' and when he wouldn't fight, he sicced his fucking bitch on me," Harley growled, spitting on the sidewalk as they left the cop shop.

"Set his dog on you, huh? That's pretty damn low, Killer," Tommy densely said.

Harley shook his head in exasperation. "Not a fucking dog, you idiot, his *woman*. She sucker-punched me in the nuts and stabbed my arm when I tried to grab her," he groused as they approached Tommy's illegally parked bike.

To Tommy's chagrin, a ticket was taped to the top of the gas tank of his chopper. "Fucking cops! Why the hell don't they put up a sign or somethin', to warn ya?" he said, pulling the ticket off, tearing it into confetti and tossing it on the ground.

Harley just shook his head at the dumb ass. The bike had been parked in a marked handicap space. Obviously, Tommy was a couple sandwiches shy of a picnic.

"Thanks for springing me, Toad. The law dogs impounded my ride, said it wasn't street legal, so, listen, I need to borrow your bike, Tommy, got some unfinished business to attend to," Harley said, holding out a hand for the key.

"Uh, I dunno,' Harley, you're kinda rough on bikes, and I just had a new paint job done," Tommy said.

"Don't make me pull rank on you, Tom. You may be a 'new fish' in the club, but you know the rules. If a member needs to borrow a bike—" Harley started. The young biker stopped him and unhappily handed over the key.

"Just drive her careful-like, if you don't mind," Tommy said, starting to climb on behind him.

"Sorry, Toad, but I'm ridin' solo. You'll have to call a cab. Later, dude," he said. The big bike rumbled to life and Harley sped away, leaving Tommy standing there cussing in the wake of his exhaust ...

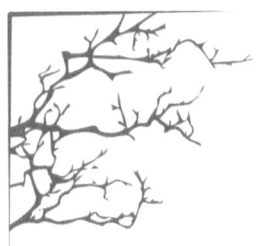

Chapter Four

North Austin

Mason started his car and pulled it around the Maserati. He drove through the opened gates and into the computer geek's back yard, careful not to hit a pair of vicious-looking Dobermans patrolling the backyard like sentries. Parking, he observed multiple vintage cars of various makes and models sitting around in differing states of disrepair. *Curious,* he thought, climbing carefully out of his car. The pair of "dobies" didn't seem interested in him as he made his way to the back door. *Some watch dogs they make,* he scoffed to himself. The gate had slammed closed behind him, making him uneasy.

The back door was unlocked, so he stepped inside and found himself in the kitchen.

Seeing no one, he called out, "Hello, Abby? April?"

He heard moaning coming from upstairs. Startled, Mason raced up the stairs, halting at the top to listen. The sound occurred again, but louder. He was about to barge into the nearest room when he realized April must be "paying" Abby for allowing him to storing his car there. A wave of jealousy swept over him. He didn't know why, since she was nothing but trouble.

He glanced once more at the door, hesitated, then turned and walked back down to the living room to wait. Looking around, he noticed shelves full of books lining two walls. He walked over to peruse the titles, pulling out one that caught his eye—H. P. Lovecraft's "Necronomicon." A small shiver ran down his spine. He'd read this as a kid, and it had spooked the crap out of him. Placing it back on the shelf, he found another that he recognized, Dante's "Inferno." There were several books on Satanic worship and human sacrifice. With growing discomfort, Mason sensed a theme that made him uneasy.

He thought back to the sign on the computer geek's front door. His gut was telling him to get the hell out of this place, pronto.

"Find anything interesting?" The deep voice made him jump. He whirled around to find Abby six feet away, staring at him with a slight smirk. The guy was stealthy as a cat; Mason hadn't heard him approach. April was nowhere to be seen.

"She's brushing her teeth. Apparently, she found my spunk distasteful. She'll be down in a moment," the computer geek said, as if reading his mind. Moving nearer to Mason, he stared into his eyes, studying him as if he were a bug under a microscope. "Do you find my books ... disturbing, Mason?" he asked, moving closer until only a foot of space separated them.

"I've read one or two before, just not my cup of tea, I'm afraid." He was determined not to be intimidated by the man.

Abby's cold, dark eyes continued to appraise him. "There's no need to be afraid. The supernatural has always appealed to me on a visceral level. There *are* things in this world that defy explanation, wouldn't you agree?" He took a novel from the shelf, handing it to him.

Mason glanced at the title, "The Devil and Daniel Webster," by Stephen Benet. He'd read it back in high school, only vaguely remembering its premise.

"I gather you're into the occult. Sorry, but I don't believe in all that crap, dude," Mason said, taking an unconscious step away from him.

"What is it you desire most in life, Mr. Rivers?" Abby asked, locking his gaze on Mason.

How did he know my last name? Mason was growing uncomfortable. *Might as well humor the guy until I can get the hell away of this creepy place*, he thought.

"I always wanted to be a great lead guitarist, but that sure as hell ain't gonna happen in this lifetime," he replied, sourly.

"Why is that?" Abby asked him.

Mason hesitated, unsure if he wanted to answer him. "Because of my little finger," he finally replied.

The geek glanced at Mason's pinkie finger, shaking his head. "Forgive me, but I don't understand. I see no malformation of the digit, and all five appear intact. So, tell me, why would that keep you from achieving your goal of 'greatness?'" he looked amused.

Mason stared at Abby as if he was an imbecile. "Well, obviously, it's too damn short."

"What's too damn short?" April asked, as she descended the stairway.

"My little finger. It won't reach across all six strings, so I'm unable to play a lot of the chords." He held up his left hand, and it was obvious his pinkie was an inch and a half shorter than his ring finger.

"Sorry, I thought you were talking about something else," April teased him, with an impish grin. She sat on the couch, pulled the bag of weed from her purse, and began rolling another joint.

"I could help you with your, uh, *little* problem, but I'm afraid the price would be prohibitive." Abby walked into the kitchen to fix himself a drink.

Mason looked skeptically at the geek. "Yeah? Well, FYI, I'm broke as a spoke. Anyway, how would you fix it—magically grow me a new fucking hand?"

Abby smiled, but it didn't reach his cold eyes. "Nothing quite so melodramatic, Mr. Rivers. There are certain procedures that could ... rectify your lamentable circumstances," he claimed cryptically. He poured a reddish colored drink from a bottle he retrieved from the refrigerator.

"So, what's the catch? Do I need to hand over my first-born child, or sign something in blood?"

Abby eased the glass away from his lips and studied him for a moment before answering. "You know, let's just forget the whole thing. I'm sorry to have piqued your curiosity, but you don't seem capable of taking my offer in earnest. Please leave now and take her with you," Abby nodded at April. "I expect you to reclaim your vehicle by tomorrow noon, no later. Goodbye Mr. Rivers," he said coldly, setting his glass down hard on the counter.

Mason was flummoxed by his sudden about-face. "Wait a minute, dammit, I wasn't trying to be rude. I'm sorry if I seem skeptical, but there's no way in hell anyone can make me a better guitarist than I am now," he said candidly.

"You seriously underestimate me, Mr. Rivers. I could arrange it so that you might attain your wildest dreams ... *if* you were willing to pay the price," Abby stated, picking up his glass again.

Mason craved what the geek offered, yet he couldn't fathom how it could be achieved. "So, if I did agree, what kinda price are we talking about?" he felt he was about to cross some invisible line with no hope of return.

"Why, your immortal soul, of course," Abby declared, with an evil-looking grin. The silence in the room was deafening. "That's the response you were expecting, isn't it, Mr. Rivers?" Abby snorted, clapping his hands to break the tension hanging in the air.

Mason laughed weakly. "Well, yeah, I guess it's what I assumed," he agreed, only somewhat relieved.

April had thus far refrained from joining the conversation. Now, she cautioned, "Be careful, Mason, Abby can be very persuasive. He could sell ice to Eskimos. He's a real smooth-talking devil," she warned, passing Mason the lit blunt. Her choice of words was not at all reassuring.

Abby reassured Mason, "You *would* need to sign a legal document to make any agreement between us binding ... but not in blood," he paused for effect.

Mason was fast approaching a crossroads within himself. *Should I do it or not?* He struggled to make a choice that he wouldn't regret for the rest of his life.

"You'll beee soorry," April said, sing-song fashion, from the couch.

Abby continued to coax him, "It stipulates that in return for your impending fame and fortune, you pay me fifty-one percent of all your earnings until the day arrives when you are no longer famous. As we all know, fame, like time, is fleeting," he ended.

"So, if I agree to do this, I'll become a successful guitarist, right? No bullshit, no other strings attached?" he asked seriously.

"One of the greatest the world has ever seen or heard, without a doubt," Abby assured him, his voice practically dripping with sincerity.

Mason figured he had nothing to lose. "What happens when I am no longer famous?" he inquired, not sure he wanted to know.

"Then your soul is mine," Abby hissed.

Mason didn't believe this bullshit for a second. "Okay, let's do it, where do I sign to get the ball rolling?" Nervously, he rubbed his hands together.

Abby smiled tightly, producing a tablet out of thin air, or so it seemed to Mason. *Must be the weed*, he thought as he walked over to sign the document.

As he took the proffered stylus from Abby's hand, the tablet came to life. Frowning, Mason paused, because the writing on the thing was in some unfamiliar language. Seeing the problem, Abby reached over, tapped the screen, and the language switched to English.

Like most laypeople, Mason couldn't comprehend the true meaning behind the contract's dense legal terms. Someone had highlighted the primary features, as if the contract had been prepared in advance or for someone else. Worse, some of the print was so small he would've needed a magnifying glass to read it. Taking a deep breath, Mason scribbled his name and the date, making it as illegible as the rest of the damn document. Abby had April sign as a witness, which she did with a scowl. Satisfied, he took the tablet back from Mason.

"There, all done," Mason said shakily. "So, what now? When does your 'voodoo' kick in?" He took a long toke off April's joint to calm his nerves.

"It began the moment you signed the contract. You should get a text from my 'associate' right about ... now," Abby told him.

At that moment, Mason's phone chimed from his back pocket, startling him. He took it out, read the message, and stuffed it back in his jeans, shaking his head.

"I don't get it. It just said for me to meet them at the Driscoll Hotel on Brazos at 6:00 p.m., sharp and to text them when I arrive. Yeah, right, like I could afford to even walk into that fancy-assed place. My wheels are in your backyard. Even if I had 'em, what would I do there?" he looked to Abby for answers.

"I think if you'll check your bank account, you'll find more than sufficient cash has been deposited there. As for transportation, you can borrow mine, provided you treat it like a lady. One scratch, and you'll pay for the damages in more ways than one," the geek flashed a shark's toothy smile.

Mason didn't believe anyone could've placed money in his account without his passwords or his pin number. Whipping out his phone, he checked the balances of his checking and savings. *Holy Shit!* There was more than 50,000 dollars in his checking account. His previous balance had been a paltry fifty-five dollars.

"Oh, ye of little faith," Abby remarked, pouring himself another glass of the vile-looking substance from his fridge. "You can't be a world-renowned rock star and be seen driving a crappy car or staying in some crack motel, now can you? You'll have to adapt to a totally different lifestyle than you're accustomed to, Mason. Here's to a long and fruitful partnership," he offered Mason a drink for a toast.

Mason shook his head, taking a few steps back. To him, Abby's reddish-colored liquid looked too much like blood for his liking. It might be plain old V-8, but who knew?

April lay half-sprawled on the couch, stoned to the bone. She sat up and yawned. "Hey, Mason, think I could tag along with you? I've never stayed at a fancy 'haunted' hotel before," she pleaded.

Everything had happened so fast, it made Mason's head swim. "What do you mean, 'haunted?'" He turned to her, puzzled.

"The place is supposed to be haunted. I've heard people have died there and ... well, you know, hung around," she shrugged.

"Here's the key fob for the car. You'd better get moving, my associate, Alal, does not like to be kept waiting." Abby pointed to the time on his gold Rolex.

Crap! Mason realized it was 5:40 p.m. Where had the afternoon gone? He'd have sworn they'd only been here for an hour, at most. Unsettled by the afternoon's bizarre occurrences, he started for the front door, April in tow, but he stopped short and turned to the mysterious coder.

"I gotta know, is Abby your real name?" He wasn't even sure why he needed to know.

"That's merely April's pet name for me. If you must know, my full name is Adriel Abbadon," Adriel said proudly.

Mason wasn't sure if he believed that. Right now, he didn't have time to debate it. If he didn't leave soon, he'd be late getting to the hotel.

"Okay, 'Adriel,'" he spoke the name sarcastically. "So, how do I contact you when I get there?"

"You don't; from now on, Alal will see to your needs. If problems arise, I will handle them. Leave now and enjoy your new life as a rock and roll god. Just a reminder—from this point forward, there's no turning back, no reneging on our contract," Adriel informed him, with what looked like his first genuine smile.

Mason felt a shiver of something run through him, but he chose to ignore it. He and April walked out to the luxurious car and climbed inside. The interior had more leg room than Mason would have thought possible for the compact sports car. When he started the engine, it roared to life, settling down to purr like a huge jungle cat. Grinning widely, he carefully reversed out of the driveway. With a squeal of tires, the crimson rocket on wheels sped down the residential street into an unknown future ...

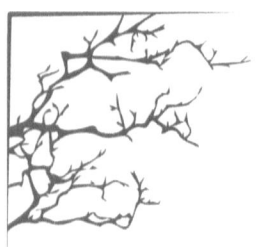

Chapter Five

The Driscoll Hotel,

Downtown Austin

At 5:55 p.m., he pulled to a stop in front of the historic Driscoll Hotel on Brazos Street, marveling at the fact that as a native Austinite, he'd never set foot inside the Romanesque building completed in 1886. Its architecture was an archaic anomaly compared to the adjacent skyscrapers towering over Austin's ever-expanding downtown sector. He didn't know if the hotel was haunted, but if a structure could possess the essence of persons who'd died there, this place would qualify. All it needed to complete the archetype were gargoyles guarding the entrance.

A uniformed valet stepped up to the driver's side window as Mason lowered it. "Good evening, Mr. Rivers, and welcome to the Driscoll. We've been expecting you," the clean-cut young man offered pleasantly.

Mason didn't know how to respond to that. Because of the cost, he'd never used valet parking before. "Uh, yeah, I'm supposed to meet someone here in the lobby at six. Do you need to see my credit card or something?" He tried to sound as if he knew what he was doing.

The young man held out his cell for Mason to sign. "No, sir, the parking fee has already been taken care of. All I'll need is your electronic signature and your key fob. Any time you call, your car will be brought to you at this spot." Awkwardly, Mason scribbled with his finger and handed it back, along with the key fob.

"How does it feel to be treated like royalty, bud?" April grinned, opening her door and climbing out.

"More than a little strange, I'm not used to being waited on," he grumbled, opening his door. He almost hated to leave the lavish interior of this expensive beast. "Please be extremely careful with her, if there's so much as a scratch on her, there'll be hell to pay," he said. *Really,* he thought grimly.

"No problem, Mr. Rivers, she'll be in caring hands, I assure you. Do you need any help with your luggage, sir?" the valet finished politely.

Crap! He realized that everything he owned was in the trunk of his car, parked behind Adriel's privacy fence. He'd been so distracted by the afternoon's events, he hadn't thought to retrieve his clothes before they'd left.

"Uh, that won't be necessary, thank you," he responded, strolling over to join April at the hotel entrance. "How the hell will this 'Alal' person know us once we're inside? They don't know what we look like," he wondered aloud, as they entered the lobby.

"I don't know, guess we'll find out soon." April was staring at everything.

Rows of massive white support columns lined the polished marble floor, while overhead was an ornate domed skylight with a Texas star as its centerpiece. The lobby was imposing and more than a little intimidating. Before today, Mason's idea of a 'luxury' hotel would've been a Hilton or a Marriott. The Driscoll exuded wealth and prestige far beyond he'd imagined. Men milled around in the lobby, most dressed in power suits and ties. Many of the women looked like models or movie starlets straight off a Hollywood film set.

Dressed only in a T-shirt and jeans, Mason felt naked and uncomfortable, out of his element, and wondered if April was feeling the same way.

"Wish I'd thought to bring a change of clothes, I feel underdressed," he groused, wishing, for once, to be invisible. As he and April walked to the registration desk, several in the small crowd watched them from the corner of their eyes. "Rich people hoping to glimpse someone famous," Mason scoffed.

"But isn't that what you aspire to *be,* Mason? Rich and famous?" a sultry voice spoke from behind him. He whirled around to find a tall, voluptuous blonde with striking blue eyes smirking at him. He'd never seen her before and had no inkling how she knew his name.

"Sorry, do I know you?" he spoke curtly, evading her question.

Dropping the attitude, the attractive woman took a step closer to him. "My name is Alal, you may call me Ally, if you wish," she said, appraising April like a lioness eyeing an appetizing meal.

April squirmed, uncomfortable under the other woman's scrutiny. "I'm April, you may call me April," she mocked sarcastically, forcing a smile.

Alal ignored her snide remark, but Mason sensed tension between the two women and moved to intervene. "So, you're the one I'm supposed to meet. Okay, I'm here, now what am I supposed to do, Ally?"

Her demeanor shifted to one of all business. "I've already checked you in, here's the key card to your suite. Try to get a lot of sleep tonight, you're going to need it. Your new wardrobe is waiting in your room. If you have further need of me tonight, you may text me at the number on your phone. If not, I'll see you in the morning at 7:00 a.m. sharp. Do *not,* I repeat, do *not* call me! I detest conversing on the horrid things, but Adriel insists upon using them." She instructed, wrinkling her nose at her phone in distaste.

"Alright, I have an important question. How am I supposed to practice my guitar riffs? Mine is in the freaking pawnshop," he inquired.

"A new instrument is waiting for you in the suite, along with an amplifier thingy. But you won't be able to use it until tomorrow," she offered, without further explanation, edging away from them.

Mason pondered why she'd left that hanging. *Maybe it doesn't have strings on it yet,* he thought, trying to imagine why he wouldn't be able to play a new guitar right away. He wanted to ask the peculiar woman, but decided not to, figuring he'd find out soon enough. He took the key card from the odd but attractive female. Without another word, Alal, or "Ally," turned and strode to the elevators.

"I don't know about you, but she creeps me the hell out," April remarked, as they watched the tall woman step into the elevator.

"Yeah, she's definitely a strange one. Let's go to our room, I'd like to get out of these clothes. All these rich bitches are staring at us like we're fucking homeless or something," he complained.

April rolled her eyes at him. "I hate to break it to you, bud, but that is *exactly* what we are," she told him.

Realizing his faux pas, Mason felt his face flush. She was correct, he'd spent the past week sleeping on other peoples' couches and floors. If it wasn't for his car—but he would not dwell on that now.

"Well, it won't be this way for long," he muttered, as they strolled over to the elevators.

Their key card was for Suite 525. When the elevator doors opened, they saw directions to the rooms were mounted on brass placards on the facing wall. They walked down the thickly carpeted hall until they stood in front of their suite. Mason slid the key card into the reader and pulled it out. The beady little LED continued glowing red. He repeated his actions twice with the same result.

"Here, let me try." Impatiently, she snatched the card from his hand. She whisked the card in and out fast, and the LED turned green. "Gotta do it quick or the reader won't cooperate." Maybe she had some previous experience.

Mason shrugged, opening the door to their suite. Hardwood floors shone with a pristine luster that must require constant polishing and buffing. Vaulted ceilings made the expansive rooms feel even larger.

They walked into the luxury suite, with a living room that could be closed off from the sizeable bedroom area with sliding doors. A large flat-screen TV was mounted on one wall, set off on either side by expensive-looking prints by famous Texas artists. The far end of the room held a minibar next to a four-foot pony wall, and a kitchenette equipped with a microwave, cabinets with dishes, and a sink. One large sofa, a smaller sofa or loveseat, and several comfy chairs were scattered throughout the living area.

On top of the bar sat a new-looking, hard-shell guitar case, while a small forty watt Marshall amp stood nearby on the floor.

"I gotta find the lady's room. Wow, this place is great, I hate to think what it costs for one night of debauchery." April couldn't stop gazing at the expensive furnishings.

Mason cringed, wondering the same thing. While she wandered into the adjoining bedroom in search of the facilities, he gravitated to the bar to scrutinize the guitar case. The case itself was generic, holding no clue to what lay inside. He tried to flip open the latches, but they didn't budge. *Shit!* The case was locked tighter than a camel's ass in a sandstorm. He noticed that all the latches were keyed. Ally's doing, no doubt. Short of prying the damn case open, it seemed he would *not* be playing the guitar tonight. Making himself a drink at the bar, he contemplated jimmying the locks, but gave it up.

Drink in hand, he walked in to check out the bedroom. A king-size four-poster bed was its obvious centerpiece. White lacy curtains canopied the entire bed, tied back with braided gold tassels. A couple of upholstered chairs, a love seat, and an antique armoire comprised the room's furniture. The living area and the bedroom each had a sizeable balcony overlooking the downtown area. He heard the toilet flush, and April walked out of the bathroom.

"*Whew*, do *not* go in there," she warned, fanning the air. Mason chuckled but didn't respond. "You'd think a fancy hotel like this would have a working 'fart-fan,'" she complained.

"Thanks for the warning," he told her. "Well, I tried to open the guitar case but the damn thing's locked. I'm guessing Ally has the key, nothing to do but wait until morning, I guess," he told her, sitting gently on the edge of the bed.

"Well, in the meantime, it's been a long time since lunch, you wanna get something to eat?" She plopped down beside him.

"I'm hungry enough to eat a bear and ask for seconds," he agreed, feeling his stomach growl at the mention of food.

"Do you want to eat in the restaurant downstairs? Or would you prefer to order room service?" he offered, remembering how they were dressed.

"I think you might have clothes in that 'do-hickey' over there that I can never remember the name of," she observed, pointing to the armoire.

He got up, walked over, and opened it. Sure enough, a few burnt orange and dark blue men's silk shirts and a pair of Gucci jeans with fashionable holes ripped in the knees hung inside. A jacket worth more than he'd ever seen in his life hung beside them. Some designer tennis shoes and purple socks sat on the bottom shelf. *Purple socks? Someone had a skewed vision of "rock star" attire, or maybe they were colorblind.* He realized that no women's clothing hung inside.

"What the hell? I thought we'd both be getting new clothes," he frowned, turning to April.

She was busy rolling a joint from the dwindling stash. "I believe she said, and I quote, 'A new wardrobe will be waiting for *you*.' She didn't specifically mention anything about *me*." She was busy lighting the doobie and taking a toke. How women could pull that memory trick continued to amaze Mason.

"Best take that out on the balcony, babe, room service might rat us out," he suggested.

"Jeez, don't be such a 'Paranoid Pete,' bud, famous rock stars stay here all the time. Does this mean we won't be going down to the restaurant to eat?" Grumpily, she walked over to the bedroom's balcony doors and stepped out.

"That may be true, but I'm not a 'rock star' yet. I'm having serious doubts that Adriel can pull this rabbit out of his hat. And yes, we'll be eating dinner here. Ally and Abby both knew you were coming with me, there's no excuse for not getting you some new shi—" His rant was stopped by a knock on the front door. *Crap! Someone probably smelled the weed and reported us*, was his first thought.

"Hang on, I'm coming," he yelled toward the door. "Stay on the balcony and stash the jay, for crying out loud," he hissed to April, pulling the French doors closed in her face. April seethed, but did as he asked. Fanning the air with his arms, Mason shut off the bedroom doors behind him. Striding to the front door, he peered through the peephole. "Who is it?" he called out.

"It's room service, Mr. Rivers," spoke a muffled voice.

"I didn't order room service. You must be mistaken," Mason fired back.

"No, sir, I have some apparel here for a Ms. Flowers. It was supposed to have been delivered earlier, but the delivery truck was stuck in traffic," the disembodied voice explained.

Mason opened the door to gape at the rack of expensive women's clothes. *Sonofabitch! More money out of his new bank account.* Several silk blouses and two pairs of jeans identical to his own, except in size, along with a pair of red stiletto heels, were carried inside by a junior staffer with blond hair and a friendly face.

"Hi, I'm Jimmy, I'll just hang them in the armoire for you," he said cheerfully. Before Mason could object, the guy opened the bedroom door, stopped, and sniffed the air like a bloodhound. "Smells like you have some primo Ganja, Mr. Rivers. Don't worry, a lot of famous people who stay here tend to, uh, indulge. Hotel management turns a blind eye and *nose*, as long as the guests are discreet and don't cause trouble," the young man carefully hung the clothes up in the cabinet. "If there's anything else you need, just call the front desk and ask for Jimmy," he said, holding out his hand expectantly.

Mason was flustered until he realized the guy expected a tip. *Crap*! He'd forgotten to get any cash at the ATM when they were downstairs. "Uh, I'm a little short on cash right now, sorry about that," he mumbled apologetically.

Jimmy didn't blink an eye. "How about you give me a couple tokes of your weed and we'll call it even," Jimmy suggested, with a wink.

"Oh, okay, no problem, I'm sure April will be happy to accommodate you, it isn't actually *my* weed," Mason sarcastically pointed out.

Taking him out to the balcony, he introduced him to April, explaining the situation. She smirked at Mason but said nothing as she re-lit the jay and passed it to Jimmy. He took two big hits, held it, and exhaled the pungent cloud, watching it drift away on the breeze.

"Thanks, much appreciated, I gotta get back to work. You need anything—and I mean, *anything*—just ask for me. Enjoy your stay," he said with a grin, pointing to the joint in April's hand for emphasis. He turned and left the suite.

"I told you, Mr. Paranoid—rich and famous people get away with this shit all the time," she carelessly tossed the roach off the railing to the street below.

"Well, as far as I know, I'm neither at the moment. Your problem is you're reckless; you throw caution to wind, and to hell with the consequences."

April frowned, crossing her arms. "Listen, bud, FYI, the world doesn't give one crap about me. So why should I conform to society's bullshit rules and regulations, when all I get for my trouble is a solid kick in the teeth? Grow a pair, Mason, you gotta take life by the balls. Otherwise, you'll never get anywhere in this fucked-up world. A life without risks makes April a dull girl."

She marched back inside in a huff. Mason followed her in, took her arm, marched her over to the armoire, and opened it. Her eyes widened at the posh clothing inside, including luxurious underwear.

"I hope you're happy now. It seems there was a delay in delivery," he said, hoping it would mollify her.

"Wow, these are fab, but how did Abby know my size? Oh, I love those shoes!" she squealed excitedly, as she held a blouse up against her.

He had to smile, she was like a kid in a candy factory. All the clothes had likely cost him a bundle. At some point, he'd need to check his bank account to see how fast it was dwindling, but right now, he didn't care. The pure joy on April's face was worth every dollar.

"What say we hit the shower, then put on our fancy new clothes and head downstairs for dinner?" he suggested.

She eagerly agreed, grabbing one of everything, she turned and headed for the bathroom. he would've followed, but she stopped him.

"Sorry, bud, no hanky-panky before dinner," she smiled, closing the door and locking it behind her. *Crap*! His anticipation of hot shower sex wilted along with his erection. Twenty minutes later, April stepped out of the steamy, luxurious bathroom and performed a little pirouette.

"Well, how do I look?" she asked. Mason was stunned by the transformation.

"You look ... absolutely beautiful—not that you weren't before," he added.

"Nice save, but thanks all the same. The bathroom's all yours, but hurry up. I'm freaking starved!" she exclaimed.

Grabbing some of his new clothes, Mason walked into the large, well-appointed bathroom and took his turn in the swanky shower. After dressing, he opened the door a few minutes later. April, curled up on a large lounger, glanced up from her phone with an appraising eye.

"You certainly clean up nicely, Mr. Tall, Dark and Handsome. Let's go before I eat the furniture," she said, taking him by the hand.

"Okay, okay, just hang on, let me get my room key and wallet," he insisted, retrieving both from his old jeans. He stared longingly at the locked guitar case as they made their way out the door.

On the first floor, Mason asked an idling bellhop for directions to the "Driscoll Grill," and he pointed to a door. Mason thanked him and they made their way into the restaurant. The room was crowded with a lengthy wait for a table, so they decided they'd eat at the bar.

While they were ordering drinks, Ally appeared, taking the seat next to him, prompting a glower from April, who sat on his other side.

"So, have you settled into your room, found everything to your liking?" Alal asked, with a crocodile smile.

"Yeah, everything's just peachy. When exactly do I get to see and play my new ax? I noticed the guitar case was locked. What's up with that?" he asked her, taking a swallow of his beer.

"You wouldn't be able to play it as is, not before tomorrow, anyway." She ordered a double shot of top-shelf tequila from the female bartender while Mason puzzled over what she meant.

"I don't enjoy playing verbal hide-and-seek, Ally. What exactly would happen to me if I decided to back out of this deal with Adriel?" he asked, tired of her evasive bullshit.

"I'm afraid that isn't an option, Mr. Rivers," the bass voice replied, startling him. Mason whipped around to find Adriel looming over him.

"Wh-What are doing here?" Mason asked nervously.

"I was concerned you might be having second thoughts about our little contract. Make no mistake, you *will* fulfill your part of the bargain—one way ... or the other," Adriel replied icily.

"Look, Adriel or Abby, or whatever the hell your name is, I don't like being threatened." He stood to face the taller man.

"It isn't a threat, Mr. Rivers, it's a fact. You've made your bed, now it's time to lie in it. There is *no* going back; from this point forward, *you're mine!*" Those two words seemed to vibrate in the air.

For the first time since all this craziness had begun, what he heard then in Adriel's voice terrified Mason. He deeply regretted ever meeting this ... *thing* posing as a human being. No amount of fame or fortune was worth losing your soul. April must've known what Adriel was before she introduced them. *So why did she do it? What was in it for her?*

He turned to confront her. "I hope you're happy, April, or whoever the hell you are," "What's your cut in this deal? You get to live forever? Or maybe you're just a shill for your pal here?"

Tossing back her double shot of tequila, April grimaced and slowly turned to face him. "I get to live a while longer, it's true. But I traded my soul a long time ago, Mason. You see, I've always believed I could be the lead singer in a successful rock band. When I saw your band ... I knew you had the potential to be truly great ..." she hesitated, a tear rolling down her lightly freckled cheek. "Anyway, to fulfill my contract, I had to bring him another soul. You're my last, best hope for a shot at stardom. If I don't achieve that by midnight of my twenty-first birthday, I ..." she paused.

Mason was still upset by her callous betrayal of their friendship, but his curiosity won the moment. "You what?" he asked, slugging down the last of his beer.

Her green eyes shimmered with tears. "I forfeit *my* soul," she said quietly, turning back to face the bar. She ordered another shot of tequila.

Mason was stunned by her words. "C'mon, April, you don't really expect me to believe all this demonic BS, do you? You seem like a smart lady, for crying out loud!" he exclaimed.

"It isn't bullshit, Mason. I told you I lost my father in a car accident—that was a lie. The terrible truth is, *I* killed him!" she sobbed.

At this point, he didn't know what to believe. "What do you mean, you killed him?" he asked cautiously.

Ally rolled her eyes and got up from the bar to join Adriel in a nearby booth. She knew April's story and had no interest in hearing it again.

April blew her nose on a bar napkin and drank her tequila before she replied. "I was eighteen when I left home for college. My dad was against it, but my mother insisted. I met Adriel at college. He showed up in my vocal music class, was good-looking in a geeky sort of way, and we struck up a friendship after class. One night after an evening of partying, he seduced me. Afterward, as we lay entwined, he asked me that question: 'What is your greatest desire in life?' Half in jest, I foolishly told him I wanted to be the greatest singer anyone had ever heard." She stopped and ordered another shot of tequila. Mason was intrigued, but remained skeptical.

"Adriel said, 'What if I could make it all happen?' I thought he was kidding around, but the more he talked, the more I believed he was serious. By the time he casually mentioned that I'd have to sign a contract to make it happen, I was too far into visions of impending stardom to think straight. The bastard really *is* one hell of a salesman," she said bitterly.

The bartender placed the shot in front of her, giving her a questioning look. It was her third in ten minutes.

"So what does this have to do with blaming yourself for your dad's death?" Mason prodded.

"As I said, part of my contract was to provide Adriel with someone else's soul," she said, tossing down the tequila in one large gulp. "My dad was a greedy bastard who worshiped money but didn't like working for it. And he was abusive when he drank, which was most of the time. He couldn't find a job and when he did, it only lasted for about a week before either he was fired, or he'd quit.

"To pay the bills, my mother began working longer shifts, and he started creeping into my bedroom late at night when she was at work or after she fell asleep. At first, he just crawled into bed with me and lay quietly beside me for a while. I was too afraid to confront him about it. As time passed, it escalated, he'd stay a little longer each time, and I'd pretend to be asleep while his hands roamed over my body like some nasty spider in the dark. I held in the tears when he pulled my panties down and forced himself inside me. I hated him for that. How could he do that to his own fucking daughter?" April stopped, trying to compose herself.

When she ordered another shot, the bartender shook her head, placing a glass of water in front of her instead. With a frown, April drank it down without comment. She already had a buzz on, felt the room growing hazy.

"One night after he'd finished, as I lay there, crying and ashamed, he whispered in my ear, 'If you ever tell anyone about this, I'll deny it and I'll make you wish you were never born.' I felt utterly numb, no more tears, just cold.

"The next day, I applied to college and was accepted within a week. I stayed at a friend's house 'til a room opened up on campus. When I made my drunken deal with Adriel the night of that party, I knew whose soul I would deliver to him. My father would pay for what he'd done to me."

Mason ordered another beer, waiting for her to finish.

"One day during spring break, I introduced my father to Adriel. And when Adriel offered *him* the deal of a lifetime, he naturally jumped at it. Unfortunately, he didn't see the fine print on his contract that stipulated he would first have to admit to my mother he'd been raping me for months. Otherwise, no money, do not pass go—a one-way ticket to hell.

"He couldn't back out, he'd already signed the contract. It was a lose/lose deal from the git-go. I had planned it that way. I knew he'd never admit he raped me. Mom would divorce him, haul his ass into jail, and throw away the key. But if he refused, he'd have to live without money for the rest of his miserable life, knowing his wretched soul was lost. Either way, it would be bye-bye, daddy," she said bitterly.

"So, what happened?" Mason asked, draining his second beer.

"He committed suicide the next day, blew his brains out with a shotgun. Mom found him sprawled in the bathtub," she said calmly.

"*Holy shit*! That must've been traumatic for your mother."

"Not so much. After we buried him, I found out she'd suspected he was doing me but couldn't prove it. When I confirmed her suspicions, she admitted she hadn't been intimate with him for over a year. She blamed herself for what happened. I couldn't very well tell her the *truth* of why he died, she would've had me committed," she insisted.

"We returned to school the following week. I couldn't study or concentrate in my classes. Without warning, Adriel dropped out and told me he was moving to Austin, but not before reminding me that the clock was ticking on our deal. I was a miserable wreck. My father deserved to be punished for what he'd done, but the guilt over having sold him out sickened me to my core. I never expected he'd kill himself.

"Desperate to find the perfect band to join, I dropped out of school two days later and purchased a one-way ticket to Austin for its burgeoning music scene. Adriel found me immediately, of course, and here I am," April finished. She gazed woozily at her reflection in the mirror behind the bar, where there seemed to be two of her staring back. *Shit! I'm plastered*, she thought, weaving on her bar stool.

"That's a hell of a story, April, but I still don't believe Adriel is the devil or a demon or whatever you wanna call him. How do you know he actually took your father's soul when he died? What proof do you have that *any* of this is fucking real?" Mason observed, reaching out to steady her.

She grinned lopsidedly at him, shaking her head, as the tequila hit her system all at once. "You don' unnerstan' ... Adriel comes to me in my dreams ev'ry night an' shows me horr'ble pi'tures of my father screamin' as he's being fucked in the ass by some hideous creature ... an' it never stops 'til I wake up screamin'. Adriel's the real deal, bud. We're ... both soo screwed," she mumbled, as she passed out cold.

Mason caught her before she fell off her stool. Picking her up, he turned to look for Adriel and Ally, but but they were gone. Paying for the drinks, he carried April to the elevators and took her up to their suite. He had to lay her on the floor while he fumbled with the key card. On his fifth try, the door finally unlocked, and he shoved it open. Cursing the asshole who'd decided key cards were better than keys, he scooped April back up and carried her into the bedroom. Gently, he laid her on the bed on her side, where she lay snoring in an alcohol-fueled coma.

Sighing, he wandered unsteadily to the living room bar and made himself a drink. He stared at the mysterious guitar case sitting in front of him, wondering if he could somehow pry it open without damaging the locks. *Maybe better not*, he thought. Drunkenly, he plopped down on a chair and fell into a troubled sleep ...

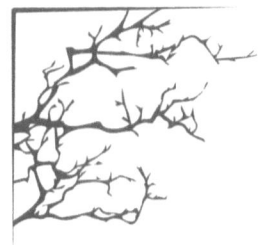

Chapter Six

North Austin

Harley had ridden around for hours, looking for Mason's car, with no luck. He was tired, ready to give it up, when he screeched to a halt in front of a two-story condo on Payne Avenue. There it sat, parked in the huge backyard, illuminated by a security light stationed above the open gate.

Gotcha, fucker! He eased the kickstand down and climbed off Toad's bike. Opening the saddlebag on the back, he retrieved a nickel-plated .44 caliber revolver from within and tucked it into the waistband of his jeans. As he cautiously entered the back yard, he gaped at the sheer number and variety of vehicles parked in the spacious backyard. Seeing and hearing no one, he walked over to peer through the window of the ancient Ford.

No one was inside the car, so the asshole and the girl must be inside the house. At that moment, the security gate behind him snapped shut with a *clack*, making him jump. The security light went dark a second later, and he was left standing in darkness. Suddenly, low, sinister growls came from his left, then from his right, raising the hackles on his neck.

Harley decided then and there that finding the bastard and his redheaded bitch was no longer a priority. Slowly, he eased backward, trying to locate the now-shuttered gate's latch in the dark while keeping an eye peeled for an attack. He retreated right into the gate, and his fingers felt for the latch, but found only smooth wood. *Shit!* The latch must be controlled from within the house. He was trapped. Pulling the magnum from his waistband, he cautiously moved toward the back door, sweeping the gun back and forth in front of him.

In the dark, he tripped over something and fell, losing the gun as he tried to break his fall. As he got to his feet, something large slammed into him, knocking him back on his ass.

"How good of you to visit, Mr. Kilroy, I've been expecting you," a deep voice came from the darkness.

"Who's there? Whoever you are, you're messing with the wrong fucking dude!" Harvey warned nervously.

"Such hostility! I'm afraid that won't do. You see—or rather, you don't—you're threatening a rather valuable asset of mine. I'm afraid I can't allow that," the voice calmly replied.

Harley was frightened, and when scared, he grew angry. "Fuck you, asshole!" He threw wild, blind punches around him. Abruptly, razor-sharp teeth latched onto his balls, ripping them out in a spray of blood as he screeched in agony. He collapsed on the pavement, shrieking until the teeth found his throat, silencing him.

"Well done, Alal, when you're finished, toss the remains to the hounds, then remove his bike from the street and park it behind the gate. He won't be needing it anymore," Adriel instructed pleasantly as he retrieved Harley's gun from the pavement.

Alal growled her reply, slashing the dead biker's torso from head to crotch with one sharp claw, to expose his viscera. Drooling in hungry anticipation, she lowered her head to feed ...

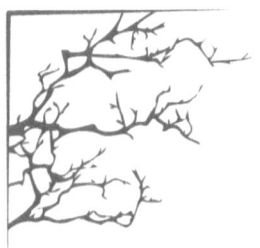

Chapter Seven

Driscoll Hotel

Around 3:00 a.m., Mason's bladder woke him from a fitful sleep in the chair. His stiff neck had a crick in it from the awkward position he had slept in for the past few hours. At some point, his drink had spilled on the carpet, and his head ached like a rotten tooth. He stumbled through the bedroom and made a beeline for the bathroom. As he unzipped his pants to piss, he noticed something weird. At first, he thought he was seeing double because of the alcohol he'd consumed.

He shook his head in disbelief as he inspected his left hand. Within the last five hours, his little finger had grown *a half inch* longer. Incredibly, a sister digit had emerged next to it as if his hand were some malignant beanstalk.

At present, the new finger was only two inches long. It sure as hell hadn't been there when he'd fallen asleep ... *had it?* Stunned, he zipped up, finally convinced April had spoken the truth about Adriel. No logical explanation existed for the huge amount of money sitting in his bank account. And now, the shocking appearance of an additional finger confirmed his worst fear. He'd actually made a deal with the Devil himself or one of his underlings. Well, he'd signed the contract, he couldn't change that. What was done was done. Might as well enjoy whatever fame and riches came his way, as it wouldn't last forever. Nothing ever did, he thought grimly as he left the bathroom.

April cried out in her sleep, startling him. He pondered what night terrors might await him in the future. Lying down beside her on the bed, he stroked her wild red hair. "I think you're right," he whispered softly, "we *are* both truly screwed," as sleep claimed him again.

The alarm on his phone jolted him awake at 6:30 a.m. Yawning, he reached to wake April, but she was gone. He heard the shower running, so he climbed off the bed and strolled into the bathroom, which wasn't locked. Without announcing his presence, he lifted the lid on the toilet to relieve his swollen bladder. Catching sight of his left hand, he gasped. *Holy Crap!* His pinkie was now the same length as his ring finger, and the recent addition was catching up fast.

April shut off the water and slid the opaque glass door open. He couldn't have stopped the flow of urine if his life depended on it. He'd never seen her naked, and she was a beautiful sight.

If she was modest about her nudity, it didn't show. Her eyes were drawn instead to the hand holding his junk. "Whoa, when did that happen?" She didn't seem shocked, as she grabbed a soft, thick towel.

"Last night. You passed out in the bar, and I carried you upstairs. By the way, you're heavier than you look," he teased her, and she shot him a dirty look. "I guess I passed out in a chair in the other room. Woke up to pee and this new little guy had popped up out of nowhere," he added, as he finished peeing.

"It's disturbing, but it might come in handy on those long, lonely nights when you don't have a woman—get it? Come in 'handy?'" she grinned, as she towel-dried her hair.

"Ha-ha, so not funny. What the hell happens if they keep growing? This is some crazy shit I got myself into," he groused, flushing the toilet.

"Gotta be careful what you wish for, bud. I found that out the hard way," April reminded him. "Remember that old song, 'Ya' can't always get what you need.'"

"I think it's, 'You can't always get what you *want*'—not what you *need*," he corrected, smiling at her musical faux pas.

"Well, if ya' didn't *need* it, why would ya' want it in the first place? Duh!" she returned, with a shake of her damp, curly head.

"You don't get ... I mean—oh, never mind—I know what you meant. Anyway, it doesn't matter now, there's nothing I can do about it. I made my wish and signed the contract, now I'll have to deal with the consequences, freakin' '*que sera sera*,'" he grumbled, leaving the bathroom so she could finish up. He dressed, and she joined him minutes later, looking resplendent in her new wardrobe.

"I hope Ally is on time, I'd like to get some breakfast," she said, eyeing the room-service menu. Mason agreed as he sat on the bed, inspecting the new appendage growing on his left hand. *How the hell will I be able to play now with an extra freaking finger instead of the usual four?* he wondered.

"This is ridiculous, I'll never be able to figure out how to chord with this extra finger," he grumbled audibly.

"Why is that?" she asked distractedly.

"There'll be no muscle memory in it, it would be like expecting a newborn baby to be able play like Jimi Hendrix, or Stevie Ray Vaughn."

"Um, who's 'Jimmy Hendrix'?" she asked innocently.

"He's—never mind, before your time."

A loud knock on the front door stopped their conversation, and Ally entered the suite with her key. Mason glanced at his watch: 7:00 a.m. Well, at least she was punctual.

"Morning, my future rock stars. I see you have a new little friend," she nodded at the recent addition to his playing hand.

"Yeah, about that, how the hell do you expect me to play like a guitar god with this *atrocity*?" he asked angrily, shaking the offending hand for emphasis. "It'll take forever to train it properly, and from what I understand, 'forever' is not exactly in my future."

If he expected sympathy from the blonde demon, he was mistaken. "Oh, ye of little faith," she sarcastically repeated Adriel's words.

Sauntering over to the bar, she produced a tiny silver key and inserted it in the lock on the guitar case. With a twist of her wrist, she unlocked and opened it for his inspection.

Eagerly, he stepped around her to have a look inside the mystery case. What he saw took his breath away. Resting on a bed of crushed red velvet lay a vintage 1958 Fender Stratocaster with a sunburst finish, in pristine condition. Taking it in, his eyes grew wide. He knew this model sold for as much as 20,000 dollars. But that wasn't what took his breath away. The guitar was embossed with lavish gold script across the body. The neck between the frets was inlaid with mother-of-pearl floral lettering that spelled out his new moniker—*Mase the Ace? Who the hell came up with that?* Then he remembered who he was dealing with.

"Well, go ahead, pick it up. It won't bite," Ally encouraged.

He wasn't so sure. He was almost afraid to touch it. Carefully, he reached down and lifted the gorgeous instrument from its sarcophagus, cradling it like a newborn baby. It felt heavy in his hands, as if made of metal rather than wood and varnish. He removed the patch cord from the back of the amp and plugged it in, flipping on the power. Propping one foot on the amp to support the guitar, he positioned his left hand on the neck, ready to try some experimental power riffs. As soon as his fingers touched the strings, a strange thrum of power surged down his left arm into his fingers.

Independently, they took off, racing up and down the keyboard as if controlled by an unseen force. Mason was both amazed and terrified as he watched his fingers fly helter-skelter over the fingerboard, cranking out faster and faster arpeggios that stung the morning air with crisp, melodic riffs. By the time he stopped, he was sweating. As soon as his fingers left the strings, the weird thrumming sensation was gone.

"*Holy shit*! What the hell was that?" he exclaimed, unplugging the guitar, placing it back in its case.

"Exactly. Of course, there had to be a few minor ... 'modifications' to the guitar to accommodate your skill set. Other than that, the rest was all you." She was making herself a drink from the bar.

Modifications my ass! Mason thought uneasily. "How do I control this ... *thing?* That shit I just played came out of nowhere. What happens when I want to perform a song I'm actually familiar with?" he complained.

Ally coolly eyed him, taking a sip of her single-malt whiskey. "You ever hear of the 'Think System,' Ace," she asked him.

Mason tried to recall where he'd heard that term before. Then he remembered. "You gotta be fucking kidding me—the 'think system' *developed* by Professor Harold Hill in Meredith Wilson's 'The Music Man?' That's nuts!" he sputtered, exasperated.

"How do you think Meredith came up with it?" she smirked knowingly.

"You're telling me that he ..."

She stopped him. "No, no, he didn't sell his soul, if that's what you're inferring. He's safely in the *other* place. A pity," she scowled her disapproval.

Mason leaned back from her. "I don't know, I've played by ear since I was seven. I can hear the notes and melodies in my head, that was never the problem. I just couldn't *play* some of the more difficult chords, because my little finger was so damn short," he explained.

"I'd say that little problem has been rectified, wouldn't you?" Ally said, nodding to his newly transformed left hand.

"I wonder if it worked as well down below," April snickered, gazing lustily at his crotch.

Mason didn't think that was at all funny. Now that she'd suggested it, he'd be stuck in a worry-loop, wondering if what happened to his hand might also affect his other extremities. *That's all I fucking need, two Johnsons.*

"Hey, look, it could be worse, you could grow another asshole, wouldn't *that* be fun?" April teased.

"Ha-freaking-ha. So, I'm supposed to just 'think' of the tune I want to play and it like, magically happens?" he asked Ally, ignoring April's snide remarks.

"Try it and see for yourself. Focus on the melody and the rest will follow, easy-peasy," Ally told him, slugging down the rest of her drink.

Mason found that hard to believe, but he picked up the guitar and plugged it back in. He concentrated on a technically challenging song that had frustrated him in the past. Again, when his fingers touched the strings, they seemed to have a mind of their own. He watched, shocked, as they performed a blistering solo up and down the guitar's neck. The fingers moved over the fretboard so fast, he could almost swear they were smoking by the time he was finished. In fact, his recent addition was bleeding a little from the strenuous fretwork, not having been 'born' with callouses.

"Wow, that was some bad-ass shredding, Ace," April crowed, seeing him in a new light. "I knew you were good before, but that ... that was awesome! When I first saw you, I knew you were the one."

Mason was still stunned at how rapidly all the right notes had flowed from his mind to his fingers. His brain had barely kept up with the lightning-fast riffs. It was truly a mental mind fuck.

"Don't go getting a big head, lightning boy, you still need to find the right band to back you. I presume you've already found your lead singer." Ally tossed her head derisively in April's direction. April scowled at the blonde bitch but didn't respond. Ally wandered out on the balcony with her fresh drink.

Mason turned to April, "I never asked, but I assume you *can* sing?" Her face turned redder than her hair.

"Of course, I can sing, you dumb ass! You think I'd waste my precious time on some hack guitarist with no fucking potential? Pick it up and play something, Mr. Hotshot," she huffed indignantly.

Mason decided he'd throw her by playing a "golden oldie" to test her. He plugged in and started playing an old rock and roll song by the sister group, Heart. When she started singing the lyrics to "Crazy on You," his jaw dropped. Not only did she have an amazing alto voice, but a stunning falsetto as well, reaching notes high enough to shatter crystal. Her performance demonstrated remarkable emotional and vocal talent.

Finishing the song, he stood there speechless, wearing a stupid grin. It had been like listening to an angel's voice, if angels sang rock and roll.

"I hope I passed the audition," she smirked, with arms crossed.

"It was incredible, you blew me away! Oh, and by the way, you're hired," he quickly added.

She rolled her eyes, but smiled at his compliment. "Thanks for the offer, but I think I'll pass," she replied coolly, strolling to the bar for a drink.

Mason's face fell like a stone. "Wh-What do you mean '*you'll pass?*'"

She delayed replying, making him sweat, before she turned, with a grin. "Gotcha!' I was only kidding. Relax, Ace, you're still way too uptight. I'm not going anywhere but to the top of the billboards, and you're gonna help me get there," she boasted.

He blew out a relieved sigh, before he realized he'd neglected to ask her something. "You never told me how long it is until your twenty-first B-day?" He was concerned about the time remaining on her contract with Adriel.

She paused to count, "I have exactly six months, three days, seven hours and twenty-three minutes to fulfill the other half of my contract. If I'm not a star by then ... well, I guess it's bye-bye, soul," she grimaced.

Six fucking months to live! Mason shuddered, thinking how uncertain both their futures were.

"Well, in that case we'd better get a band put together quick. Do you and Adriel have some mysterious 'master' plan, Ally? Or do we just wing it from here on?"

"What a stupid question, of course, we have a plan. You and the golden warbler here get rich and famous, then we get your souls. It seems obvious to me," Alal said, walking back inside.

"What about your old bandmates, Mase—they good enough to back us?" April asked, finishing her small whiskey.

He hesitated before answering her. "Yeah, they're good; I'm just not sure they'd be willing to do it. I left on shaky ground when they gave me the boot. On my way out the door, I, uh ... might've *accidentally* trashed some of their instruments. It's all sorta hazy, I was pretty wasted," he mumbled sheepishly.

At his admission, April rolled her eyes. "That's just frickin' great. Well, I suggest you do everything in your power to make amends, we don't have a hell of a lot of choices right now, and the clock is ticking!"

Ally chortled wickedly at the simmering animosity between the two. She so enjoyed watching stupid humans fight, especially when their souls were on the line.

"Enough with the bitching, get something to eat. I'll meet you back here in an hour," she snapped, turning to leave. As soon as her back was turned, April flipped her the bird.

"She's right, I can't think on an empty stomach," Mason said. "You want to order room service or go downstairs?" he asked April.

"What*ever*," she huffed, worried his bandmates wouldn't want to join their band.

"Let's eat here; that way, I can make a few calls," he pulled out his phone. "What do want to eat?"

"Don't care, long as it's not cold when it gets here." He was already scrolling through his phone.

April went to the bedroom and flopped down on the bed to peruse the hotel menu, while he took a deep breath and called the first number on his list.

"Hey, Jeff, it's ... it's Mason. Wait—wait—hold on ... chill, please, dude! I—yeah, I know I'm an asshole, and—you know that's physically impossible. Just listen to me for a minute, okay? If you'll calm down and hear me out, the opportunity of your lives is waiting for you and the guys. Something amazing has happened to me, but I need you guys with me for it to succeed. I—no, I'm not drunk or stoned ... yes, I'll buy all of you new instruments, amps, whatever you want. If you'll only meet with me, I'll explain everything," Mason said, pleading his case ...

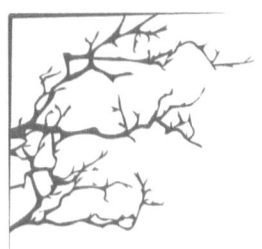

Chapter Eight

Mason's former bass player, Jeff Huntsman had been the most vocal of the group insisting that Mason clean up his act or he was history, so Mason knew he'd be the hardest sell among the three remaining members. Grudgingly, Jeff agreed to a meet. Reassured, Mason told him where he was and his room number.

"You gotta be kidding. You're stayin' at the fucking Driskill? How the hell can you afford that place? They cater to the rich and famous. Just what the blue-eyed hell is going on?" Jeff skeptically inquired.

Mason knew if he tried to explain the situation over the phone, he'd lose him forever. "I know it sounds crazy, but I've changed—*literally*. If you'll come to the hotel, you'll see and hear for yourself. You won't regret it, I swear."

Jeff finally agreed and told him he'd be there in an hour.

"One more thing. Do me a favor, call the others and try to convince them to come. They'll listen to you, Jeff, and it's important that you all have a say in this deal," Mason added. Jeff said he'd try, but no promises, and disconnected.

Mason sighed. He didn't know what they'd think or do when they saw his altered hand, much less when they heard him play. His thoughts were interrupted as someone knocked at the front door. He walked over and peered through the peephole at Jimmy, the room service guy. Mason opened the door for him and his cart.

"Hey, Mr. Rivers, got your breakfast here, where do ya' want it?" Jimmy walked in with his usual smile. With his phone held in his right hand, Mason pointed to the bedroom with the left.

As his eyes fell on Mason's hand, the smile on Jimmy's face faltered. *The guy has six freakin' fingers! How did I not notice that when I was here yesterday?* Noticing Jimmy's face, Mason shoved the hand into his pants pocket as he followed him into the bedroom, where April lay scrolling through her phone.

"Hey, Ace, did you know this suite is supposed to be the most haunted one in the entire—" she said, as the aroma of the food pulled her attention from her phone, and she looked up.

"That's great," Mason muttered, "we've got the devil and spooks, what next, witches and warlocks?" he grumbled under his breath.

Jimmy gave him a cautious look. "You have something against warlocks, Mr. Rivers? 'Cause I happen to know one, personally," Jimmy said casually, parking the cart by the bed. Somehow, Mason was not surprised to hear that.

"No shit?" April added casually, as if speaking of the weather. "I guess they'd come in handy if you, like, wanted to put a curse on someone or turn 'em into a toad or something, huh?"

"Nah, it's nothin' like you see in the movies or on TV. Actually, I'm a warlock in a local coven here in town. We practice what you might call 'white majicks.' We primarily worship the 'triple-horn Goddess' and the 'horned one,'" he stood, waiting hopefully for a tip.

Luckily, Mason had remembered to grab some cash at the ATM. He dug out a twenty and handed it to Jimmy.

"Thanks, Mr. Rivers, enjoy your meal. If you need anything else, you know who to call," Jimmy offered, with a wink and a smile.

"I'll do that—say, wait a minute. Actually, there *is* something else," Mason said.

"Yeah? You name it, I'll do it," Jimmy replied.

"Some guys from my band are headed this way soon," Mason explained. "Any possibility of scoring me some decent herb ... say, in the next thirty minutes? I can make it worth your while," he imagined wheels turning in Jimmy's head as he pondered the idea.

"Not a problem. How much ya' need?" Jimmy inquired.

"What would a quarter cost?" Mason asked.

"For the stuff I normally get? It'd be a hundred and forty bucks, and I'll even throw in some rolling papers."

Mason thought the price was a little high, no pun. Jimmy had inflated the cost, intent on padding his own wallet.

"Okay, deal. Not that I don't trust you, but I'll give you half now, the other half on delivery. I presume you can cover the rest?" Mason said.

Jimmy didn't hesitate, "You bet, be back in a flash with your stash."

Mason counted out some bills and handed them over. Jimmy stuffed them in his wallet and left the suite. Mason sat down on the bed next to April, who was chowing down on a breakfast taco.

"Is that all you ordered? Where's mine?" he asked, frowning at the empty serving tray.

"Sorry. You snooze, ya' lose," she mumbled around a mouthful of taco.

He watched while she popped the last bite in her mouth and made a production out of savoring it, rolling her eyes and groaning in mock ecstasy.

Disgusted, he stood up to get himself a beer from the mini fridge, as the sound of giggling stopped him. "What's so funny?" he asked, turning back.

"You are so damn gullible, Ace. Sit down and eat your breakfast," she chuckled, handing him two tacos she'd secreted off the serving tray.

"Real funny," he grabbed them. He sat back down and dug in, taking a large bite. "It's already cold!" he complained, wolfing it down anyway.

"There's a freakin' microwave behind the bar, for crying out loud. Quit your bitchin' and go nuke it," she scolded him.

Standing, he got up, wandered into the living area, and found the microwave. Uncertain how long to heat one taco, he nuked it, removed it, took a huge bite, and burned the crap out of the roof of his mouth. Cursing, he grabbed an ice cube from the bin under the bar and stuck it on his scalded tongue to ease the pain.

"Did you find it?" April called out.

"Yeah, I found it," he yelled. If she knew what he'd done, she'd only laugh her ass off. He strode back to the bedroom, hoping the pain would subside soon.

About thirty minutes later, Jimmy returned and rapped on the door. Mason opened the door to let him in, closing it behind him.

"Here you are, Mr. Rivers—best herb in town, if I say so myself," he bragged. He handed Mason a small zip-lock bag, along with a pack of rolling papers.

Smelling the skunky aroma emanating from the bag even before he'd opened it for inspection, Mason was impressed. "You did me righteous, Jimbo, appreciate it. Here's your money and a little extra for your trouble," Mason said, forking over the cash, slipping an extra twenty on top.

"No problemo, if you need anything else, call me. You have my private number now, I sent it to your phone," Jimmy grinned.

Mason raised an eyebrow at that. "Yeah? And how'd you get my number? I don't recall giving it to you," he said guardedly.

"Just a little 'white magic,' but don't worry, I won't give it to anyone else. Enjoy your stay, Mr. Rivers, ma'am," he nodded to each of them, grabbing the dinner cart and rolling it out the door.

Mason walked back to the bedroom, handing the bag to April. "Roll us up a couple, the boys should be here soon. I only talked to Jeff, but I'm hoping they'll all come. I want to give them a little peace offering to help break the ice, so to speak," he said, sitting on the bed next to her.

"How do you plan to explain your newfound ability and the extra finger?" she asked with a smirk.

"Good question. I could tell 'em the truth, but if I do, they'll freak out for sure," he breathed out a sigh.

"Maybe after they smoke some of this stuff, they'll be too buzzed to notice," she offered.

"No way! The second I play, they'll know. I need to come up with something fast, they'll be here any minute." Unfortunately, he couldn't think of any way to explain the phenomena.

April shrugged and continued rolling in silence. Mason stood and paced the room, wracking his brain for a believable explanation, rejecting different scenarios as fast as they popped into his mind.

A knock at the door interrupted his thoughts. Taking a deep breath, he started toward it. Before he got there, it opened and Ally walked in as she always did.

"Listen, I have a slight dilemma," he said, closing it behind her.

"What's the matter, Ace? Concerned about how to explain your new 'talent' to your old bandmates?"

Shit! Can she read my mind? he wondered.

"Well, if I tell them the truth, they'll think I'm nuts. I've got to—" he was stopped by another knock at the door. "Fuck it all, they're here. What the hell am I gonna do? I didn't think this through before I called Jeff."

The blonde demon chortled at his predicament. "The truth might set you free, Ace, but it won't keep you out of hell. Good luck, lightning boy, you're on your own. Just remember the clock is ticking." She gave him an wicked smile.

"Maybe it would be easier to start fresh with new band members, Mason," April suggested, joining them. "You wouldn't have to worry about explanations, no one would know the difference. People are born with extra fingers and toes all the time."

He hadn't thought of that, it could be the best way to handle the situation. The hitch was it would take forever to vet three new members, and they wouldn't know any of his songs. He was running out of options, and Jeff was now banging on the door.

Ally stood at the bar with a fresh drink, relishing his indecision.

"I'll just tell them the truth. If they can't handle it, fuck 'em. We'll just have to find some new talent," he finally decided. He opened the door and was relieved to see all three of the guys. "Hey, guys, sorry to keep you waiting. Good to see y'all, come on in," he waved them inside.

Jeff walked in with a frown. Warily, he and the other two entered the suite, while Mason shut the door.

He introduced April and Ally and told the three to help themselves at the bar. Larry, the rhythm guitar player, was ogling Ally, while Davy, the drummer, had his eye on April.

Jeff was the first to spot Mason's altered left hand. He did an instant double take. "What the holy fuck happened to your freaking hand, Mase?" His jaw dropped in astonishment. That got the others' attention.

"It's a long story. The short of it is, I, uh … stupidly made a deal with an actual … demon, in exchange for *this*," he said straight-faced, holding up his hand.

The silence in the room was deafening. Jeff was the first to speak. "Mase, you really screwed the pooch this time. You dragged us all the way up here to feed us some crap story? I feel sad for you, you've finally lost your freakin' marbles, dude. C'mon, guys, let's get outta here," he said, shaking his head sadly.

"Wait! It isn't crap, Jeff. I can prove it," Mason exclaimed, stepping in front of them to stop them.

"Okay, Mase. You have thirty seconds to impress me before we're history," Jeff crossed his arms impatiently.

Mason agreed. Pulling out the "slightly modified" Strat, he plugged it in. When they saw the guitar, all their eyes nearly bugged out. Mason picked a song they all knew and placed his fingers lightly on the strings. The digits took off, the music soaring as they raced up and down the frets. Intricate leads and riffs that would have been impossible before poured from his soul in a torrent of stunning arpeggios laced with tight flourishes. When he finished, his former bandmates just stood there in shocked silence.

"Still think I was bullshitting you?" he asked.

"H-How the hell did you learn to play like that? It's only been a freakin' week since we kicked you. *Nobody* could master the stuff you just played in a week's time, plus what's up with the fingers? What the fuck's going on here, Mase?" Jeff sputtered uneasily. Davy and Larry stared at him like he'd just arrived from another planet.

"I told you, I sold my freakin' soul to a devil, and in return, I'm gonna be one of the greatest guitarists in the world," he said patiently.

"Wait a second, you said '*a* devil,' you mean there's more than one?" Jeff asked incredulously.

"Yeah, 'fraid so. This one goes by the name Adriel. I think he's one of many walking this earth. But I assure you, he's the 'real McCoy,'" he replied solemnly.

"I can vouch for that, boys. Your buddy Mason is a very perceptive fellow," Ally said with a smirk. At that same moment, the demoness revealed her true face to them for a split second.

Viewing her monstrous visage, Larry and Davy each turned white as a sheet. Jeff shrieked like a little girl. Mason had his back to her and didn't see the brief transformation, but April did. She fainted, slipping to the floor in a heap. Puzzled by everyone's strange reaction, Mason whirled around to face Ally, but was too late. She merely shrugged, chuckling inwardly at his befuddlement.

"What the hell just happened?" he asked her.

"I haven't the foggiest, all I did was give them a smile," she replied innocently.

He didn't believe that for a second. He ran to April and kneeled down, patting her cheeks until she came to and batted his hand away.

"Well, that's something you don't want to see every day, thank you very little," she remarked, sitting up.

The guys eventually came to their senses, scrambling pell-mell for the door to escape this insanity.

When they reached it, Ally waved her hand, and no matter how hard they yanked, the door wouldn't budge. "Leaving so soon? That would be terribly rude. Humans are so overly reactionary," she clicked her tongue at them, then downed a shot of tequila.

"W-What t-the hell are you?" Jeff screeched at her, terrorized. Larry's and Davy's eyes rolled while they kicked and beat on the sturdy door in vain.

"I've often wondered that myself. When the facade slips, everyone sees me differently. Safe to say, it won't happen often. Allow me to introduce myself. I am Alal, the demoness, destroyer of men's souls. Henceforth, however, you will address me only as Ally, the band's new manager and promoter, extraordinaire," she replied coolly.

"Th-This is fucking insane! Y-You're just an illusionist or something, pulling a David Copperfield or some shit on us!" Jeff exclaimed, hoping to convince himself. "I don't believe in the f-fucking devil or d-demons, or whatever the hell you claim to be. P-Please just let us go!" Jeff stammered, frightened and angry.

Ally smiled nastily. "Oh, Adriel, wherefore art thou, master?"

"You called?" a deep bass voice answered from the hallway outside. The door opened and Adriel strolled in, smirking at the stunned look on the newcomers' faces.

Walking over to the three shaking musicians, he produced a thick roll of money out of the air, holding it aloft so they could see the denomination of the bills. "I'm offering you $30,000 in cash, ten grand apiece, to cover the loss of your equipment from Mr. Rivers' drunken tantrum and then some," he said coolly to the trio.

Calming down, Jeff glanced at Larry and Davy, then back at the hand holding the cash. Gathering his courage, he asked cautiously, "Wh-What's the catch, mister?"

"Catch? There is no catch. This is simply payment for the damage done by your former bandmate. I think the amount is sufficient to cover all your losses," he replied. Jeff looked at the others, who nodded their approval. Hesitantly, he stepped forward to take the money.

When he reached for it, however, Adriel tightened his grip on it. "In return for my generosity, I merely ask a favor from you," he said with a tight smile.

"Yeah? What kind of favor are we talking about?" Jeff asked skeptically, not trusting the guy one bit.

"Mr. Rivers and Miss Flowers are both ... clients of mine. If you'd be willing to let bygones be bygones, re-form your band and include them in it, I would be *very* grateful indeed. It would be very profitable for you, as well. As you all saw and heard, Mason is truly a changed man," Adriel replied smoothly.

"W-We could do that, right, guys?" Jeff asked, turning to the bass player and drummer. Larry and Davy glanced at one another uncertainly, before nodding their heads in reluctant agreement.

"A-Are you really a d-devil, mister?" Davy asked him.

"I'm a legitimate businessman, sir. If you mean to imply that I'm some mythological creature from the Old Testament, you're sadly mistaken," Adriel indignantly replied.

None of them looked totally convinced, but Jeff took the money from him and quickly divided it between them.

Adriel waited until they'd pocketed the cash before speaking again. "There's merely the small matter of a legal contract that you all need to sign before you leave today. It isn't complicated. It simply states that Mr. Rivers and Miss Flowers are to remain in the band until they've fulfilled their contracts with me," Adriel explained coyly.

Jeff didn't like the sound of that. "What happens if we have to kick him out again?" he asked guardedly.

"Then you walk away from the fame and fortune which would've been yours," Adriel said deceitfully.

Mason saw where this was heading and tried to warn them. "Be extremely careful, guys, this dude is as slippery as snot on a glass door knob. Make sure you read all the fine print before you sign anything," he urged. He could almost see the dollar signs in their eyes and hated to see them making the same huge mistakes he and April had.

"Let's have a look at that contract, mister, then we'll see what's what," Jeff said, crossing his arms once more.

"Excellent, just give me a moment ..." Adriel produced a tablet from his jacket and handed it to him.

Jeff looked excitedly at Larry and Davy, who were sweating profusely despite the cool temperature of the room. The three huddled together with Mason and April to analyze every word and phrase in the contract, carefully examining it for any hidden clauses or meanings.

Twenty minutes later, Jeff handed the tablet back to Adriel. "Well, there's nothing in there that mentions 'selling our souls' or words to that effect, in re-forming the band, so I suppose it's legit." Mason could tell Jeff still wasn't fully convinced.

"I assure you, everything in the contract is completely on the up and up," Adriel wheedled. "All I need is your signatures, and fame and fortune shall be yours," Adriel enticed, a beguiling smile on his face.

Mason groaned, as first Jeff, then the other two took the stylus and signed their names to the contract.

"With that all settled, I'd like to propose a toast," Adriel announced, pulling a small flask from his jacket pocket. Pouring measured shots of a crimson liquid into shot glasses, he handed them to the three. It appeared to be the same mysterious beverage Mason had seen Adriel imbibe at his condo. "Here's to a long and prosperous future together. I promise you, it'll be one hell of a time," Adriel toasted, downing his shot.

The three doubtfully followed suit, grimacing at the noxious taste of the liquid. "What the hell was that?" Davy asked, making a face.

"My own special blend. Something I've been working on over the course of many, many years. I call it 'The Devil's Brew,'" Adriel replied slyly, with a wink.

None of them thought that was funny. "Seriously, what the hell did we just drink?" Jeff demanded anxiously.

"The essence of your fellow man—a few choice herbs and spices, fermented with a smidgen of my blood. Needless to say, the elixir's effects are permanent," he chuckled coldly.

At that, Jeff tossed his glass on the floor and was moving toward Adriel to punch his lights out when Mason stepped forward to stop him.

"Calm down, Jeff, he's bullshitting you. It's only V-8 juice and vodka, right, Abby?" he barked, restraining Jeff with both arms.

"If you say so," Adriel agreed calmly, with a crooked grin. Jeff didn't seem convinced, but he stopped struggling to break free of Mason's embrace.

"I feel sorta strange, Jeff. That wasn't like any damn V-8 I ever tasted," Larry said anxiously, rubbing his eyes to try to clear his vision.

Davy was also feeling odd. "I don't like this, guys. What's happening ... I feel something, like, *moving* inside me!" Davy screeched, clutching his stomach with both hands.

Furious, Mason whirled on Adriel. "What the hell did you do to them, you smooth-talking son of a bitch?" he growled, taking a menacing step toward him.

"It's only a little insurance against any future rebellion on their part. I can't have them suddenly changing their minds—as you humans tend to do—when they discover they received less than they bargained for," he shifted backward slightly.

Mason watched in horror as his former band members convulsed and collapsed on the floor, writhing in agony.

"Stop it now, Adriel, you're killing them!" April screamed in dismay.

"Nonsense, they'll be fine. The side effects only last a few minutes in most humans," he disputed, unconcerned.

"Fuck you," Jeff moaned from the floor. Davy and Larry were also clutching their stomachs, rolling on the floor.

Pacing the floor in front of them, Mason felt deceived and helpless. Eventually, their spasms eased, and they sat up, still gasping for breath. Mason and April rushed over to help them all get to their feet.

"I'm sorry, guys, I had no idea he was going to do that to you," Mason apologized to them.

The three glanced at one another with puzzled looks. "Uh, do *what* to us? What the hell are you talking about, Mase?" Jeff asked, confused.

"The drink he gave you, it was obviously spiked with something toxic," Mason replied, glaring at Adriel.

They all stared at Mason like he'd grown a third eye. "Don't know what you're babbling about, Ace. The last thing I remember was signing that contract," Jeff said, shaking his head. Mason looked to Adriel for an explanation.

"It's nothing really, a little something to ensure that they uphold their end of our bargain. Amnesia is an unfortunate by-product of the elixir. I'm still tinkering with the formula, perhaps I'll perfect it in the next millennia or two," he clarified, with an evil grin.

Ally abruptly changed the subject. "I strongly suggest all of you start rehearsing immediately—you're booked to play in 'Battle of the Bands' this Saturday. First prize is a recording contract with Sony records and $5,000 cash," she cheerfully announced.

Mason and the rest were stunned. "S-Say *what*? That's—only three days away. That won't give us nearly enough time to practice. These guys have day jobs, for cripes sake!" Mason exclaimed.

"Not any more—this is their only job now," Ally asserted. "They need to understand that this gig is for all the marbles. You have one shot at stardom, and this is it," she replied coolly.

Mason didn't like it, none of them did, but what could they do?

"So, go now and purchase the instruments you need, to be delivered only to this room," Adriel directed the three men. "I've arranged with the hotel management to move your closest neighbors away, so you can practice as long as you want. The clock's ticking, guys," Adriel commanded, pointing toward the door.

Without a word, Jeff and the other two turned in unison and strode to the door, which now opened freely.

When they'd gone, Mason turned to Adriel. "Those guys are acting like freakin' robots, what the hell did you do to them?" he hissed.

"You worry too much, Mr. Rivers," Adriel advised. "If I were you, I'd be more concerned with my own future. You and Miss Flowers need one another to prevail in this endeavor. Your fellow bandmates' actions are of little consequence to me, as long as they make me money. I win whether you succeed or fail. You both should've read the fine print on their contracts," Adriel gleefully rubbed his hands together.

Mason and April were both stunned. "B-But ... I read the damned contract, too, there *was* no 'fine print,'" he protested.

"Ahh, but there *is*," Adriel pointed out. "You just have to know where to look," he produced the tablet containing their contract. Opening the page, he scrolled down until he found what he wanted, handing it to Mason for his inspection. "Oh, and you might need this," Adriel said, handing Mason a large magnifying glass.

Mason took it and scoured the contract until he finally found it. The writing was so tiny the naked eye would've missed it altogether. At the bottom of the last paragraph was one more sentence.

"*Shit*!" He looked over at April. "This states that if for any reason, they quit the band before you and I complete our part of the contract, we—we lose everything," he sputtered.

"What do you mean by *everything?*" April asked.

"It means we're fucked, is what it means," Mason irritably snapped, throwing the tablet and the magnifier at the smug-looking demon who, somehow, caught both.

"Temper, temper, Mr. Rivers," he chided. "I'm afraid it will be up to you and Miss Flowers to keep the others motivated until you reach your goal. The elixir will help, but it won't work without the proper incentive. Now that you have that carrot, I suggest you use it wisely. I have business to attend to, I'll leave you in Alal's capable hands. Afternoon," Adriel turned and left the suite, closing the door behind him.

"When the guys get back, I'm gonna tell 'em the truth. They should know what they signed up for—not that it'll do them any good. This is all my fucking fault, I never should've called them. I knew that asshole Adriel couldn't be trusted," Mason growled, marching over to the bar for a drink.

"I don't think that's such a good idea, Ace. If you tell them the truth, they're likely to rabbit and doom us all. Personally, I'd like to live to see my twenty-first birthday, thank you very much," April pointed out.

He saw her logic and was embarrassed; selfishly, he'd been thinking only of himself. "You're right; we can't tell them about the hidden clause. What they don't know won't hurt 'em, right?" He looked at her, hoping she'd agree and assuage his guilt. She didn't, which made him feel like crap.

"It wouldn't change things, just make them worse," she said, frowning. "We've got to get our shit together and fast, if we're to have any chance of winning that freaking contest."

"Listen to your girlfriend, Ace," Ally chimed in. "You'll need a miracle to win that contest. You'll be playing first in the lineup on Saturday, and— I'm really not supposed to tell you this—but yours is not the only band Adriel has made a deal with," Ally revealed, with a satisfied smirk.

Looking at April, Mason saw she was as shocked by Ally's update as he.

"First, she is *not* my girlfriend. Second, why didn't you tell us about this before I let the other guys sign Adriel's fucking contract? This is *such shit*!" he shouted, livid that she'd kept them in the dark.

"Where's the fun in that? This certainly gives you more incentive to win, doesn't it?" she challenged smugly, pouring herself yet another shot of tequila.

"This is fucked up on so many levels," Mason cried, grinding his teeth in frustration.

"Just so you know, my money's on the other band," Ally grinned, rubbing salt in the wound.

April tried to console him, but he was not having it. "You're a filthy, wicked cunt, you know that, right?" she snarled at Ally.

"Why, thank you, I do my best. Do you realize that you're *so* much more attractive when you're angry?" Ally countered, with a lascivious lick of her lips.

"Fuck you, bitch!" April shot back.

"You'd enjoy that, but I'm afraid it'll have to wait. Work first, play later," the blonde demon responded.

"In your dreams, you fucking harpy!" April sniped. Lighting a cigarette, she blew her exhaled smoke in Alal's face, turned, and walked away in a huff.

Aware that his timing was terrible, Mason chided April, "You know, you really shouldn't smoke, it's bad for your health, not to mention your pipes."

April whirled around, staring daggers at him. "If we don't win that damn contest, I won't *have* any health to worry about, will I? Just leave my bad habits alone, if you don't mind!"

Mason threw up his hands in surrender. "You're right, I'm very sorry. I can be a righteous asshole sometimes," he tried expressing regret.

"Face it, Ace, you've been an asshole *most* of the brief time I've known you. Don't sweat it, you are who you are," April said bluntly, stalking out onto the balcony to finish her smoke.

"For someone so sorely lacking in the girlfriend department, you really should get a clue, Ace. Even assholes get laid occasionally, but it helps if you don't cut off your dick to spite your face," Alal advised, downing another shot. It amazed Mason that she was still conscious and standing. It had been her fifth or sixth large shot of tequila, and she wasn't even slurring.

"Ah, don't you think you ought to take it easy on that stuff?" he lectured her. "It's not even noon and—"

Her icy glare stopped him cold. "Listen, you pathetic human, the day I get drunk drinking this horse piss is the day I quit my job and become a nun, which ain't gonna happen, for obvious reasons," she said icily, tossing back another shot.

"Great," he muttered to himself, walking away. "Just what we need, an alcoholic demon in denial."

An hour passed before the guys arrived back at the suite. They all helped themselves to the whiskey at the minibar.

"That was the weirdest shopping trip. Never had that much money to spend on a decent guitar. I snagged myself a sweet, custom Fender Bass and amp," Jeff bragged, wincing as the whiskey burned a trail down his throat. Davy and Larry had also done well, purchasing a Tama Drum kit, a Rickenbacker 620 twelve-string, and a Marshall stack to complete their shopping spree.

"We also grabbed a Peavey PA system on sale with mikes and stands included," Jeff added.

"They should've delivered it all by now, man. I hope I gave 'em the right room number," Davy worried.

Mason felt lower than an ant turd for not telling them the odds they faced in the upcoming contest.

A rap at the door signaled the arrival of their loot. When Mason opened the door, Jimmy and a couple of helpers hauled all the new equipment inside, placing it in the center of the living room. When they left, Mason tipped them all well.

"Okay, guys, let's get to work, we've got to cram two weeks' practice into forty-eight hours," he said, helping them unbox the instruments. Twenty minutes later, they were all set up and ready to go.

April walked in, saying, "Hey, guys, listen to this. I'm looking at the contest web page, and the rules state: 'Each band will be limited to only two songs or ten minutes, whichever comes first.' If you go over the ten-minute limit, you're immediately disqualified!" April pointed out as she walked in.

"Man, that sucks, I thought we'd get to play at least three," Larry groused.

"I suggest we play the last two I wrote before my ... ah, 'departure.' Those both rock pretty hard, and with April's vocal chops, we'll knock 'em dead on the harmony," Mason said, as they tuned up.

Fortunately, April had heard them perform the songs in clubs around town, so she was familiar with the tunes, if not the lyrics. The third time they played them, she had memorized half of the words, and by the fifth, she was singing lead and adding delicious harmonies on the bridges.

They continued rehearsing for another three hours before breaking for lunch. Mason ordered food for everyone except Ally, who seemed content drinking hers. After eating, they resumed playing until, after hours of mind-numbing repetition, April's voice began to falter. At that point, they agreed to stop for the day. Jeff and the other bandmates joined Ally at the bar.

"If I have to sing that song one more time today, I'll throw myself off the freaking balcony and be done with it," April moaned, collapsing on the couch, exhausted.

"I think we're all worn out. We sure won't be doing ourselves any favors if you lose your voice," Mason said, sitting down beside her.

"You really think we have a chance in hell of winning this frickin' contest?" April asked him quietly, watching the other three guys stand around the bar, drinking and laughing.

"If we don't, our options aren't looking too good. Hey, look on the bright side—worst happens, we'll spend eternity together," he joked, trying unsuccessfully to lighten her mood.

"Not funny, asshole," she said, punching his arm. "I'm serious, what happens to us if we lose? I don't trust Adriel not to welch on our deal. Even if we should win, he could change the rules of the game on a whim. Look what he did to your band buddies, what makes you think he won't do something worse to us?" Shakily, she lit a smoke from her purse.

"Honestly, I don't have an answer to that. We'll just have to hope he keeps his word. He's got us by the short hairs, and short of killing him, I don't see any way out of that freakin' contract," Mason snorted derisively.

She turned to stare at him until he was unnerved. "Wait, you're not actually suggesting we—" he began.

April held up a finger to her lips to silence him. "There's gotta be a way out of those contracts we signed," she almost whispered. "Maybe some supernatural ritual, an exorcism, or something. Hell, I don't know, I'm grasping at straws here." She shrugged, stood, and walked over to the bar.

Mason sat in the living room, pondering possibilities, while the guys, drinks in hand, wandered out onto the large balcony, as far from Ally as they could get and still be in the same building. Motioning April to follow him, he got up, and they moved to the bedroom for privacy.

"I might have an idea. That Jimmy dude from room service said he was a warlock, right? Maybe he could help us. If he's a witch, maybe he could, I don't know, put a spell or a curse on Abby and send his ass back to hell, or wherever he came from," he suggested quietly.

"Jimmy said he's a member of a Wiccan coven, Ace. Last I heard, they don't practice 'black magic.' You need someone who's an authority on satanic rituals, someone who practices the dark arts, not some tree worshiping bellhop," she rolled her eyes at him.

"Well, if you have a better idea, let's hear it. Murdering demons isn't exactly my forté, alright?" he said, amazed that they were even having this conversation.

"Jimmy might know someone, it's worth a shot, don't you think?" she suggested.

"I don't know—possibly. Speaking of shots, our newly anointed manager from hell in the other room drinks like a fish. If we could get her drunk enough, she might let something slip that could help us get rid of them both."

"Have you seen how much liquor that *creature* can hold? She'd drink us under the table in a heartbeat, bud," she shook her head at the idea.

"Yeah, you're probably right. *Shit*! There's gotta be something, some Achilles heel we can take advantage of. After she and the guys leave, I'll send for Jimmy, and we'll see what he has to say," Mason said decidedly.

Jeff, Larry, and Davy came back inside, looking a little wobbly from all the booze and weed they'd consumed. Mason realized it was nearly six p.m. The afternoon had flown by in a blur, and his stomach was rumbling hungrily.

The guys said their goodbyes and stumbled their way toward the door. Ally demanded they all return at seven sharp in the morning as she polished off the last drop of tequila in a bottle.

"Well, I'd love to stay and chat, but I have important things to do," she stated. "I don't understand why humans like this crap, all it does is leave a nasty taste in your mouth," she scoffed, giving the empty bottle a contemptuous shake.

"*Some* people actually enjoy the flavor, but it's an acquired taste. A little salt and lemon help to counter its sweetness," Mason told her, impatiently waiting for the demoness to depart.

"Whatever. I'll see you two in the morning. Get some rest, you'll need it tomorrow." She walked out the door.

Right away, Mason ordered them some dinner, asking that Jimmy bring it. He was told Jimmy had left for the day and wouldn't be back until morning.

"Just text him on Instagram, maybe he'll come back tonight if you give him a little incentive." April made an 'O' with her left thumb and forefinger, poking her right index finger in and out suggestively.

"What are you suggesting? We drag him back up here and you screw him for information?"

"In my experience, a little poon will open doors quicker than weed or booze any day of the week," she said with a shrug.

He hadn't given it much thought, but he had to agree with her. He figured most men would jump at the offer of sex with a beautiful woman. He was feeling a little jealous at the thought of her and Jimmy rolling in the hay together, since she didn't seemed at all interested in sex with *him*. Since the BJ she'd given him in his car, she'd shown little interest in his obvious desire to bed her.

"Stop it, Ace! I know what you're thinking, but this has nothing to do with lust. We need information, it's just the quickest and easiest way to get it," she assured him.

He wasn't so sure about that. "So, what'll I tell him, 'Come up for some drinks, oh, and you might bring a rubber or two, hint-hint?'" he said sarcastically.

"Actually, that's not a bad idea. Maybe three rubbers; he's young, it could take a while to get him to talk," she said with a straight face. Mason did a slow burn until he realized she was teasing him again. "Seriously, Ace, just tell him we need to talk, and it'll be worth his while to come, no pun intended," she advised solemnly.

"What if I just straight out tell him about our situation? He might know someone who could help, and you wouldn't have to sacrifice your, uh, 'virtue,'" he suggested.

"FYI, my 'virtue' is not at stake, but if it bothers you for me to screw him for info, that's your call. Personally, I think my way would be quicker," she said.

The knock at the door meant that their dinner had arrived. While Mason was busy composing a text to Jimmy, she got up to open the door, surprised to find Jimmy standing there by the serving cart, with his usual grin.

"Well, hello there, handsome." April beamed up at him. The young man's face blushed crimson at her compliment. "We thought you'd gone for the day, what's up?" she asked him.

"One of the guys called in sick, and they asked me to come back and cover his shift. So, here I am," he replied, grinning like a possum.

"Well, that's actually perfect timing," she said. "C'mon in," she led him toward the bedroom. "Hey, Mase, look who's here," she said brightly, as Jimmy wheeled the cart in.

Mason glanced up from his phone. "Hey, I was just about to text you. If you have a few minutes, we'd like to ask you for a big favor," he waved Jimmy into the bedroom.

"Sure thing, Mr. Rivers, be glad to help anyway I can," he said, stopping the cart in front of them.

Mason started hesitantly, "I know this will sound crazy, but ... do you know anyone who practices, ah, 'black magic,' perchance?" he asked hesitantly.

As he considered Mason's request, Jimmy's smile dimmed. "Why would you need someone like that?" he asked cautiously.

Taking a deep breath, Mason described what that had transpired in the past few days, leading to their current situation. When he finished, Jimmy was quiet for a moment, deep in thought. If he was shocked by Mason's tale, it didn't show.

"If this Adriel dude really is a demon, bustin' a cap in his ass won't work. I could get you a gun, but it'd be useless against him and his kind." He frowned, pondering their dilemma. "I know this dude who's the lead guitarist for this heavy-metal band here in town. He's like this grand pooh bah of his coven. We don't hang anymore, for obvious reasons. He's the only guy I can think of who could maybe help with your, um, 'problem,'" Jimmy said.

"How do we get hold of him? You have his number by any chance?" Mason asked hopefully.

"Nope. Went to school with the dude. We struck up a friendship through a mutual friend 'til I found out he was a demon worshiper. That's not the way I roll." Jimmy shook his head.

He saw the disappointment on their faces at his news. "But hey, I think his band is competing in Saturday's 'Battle of the Bands.' You could probably find him there. Just don't say who sent you, I don't need any blow-back from him or his coven," he snorted scornfully.

Mason glanced at April and knew she was thinking the same thing he was. "Yeah, ya' know, we're also scheduled to play in that contest. What's his name and the name of his band?" Mason asked, growing uneasy.

"His name's Johnny Ripper. The band is 'Jack and the Hell Rippers,'" Jimmy replied.

"How original," April remarked. "What do you bet they're the ones Ally was telling us about earlier?" April turned to Mason indignantly. "If you recall, she said Adriel also had a deal with another band—it's gotta be them. *Shit!*"

Jimmy looked puzzled. "Wait, you saying you're gonna be competing against the Rippers?" he asked, surprised. They merely nodded miserably. "I hear they're one of the favorites to win. Johnny's always been a decent ax man, but his band sucked the big one last time I heard 'em play. Then, maybe six months ago, they re-surfaced as one of the premier death metal bands in town. I haven't heard 'em lately—not my kind of music—but all the metal heads are raving over 'em." Jimmy fidgeted with his key card.

"Fucking Adriel! He's gonna pit us against Ripper's band, I know it. This is just a game to him. He wins no matter who comes out on top," Mason swore, grinding his teeth.

"What happens if you lose?" Jimmy asked hesitantly, not certain he wanted to know.

"I'm not sure, but I doubt it'll be pleasant for the loser," Mason replied soberly.

Jimmy didn't know how to reply to that. "Well, in that case, I really hope you win, Mr. Rivers. I wish I could've been more help," he said lamely. In his pocket, his phone chimed. "Sorry, but I gotta go, the supper rush is on, and they're wondering where I'm at. Best of luck on Saturday. My girlfriend and I have tickets, so we'll be there, cheering you on," he said, turning to leave.

"Thanks, Jimmy, we appreciate that. Thanks for the help," Mason replied, tipping him generously.

When Jimmy left, Mason turned to April, who was rolling a blunt on the bar top. "I guess asking Johnny Ripper for advice is out of the question," he sighed.

"Not necessarily, Ace," she disagreed. "It's unlikely that Ripper knows you or your band. As long as you don't drag Adriel's name into the conversation, how would he possibly know who you were talking about?" She lifted the cover from their supper.

"C'mon April, give me a break. I don't believe for a minute that Adriel isn't playing both sides of the field. Ally's probably with Ripper at this very moment, telling him everything she told us," he grumbled.

"But what if Ripper's band *isn't* the one Adriel made a deal with?" April said. "What if it's another band entirely? Unless you talk to him, you have no way of knowing. What's the worst that could happen?" she asked, grabbing a few bites of the burger and fries Jimmy had brought for supper.

"The worst that could happen is he tips off Adriel that we're planning to kill him. If he gets wind of that, we're truly fucked!" he growled, pacing the room.

"I've got news for you, Ace, we've been 'truly fucked' ever since we signed those contracts. If we can't figure out a way to get rid of him and Ally, our souls will be lost forever. Personally, I don't envision spending eternity with that demonic asshole, thank you," she said between bites.

"I guess it's worth a shot. *Shit*! This burger's cold," he groused, finally taking a bite of his food. He walked over and stuck it in the microwave to heat.

"How about we forget about all this for tonight and do something exciting for a change," she suggested.

Mason's brain instantly switched to potential sex mode. "What exactly did you have in mind?" he smiled, arching a brow.

"I was thinking we should go clubbing down on Sixth Street. Some of the bands in the contest will likely be playing there tonight. It could be a chance to see and hear what kind of talent we'll be facing in the competition," she replied, lighting an after-dinner smoke from her purse.

Mason's face fell, along with any hope he had of getting laid. "I suppose you're right. Just so you know, I've never been much of a dancer. The only rhythm I have is in my hands," he said, tossing most of his uneaten burger into the trash.

"Well, maybe you can put them to good use later tonight," she replied, licking her lips suggestively. Mason got hard just thinking about it. "Let's go. Nice as it is, I'm getting cabin fever in this place," she grabbed her purse off the couch.

Mason called the valet to bring his car around, and they left the suite ...

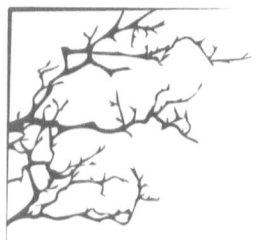

Chapter Nine

North Austin

Tommy "The Toad" Truman sat alone in a dark bar, a warm beer in his hand. He was troubled, since he hadn't heard from Harley in nearly two days. His concern mounted as the hours passed with no contact. Something bad must have happened to the big dude. Tommy's only hope was that his bike was still in one piece wherever Harley had left it. If Harley hadn't had seniority in the club, he never would've lent him his bike. None of the other members had heard from him lately, either. He'd called around, checking all the local hospitals and the county jail with the same result. No one had seen him. He'd already checked with the local bars where they hung out, to no avail. *So, where the hell is the big bastard?* he wondered, placing a twenty on the bar to pay his tab.

Frustrated, he left the Poodle Dog, self-consciously straddled his old Honda 750cc, and hit the electric start. The engine purred to life with hardly a sound, unlike his Harley-Davidson. If he was seen riding the Japanese pussy-bike around town, his rep would take a big hit—but it still beat walking in the oven-like heat that passed for summer in Texas. A few blocks away, he pulled into Little Joe's driveway and killed the engine.

"Little Joe" Hampton was anything but little. The oldest member of their club stood six feet, six inches tall and weighed nearly three hundred pounds. Pushing seventy years of age, most of his muscle had gone to flab, but nobody dared say it to his face. He was still one of the meanest, toughest men Tommy had ever met. He was also smart as a whip and had ruled over this local chapter of the club for the past twenty-five years. Harley and Little Joe had ridden together for fifteen years, so if anyone could find Harley, it would be him. Tommy got off the Honda, walked up to the unassuming one-story frame house, and knocked on the front door. When no one answered, he knocked a little louder.

"Hold yer fuckin' horses! I'm comin,'" a voice inside yelled. The outside light came on, the front door opened, and Little Joe stood there, squinting down at Tommy until he finally recognized him. He yanked him inside. "What the hell'r you doin' here, Toad? Good way to get your balls blown off, comin' here unexpectedly at night," Joe growled, easing the hammer down on the forty-five caliber semiautomatic he held behind his back.

"Sorry about that, Little Joe, it's just ... Harley's missing. I bailed him outta jail yesterday, and he borrowed my ride to go find some asshole that messed up *his* bike, and I ain't heard from him since. I've tried ta call him more'n a dozen times, but it just goes to voice mail. I think he may be in trouble. I done called the hospitals and jails, he ain't in any of them," Tommy rambled nervously.

"*Crap*! Did you check all the bars? He's probably just wasted and shacked up with some scurvy bitch." Joe exclaimed, easing his large butt into in his ratty recliner.

On a glass-topped coffee table in front of him sat a mound of a white crystalline substance with a scale and a pile of small plastic bags beside it. Tommy knew it was meth. The gang was a large distributor of the drug, supplying about twenty percent of the county's junkies with their daily fix. The Mexican cartels provided the rest. Each side had their turf clearly staked out, neither messed with the other.

"Sit your ass down, kid, you're making me nervous, and Little Joe don't like to be nervous," Joe growled, cocking and unlocking the hammer on his pistol. Tommy grabbed a seat on a small couch beside him, unsure of what to say to the terrifying geriatric biker.

"If ya' want a snort, help yourself. Just be careful, it ain't cut yet," Little Joe offered gruffly.

"Uh, no thanks, I had some earlier, I'm good," Tommy respectfully declined. He knew better than to insult the man, but he was also aware that snorting the stuff until it had been 'stepped-on' was dicey, at best.

"Suit yerself," Little Joe said, laying the gun on the table in front of him.

Terrified, Tommy looked from the gun to Little Joe and back. *What did I do? Why does the old geezer expect me to shoot myself?* he thought, feeling his sphincter tighten a couple of notches. He'd fucked up somehow, insulted the leader of his club, and now it seemed he'd pay the ultimate price for his unknown blunder. With a trembling right hand, he reached over to pick up the gun, when Little Joe's gravelly voice stopped him.

"What the fuck'r you doin'?' *Nobody* touches my piece without my permission!" Joe snarled, snatching the gun from Tommy's hand and pointing it at his nose.

Tommy's bulbous eyes bugged out as he stared down the barrel of the forty-five. "B-But I-I was just doin' what you t-told me to do, Little Joe. I-I'm sorry if I insulted you, p-p-please d-don't s-shoot me!" Tommy stammered, pleading for his life. A nasty, warm wetness spread from his crotch as his bladder emptied into his jeans and ran down his leg to puddle inside his boot.

"What the hell ya' talkin' about, Toad? You ain't makin' any fuckin' sense." Joe frowned, but he lowered the pistol, to Tommy's relief.

"Y-you told me to shoot myself, I-I was just f-following your orders, Little Joe," Tommy stammered.

The old biker stared at him for a second. "You dumb ass, I said 'suit yerself,' not 'shoot yerself.' You'd best clean out your fuckin' ears, ya' just about got your stupid ass killed," Joe pointed out. "Anyway, Harley has one of them tracking Apps on his phone, I'll call this number, enter the password and bingo! It'll locate his ass," Joe said, punching in the code on his phone.

It took a moment for the GPS to load and respond. When the results popped up, Little Joe scowled at the phone. "This thing says he ain't very far from here," he said, squinting at the screen. "Says he's currently on Payne Avenue. What the hell would he be doing over there?" He glared at Tommy, as if he would know.

"Beats me, Little Joe. But whatever he's doin', he ain't answering his freakin' phone," Tommy shrugged.

"Well, get yer ass over there and find him. Tell him to call me ASAP!" Joe demanded, giving him the address.

Tommy did not hesitate; rushing out the door, he climbed on his bike and sped off to locate Harley ...

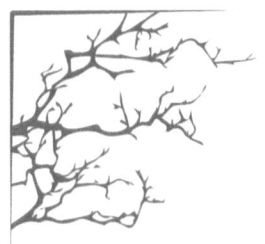

Chapter Ten

The Driskill Hotel

Mason and April were halfway across the hotel lobby when they realized they wouldn't need the car, as Sixth Street was only half a block away. He instructed the valet to return the car to the garage, and they strolled down the sidewalk. They walked up the street and entered the first bar they came to, a place called "Crooked Dick's," where heavy metal music was blasting from the PA. The beefy doorman/bouncer took their ten-dollar cover charge, and they waded into a crowd of college kids, with a few die-hard baby-boomers and hipster wannabes sprinkled throughout. Finished with their first set, the band onstage were taking "a pause for the cause," which usually comprised a few tokes in a back room, a shot of whiskey, or both.

Mason ordered a beer for himself and a Sex-on-the-Beach for April, hoping she'd take the hint.

She shook her head, smiling at his lame attempt at subliminal messaging. "You really want it *bad,* don't you, Ace?" she chuckled.

Feeling his cheeks flush, he didn't respond. It seemed like a month of Sundays since he'd been laid, and he was hornier than a puppy with two peckers.

"What band is playing?" he changed the subject.

"I don't know who's playing, ask the freaking bartender, for crying out loud. I gotta find the little girls' room." She left him standing at the bar.

Mason approached a young blonde standing nearby. She had so many shiny studs in her nose and lips that he was surprised she could breathe or talk. The band picked that moment to start their next set, so when Mason asked her who was playing, he had to cup his ear and lean down to hear her reply.

"It'th tha' Hell Wippers t'night," she lisped loudly over the music.

Mason nodded, turning his attention to the band, whose lead vocalist and rhythm guitarist seemed to be a slender young woman dressed head-to-toe in grunge-goth. Her long, frizzy, multi-colored hair bounced to the beat of the music as she belted out unintelligible lyrics. A flowing black cape swirled around her tattooed neck and arms as she moved sensuously around onstage. A silver medallion in the shape of a pentagram hung from a chain around her neck, swinging back and forth like a metronome. The lead guitarist was a diminutive dude, but the riffs he was playing were jaw-dropping in their complexity. This had to be Jack Ripper, the band's namesake.

April returned from the restroom and ordered another drink, this time a Jack and Coke, a silent rebuke to Mason for ordering the fancy drink earlier. He frowned but didn't speak to her. She wouldn't have heard him over the ear-pounding music, anyway. The band played a few more originals, then ended their second set with a cover of the metal band, Death's "Lack of Comprehension," to the crowd's enthusiastic approval. When the music stopped and they could hear again, Mason and April pushed through the crowd to a table reserved for the band. The bass player and the drummer had gone in back to indulge in one illicit drug or another.

Mason introduced April and himself to Jack. "I hear you're playing in the contest Saturday. Is there somewhere we can talk that's a little more private? I'd like to ask you something a little odd," Mason inquired, his ears still ringing from the amplifiers.

Jack gazed at him with suspicion before speaking. "Dude, I'm not gay, and no matter what you've heard, I'm really not into threesomes. We cool on that?" Jack took a swig of his beer.

Mason glanced at April, who was smirking. "Uh, that's not what we need at all ... we need help with a sticky situation we're in, and I was informed you might be the one who can do it. I could make it worth your while," he replied evenly.

Jack studied the two of them as he took another drink of his beer while contemplating his answer. Deciding to listen, he stood up. "I'll give you five minutes, then we gotta play our last set. Follow me," he led them down a narrow hallway past the restrooms. Stopping at the last door, he knocked twice and entered. When they walked inside, the drummer was passing a joint to the bass player.

"Hey, guys, take it outside, and give us the room," Jack ordered. They nodded and left, closing the door. "So, what the hell is this about, and what makes you think I could help?" Jack asked pointedly.

Taking a deep breath, Mason said, "I was told you're someone who knows quite a bit about satanic rituals and practices, is that right?"

The dark-eyed lead guitarist just stared at him in silence. "Dude, if you want to join my coven, you'll find an application on our website. But you'll have to wait until the contest is over." He leaned back in his chair.

Mason shook his head. "That isn't why we're here ..." he paused to think. "We need to know if there's a way to ... how should I put this? We need to know if it's possible to kill a demon?" he deadpanned.

Jack wondered if he was joking, finally deciding he wasn't. "You out of your fucking mind, dude? We don't kill demons, we *worship* them! I wouldn't tell you, even if I could. You came to the wrong fucking person. Now I've gotta get back onstage," he coolly said, dismissing them both, opening the door to leave.

"Wait! I said I'd make it worth your while, and I meant it. I'll pay for any useful information," Mason added.

Attentive, Jack turned back to him. "Yeah? How much are we talking?" he probed.

Mason glanced at April before answering. "I'll pay you two grand, half up front, the rest when the deed is done," he replied.

Jack smiled coldly, shaking his head, "You'll have to do better than that. If word got out I'd betrayed my oath of secrecy, I'd be risking my position in the coven, possibly my life. Five grand, or no deal," he demanded, his hand on the doorknob.

Mason picked up on the guy's greed, but where else could they go? "Okay, five grand. Tell us what we need to do to get this thing done," he agreed uneasily.

The guy grinned nastily, displaying teeth that had hadn't seen a toothbrush in years. "Okay, here's what you'll have to do ..."

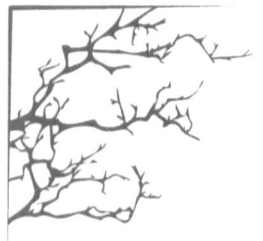

Chapter Eleven

Adriel's House

Tommy pulled his bike to a halt in front of the two-story house on Payne and killed the engine. He didn't see any sign of Harley or his chopper in the driveway. The home had security lights in the back, but being short, he couldn't see over the eight-foot privacy fence separating him from the backyard. Dim light leaked from windows on either side of the front door, but that didn't mean anyone was inside. He knew lights might be on a timer.

So, if his phone is here, where the hell is Harley and my bike? He thought, climbing off the Honda. He stood dithering, wracking his brain for the safest way to proceed. Old Harley could be shacked up with some bar slut—but he might also be in real danger. Toad peered into the dark front windows before knocking on the front door, with no response. With a sigh, he walked around to the tall privacy fence, approached the gate, and tried the latch. Much to his astonishment, it opened. Cautiously, he stepped into the yard, and looked around. He was amazed by what he saw. The place was a junkyard filled with all kinds of vehicles. In the furthermost reach of the security lights' illumination, he spied his bike leaning up against an old metal shed. Seeing no guard dogs to contend with, he slipped into the yard. As he walked toward the back, however, the gate snapped shut behind him with a resounding *clack,* making him jump.

Cautiously, he monitored the back door of the house for a sign that its closing had alerted anyone inside. When a minute passed with no one appearing, he wove his way between the abandoned cars to his bike.

The security light suddenly flickered and died, leaving him in the dark. *Shit*! He hadn't expected his luck to hold for long; sadly, he was right. The low warning snarl of a large dog rumbled in the surrounding night. He froze in his tracks as the growling drew closer. He could either try to make it back to the gate before the damn dog attacked, or he could stand and try to fight an animal he couldn't see with only his buck knife as a weapon. He didn't like his odds of making it to the gate, but it would be better than having a freaking dog tear his balls off. Steeling himself to make a dash toward the gate, a second growl joined the first, stopping him mid-stride. *Crap!* It appeared two of them were stalking him. The second one had flanked him, and he was trapped in a narrow gap between vehicles with nowhere to go.

"Brutus, Cerberus, heel," a deep voice called out from the dark.

If he hadn't already pissed his pants at Little Joe's, Tommy would have done so at the sound of that voice. Instead, his sphincter tightened a few notches.

"Call off your dogs, dude, I'm comin' out," he yelled, working his way back through the cars. As he did, he opened the four-inch blade of his knife, holding it down by his side, in case one of the dogs attacked. "Where the hell is Harley? He must be here because that's my fucking bike you have stashed by that shed, asshole!" he yelled with more bravado than he felt. He saw the silhouette of a tall figure standing a few feet away.

"Where the hell, indeed? The more pressing question is, what should I do with you, Mr. Truman?" the dark figure spoke coolly, but malevolently.

Tommy didn't like the sound of that. *How does the fucker know my name?* "Listen, Mister, I got a blade. I don't want to hurt you, I—I don't care about Harley, all I want is my bike back," he pleaded, nervous sweat soaking his shirt.

"Unluckily for you, it seems my esteemed associate, Alal, was unaware of the GPS tracking capability on phones nowadays. That was an oversight on my part. It's difficult to keep up with human technology, is it not, Alal?" the dark figure chuckled.

Who the fuck is Alal? was Tommy's final thought as something leaped from the shadows, knocking him flat on his back. Wicked teeth, sharp as razors tore out his throat in a spray of crimson before he could react. Unseen in the darkness, hot blood spurted from severed arteries in his neck, pooling around his twitching body. Eagerly, Alal kneeled and pressed her gaping maw over his wounds, gulping down the blood as it pulsed out of his ever-weakening heart. When he was dead, she stood up, walked over to Adriel, and kneeled before him.

"I am sorry, master. I forgot to destroy the pathetic human's phone. I am not worthy to serve you, do with me as you will," the demoness said resignedly, bowing her head in subservience.

"Rise, Alal. It was a lapse in judgment on my part, as well. I assumed you knew about the tracking capabilities built into the wretched devices, that's on me," Adriel said neutrally.

"What do you wish me to do with him?" She nodded to the cooling corpse at her feet.

"We need to discourage any more of his kind from sniffing around. It's becoming quite the nuisance," Adriel reached down to search the dead biker. Taking Tommy's wallet and his phone, he stuffed the wallet in his jacket pocket.

The phone wasn't locked or password protected, so he opened the contacts section and quickly found what he was looking for. After giving Alal her orders, he destroyed the cell, crushing it with one mighty squeeze of his hand. He dumped the remnants in a garbage bin and ambled back inside the house. Alal retrieved her pickup from the street and backed it up to the gate.

She easily lifted Tommy's body with one hand, tossing it roughly into the bed of the truck. Climbing into the cab, she closed the door and sped off down the road. She wasn't worried about being pulled over by some nosy cop. If it happened, she'd take care of the problem. The truck had been stolen in New Mexico and was registered to a person long dead. Additionaly, the license plates had been changed several times in the past six months. If a cop stopped her and called it in, she would eliminate him, and leave the truck and the body. Neither one could be traced back to Adriel or her. Five minutes later, she arrived in front of the address Adriel had provided.

Parking the truck in front of a neighbor's house, shed patiently waited. Two hours slowly passed before the lights went off inside the house. She waited another forty-five minutes to give its owner time to get to sleep before exiting the truck's cab. Reaching into the bed of the truck, she lifted the dead biker out as though he weighed less than a sack of potatoes. After accomplishing her task, she climbed back into the truck and drove away. As she imagined the expression on the face of the house's lone occupant when he awoke the following morning, she cranked up the volume on the radio, smiling at the song that was playing—the Stones' "Sympathy for the Devil."

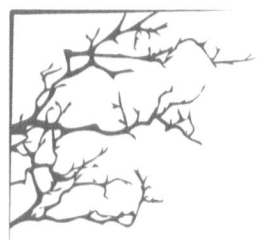

Chapter Twelve

Sixth Street, Austin

When Jack and his band started their last set around midnight, Mason and April left the bar. They walked back to the hotel looking glum. They'd hoped the information Jack provided would solve their predicament. The problem was, the sacrifice of an innocent human was an essential part of Jack's solution—something neither of them would do. Jack had shrugged, demanding half the fee up front which Mason had promised. Mason told him to go fuck himself.

Jack had pointed out that whether or not they acted upon it, he'd offered them the solution and insisted upon being paid. Unwillingly, Mason had finally agreed, telling him he'd be paid when the coming contest was over.

"I still think we'd be better off finding a priest to perform an exorcism, or something similar. If he really expects us to kill an innocent person, he's a metal-headed moron!" April argued as they entered their suite.

"Maybe we should attack this from another angle. I don't know what else to do, we're kinda between a rock and a hard place," Mason said, making himself a nightcap at the minibar.

"Or maybe we just need to find someone who *isn't* innocent," she said, only half in jest.

Glancing at her, he saw desperation that mirrored his own in the depths of her eyes.

"You, ah, have a suggestion?" he said, assured that she did.

"I can only think of one person," she replied.

"Yeah? Who are we talking about?" he asked, taking a drink from his glass.

"That fucking cop who raped me, Officer Dipshit, the one who pulled us over the other day," she snarled, causing Mason to spew his mouthful of whiskey on the floor.

"Are you outta your mind? You can't kill a freaking cop. They'll ... " He sputtered to a halt, unable to finish the thought.

"They'll *what*? Throw me in jail, give me the needle? If we don't find a solution to this and fast, it's only delaying the inevitable, Ace. I'm screwed either way," she sat there, staring at him.

"There must be some other way; we still have time to come up with something."

"Look, I know where that bastard lives. He deserves to be punished, Ace. I can't think of a more deserving person to sacrifice."

"He doesn't deserve to die for committing rape, the punishment doesn't fit the crime. Prison, sure, but you're talking about premeditated, cold-blooded murder, for cripes sake!" Mason countered angrily.

"If you don't have the balls for it, I'll do it by myself. I recorded everything Jack told us tonight with my phone, so I know how the ritual's performed. If you won't help me with this, Ace, we're through!" she growled. Lighting a cigarette, she angrily strode out onto the balcony to smoke.

Mason was thoroughly wasted. This evening hadn't panned out as he'd hoped. He'd assumed the satanist/lead guitarist would provide a simple solution to their problem, but he should've known better.

"You can't quit now, April. I won't condone killing someone who doesn't actually deserve it—even to save my soul or yours," he defended his position, walking out behind her.

April stared down at a small crowd of people passing on the sidewalk below them.

"I wonder if it would hurt much," she whispered, gauging the distance down to the sidewalk. Mason heard and knew what she was contemplating.

He embraced her from behind, pulling her close. "That's not the answer, babe. C'mon, let's go inside, we'll figure something out tomorrow. In the meantime, we need to get some shuteye," he said with a yawn.

She finished her smoke, and they went inside. While she was taking a shower, Mason plopped down on the bed and turned on the TV to distract himself from their impasse. Aimlessly, he flipped through the channels, close to falling asleep, finding nothing to his liking—'til something grabbed his attention.

A young female with hair the same color as April's lay naked on a bed, hands tied behind her back, while some dude screwed her in the ass. Mason was ready to change the channel when the camera focused in tight on her face. He sat up, awake and alert. *What the hell?* She was the spitting image of April. He hit the volume button on the remote, but no sound accompanied the video, which seemed odd.

The woman in the video was in distress, crying, tossing her head in obvious pain while the guy pummeled her like a rabbit in heat. As the camera pulled back, the man's face became visible, and Mason instantly recognized him. The cop who'd pulled him over for speeding was the person raping her.

Hearing a gasp, he turned to see April standing in the bathroom doorway, a horrified look on her face, transfixed by the sordid scene unfolding on the giant screen. With a shriek, she ran over, snatched the remote from his hand, and hurled it with all her might at the screen, smashing the remote into pieces as the TV went blank and died.

Sobbing, she turned to a stunned Mason and fumed, "That fucking bastard— he filmed the rape," she raged, as she irritably paced the floor.

A bizarre thought occurred to him, "What if Officer Dipshit is actually Adriel? I mean, if he's truly a demon, couldn't he change his appearance at will?" Mason suggested, still shocked by the pornographic images he'd witnessed.

"I—I suppose it's possible. But why? Why would he do such a horrid thing?" she asked, wrapping her arms around her slender frame.

"Which horrid thing, the rape or the video?" He asked her, trying to clarify.

"Both. What does he hope to gain by humiliating me over and over on some goddamned porn channel?" she demanded.

Mason was silent for a moment. "Well, we know he gets off on making people suffer," he offered, with a shrug.

She thought about it for several minutes. "It's suppose it's not inconceivable," she said, as she grew calmer. "Adriel and Officer Dipshit— it's possible. The only way to be certain is to sacrifice the cop. If he doesn't die, we'll know it was all Adriel, and we're screwed. If he dies, he'll get what he deserved in the first place—and we'll rid ourselves of Adriel and his bitch, Alal. Either way, if we don't at least try, we're doomed."

He was having a hard time wrapping his head around her logic. "I guess you're right. We have to do something. After seeing that horrible video, I agree the cop should pay for what he did. I wish there was some other solution, but I can't think of one. Maybe you could call APD and find out if he's really a cop, that would answer your question. Adriel can't be in two places at the same time. You *do* know the cop's name, right?"

"His name's Craig Gleason. At least according to the name tag pinned on the bastard's uniform," she said through gritted teeth.

"Okay, call and see if there's a cop with that name. If there is, we can safely assume he's not Adriel. Then we can decide what to do next," he advised.

"That could work, I hadn't thought of that," she agreed, with a shrug. She picked up her phone, then hesitated. "They're going to want to know why I'm asking, what can I tell them?"

"Tell 'em the truth. Tell 'em he forced himself on you, and you want to file charges on his sorry ass. Or better yet, just say nothing. People call all the time to check on cops' identities. I'm sure they can verify whether he's legit," he said with a wide yawn.

"*Shit*! I don't remember his badge number, and on top of that, now that I think about it, there's probably no one there to ask at this time of night. All I'll get is the 311 operator, and they won't know crap," she sat down unhappily.

Mason didn't know what else to suggest, so he got up, went to the bathroom to relieve his bladder, and took a quick shower. When he returned, she was sprawled out on the bed, sound asleep and snoring. He covered her with the comforter and then laid down beside her. Setting the alarm on his phone as sleep tugged at his eyelids, he wondered if his soul had not truly been lost the first moment he set eyes on the woman lying next to him.

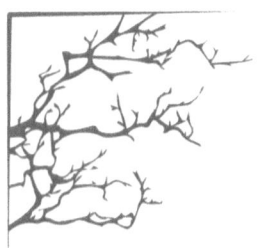

Chapter Thirteen

Little Joe Hampton's Home

"Little Joe" Hampton crawled out of bed at 7:00 a.m. He slept very little anymore, due to his age and his traitorous bladder. Sampling his "product" late at night didn't help. He traipsed into the filthy kitchen and opened an ancient refrigerator to retrieve his breakfast, a sixteen-ounce can of Lone Star beer. In one huge gulp, he drained the beer and let out an enormous belch, tossing the empty in the sink to join a pile of dirty dishes. He hadn't heard from Toad again after he'd left last night, and he was concerned. The fierce barking of his mangy old dog, Buckshot, got his attention. Despite complaints from his nosy fucking neighbors, he kept the dog tethered day and night to a leash behind chain-link fencing that surrounded his lot.

Grabbing his pistol, he marched over to the front door and opened it to see what the racket was about. At first glance, everything seemed normal. Stepping out to have a look around, he found Toad. He was sitting on Little Joe's bike, slumped over the gas tank, as if asleep. Joe was about to yell at him, when something stopped him. A warning bell sounded in his head as he moved closer to his bike and its rider.

"Hey, Toad, wake up. Did you find Har—" he stopped, as he got a closer look. "What the holy hell?" he gasped, quickly stepping away from the mutilated corpse.

Tommy's throat had been torn to shreds, but that wasn't the worst of it. The bloody remains of his cock protruded from his mouth, dangling like an obscene second nose. A scrap of paper had been pinned to his forehead by a small black stiletto buried to the hilt in his skull. The note, written in blood, read:

'Back Off, or UR next!'

That enraged Little Joe, he didn't take shit off anyone. Whoever did this was a dead man ...

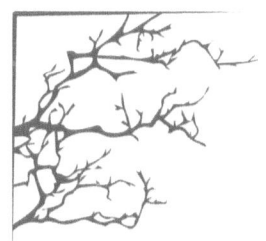

Chapter Fourteen

The Driscoll Hotel

Mason's phone alarm went off at 6:45 a.m. Groaning, he heaved himself up, his head pounding like a bass drum with every beat of his heart. April was already up and dressed, standing on the balcony having a smoke. Mumbling to himself, he staggered to the minibar and grabbed a beer out of the little fridge. A little hair of the dog to start the day.

April stepped back inside and announced, "I've figured it out."

"Figured what out?" he asked sleepily, sinking slowly onto the sofa.

"Figured out how we can get to Officer Dipshit and do the deed," she sat down next to him.

"Wait—I thought you were gonna call to confirm his identity before we did anything rash?" he sat up, instantly awake.

"Already done, he's a legitimate cop. I talked to a supervisor before you got up," she said, yawning.

"I suppose that rules out Adriel and him, being one and the same," he said, uneasy about her next step. "So, what's your plan? We can't do it here at the hotel, way too risky," he stood up, pacing anxiously.

"No, not here, it needs to be on his own turf, somewhere he'll feel comfortable. It should be at his house. Naturally, he'll be suspicious why I would choose to contact him after what he did to me. He knows I hate his sorry ass," she considered, frowning.

"So, what do you plan to say, 'Hi, let's let bygones be bygones—oh, and by the way, would you mind lying on the floor while I draw a pentagram around you and cut out your fuckin' heart?'" he asked sarcastically.

"Not what I had in mind, no. He's a guy, and like most guys, the 'little head' does most of his thinking. It shouldn't be hard to persuade him to let me in. I'll offer to give him a hummer for that fucking video he made. If he says 'no,' I'll just fry his sorry ass with *this*," she replied smugly, opening her purse.

From inside, she produced what looked like a phone. She depressed a hidden trigger, and a blue arc of electricity crackled between hidden electrodes which appeared from inside it.

"Where the hell did you *get* that?" he asked, staring at the device.

"I ordered it off 'Amazon' yesterday. The latest model, it's specifically designed to look like a phone, so you could probably even get it on a plane. It was delivered this morning while you were still asleep," she gave him a sly smile.

"Well, you've been quite the busy bee, and the day's barely begun. So, when is this all to take place, and what part would I play?" he asked, absently scratching his balls.

"I'm thinking tonight, after he gets off work. I found out he works the three to eleven shift weekdays, so we can expect him home around 11:30 p.m. You'll need to wait in the shadows 'til I give you the signal to come inside."

"Suppose he isn't alone? How would you explain your reason for showing up unannounced on his doorstep?" he asked, playing "devil's advocate."

"I'll ... I don't know, make up some lame excuse on the fly. Damn it to hell, Ace, I can't think of every little thing that might possibly go wrong. If I did, I'd never have the nerve to go through with this craziness," she snapped.

"Sorry, just trying to find holes in this so-called plan of yours. Remember, 'if anything *can* go wrong, it *will*,' that's 'Murphy's Law.'"

"We'll just have to make sure that it doesn't," she replied tersely. "Listen, if we lose that contest on Saturday, there's no telling what Adriel might do. We need to strike fast and hard, get this done, the quicker the better."

"*If* we do this thing, there's no guarantee it'll work. A million things could go wrong. I trust that asshole, Jack, and his black magic about as far as I could throw him. What if we kill the asshole and nothing changes? What the hell do we do then?" he asked, still worried about her questionable "plan."

"I don't know, okay? We'll just have to play it by ear, you're pretty good at that, so it shouldn't be a problem," she challenged him.

He wasn't at all sure about that. Her allusion worked only as far as music was concerned—in his life overall, not so much. He'd been playing life 'by ear' for the past twenty-seven years, and look where it had gotten him.

"We can continue this discussion later. Let's order some breakfast, I'm starving." He changed the subject with relief.

Shrugging, she got up to retrieve the menu without another word. There was a knock at the door, and Alal let herself in, looking way too perky for 7:00 in the morning. Maybe demons didn't need sleep.

"I see you're awake, good. I've ordered breakfast for everyone, so don't bother. Your bandmates are late, and I won't tolerate tardiness in you pathetic humans. If they're not here in five minutes, I'll—" The knock at the door ruined her diatribe.

Impatiently, she turned and opened it. Jeff and the others stood there, bleary-eyed and disheveled, looking as though they'd slept in their clothes.

"Mornin'," Jeff mumbled as they shuffled inside and closed the door.

"You're late. Don't let it happen again," Alal growled.

"What if it does?" Larry bitched. "I mean, shit, we can't control the damn traffic," he was eyeing the minibar, not Alal.

She narrowed her icy blue eyes at him. "*If* it does, there will be rather unpleasant consequences," she answered.

Glancing tensely at the others, Larry wisely chose not to pursue his argument with the demoness. Their breakfast arrived minutes later, and everyone ate in cowed silence. Mason was the first to break it.

"Let's get started. We need all the practice we can get if we're to have any chance of winning that contest. We scoped out one of our main competitors last night, and their band is gonna be tough to beat," he stated, opening his guitar case.

"Better listen to him, guys. Jack and the Hell Rippers are odds-on favorites to win that contest. We can't let that happen," April added firmly.

They quickly tuned up, while Alal opened a fresh bottle of top-shelf tequila. Practicing the same two songs for over two and a half hours, they finally took a break.

"I don't know about you guys, but I've got to rest my cords. If I blow out my voice, I won't be of much use on Saturday," April said, moving to the bar to make herself a small drink.

Alal was already on her fifth shot and bored shitless. She consumed tequila like it was water, with no ill effects. "I need to leave for a while, I have … an errand to run. Consider this a brief intermission. I'll return right after lunch, then you may continue your boring little practice sessions, ta-ta," she jeered, taking one more shot for the road. Once she was gone, everyone relaxed visibly.

"Does she really have to be here the whole time we jam?" Jeff groused, snagging a beer from the fridge. "She scares the crap outta me, and it's making it difficult for me to concentrate."

"She drank enough tequila to kill a horse. Maybe she'll stumble and fall in front of a bus," Larry said hopefully.

"We should be so lucky," Davy grumbled, shaking his head.

"She's Adriel's toady, she can do whatever she pleases. We're at their mercy—for the time being, at least," April glanced pointedly at Mason.

"She's right. That could change, but right now, we need to play nice with the evil bitch and do what she says," Mason reminded everyone firmly.

April got up and motioned him to follow her out on the balcony for some privacy.

When they were alone, she turned to him and asked, "Should we tell them about our plan? We might need help to do this tonight," she said quietly.

"No way, the fewer people involved, the better our chances are of pulling it off," he hissed adamantly. "The more people involved, the greater the odds that something will go wrong—and something definitely *will* go wrong, I can almost guaran-fucking-tee it!"

They each had valid points; neither would concede to the other. They stood glaring at one another until she finally caved on the matter.

"Alright, but just so you know, if this thing goes south tonight, it's on your stubborn head, Ace," she growled, storming back inside.

He sighed and leaned over the balcony to watch the people passing on the sidewalk far below. For a second, he wondered how much it would hurt if he had the nerve to take a header to the sidewalk, as she had contemplated earlier. With his luck, he figured he'd do just enough damage to end up as a fucking vegetable for the rest of a long life. Disgusted by his own cowardice, he turned and entered the suite to join the others …

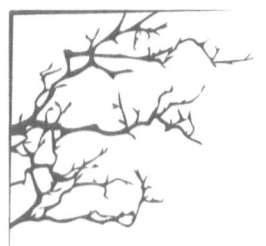

Chapter Fifteen

Little Joe's House

"Little Joe" hastily covered Toad's mangled corpse with an old blue tarp, then went back inside to calm down and think about his next step. He popped the top on another can of beer, then called two of his top lieutenants. He told them to drop whatever they were doing and get their asses over there ASAP for a war council. Whoever had killed the Toad had likely done the same to Harley. They'd screwed with the wrong people. While he waited for them to arrive, he snorted a couple lines of crank to help clear his head. A few minutes later, he heard the thundering rumble of Harley-Davidson motorcycles approaching the house. Billy Ray Hansen and his older brother Daryl arrived and entered the house without knocking.

Billy Ray was tall and skinny as a rail, whereas Daryl was short and shaped like bowling pin on steroids. But looks could be deceiving, both were tough as nails and more dangerous than a bag full of rattlesnakes.

"Yo, what's the fuckin' emergency? I was in the middle of copping a nut with my old lady when you called," Billy ray grumbled.

"We've got us a major problem and it needs to be taken care of, pronto. Toad's dead and Harley's missing, I reckon he's dead, too. I sent Toad to find him last night at this address over on Payne Street. Harley's phone pinged from there then, but I got nothing from the location when I tried it this morning." Joe told them.

He got up and led them back outside to the carport. Pulling back the tarp, he angrily ripped the bloody note from the dead man's forehead.

"*Holy shit!*" Billy Ray exclaimed as he studied the grisly remains.

"Sonofabitch! Whoever did this is a fucking dead man," Daryl growled, angrily kicking the back tire.

"Fuckin' A, right! I want the head of the bastard that did this, gonna feed his brains to Buckshot. Take whatever weapons you need and find the motherfucker. But first, get rid of this body, it's beginning to stink. Take him to out to the quarry, you can use my old truck." Little Joe turned to go back inside.

BILLY RAY BACKED THE old Ford F-350 heavy-duty under the carport and together, they lifted Tommy's body, wrapped in the tarp and tied with rope and tossed it in the truck's bed. Daryl added a couple of cinder blocks and a length of rope. Hopping in the the truck, they drove out toward an abandoned limestone quarry west of town. Billy Ray was careful to obey the speed limit; they sure as hell didn't need to be pulled over with a dead body in the back.

"You reckon the asshole who whacked Toad and Harley is really gonna hang around after killing them? I was him, I'd be on a freakin' plane with a one-way ticket to South America by now," Billy Ray said conversationally.

"We'll find out when we get there. First, we take care of Toad. We'll deal with that prick after we're done with him," Daryl replied.

They were about a mile from the turnoff to the quarry when the *whoop-whoop* of a police siren drew Billy Ray's attention to his rearview mirror.

"*Shit*! He's pulling me over! I was doing the damn speed limit. What the hell are we gonna do now?" Billy Ray demanded.

"Stay chill, bro. If he gets suspicious about the tarp, just tell him it's a rug. If he wants to have a look, I'll take care of him," Daryl said, chambering a round in his Glock Nineteen pistol.

Billy Ray swore, pulled over to the shoulder of the road, and parked. He'd done a lot of crappy things in his life, but he'd never popped a cop.

"Whatever happens, *don't* shoot the fucker, bro. I'm serious as a heart attack, I ain't gonna to take the needle for you or anyone! You shoot him and we're as good as dead!" he hissed. Daryl glared back at him, but didn't reply.

The police car came to a halt about ten feet behind them, and a female cop got out. The stout officer approached their truck while talking into her radio. Fortunately for them and her, she was shorter than the truck's bed and couldn't see its contents.

Billy Ray lowered the window to talk, "Morning, Officer. Is there a problem? I swear I wasn't speeding," he said nervously.

The dark-haired cop stared at him through tinted sunglasses. "Sir, I'll need to see your license and registration, please," she stated neutrally.

"Sure thing, ma'am, just give me a second while I dig that out of the glove box," he replied. Reaching over and opening it, he nearly shit his pants.

Sitting on top of the needed paperwork was close to an ounce of crystal meth—obviously, one of Little Joe's private stashes. The zip-lock bag contained enough crank to send them both to prison forever. Calmly, Daryl pulled the registration out from under it, gave it to his brother, and closed the compartment from view. Billy Ray handed it and his driver's license out the window to the impatient cop.

She looked it over, then handed it back. "Mr. Hansen, are you the owner of this vehicle?" she asked, her right hand resting casually on the butt of her service weapon.

Billy Ray was sweating as he contemplated his answer. "Uh, no, ma'am. This here is my friend's truck, we, uh, just borrowed it to run some errands. Ain't no law against that, is there?" he countered.

The cop just stared at him for a long moment. "No, sir, as long as you have the owner's permission, you're fine. However, this vehicle has been reported as stolen. I'm going to have to ask you to step out of car, keep your hands where I can see them," she commanded, drawing her service weapon.

Shit! Shit! Shit! We are so screwed! Billy thought, panicking. Glancing over at Daryl, he saw his eyes turn cold and calculating. If he didn't think of something quick, his brother would almost surely waste the cop, and life as they knew it would be over.

"Officer, there's been some mistake, this truck belongs to Little Joe Hampton. He's had it for ten freakin' years, I can prove it's his, if you'll give me a chance," he begged, watching the passenger door open as Daryl quietly slipped out of the truck.

Obscured by the truck's body, Daryl crept to the rear. Easing up behind her, he raised his gun. One wrong move on her part and she'd never hear the shot that killed her. Meanwhile, Billy Ray eased out of the pickup with hands raised. When he saw Daryl standing behind the oblivious cop, he tried to signal him with his eyes to stand down without giving his presence away.

"Listen, Officer, uh," he squinted to read her name tag, "Officer Jenkins, I swear to you that you're making a big mistake, I—" he said, as she cut him off.

"Hands behind your back and face the truck, *now*!" she barked, taking a step forward.

Shaking his head in frustration, he did as he was told. That's when she saw Daryl behind her in the over-sized door mirror, pointing the muzzle of a gun inches from the back of her head.

She froze and tried not to panic. The road where they were parked was located off the main highway, with little to no traffic on it at this time of the morning. The bastard behind her could shoot her right now and no one would be the wiser.

"Mister, drop your weapon now, and no one will get hurt," she said, with as much authority as she could muster. She knew if she didn't get the situation under control fast, it could turn deadly in a heartbeat. She had to get him to lower his gun before all hell broke loose. "Mister, I won't ask you again, drop the weapon and get on the ground, *now*!" she demanded, her adrenaline pumping like mad.

As Daryl gave her icy smile, she knew she was dead. Frantic, she desperately tried to key her radio mike to make a distress call of "officer down" before he pulled the trigger. Blood and brains splattered Billy Ray as the hollow-point bullet exited the front of her skull, leaving a golf ball-size hole above her left eye. The force of the impact blew her off her feet, and she crumpled to the ground. A pool of crimson spread across the filthy pavement as she bled out.

Billy Ray had known Daryl was going to kill the cop as soon as he'd left the truck. His brother was a cold-blooded killer who didn't think twice at taking a cop's life.

"Well, I hope you're fuckin' happy, you've screwed us but good! Now we got two bodies to get rid of, you trigger-happy asshole!" Billy Ray raged, wiping bits of bloody brain tissue from his face.

"She gave me no choice, little brother. If I hadn't, she'd have found Toad's body and the crank in the glove box. I ain't going back to that hell hole in Huntsville fer the likes of her or nobody. Quit yer bitchin' and grab her feet. Help me put her in the trunk of her car, 'fore somebody sees us." He growled, tucking the gun in the back waistband of his jeans.

Billy Ray didn't argue. Glancing around for approaching cars, he dragged the cop's body to the rear of her cruiser. Daryl popped the trunk lid and whistled at what he saw inside. The dead cop had an M-4 fully automatic assault rifle locked on a rack inside.

"Sure would like to have that baby, but there's no time to look for the key. Help me get her inside," he grunted as they lifted the corpse and tossed it inside. He slammed the lid shut just as a car came barreling down the road towards them. It slowed as it passed them, either out of idle curiosity or because of the police car, then continued on its way without incident. "Get in the damn truck!" Daryl ordered coolly. "I'll drive the cop's car and follow you to the quarry, now move yer ass!"

Billy Ray did as his despicable brother demanded and climbed back inside the cab. If caught, he'd rat his brother out and turn State's evidence against the crazy bastard, anything to keep himself off death row. This was so screwed up, he knew in his bones there was no chance in hell they'd get away with it. He sped down the one-lane road to the entrance of the old quarry, with Daryl close behind.

Years ago, the owners of the water-filled pit had installed a flimsy metal gate at the entrance, which now lay mangled on the ground, the victim of scores of drunken teenage drivers looking for a cool place to make out and party. Teenagers, and more nefarious individuals like they, themselves, used it for fishing and as a dumping ground for stolen cars and the occasional body or two. Today would be no different—the only exception being that one of the bodies was a cop.

When Daryl pulled the trigger, they'd crossed a forbidden line. Their motorcycle club had an uneasy relationship with local law enforcement at the best of times. His brother had literally shot that all to hell. Billy Ray scanned the surrounding area for any sign of trespassers. Seeing no one, he backed the truck up to the edge of the cliff overlooking the pit's dingy green water.

Daryl pulled the police car to a stop a good thirty feet from the lip, put it in Park, rolled down all the windows, then got out. Climbing into the bed of the truck, he pulled out a switchblade. Inserting the blade just below Toad's sternum, he sliced him open to his navel, slitting the stomach open to relieve gas buildup from decomposition. The last thing they needed was for Toad to make a surprise appearance in a few days' time. Daryl cut the rope they brought into two equal lengths, tying one end around Toad's waist and the other around the two cinder blocks. Together, they shoved Toad and his makeshift anchor off the end of the open tailgate and into the murky water far below. The body sank rapidly, disappearing in seconds.

"Well, that takes care of Toad. Now we get rid of the bitch and her car," Daryl said steadily.

He jumped down and searched the ground until he found what he was looking for. Hefting a large rock, he opened the driver's door and wedged it against the accelerator. The engine raced as the RPM's climbed to a deafening roar. Placing his right foot on the brake, he moved the gear shift into Drive and leaped back. A rooster tail of dirt and gravel sprayed the air as the cruiser leapt forward. Speeding over the cliff, it hit the water nose first with an enormous splash.

It took nearly five minutes for the car to sink below the surface and vanish, leaving a trail of air bubbles to surface in its wake. Billy Ray felt slightly relieved that they hadn't been caught yet. Then, an alarming thought occurred.

"Hey, Daryl, what about the cop's body cam?" he asked uneasily.

"Yeah? What about it?" his brother asked, as they climbed into the truck.

"It'll have video of the whole damn mess, is what! I'm the only one on it and I'm not going down just because you can't control your fucking trigger finger!" he snarled angrily.

"Chill, little brother. You need to back the hell off! The water will destroy the electronics, ya' got nothin' to worry about," Daryl growled.

"Easy for you to say, it wasn't *your* face caught on video, you fucking moron!" he snapped, as they sped from the scene. Daryl did a slow burn but didn't reply. "Little Joe ain't gonna be a happy camper when he hears about this," Billy Ray pointed out.

"That's why we ain't sayin' shit about what went down today. Less he knows, the better for us," Daryl replied, lighting a cigarette.

"You mean the better for *you!* If he finds out you killed a damn cop, he'll roast your chestnuts over a fire while they're still attached," Billy Ray snorted smugly.

"Just shut the hell up and drive. We need to grab that asshole on Payne and take him to Little Joe. Make him pay for what he did to Harley and the Toad," Daryl said, changing the subject.

They exited the highway, drove to North Lamar Boulevard, and headed south until they spotted the familiar landmark of the "Purple Iris" topless bar. He took a right turn on Brentwood at the light, then a left on Wild, and followed it to where it dead-ended with Payne.

"According to the GPS on my phone, the house is on the right," Daryl commented.

Billy Ray pulled to a stop in front of a neighbor's home and parked. They sat and watched the target house for a few minutes before deeming it safe to approach.

AS THEY GOT OUT OF the truck, Billy Ray shoved a snub-nosed forty-four caliber revolver into the waistband of his jeans as insurance in case the asshole put up a fight. Casually, they walked up to the front door of the condo, glancing around for prying eyes. They first thing they spied was the sign on the front door, *"Abandon all hope, ye who enter."* Apparently, the asshole had a warped sense of humor. Billy Ray knocked three times on the metal door and waited for a reply from within. When it seemed clear nobody was going to answer, he knocked again, louder this time.

"I don't think there's anyone home, bro," Billy Ray said quietly.

"Would *you* answer the door if you'd done what they did to Harley and Toad? Get real, little brother. Step aside, we'll do this my way," Daryl hissed.

He took a couple of steps back, preparing to kick the door in, when Billy Ray held out his arm, stopping him.

"Maybe he's out back, there's a gate on that privacy fence over there. We should see if it's locked before you go busting in. Plus, if anything goes down, it's hidden from any nosy neighbors," Billy Ray said logically.

"You surprise me sometimes, little bro, that might actually be better, less noise when I break the asshole's arms," Daryl grunted.

They approached the gate, and Billy Ray tried the handle. The gate wasn't locked, which set off warning bells in Daryl's head. *This could be a trap!* he thought, as the gate slowly swung open. They observed the assortment of cars that cluttered most of the yard. Billy Ray spotted Harley's bike parked by an old metal shed toward the back. Harley had evidently ridden it here, but there was no other sign of him. Daryl closed the gate behind him, gawking at the junkyard in front of them.

"What the hell? It looks like the asshole's running a salvage yard," Daryl observed.

"That, or he's selling parts to a local 'chop-shop,'" Billy Ray added, moving forward cautiously. "Hey, ain't that Toad's old Honda over there?" he asked, spotting the bike wedged between a battered Ford Fiesta and a Mercedes Benz with Colorado plates.

"Sure is, this sonofabitch is gonna die a slow fucking death!" Daryl growled angrily. A sudden noise made them whirl around.

A tall, dark-haired dude stood watching them from the back door, a twisted smile on his face. Both brothers whipped out their guns and pointed them at the man.

Adriel raised both hands and grinned in mock surrender. "Well, that certainly doesn't seem friendly. I believe you're the Hansen brothers, right?" he asked, pleasantly, taking a step toward them.

"Don't know how you got that info, shithead, but if you move another muscle, I'll drop you where you fucking stand!" Daryl warned, his finger on the trigger.

"What the hell did you do with Harley?" Billy Ray snarled.

"Honestly? Something that should have been done a long time ago. I can't think of a more deserving fellow, can you, Alal?" Adriel retorted with an evil grin.

The brothers were confused by the name. "Who the fuck is Alal?" Daryl demanded.

"That would be me. You miserable humans are all alike," said a female voice from behind them.

Daryl and Billy Ray pivoted on their heels to find a gorgeous blonde with huge tits pointing a double-barreled, sawed-off shotgun at them.

"Drop your weapons on the ground. One false move and I'll blow your balls—if you have any—into the next county," she warned, smiling.

Daryl gave Billy Ray a disgusted look as they slowly lowered their weapons, placing them on the pavement. This whole thing smelled like a set-up. He should've trusted his gut when they'd found the open gate. Not only had they lost the element of surprise, now they were at the mercy of the asshole they'd come here to kill. This day had gone from bad to worse in a heartbeat. If they somehow got out of this cluster-fuck alive, Daryl planned to kill Little Joe with his bare hands, then haul ass to Mexico for the foreseeable future.

Alal marched them inside the condo at gun point, Adriel following close behind.

"You're making a big mistake, mister. You're gonna be in a world of shit when Little Joe gets ahold of your stupid ass! He knows where you live, you're one dead motherfucker!" Daryl snarled.

"Alas, I live in a world of shit, Mr. Hansen. As for your boss, 'Little Joe,' I look forward to meeting him soon. Unfortunately, I rather doubt you and your brother will be around to enjoy that little tete-a-tete," Adriel said, with an icy smile. Hearing this, Billy Ray's anxiety blossomed into full-blown panic.

"Alal, please escort these gentlemen inside, and place them in the 'Fun' room. I intend to make this a truly memorable experience for our guests," Adriel instructed, holding the door open. Producing a pair of plastic zip ties, he roughly cuffed their hands behind their backs.

Alal marched them into the house at gunpoint.

"Listen, mister, w-we have a shitload of money, you can have it all, just let us go and I'll—" Billy Ray begged.

Daryl cut him off, "Shut the hell up, little bro. We ain't giving 'em shit! If they kill us, Little Joe'll burn 'em to the ground. They won't get away with—"

Daryl shouted, before Alal slapped duct tape over his mouth to stop him. When Billy Ray started to protest, she taped him, as well.

"Ahh, silence is golden. Put them in the room and make them comfortable. I think it's time we pay a visit to their benefactor and finish this, once and for all. These human roaches continue to come out of the woodwork, and it's vexing me," Adriel said, frowning.

Alal forced the brothers inside the room and turned on the light. The first thing they observed appeared to be an ordinary dentist's chair in the center of the room. A metal cart sat adjacent, holding a vast array of wicked-looking instruments. A dentist's drill hung from a hook on a hospital IV pole, along with a bag of some red liquid that looked an awful lot like blood. Then, they noticed the drain hole in the floor.

Billy Ray's eyes filled with horror as he realized what they intended to do. Dental chairs were his own worst nightmare. As a child, he'd had a terrible experience at a dentist's office, and his rotting teeth were partially due to his dental phobia.

"Mmphh!" came his muffled feedback as she shoved him toward the dreaded chair.

Daryl could see what was coming and decided if he was going to be tortured and killed, he'd do whatever it took to escape—even if it meant sacrificing his brother. He swiveled his head to see if Adriel had followed them inside, but it appeared he hadn't.

While Alal was occupied placing the terrified, struggling Billy Ray in the chair, Daryl slyly squatted until he could reach inside his right cowboy boot. Grimacing as the zip ties cut into his wrists, he dug out a small hunting knife from its hidden scabbard. Standing, he maneuvered it until the blade rested against the plastic cuffs.

The difficulty was having sufficient time to cut through his bonds before his captors discovered the knife. While he attempted to slice through the tough plastic, his brother thrashed around in the chair, trying to avoid the inevitable. The blonde bitch inserted a hypodermic into Billy Ray's jugular, injecting him with God knows what. His muffled shriek of terror echoed through the room.

Daryl glanced over his shoulder for the tall bastard, expecting him to enter the room any moment. When he turned to look at his brother, he saw that Alal had strapped Billy Ray tightly in the chair, and he had stopped resisting. Whatever drug she'd administered must be working. Sweat beaded on Daryl's forehead as he sawed feverishly with the knife, nearly losing his grip on it.

"I've given you one cc of Succinylcholine. You won't be able to move, but you'll still be able to experience pain," the demoness remarked gleefully. If Billy Ray heard her, he didn't show it.

Daryl thought he felt a little give in the plastic tie as he continued cutting. *Come on, come on, almost there*, he thought, straining with all his might against his restraints. Without warning, he was freed, though both his palms were slick with blood and sweat from his exertions. He tried to keep his grip on the knife, but it slipped from his fingers and clattered to the floor, alerting Alal to his newfound freedom. *Shit!* Leaning over, he scooped it up. With a muffled roar of anger, he charged the blonde demoness, raising the knife to gut her where she stood.

Alal laughed and did nothing to stop him as he plunged the knife into her torso multiple times until he was exhausted. He was stunned—he'd stabbed the bitch dozens of times, and she was still standing. She wasn't even bleeding.

Fast as lightning, she snatched the blade from his hand and tossed it across the room. With a savage growl, she grabbed him by his throat with one hand, lifting him up to dangle helplessly a foot above the ground. His eyes bulged from their sockets as he clawed at the steely grip on his throat, slowly suffocating.

Adriel stepped into the room, saw what was happening, and told her to stop.

Hesitating briefly, she dropped him on the floor, where he lay coughing and gasping for air. Adriel stooped down and ripped the duct tape from his mouth.

"He had a hidden knife, probably in his boot. He tried to kill me, and I lost my temper. I'm sorry, master," Alal apologized somewhat reluctantly.

"I stabbed you—a hundred times, it's— impossible, you should be—fucking dead!" Daryl rasped, massaging his bruised throat.

"Sorry to disappoint you, you despicable piece of shit. You can't kill a demon with a puny knife," she stated. With an inhuman smile, she revealed her true visage.

If Daryl could have screamed, it would've shattered glass. The sheer look of horror on his face amused Alal. The biker had pissed his pants, scrambling away from the beast posing as a human female. She chuckled wickedly, drinking in his terror like a physic vampire, savoring its sweet taste. Daryl tucked himself into a protective ball on the cement floor. His consciousness retreated to a tiny safe corner of his brain where creatures like Alal didn't exist. His eyes rolled madly in their sockets, as he repeated a childlike mantra used to ward off monsters, *"No boogie, no boogie, no boogie, Mama!"*

"Apparently, our troublesome guest has forfeited what little mind he arrived with," Adriel observed. "Please dispose of him, he's the more dangerous of the two. Feed the remains to the dogs when you're done," Adriel instructed, turning to the semi-comatose biker in the chair.

Approaching Daryl's quivering body, Alal eagerly licked her lips. Reverting to her true form, the bones in her jaw cracked and extended as her face transformed into an unspeakable monstrosity. Multiple rows of razor-sharp teeth dripped saliva onto his horror-stricken face. Long clawed hands jerked his head back, exposing his throat. Somewhere in the depths of his terrified mind, he realized he was about to die and said a silent goodbye to his brother. In a flash, the creature's wicked jaws ripped out his throat, A fountain of fresh blood spurted from the gaping wound, which she greedily drank down to the last beat of his heart.

When she'd had her fill, she carried the body out back and let the dogs out of the metal shed. They'd been placed there earlier to keep them from barking and discouraging the Hansen brothers from entering the yard. Hungrily, they tore into Daryl's mangled corpse and made short work of him. When she returned, Adriel was having his "fun'" with the remaining biker.

The loud, high-pitched whine of a drill filled the room. A dental wedge had been placed between Billy Ray's front teeth to hold his mouth open. Adriel grinned and lowered the tool until the bit began boring a tiny hole in one of the biker's rotten molars. Had he not been paralyzed by the drug she'd given him, he would've shrieked in agony. Acrid smoke began to pour from his mouth as the drill bit slowly burrowed into the enamel, until reaching the nerve. Billy Ray's only reaction was the constant river of tears streaming from his eyes.

"Give him the antidote now, I want to hear him scream!" Adriel growled to Alal.

"There is none, but the effects of the drug should wear off soon, it's only temporary," Alal replied, moving to stand beside him. Right on cue, Billy Ray's strapped-down arms and legs twitched in the chair. His eyes rolled in their orbits like those of a frightened mare as Alal ripped away the duct tape from his mouth, and Billy Ray screeched in repressed agony.

"You'll tell me what I want to know, or I'll continue this until I run out of teeth. By the way, your brother sends his regards from hell. I believe he's roasting as we speak. So, tell me, Mr. Hansen, and don't lie—it will merely prolong the inevitable, does anyone else know you're here?" Adriel asked, applying pressure to the exposed nerve with a dental pick.

Billy Ray's body tensed as he shrieked, the pain so intense, it was beyond description. "Stop—p-please ... no more! Little Joe—just—L-Little Joe. He—sent us to— bring him—your head—for killin' Harley and Toad. P-Please ... it's the truth—I swear to God!" he gasped out, between waves of throbbing pain.

Adriel looked as though he'd been slapped in the face. "How dare you invoke *his* name in my presence, you worthless sack of shit! If you're lying, you'll be joining your brother sooner than later," he snarled, his eyes glowing red.

As Adriel dug deeper into the exposed cavity, Billy Ray screamed. He simply wanted the pain to end. He knew they would kill him, regardless of what they said.

"Fuck you and your bitch, you bastard! I ain't sayin' another word, so go ahead and kill me, I'd rather die than look at your ugly damn face another second," Billy Ray spat defiantly.

Adriel roared in anger. Without warning, he grabbed Billy Ray's jaw in one large hand, and with a tremendous yank, ripped his lower jaw from his face, tossing it onto the concrete floor. Billy Ray's torso went rigid with shock as hot blood spurted. Alal pounced at him, opening her maw wide to catch the blood as it poured from his raw, gaping wound.

"Dispose of him, Alal, we need to pay this Little Joe a visit. Now!" Adriel growled, pissed at himself for losing his self-control. He would've enjoyed torturing the biker for much longer before killing him. Fortunately for Billy Ray, demons had extremely bad tempers and very little patience. "Oh, and please make yourself presentable before we leave. I doubt this Little Joe will fully appreciate a beautiful woman covered in his underling's blood," he added, wiping his bloody hand on a towel.

Looking annoyed, Alal heaved Billy Ray's corpse over her shoulder, carried it to the back door, and flung it to the waiting hellhounds. She took a hot shower, dressing in a black leotard that accentuated her perfect breasts and long sensuous legs, and joined Adriel downstairs.While he locked up, she climbed into Little Joe's truck and started it.

"Let's go make this 'Little Joe' a deal he can't refuse," he chortled nastily. Grinning, they sped off toward their destination. Adriel jumped into her truck, ready to follow her.

LITTLE JOE WAS GETTING more enraged by the minute. He hadn't heard from Billy Ray or his hot-headed brother for over four hours. They were way overdue, and he was getting antsy. He'd given them one simple task to perform and it appeared they'd screwed it up. He knew his old truck was "hot," but he'd never been stopped, so he hadn't even thought about that. He seldom drove it unless he was making a trip to pick up "product," otherwise he rode his bike. If they'd gotten stopped, he'd have to go down and bail them out of jail.

So when his old Ford barreled into his yard, mowing down and crushing his treasured set of garden gnomes, he was more than a little agitated.

"Motherfucker!" he shouted, grabbing his gun off the table, rushing to the door.

Infuriated, he swung it open and saw not Billy Ray or Daryl behind the wheel but some blonde bitch who'd blatantly destroyed his precious gnomes. An icy harbinger of dread ran its bony finger down his spine as a newer pickup arrived to park behind his truck. A tall, dark-haired dude got out to join the smirking blonde bombshell as she exited his truck. He understood then that Billy Ray and Daryl were likely dead, and this was the man he'd sent them to kill. Well, he'd settle his hash here and now, by God.

As Little Joe leveled his Glock, ready to fire, the dude and the woman raised both their hands. "Stop right there, asshole! You have ten seconds to explain why that bitch is drivin' *my* fuckin' truck instead my crew, or I'll send you to hell and back!" Little Joe snarled.

"Sorry, been there, done that. Personally, I've always found those gnomes a bit creepy, but I suppose there's no law against poor taste in lawn décor, is there, Mr. Hampton?" With a slight shrug, Adriel pointed to the remains of Little Joe's lawn gnomes.

"You have exactly five seconds to tell me where Harley and the rest of my boys are, asshole, or you and your blonde bitch will be pushin' up daisies," Little Joe growled, finger tightening on the trigger. His mutt, Buckshot, picked that moment to bark his head off at the strangers. Little Joe turned his head to tell the dog to shut the hell up, and when he did, Alal moved at preternatural speed to disarm him.

"Let's take this conversation inside, shall we?" Adriel suggested, no longer smiling. "We don't want to disturb your neighbors with any unnecessary gun play."

Alal gripped the Glock in her right hand, prodding Little Joe with the business end for emphasis.

Shit! What choice do I have? he thought grimly. Resignedly, he raised his hands and turned to go inside, the demons following behind.

"I don't have no valuables if it's money you're after." He sat down in his recliner.

"Unfortunately, for you, it isn't. Normally in a situation like this, I'd be inclined to make you an offer of a lifetime, but not after today. You and your thugs have meddled in my affairs for the last time. You profit from the misery of others. All those wretched humans you keep addicted to your white poison will be much better off without you," Adriel pointed out, taking a threatening step closer.

"Here, you can have your peashooter back now," Alal said with a smirk.

Little Joe took it and saw she'd removed the magazine, along with the chambered round. Disgusted, he tossed the useless weapon on the couch. "At least tell me what you did with my guys. Some of 'em had families to support," Little Joe grunted, trying to postpone the inevitable.

"Then they should have chosen a better line of work. In my *humble* opinion, humans reap what they sow. I imagine they're being buggered by some of our 'associates' as we speak," Adriel replied cheerfully, his face transforming, to Little Joe's horror.

A little later, a neighbor would report hearing inhuman screams coming from the old biker's house ...

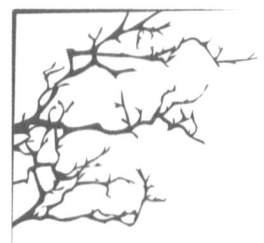

Chapter Sixteen

The Driscoll Hotel

Alal returned to the Driskill a little past 3:00 p.m., to find Mason and the others standing around talking. "Why are you not practicing? I'm gone for two minutes, and you worthless bunch of slackers take advantage of it. At the rate you're going, you'll never win that contest," she scoffed, approaching the bar.

"You've been gone for over three hours, and FYI, we've been practicing our asses off, thank you," Mason replied. *Demons must have no sense of time,* he thought.

"We expected you back after lunch, what happened?" Jeff asked her.

"None of your fucking business! I had important matters to attend to. I suggest from here on, you keep your nose to the grindstone and out of my affairs, if you know what's good for it." Danger lurked behind those icy blue eyes.

"Okay, okay, you don't have to bite my head off, for Pete's sake," Jeff replied, instantly regretting that phrase.

"Don't tempt me, you miserable little weasel. You'd be nothing but an appetizer to someone like me," the she-demon snapped.

He shrank at her words, thinking it would be healthier in the future to keep his stupid mouth shut.

With an audible groan, they picked up their instruments and practiced for another two hours before finally calling it quits. April was getting irritable, and Mason's new finger throbbed like a bad tooth.

"That's enough for today, guys. My fingers are toast. We'll meet back here tomorrow, same bat time, same bat channel," Mason told them, referencing the corny old TV series from the Sixties.

"What the hell is 'bat time?'" April asked.

"It's—never mind, I doubt you watch reruns of old TV shows. It just means we'll meet here at the usual time to prepare for tomorrow's contest," he explained patiently.

With a shrug, she walked out to the balcony to have a smoke. Jeff and the others said their goodbyes and filed out, promising to be on time in the morning. None of them wanted to invoke the wrath of the blonde demoness. Alal was the last to decamp, of course. She'd struck up quite the friendship with Senor Jose Cuervo, seeming reluctant to leave him behind. Mason and April were eager to be rid of her in more ways than one. After eight or nine shots, she finally appeared a bit unsteady on her feet. Demons might have a stronger constitution than humans, but apparently, they were also susceptible to the effects of alcohol.

"Why don't you take the bottle with you? We're not gonna drink any more tonight," Mason suggested, hoping she'd take the hint.

Alal paused, the next shot almost to her mouth. "What? You tryin' ta get rid of me?" her eyes narrowed suspiciously.

If only, he thought, gritting his teeth. "Not at all. Just didn't think you'd want to join us in a game of Monopoly. It usually takes four or five hours to—"

She waved him to stop, "'Nough! I'd rather be boiled in oil. I'll leave you 'n' 'Adele' to your petty gamesh, I've got 'portant things ta do," she slurred.

April stared daggers at the demoness as she started toward the door. Alal suddenly stopped, turned, and snagged the half-empty bottle of tequila from the bar. Swaying unsteadily, she opened the door and left, slamming it shut behind her. When she was gone, Mason breathed a sigh of relief.

"Can you believe that wicked bitch compared me to Adele? I don't know who should be more insulted, Adele or me," April blurted huffily.

"Forget her, she's drunk as a skunk. When the bottle's empty, she'll probably shove senior Cuervo up her demonic twat, they seem to make a cozy couple," he observed sarcastically. "So, when do we pay a visit to Officer Dipshit and get this thing done?" he inquired.

"Chill, Ace. It'll be a while before his shift is over. We should be in position no later than 11:15. In the meantime, though, I'd like you to screw my brains out," she stated abruptly.

Mason's jaw almost hit the floor. "Wh-What changed your mind? Why now?"

"If something bad happens tonight, I don't want to die a virgin, okay?" she snapped.

He looked stunned. "How is that possible? You've already done the deed with Adriel and the cop, I know that for a fact," he exclaimed jealously.

"You don't know shit! He and Officer Dipshit both prefer anal sex, and they're the only ones I've ever done that with. I was saving myself for someone I really cared for," she replied indignantly.

He was about to say something derogatory when he realized she was talking about him. "Y-You really care for me that much?" he stuttered, finding it hard to believe.

She rolled her eyes, grabbed his head and pulled him to her, kissing him deeply. He responded passionately. Breaking the kiss, he scooped her up in his arms and carried her to the bedroom. Quickly stripping off their clothes, they lay naked on the enormous bed, entwined in one another's arms. He was more than ready, as she guided him into her wet core. She arched her hips and gasped as he thrust himself deep inside and felt her hymen give.

He stopped. "Are you okay? Did I hurt you?" he asked, breathing hard.

"No, no—don't stop, you idiot," she hissed, urging him on.

As their hips found a rhythm, he kissed her fervently, his hands tweaking her sensitive nipples, making her moan with ecstasy as he plunged rapidly in and out. She climaxed twice, making him groan with pleasure as her inner muscles convulsed and contracted, milking his manhood until he cried out, burying himself to the hilt and filling her with his hot seed. Muscles quivering, he collapsed on top of her, trying to catch his breath.

"That was—wonderful! I hope—you thought—to use a rubber," she said breathlessly, as her inner muscles continued to spasm around his semi-hard cock.

"Say what?" he asked, losing what remained of his erection.

"Just kidding, Ace, relax. I'm on the pill," she lied, and Mason visibly relaxed.

She had never bothered to get a prescription. She'd wanted to wait until she found the right guy to give her virginity to, but then she'd made her deal with Adriel. Now, having met Mason, and with time possibly expiring for both of them soon, she'd decided to throw caution to the wind. "Think we could do it again, or do you need some time to reload?" she asked hopefully.

"I think so, though I may need a little help," he replied, wriggling his eyebrows suggestively.

She laughed and rolled him onto his back. "I think 'Mr. Happy' just needs a little TLC," she teased. Opening her mouth, she took his entire length into her throat, burying her face in his pubes.

He groaned as she squeezed and caressed his swollen nuts, her head bobbing over his crotch, her smoky gaze locked with his, as he quickly got hard again.

"Better—stop—unless—you want a mouthful," he warned, breathing hard.

Grinning around his member, she pulled away to mount him and ride him like a stallion. She lowered her mouth to his, thrusting her tongue deep in his mouth while he gripped her writhing hips, urging her on. Reaching back between his quivering thighs, she inserted her middle finger deep in his rectum, massaging his prostate as he moaned.

"Can't—last—much—longer," he warned. She pulled out her finger and flipped her sweating body around, pushing her sex against his panting mouth and swallowing his cock to the root. His tongue buried itself deep within her, triggering her climax. Warm liquid flooded his face as he joined her, filling her mouth with his essence. They lay entangled until they each caught their breath.

"I—think—I—love you," Mason declared breathlessly. Stiffening at those words, she pushed him away and jumped off the bed.

"Don't say something you don't mean, Ace. We both needed the release, and yes, the sex was great. And I *really* like you ... well, most of the time, but don't go throwing the "L" word around unless you're serious, okay? I don't need a broken heart, on top of everything else." She stepped out onto the balcony for a smoke.

He mentally slapped himself. *What the hell am I thinking?* True, he'd only known her for a couple days, but somewhere along the way, he had fallen hard for the redheaded spitfire. With a sigh, he got up to join her on the balcony.

"I'm serious, April. I've never met anyone quite like you and ... even though you can be a royal pain in the ass, I—I don't want to lose you. I love you, April Flowers," he whispered in her ear. He wrapped his arms around her, pulling her close.

She turned her face to him, her sultry green eyes staring deep into his. "I think I love you, too, and it scares me shitless, Ace. If we don't pull this thing off tonight, we may not have a lot of time together. I don't want to waste another minute, so let's love one another while we can," she replied, tugging on his cock for emphasis.

He led her back to the bed, where they made slow, passionate love until they finally fell apart, exhausted. She dragged him to the bathroom, and they showered together, soaping one another under the hot spray, kissing, hands exploring the other's supple body.

"Sorry, babe, we'd better stop. My pecker's so sore, it feels like it's gonna fall off any second now. I'm going to have to give him a rest," he apologized.

"Don't you have a name for it? I thought all guys named their dicks," she joked with a smile.

"I never really thought about it much, to tell you the truth. I suppose 'Mr. Happy" is as good any. I know he's delighted right now," he replied, planting a quick kiss on her lips.

They toweled off and dressed for the evening's project, her in black leotards, him in dark T-shirt and jeans. They discussed her plan, going over and over it for unseen pitfalls, until it was almost time to leave.

"We don't have to do this, you know. We can forget about Officer Dipshit and try to find some way to do this without killing him," Mason offered weakly, grasping at any alternative.

"You're not getting cold feet, are you?" she asked him, frowning.

"I just wish there was a better solution to our situation. If the sacrifice works, we're guilty of murder. If it doesn't work, we're still guilty of murder, *and* we'll spend an eternity in hell, wondering if there was something we could have done differently," he sighed.

April wasn't at all sure of her plan, but barring a miracle, she couldn't see any other way to rid themselves of their supernatural adversaries. "It has to work, Ace. Let's go, before we talk ourselves out of it." She reached for her purse.

At that point, a new and troubling thought occurred to him. "What if that ass-wipe Ripper lied to us about the ritual?"

"How do you mean?"

"What if he flat-out lied—and it doesn't work? We'll have killed the cop for nothing, and it's either the needle or we get to spend eternity with that asshole Adriel and his toady bitch," he pointed out.

"We've already been over this, Ace, you're over-thinking it again. Either we commit fully, or we stop now, it's your call."

He'd searched his soul for another solution, but none was forthcoming. Go figure. "Okay, let's do it. I must be outta my freakin' mind, but let's take care of it," he said grimly.

THE COP RESIDED IN a two-story condo in an upscale neighborhood catering mostly to upper-middle-class families. Fifteen minutes later, the Maserati purred to a halt near the front door of a condo. Mason wondered how Officer Dipshit, on a cop's salary, could afford such fancy digs all by himself. In a town where the average cop's salary started around $50,000, it seemed suspicious. It was 11:16 p.m., and they were both stressed.

"Okay, remember the plan. I'll knock on the door. He'll be leery when he sees it's me. When he lets me in, that's your signal to come to the door and stand ready. If things don't go smoothly, I'll scream and you rush in, got it?" she instructed.

He nodded, gripping the steering wheel to keep himself from screaming. "You have the knife and chalk?" he asked.

Jack Ripper had given them instructions about how to perform this ritual, but nothing could've truly prepared them for this moment. Until now, it had only been a mental exercise. The enormity of what they were about to do was both terrifying and sobering.

"Yeah, they're in my purse. *Crap*! There's his car, he's home early," she whispered.

A large, blue SUV pulled into the cop's driveway and parked. Officer Craig Gleason climbed out and a security light came on, illuminating his vehicle. A tall, blonde clad in a blood-red power suit opened the passenger side door to join him at the front door. Mason couldn't believe his eyes. If that wasn't Alal standing there with her arm looped casually around Gleason's waist, it must be her evil twin.

"Is that who I think it is?" April asked incredulously.

"Sure looks like her. What the fuck is she doing here? There's no way in hell she could've known we were planning this," he muttered.

"I think you just stated the obvious—the key word being 'hell.' You think she can really read our minds?" she asked.

"Either that or someone overheard us discussing our plans and told her, but who?" Personally, he was grateful their scheme had unraveled when it did. He'd known he didn't have it in him to murder someone in cold blood, even if their lives had depended on it.

"Well, crap! This fucking sucks!" April said irascibly. Since Alal was with the cop, there'd be no way she could get to him. "Guess we might as well head back to the hotel. Maybe she'll screw him to death," she murmured resignedly.

"We should be so lucky. Forget about that asshole, he'll get what's coming to him at some point. We need to concentrate on winning that damn contest tomorrow night. If we don't, it doesn't matter whether Officer Dipshit lives or dies, we'll still be in a world of shit," he said, starting the engine. Their trip back to the Driskill was a quiet one. Leaving the luxury car in the valet's capable hands, they wandered back up to their suite.

DISPIRITED, APRIL PLOPPED down on the fancy couch and rolled herself a doobie while he grabbed a beer from the mini-fridge, downing it almost in one large gulp.

"I'm starving. You know, we forgot to eat earlier," she stated, lighting the joint.

"I, for one, did not relish stalking that asshole on a full stomach, but yeah, now that you mention it, I'm famished, too," he said, taking a hit off it.

They ordered a large pizza from a local franchise. Waiting for it to be delivered, they turned on the TV to watch the news. Midway through the broadcast, a "Breaking News" alert in blood-red letters filled the screen.

The bleached-blonde anchorwoman announced, "This just in: An apparent homicide tonight in the West Lake Subdivision of Rollingwood allegedly involved an officer with the APD. At this time, details are sketchy, but we'll update you with more information as it becomes available. Now for the weather ..." Mason muted the sound.

"*Crap*! We were in Rollingwood a half hour ago. Do you think it's possible ... no fuckin' way!" He tried to wrap his head around this.

"I don't know, but I don't like it. Not that I give two shits if it *was* him; but if so, it means Alal's involved, and that can't be good," she replied apprehensively.

Their pizza arrived, and they monitored the news while they ate. Another homicide had been discovered earlier on the north side of town. Some old biker's body had been found by a neighbor, half-eaten by his own poor, starving dog. Police reported there was evidence of foul play, but no suspects were in custody.

"Think they're connected?" she mumbled around a large slice of pepperoni pizza she'd shoved in her mouth.

"Wouldn't surprise me in the least," he replied. "The house where they found the dead biker is maybe half a mile, as the crow flies, from Adriel's. The larger question is why, and what connection might there be between this dead guy and us? As I've said, I don't believe in coincidence," he added, reaching out to snag the last piece.

Toward the end of the broadcast, there was an update to the story about the homicide in Rollingwood. The camera cut to a reporter on the scene. Mason felt his stomach roil as he saw she stood on the very porch of the condo they'd staked out only an hour earlier. Yellow crime scene tape was being installed around the property while the reporter interviewed an older cop. Mason turned up the volume.

"I'm here with Sergeant Lewis of the Rollingwood PD. Officer Lewis, can you tell us the name of the victim found here tonight, and do you have any suspects at this time?" she asked, shoving her microphone in his solemn face.

"I can only tell you that the deceased is ... *was* an officer with APD. We're not releasing his name, pending notification of next of kin," he paused to get control of his emotions. "As for suspects, I can't comment on an ongoing investigation. I can only say that whoever committed this terrible act will be caught and punished to the fullest extent of the law," he advised, with anger in his voice.

"Should the public at large be concerned?" The reporter inquired.

The cop shook his head in the negative, still struggling with his outrage at the senseless death of a fellow officer. "We believe this was an isolated incident. We don't think the public is in any danger. When we know more, we'll update you. That's all for now," he said, turning to leave before the camera cut away.

"*Holy shit*! Alal *must've* killed him. But why?" April exclaimed, feeling nauseous.

"I can think of several reasons, none of them good. We can't very well question her about it without acknowledging our own presence there tonight," he said, with a frown.

"What if it wasn't her that killed him?" April said, worriedly chewing a nail to the quick.

"Seriously? We saw them go inside together, who the hell else could've done it in that brief period of time?"

"This isn't good, Mason. Somebody might've spotted us sitting in that ridiculously expensive 'boy toy' you call a car," she worried.

"I don't think so, the windows are heavily tinted. They might have noticed the car, but I doubt they could have seen anyone inside at night," he asserted, hoping it was true.

"That fucking bitch must have known what we were planning. She probably overheard us talking and killed him herself before we could follow through with our plan. *Shit*!" She surmised, trying not to panic.

"I don't know how or why, but we have to assume she knew about it. Okay, think, what's the worst that can happen? The cops can't place us there at the exact time of the murder. The car is registered to Adriel—that is, if it isn't hot, which is a distinct possibility," he said.

"Don't you think Alal would've recognized Adriel's car as they pulled into the cop's driveway? All she'd have to do is point the cops in our direction and we're fucking toast." April's agitation was growing.

"We both need to settle down and try to remain calm. We've got to think this through rationally. The only one who knows we were out tonight for any length of time is the valet. We have to stop acting guilty—I mean, it's not as if *we* killed anyone," he reasoned.

"That demoness could blackmail us in a heartbeat, Mason. I don't know about you, but I don't care to stand around with my thumb up my ass, waiting to be arrested for a murder I didn't commit. I say we beat feet, blow this town, and haul ass to Colorado while the gettin's good. To hell with the contest, screw Adriel, and screw his bitch! I've got friends in Boulder who can hide us 'til this cluster-fuck goes away." She declared.

At that point, they'd both worked up a sweat. "And then what?" Mason argued. "Running won't do any good, it's likely they'd find us wherever we go. If you think Adriel's just gonna tear up our contracts and let us go our merry way with no repercussions, you're outta your freakin' mind," he asserted.

"Listen Ace, I'm not gonna rot in some hellhole of a prison because of that demonic twat! As it is, I likely have less than six months to live. Damned if I'll spend the rest of it locked away in some crappy eight-by-ten-foot cell with a bunch of hard-assed killers. I'd rather take my chances in Colorado, with or without you. Your choice, but make it snappy. I wanna be in New Mexico by sunrise!" she stated, snatching her old clothes from the armoire.

He was torn; she had a valid point. If they slipped away tonight, they had a decent chance of making it to the New Mexico border before Adriel and Alal discovered them missing. If, however, either of the demons actually *could* read their minds, they'd never make it out of the hotel, let alone to Boulder.

He had only moments to decide. Stay and hope this shitstorm goes away, try to win the stupid contest tomorrow; act as if nothing had happened—or, follow the woman he'd fallen in love with into a shaky future in Colorado. If they left now, he'd be abandoning his bandmates to the wrath of those two evil creatures posing as humans. If he remained here alone, they'd be losing their lead singer, and likely, the stupid contest as well.

A sudden knock at the suite's front door startled them both. *Shit! Who could that be at this hour?* He glanced at the time.

"Don't answer it, Ace! It can't be anything good at this time of night," she hissed warily.

Before he could respond, the door opened and in walked Alal, wearing the same red power suit she'd worn at the cop's condo. Only now, it was spattered with crimson splotches no designer had provided. "I thought I heard conversation as I was walking to my room. I hope I'm not intruding on your plans for the rest of the evening?" the demoness said with her trademark smirk.

Shit! She knows, he thought, grimacing. "Well, we were just about to hit the sack," he snapped brusquely.

"I'm sure you were. I'd join you for a delicious little threesome, but I need to get out of this dress. Red wine stains can be such a pain in the ass to get out, don't you think?" Alal remarked, watching his face.

"Whatever you say," he agreed. Then, tired of the charade, he said, "Look, let's cut the bullshit. We both know what happened tonight, it's all over the fucking news. So, why'd you kill him?"

"I haven't the slightest clue what you're talking about. I don't watch human television ... too much *violence*," she mocked, with a sardonic grin. "I had the most delicious date earlier, he had excellent taste ... in wine. A pity my date was so short-lived, but he showed me a fascinating home video he'd made," her glance lit on April, who cringed inwardly. "Funny thing, the woman in it reminded me of someone. Watching him plow her back forty made me wet. It really looked delightfully painful," Alal ogled her gleefully.

"Fuck you, you demonic harpy!" April snarled. Before Mason could stop her, she charged the demoness. Clutching the knife she'd taken from her purse, she thrust it deep into the evil creature's core, giving it a vicious twist.

Unfazed, Alal flashed a malevolent smile, pulling the dagger from her chest and tossing it on the floor, to April's bitter disappointment.

"You stupid little bitch! Did you really think your puny knife could kill, Alal, the Destroyer of Men? I'm going to thoroughly enjoy watching that pretty 'brown Betty' of yours being torn to pieces over and over for all eternity. If you try anything stupid like this again, I'll *end* your wretched existence, contract or no contract!" the demon snarled. Grabbing April by the throat, she shook her like a rag doll.

"Stop it, Alal, you're going to kill her!" Mason screamed, rushing to April's defense as her face turned from dark red to deathly pale.

As Alal grudgingly released her death grip, April collapsed on the floor, clutching her throat, gasping for breath. Mason kneeled by her to help her shakily to her feet.

"Sorry," Alal said insincerely. "I have a wicked temper, comes with the territory. My date tonight found that out the hard way. Just so you know," she pointed to April, "if you try to run, we'll find you, and when we do ... well, let's just say, you won't be singing. Were it not for your contract with Adriel, I'd have torn you limb from limb and devoured your bloody corpse. Oh, and if you have any more stupid plans to get rid of us, forget about it. We'll know—and it won't bode well for either of you. Have a nice fuck, and I'll see you in the morning. Remember, tomorrow's the big day." She smiled coldly, turned, and walked out.

"It was stupid to believe I could kill that bitch with only a knife. She just pushed the wrong button, and I-I lost it," April rasped bitterly, massaging her bruised throat. "She must be able to read our minds, there's no other logical explanation, unless she has the entire suite bugged. How else would she know we were planning on skipping town?".

"I suspect you're right. We have no way to know how powerful she or Adriel actually are. Did she hurt you badly?" he asked, gently touching her throat.

She winced and whispered, "I'm not sure. The bitch had a grip of steel, I felt she could've crushed me like an insect. I need something to drink, maybe some whiskey and lemon juice would help." Her voice sounded as if she'd swallowed broken glass.

"*Shit*! I hope she didn't damage your vocal cords. If you can't sing, we'll have no hope of winning tomorrow." Grabbing a lemon from beneath the minibar, he sliced it, adding the juice to a large shot of whiskey, and handed it to her. She made a face as the concoction burned its way down her throat. Then she walked to the bedroom, returning with her phone.

Mason gave her a curious look and was about to ask what she was doing when she shook her head, placing a finger to his lips to silence him.

In case the rooms were actually bugged, she sent a text to his phone: '*We need to find a priest.*'

He read the words, frowning, then wrote: '*Why? You wanna get married?*'

She rolled her eyes in frustration, then typed and sent one word: '*Exorcism*'

Now it was his turn to shake his head. He wrote back: '*Won't work. No time to find one, even if we did, he'd think we R crazy!*'

'*It's our only hope, Ace,*' she wrote.

'*U know if she can read our minds, texting won't help, she'll still know and stop us,*' he texted.

'*Betting rooms* have *been wired for sound. Think about it, she got us this suite. Had plenty time to plant bugs. Suggest we search rooms now. Need loud music to block conversation,*' she typed.

"For both our sakes, I hope you're right," he said aloud. Connecting his phone to an amp via Bluetooth, he selected some Metallica, cranking up the volume to provide cover for any verbal communication between them. While James Hetfield belted out the lyrics to a well-known song, they explored every room, starting at the front door.

They found the first bug under the minibar. The second one, attached to the metal frame of the bed, took a little longer. The third one was the hardest to locate. Alal had hidden it behind the bathroom light fixture. They did one last sweep of the rooms but found nothing else. The suite looked like a tornado had blown through it, furniture overturned, mattresses and bedding in disarray, curtains piled in a heap on the floor. April could think of only one other place they had yet to search—the living room balcony. With the music of "Enter Sandman" blaring throughout the suite, they opened the door to the terrace and stepped out. That's when they spotted the last one. The irony was that it was an actual bug, at least, it resembled one.

A large cockroach clinging to the limestone facade above the doorway didn't run or fly when Mason swatted it with his hand. It fell at their feet, landing upside down, legs in the air. Leaning over to examine it, he discovered a tiny transmitter embedded in its fake carapace. Hating roaches; he crushed it under his heel.

Satisfied they'd found the last of the hidden devices, he turned to face April. "I think that's all of them," he said skeptically.

"We can hope. We'll need to keep up the charade of ignorance, just in case we missed one, and continue to text our important conversations when we're inside," she said wearily.

They shuffled back inside, and Mason turned off the music.

'Should I look up a priest?' he texted her.

'Sooner the better. U can call first thing in morning. Right now, need go to bed, I'm beat,' she responded.

He agreed—but before they could crawl into bed, they had to put the rooms back into some semblance of order, since Alal tended to arrive early most mornings. When that was done, they made urgent, desperate love. Exhausted, they fell into a deep post-coital slumber, where nightmares lurked in the shadowy realm of their subconscious, waiting to be unleashed ...

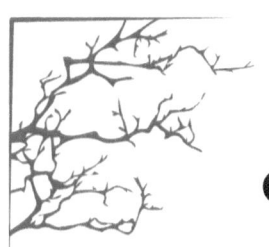

Chapter Seventeen

Mason awoke at 6:00 a.m., to find April up already. The TV was on with the sound muted. Apparently, she'd had room service deliver another TV and remote to replace the ones she'd smashed. Currently, she sat on the edge of the bed with her back to him, scrolling through her phone. He rolled over and wrapped his arms around her, pulling her down beside him to nuzzle her neck. Overnight, dark circles had formed beneath her eyes, making her appear like some refugee from a horror flick.

"Rough night again? I thought I heard you moaning in your sleep," he said, yawning.

"Yeah, same freakin' nightmare with my father. It gets worse each time I have it. I'm to the point where I dread falling asleep. The dreams are horribly vivid, and there's nothing I can do to stop them," she said miserably.

At least, her voice sounds normal again, he thought, somewhat relieved.

Handing him his phone, she texted him: *'Been awake for an hour, found a priest. Set up meeting 2:00 pm. Now we wait. If Alal tries to stop us, we'll know that bugs were red herring,'* she typed.

'Where Is the meet?' he typed.

'St. David's on Burnet Rd. Father O'Hennigan is priest's name,' she replied.

Mason nodded and got up to pee. When he returned, he saw a "Breaking News" alert pop up on the TV screen. "Turn up the sound, babe," he said, sitting beside her.

The news reporter stood in front of a large water-filled quarry, surrounded by a small phalanx of police. A large crane was lifting a dripping police cruiser from its murky depths.

"—and police are confirming this is the missing officer's squad car," the reporter commented. "She had not reported in since starting her shift yesterday. Our sources tell us the police suspect foul play, although they would neither confirm or deny it. Divers are currently searching the water for the officer's body as we speak," the reporter droned on.

"That's two cops in one day. You don't suppose Alal had anything to do with this one's disappearance, do you?" Mason asked, watching as the crane gently set the water-logged cruiser down on dry land.

"No way to tell. All I know is we'd better grab something to eat before rehearsal starts. She and the guys will be here at 7:00," she said, perusing the hotel menu.

They ordered Eggs Benedict and continued watching the news until Jimmy delivered their food. Neither of them had much of an appetite. The upcoming meet with the priest had them worried and with good reason. When they'd finished eating, she stepped out on the balcony for a quick smoke. Mason walked out to join her, and together they watched the rising sun break through the early morning clouds to bathe them in golden light. It would be another scorcher of a day. Forecasters were predicting storms with an approaching front later this evening. Mason hoped it would hold off until after the contest. He didn't relish transporting their new instruments in the pouring rain.

Alal and the rest of the band showed up promptly at 7:00. They tuned up and began the practice session, keeping a watchful eye on the demoness as she opened a fresh bottle of tequila. By the time they'd finished rehearsing their two-song set for the second time, Alal had drained over half a bottle of the expensive blue agave liquor. When they stopped for lunch, the demoness was leaning against the bar for support.

"Looks like someone needs a fresh bottle of joy juice," Mason grumbled under his breath. He wished she'd drink herself into a coma and die, but knew they'd never be that lucky. Placing his guitar on a stand, he approached the back of the bar and produced another bottle of tequila.

"Didn't want you to run out, so I ordered a couple more. You really ought to slow down on that stuff," He set the bottle in front of her. He figured using reverse psychology would piss her off, and it worked.

"Mine yer own fuckin' bisshness, ya' six-fingered freak! I'm doin' jush fine, I ken drink yer scrawny human ass unner tha table any day of tha millen'um," she slurred angrily, struggling to open the fresh bottle.

Jeff motioned Mason to the balcony with him, out of earshot of the sloshed demon. "Do you really think it's wise to antagonize her like that? I mean, you're just adding fuel to the fire," he muttered quietly.

"It's a calculated risk; I'm hoping she'll drink enough to pass out. April and I need to be someplace at 2:00 p.m., and I don't want her asking any questions about it. You think you and the others could stick around to keep her distracted while we're gone?" Mason kept his voice low.

"I guess so, but you'll owe us big time. Five minutes alone with that blonde monstrosity feels like an eternity," he groused, frowning.

"Great, I really appreciate it, bro. Let's grab something to eat and hope Jose Cuervo works his magic on the belligerent bitch," Mason said with some relief.

When they stepped back inside, they found that April had ordered sandwiches for all. Well, all except for Alal, who was weaving unsteadily on her feet. After they ate, they picked up their instruments and resumed the practice session, finally stopping at 1:40 p.m.

Alal had nearly polished off the bottle of tequila Mason had provided. Much to his dismay, she continued to defy the effects of gravity and remained on her feet. Mason glanced at April, and she nodded. It was time to find out if Alal could truly read their minds.

"Mason and I have an errand to run. We'll be back by 4:00 p.m.," April announced, holding her breath for Alal's reaction.

The drunken demoness merely waved them away without suspicion or any badgering comments for a change.

Mason exchanged nervous glances with April as they left the suite. "So, I suppose this proves she isn't a mind reader," she said as they entered the elevator.

"EITHER THAT, OR SHE'S just pretending to be drunk. If she were human, they'd be carting her ass to the morgue by now. I trust that conniving bitch as much as I would a rabid dog."

When they stepped outside the Driscoll, the valet had Adriel's car waiting for them. Fifteen minutes later, they arrived at the Catholic church in North Austin. Mason parked, and they burned five minutes trying to find the rectory, where a middle-aged woman sat perched behind a small desk.

"Hello, may I help you?"

"Uh, yes, ma'am, we've a two o'clock appointment with Father O'Hennigan," April replied.

"Please have a seat, and I'll let him know you're here," she said.

They sat and fidgeted while she called him on the intercom to announce their arrival. Moments later, a door behind her swung open, and the tall priest appeared, motioning them to enter. Father O'Hennigan was an elderly man with a kind, care-worn face. His silver-gray hair was cut in a flat-top—a style popularized in the Fifties—and he sported a belly to rival St. Nick's.

"Please, come in and have a seat. Can I get you some coffee or water?" he ushered them into his office.

"No thanks, Father, we're fine," Mason answered tensely. They sat opposite him in a couple of leather, high-backed chairs, with a small, mahogany desk covered in books and religious literature separating them.

"First off, you can call me Father James; O'Hennigan is a mouthful and a bother. I take it you need counsel today?" He folded his large hands over his portly stomach.

"That's correct, Father. I'll come straight to the point. Do you believe in the existence of demons?" Mason asked him.

The elderly priest stared thoughtfully at the two young people sitting across from him, contemplating his answer. "I believe that evil appears in many forms in this life, if that's what you're asking. Creatures such as demons and malignant spirits may exist, though I admit, I've never come face to face with such an entity in all my years as a priest. Why do you ask?" He arched a brow.

Mason glanced uneasily at April, then ventured, "What if I told you Ms. Flowers, April, and I each signed a contract with one these... creatures, and that our lives, no, our very *souls* are in peril because of it?"

Father James' pale blue eyes widened in mild alarm at that startling statement. Mason and April held his inquiring gaze, waiting for his reply.

"I—I honestly don't know what to say. Do you have any verifiable proof of this creature's existence?"

Crap! In their rush to talk to him, they hadn't thought about that. Neither of them had any concrete evidence to back up their claim. Their contracts existed only on Adriel's tablet; everything else was hearsay. They had only their testimony that they were telling the truth. Until it hit Mason that he *did* have corroboration of a sort. He held up his left hand for Father James' inspection, wiggling his six fingers.

"A couple of days ago, I only had five of these. That was before I met Adriel," Mason proclaimed, waving the sixth digit. Father James' eyes grew a little larger as he peered at the newly minted finger. They explained each of their backstories, describing how they'd met and what had occurred since, leading to their desperate visit to him.

"So, you see, Father, we don't have anyone else to turn to. We've both made many mistakes in our lives, but this is by far the worst. If we lose this contest and are unable get rid of these demons by tonight, we're doomed," he asserted grimly.

The small room was silent, save for the ticking of a clock on the wall above the priest's desk. The ball was in the priest's court, as they patiently awaited his response.

"I'm going out on a limb here—are you actually asking me to evaluate and perform an exorcism on these people?" he inquired.

"We're not asking, Father, we're begging. As incredible as it all sounds, we're telling the God's truth, I swear on my departed father's soul," April replied earnestly. As she mentioned her father, tears flowed, and the priest nudged a box of tissues close to her.

Father James sighed and shook his head sadly. "I'm afraid you don't understand the Church's position on this matter. Evaluating a candidate for the ritual of exorcism can take days or even months to complete. The ritual is to rid a *human* host of possession, *not* a demon assuming a human form. If the creature took that form without first possessing another, I don't know if an exorcism would work. Banishing such a powerful being might prove impossible, and quite dangerous to the priest performing the ritual," he explained patiently.

"Got it, then I guess we're screwed, pardon my French, Father," Mason said dejectedly.

"I'm sorry we wasted your time, Father. Let's go, Ace. We might have time to find another priest if we hurry," she stood to go.

As they turned to leave, the priest stopped them. "Wait a moment, Mr. Rivers. I'm not unsympathetic to your plight. I truly believe what you're telling me is the complete truth as you know it. It would be unethical for me to send you into harm's way without trying to help with your unorthodox problem. I could lose my parish and my collar for this, but ... this one time, I'll skirt the red tape and attempt to do what you ask," he said resignedly. "After all, no one lives forever, right?" He smiled.

Hearing this, Mason sighed with relief and April's face lit up. "Thank you for believing us, Father, we had no one else to turn to. The cops would never believe us, and they wouldn't be much help even if they did. I tried to kill one of these things with a knife, stabbed her, and all she did was laugh in my face and try to strangle me. Believe me, neither Adriel or Alal are human," she said, touching her bruised throat.

"Wait a second, did you just say *Alal,* as in 'Alal, the "demon destroyer of men?"' he asked, instantly alert.

"Yeah, she did call herself that," April sat back down.

"What about this Adriel, does he have a last name?" the priest asked her.

"It's Abaddon, if that means anything to you. He's Satan personified, Father."

"*Abaddon of the bottomless pit,*" Father James hissed, shaking his head. "If these creatures are truly what you say they are, they'd be formidable indeed. I'll need to do some research on these entities before we proceed any further. Let me ask you, are they aware of your presence here today?" he asked soberly.

"We certainly hope not," Mason responded. "Earlier, we found bugs in our suite—listening devices. Before that, we thought they might be reading our minds, but if that were true, surely they would have prevented us from coming here today," Mason replied.

"Or maybe she was too wasted on the tequila, and it simply slipped her mind. By the time we left, she'd drunk enough to kill a small elephant.

Apparently, demons don't process alcohol the way we humans do," April added.

"That doesn't surprise me. From the little I've read on the subject, it's likely demonic entities would have a high tolerance to alcohol and drugs," the priest said. "Sad to say, in today's worldview, the church has little vested interest in matters of exorcism. We've been bleeding parishioners for years, due to all the scandals in the news. Well, if we're to do this, I'll need time to prepare properly. How did you propose to get them in the same room with a priest and not raise their suspicions?"

They looked at each other with no clue. Then April looked at Mason and blurted out, "You said 'propose' ... we'll say you're there to marry us. It'll sound legit and hopefully catch them off guard. We'll ... uh, say we need them as witnesses. That could work, right?" she asked uncertainly.

Mason had concerns of his own. "Wait, what about rings? We don't have any, and I believe those are important in any marriage ceremony," he pointed out.

The priest slid open a drawer on his desk, pulled out a cigar box, and opened the lid. Producing two fat Panatella cigars, he removed the wrapper bands and handed them to Mason.

"Those should suffice in a pinch. It's not the first time I've been called upon to improvise in somewhat similar situations," he said with a smile.

"Thanks so much, Father," Mason said, vigorously shaking the priest's large hand. "So, the contest starts at eight tonight. If you agree, we'll need you in place by 10:00 p.m. at our suite at the Driskill. Win or lose, we should be back by 10:30 at the latest. I'll leave word at the front desk that we're expecting you and have them issue you a key card. We'll have to play this thing by ear. Hopefully, they'll go along with the ruse until it's too late for them to escape."

"A word of caution, Father," April said. "Should things go south later tonight, we don't expect you to hang around to watch the bloodbath. Nobody wants you to get hurt ... or worse. If this exorcism doesn't work, they may very well kill us on the spot, and we won't be able to help you. We appreciate you're taking a risk by helping us tonight, but please 'beat feet' if you feel your life's in danger." She gave him a big hug.

The portly priest smiled and hugged her back, "If I didn't help someone who truly needs it, I'd be shirking my oath as a priest and a devoted Christian in the service of our Lord, Jesus Christ. Go with God, child, and I'll see you both tonight," he waved them out, smiling.

The second they were out the door, the smile left his face. Picking up his phone, he called a number from his contacts.

After two rings, it was answered. "Yes?" the voice on the other end curtly inquired.

"We have a problem. They just left. They asked me to perform an exorcism tonight, and I've reluctantly agreed," the priest nervously said, sweat rolling down his cheeks.

"Excellent. Did they mention when and where this would take place?"

"10:30 p.m. in their suite, after this contest," Father James replied.

"You've been most helpful 'Father.' I was right to place a tap on the bitch's phone, she can't be trusted. Lucky for me, she called *you* instead of one of the other pedophilic priests entrenched in your so-called 'church.' I'll save you an especially warm place in hell when this is all over. See you tonight; don't be late!" Adriel said coldly, before disconnecting ...

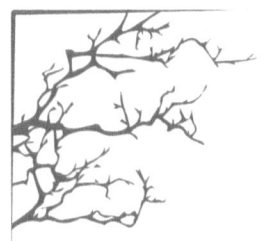

Chapter Eighteen

The Contest

Mason and April returned to the hotel at 3:50 that afternoon, to find all the guys passed out on the floor of the living area, empty liquor bottles lying around them.

"What the hell?" Mason scanned the room for Alal. He walked over to Jeff, who was leaning back against the bass drum kit, snoring. Mason nudged him with his shoe to rouse him.

"Whassup?" Jeff mumbled drunkenly.

"Wake up! What the hell happened while we were gone?" Mason asked him irately.

"Uh, well, you tol' us to distrac' tha bitch. So, bein' bored, we challenged her to a drinkin' contes.' Tha's wha' happened!" he replied thickly. He tried to sit up, and the room spun so he sat back down.

"Well, that's just wonderful. So, where's Alal? I don't see her here," he asked in frustration.

"Dunno, she wassh standin' by the bar when I guess I passed out," Jeff mumbled. "I think Davy wassh the las' to see her. Larry din't stan' a chance, three shots 'n' he wass down for tha count."

"*Shit*! I should have known better than to leave you all alone with that conniving bitch. Look, we have exactly three and a half hours before the contest starts. So, get up off your drunk ass and help me sober these two up. April, please order some food and coffee for them. Cold showers for everyone!"

He roused the other two roughly from their drunken slumber. Groaning and cursing, one by one, they stumbled unsteadily to their feet.

"Davy, where's Alal?" Mason asked, helping him to the couch to wait his turn in the cold shower.

"Dunno, don' care. My head's gonna explode any second now. No more booze, *ever*," he moaned miserably.

Mason shook his head in frustration. "It's my fault, I should've known she'd do something like this to screw us up. If we lose tonight, I won't blame anyone but myself. Food and coffee is on the way, just hang on 'til we can get something in you to help sober you up," he told him.

"I ordered some Menudo, with some extra greasy Churizo tacos on the side, April announced, with an evil smirk. "They should be here in a few minutes."

Both Davy's and Larry's faces turned unhealthy shades of green. Stumbling to his feet, Davy groaned, lurched his way to the balcony railing, and puked over the edge, unconcerned who it might land on. A loud, disgusted cry erupted from the sidewalk below, followed by harsh language.

The smell wafted in with the late afternoon breeze, pushing Larry over the brink. Grabbing the first thing he came to, he barfed his brains out, leaving a nasty, stinking mess inside his empty bass case.

"Did you really need to be so specific?" Mason groused to April. "You definitely have an evil sense of humor, woman."

"Why? I only told them the truth. Menudo is supposed to work wonders for a hangover. It has choice ingredients in it, like—"

He put his hand over her mouth. "I *know* what it's made from, thank you very little. Let's just get these dudes into the shower as fast as possible, shall we?" he said, trying not to think about those *choice ingredients.*

A primal scream issued from the bathroom when Jeff stepped under the cold shower. Room service arrived, and Jimmy wheeled the food cart inside. Mason tipped him and he left in a rush, this time without a word. The smell of the Menudo was enough to turn Mason's stomach, even sober.

April grimaced, backing away from the cart as if it were radioactive. Unwillingly, Davy and Larry took their turns under the icy water. When they were all back in the living room, Mason served them each a bowl of the steaming Mexican soup, along with some of the greasiest looking tacos he'd ever seen. They tasted way better than they looked. Davy had never eaten Churizo before and naively asked what it was made from.

April cheerfully informed him about the *"choice ingredients"* used in its creation. Larry expelled his mouthful of taco and ran to the bathroom to feed "Oorrrgg, the toilet god." None of this bothered Jeff, who actually liked the soup, as was evident as he helped himself to seconds.

On their way back to the hotel, she and Mason had decided they should fill the guys in on their plan for an exorcism, so while the three sobered up, they explained what they planned. The guys were so hung over that all they could do was barely nod.

Over the next two hours, Mason ensured everyone was plied with multiple cups of coffee. By 7:00 p.m., they'd seen no sign of Alal. Mason had hoped the demoness drank herself back to hell when she entered the suite without even knocking, shadowed by Adriel. She looked like she'd dressed for an S/M convention in a black turtleneck and jeans, sporting a black leather jacket studded with star-shaped sequins that shimmered under the light.

Adriel wore black designer slacks and a dark T-shirt silk-screened with the face of a smirking red devil holding a pitchfork, with the caption, "I'm a horny little devil!"

"Ready to rock 'n' roll?" he asked, draping his arm over Alal's shoulder to squeeze an ample tit, making her chortle.

"Ready as we're going to get. We'll need help getting all this equipment loaded and—" Mason said.

Adriel stopped him. "That won't be necessary, all you'll need are your guitars. The venue will provide the rest. The bands will share amps, mikes, and drums for quicker turnaround between sets."

Larry had spent the past hour cleaning the vomit out of his bass case and was still pissed at himself. "Dude, I can't play my bass, it still smells like puke. It'll make me sick all over again," he groused miserably.

"That's what you get for challenging a demoness to a drinking contest, foolish human," Alal sneered with a sly smile.

"Spray some Lysol or something in the damn thing," Jeff told him. "It's only for two songs, and we're going first. It'll be over before you know it, so suck it up,"

"There's been a slight change in the order of appearance," Adriel smirked. "Jack Ripper and his band are playing first; your little group will be the last to play. An unfortunate scheduling error, I'm afraid, but it shouldn't be a problem—should it?"

Glancing at April, Mason saw she was fuming, thinking the same thing he was. *This whole contest had been rigged from the start!* Not only was the order of their appearance changed, it could throw them late getting back to the suite. Father James would have to wait—they had no choice but to go with the changes.

"Don't worry about us," Mason said, trying to bolster some enthusiasm in his ragtag group. "We're ready to kick ass tonight, right guys?" The three vaguely concurred, muttering, "sure," and "yeah."

Mason decided to change the subject. "I forgot to ask where the contest is being held."

"It's at the 'Long Center.' As I mentioned before, top brass from several record companies will be in attendance. The winner will receive a recording contract and the prestige of being chosen as the best new rock band in Texas," Adriel crowed.

"Uh, what does the loser get?" Davy asked densely.

Adriel's face darkened, his eyes seeming to suck all the light from the room. "Are you really that obtuse, little drummer-boy? Would you like a little preview of what's waiting behind door number three should you lose?" he barked, rubbing his hands together in anticipation.

Davy refused, recoiling from the demon. "Sorry I asked," he muttered.

"All right, let's get this show on the road, shall we?" Adriel said tersely.

They packed up their guitars in a hurry. Trying to mask the nasty smell inside his case, Larry had sprayed it liberally with some complimentary cologne he'd found in the bathroom. Now, it smelled like "Eau de Vomitte."

Gathering what they needed, they left the hotel. When they stepped outside, a hotel courtesy van was waiting at the curb. Mason observed several brilliant flashes of lightning in the distance as a strong, cold front approached from the west.

"*Shit*! Looks like a turd floater's headed this way. Better haul ass or we'll get soaked; I sure as shit don't want to be electrocuted onstage," he told the driver. The van sped away from the curb and merged into traffic.

MINUTES LATER, THEY reached the Long Center for the Performing Arts and scrambled out, racing to beat the approaching storm. Thunder cracked and rumbled overhead, as a powerful gust of rain-cooled wind brought the aroma of cedar trees from the neighboring Hill Country and the rain began to pour in earnest. Large, fat drops pelted them as they ran for the covered entrance. Lightning struck an adjacent telephone pole, the resultant blast of thunder causing everyone to cringe as they scurried inside. Everyone, of course, except Alal and Adriel.

The interior buzzed with the noise of the sizeable crowd gathered for the event. When they asked an attendant manning the ticket counter for directions to the backstage area, she pointed to a door and told them to follow the signs. They shoved through throngs of attendees waiting in line to buy over-priced alcoholic beverages and snacks and proceeded down a dim hallway. A burly security guard near the backstage entrance stopped them.

"I'll need to see everyone's ID. Only band members are allowed past this point. I have to issue each of you badges before you can proceed any further," he said curtly. Each of them pulled out their IDs, handing them to the guard while he checked off their names on his list.

Without a word, Adriel turned and left them. "See you after the contest, break a fucking leg—really," Alal sneered, turning to follow him to their seats in the front row.

Satisfied, the guard issued them badges with lanyards. Donning them, they followed him backstage, passing small clusters of musicians idly chatting and tuning their instruments. Mason spotted Jack Ripper and his band lounging near the enormous curtain that hung over the stage.

"How many bands we up against, Ace?" Larry asked, setting his malodorous guitar case on the floor.

"Not sure, maybe ten, I'd guess."

"Nope, there's fifteen bands registered, but not all of them will show," Davy reported. "According to the program notes, every member of a performing band *must* be present, otherwise, the entire band will be disqualified," he reported.

"Well, we might as well get comfortable, it's gonna be a long wait until we're up," Jeff commented. They looked around for chairs, finding all were taken. The contest began fifteen minutes later. Jack and his Hell-Rippers took the stage and tore into a draconian death-metal song they'd written, called "Brain Eater."

Mason timed Jack's set, hoping they'd go over the ten-minute time limit and be disqualified, but no such luck. Jack ended the set with an incredible flourish of soaring leads that had the mostly young crowd on their feet, cheering for more. The band following them onstage didn't look happy.

As Jack left the stage, he passed by Mason's group and smirked nastily at him. "Thought I might see you here. Good luck tonight, dude, tough break drawing last place. Hope you've got your groove on, you'll need it to have any hope of beating us," he sneered.

As he was about to walk away, Mason grabbed his arm. "Listen you satanic asshole, I *know* Adriel has you under contract. Did he tell you we had one, as well?" Mason hissed.

Hearing this, the cocky grin on Jack's face wavered momentarily, but he quickly recovered. "Don't know what you're talking about, dude. I don't know anyone named Adriel, and I'd appreciate it if you'd let go of my arm or I'll call security," Jack grumbled, yanking free of Mason's grasp. He stalked off to join his band members for a quick toke.

April took Mason's arm, pulling him away before he said or did something stupid and got them kicked out of the contest. "Chill, Ace. What if he's telling the truth? What if it's another band entirely? You have no proof that Jack is the one in Adriel's pocket," she pointed out.

"Oh, c'mon, give me a fucking break! I seriously doubt Adriel would waste his time on any of these other bands, none of them have Jack's level of talent," he angrily exclaimed.

"*We* do, and I believe we're the best band in town right now!" April declared. "It doesn't matter *who* Adriel has in his pocket, we're gonna rock their socks off and win this damn thing!" she declared, raising her hand for a high-five.

They all joined in and slapped skin. Mason wasn't sure he shared her enthusiasm, but she was right. They *had* to focus on winning the contest to have any chance of surviving the night with their souls intact. They all soon learned that two of the bands had been disqualified because one or more members had been delayed by the stormy weather. That left ten bands to go before they were up. As the evening wore on, two more were disqualified when their lead singers blew out their voices before finishing their set. The band proceeding them played over the ten-minute deadline and were immediately disqualified.

Finally, the emcee took the mike to introduce them. "Folks, we're down to our last band of the evening. Please give a Texas-size welcome to one of Austin's hometown favorites, 'Stark Naked and The Car Thieves,'" he bellowed into the mike, as Mason plowed into the first power chord of his song, "Makin' Bacon."

The spotlight was on April, her copper red hair bouncing while she belted out the lyrics. Some in the crowd knew the words and sang along, others clapped their hands to the rhythmic beat as Davy pounded the bass drum's skins.

Mason's six fingers went into overdrive, smoking the frets as they raced up and down the neck of his guitar. He was concentrating so hard that the veins on his neck popped out, giving him the appearance of a power lifter straining under the weight of a five-hundred-pound barbell. Sweat flew from his face to spatter the spectators sitting in the first row of seats, including Adriel and Alal, who appeared disgusted as they wiped it away.

Mason couldn't believe the speed of his fingers as they flew over the frets in a frenzied blur of motion. They produced the notes faster than his conscious brain could process using pure muscle memory, with more than a little help from the recent additions. April's vocal theatrics left the young audience stunned by her intensity and the raw emotion pouring from the soul of this petite, redheaded firebrand cavorting all over the stage.

When the song was over, the crowd leapt to its feet, cheering wildly and holding their phones over their heads, videoing the sweaty band onstage as they dove into the last song of their set. As the first chords of Mason's song, "Rabid Lust," rang out, the crowd went crazy. It was the band's signature song—the crowd ate it up and asked for seconds.

Mason had carefully timed it down to the last second, and as the last notes from the amplifiers echoed in their ears, resounding applause took their place. Adriel and Alal were the only ones remaining in their seats. From the dour looks on their faces, the demons had never expected such a enthusiastic reaction from the crowd, and it caught them completely off guard.

Taking a quick bow before leaving the stage, Mason and his entourage were ecstatic. "Dude, did you hear that fucking crowd? We could've played another set and really blown their doors off!" Jeff said excitedly, as they put their instruments away.

Mason was staring at April in awe. "You truly have the pipes of an angel, Babe. Even if we lose tonight, we've won. Think of all the new fans we made tonight. You were absolutely amazing!" he babbled, high on adrenaline.

"You weren't—too shabby—yourself, Ace," April gasped, trying to catch her breath. "All of us—we kicked ass—did our best. When it comes down to it, that's all that counts. We gave it our hearts and souls."

"Hopefully not our souls, but yeah, we did better than good," Mason agreed, giving the band a group hug.

The emcee stepped back up to the mike and said, "Folks, there'll be a short intermission while the judges tally their votes. Please visit our concession stand as we await their decision. How about another round of applause for all our contestants tonight?"

The crowd cheered as each band paraded across the stage one last time, each vying for the judge's votes. Mason and his band were the last to take a bow in front of the impassioned sea of rock and rollers who made up the majority of the audience. As they made their way back behind the curtain, Mason sagged against a wall, feeling drained as the adrenaline left his body.

"Now it's hurry up and wait. I haven't been this nervous since I first played in front of an audience when I was ten years old," he admitted, pacing the floor.

After what seemed an eternity, the house lights blinked off and on, signaling intermission was over. The crowd returned to their seats, and murmurs of eager anticipation reverberated around the venue as the judges handed the emcee the name of the winning band. He paused for a moment, keeping the packed venue in agonizing suspense until he finally spoke into the mike.

"Ladies and gentlemen, I have a surprise for you. The judges have declared the contest a tie. There will be an old fashioned 'head cutting' between the two selected bands to determine the winner," he proclaimed, receiving a rousing chorus of boos from the crowd. Mason stood up and wrapped an arm around April's shoulder as they waited to hear which bands had been chosen.

"The first band to play will be 'Jack and the Hell-Rippers,'" the emcee said, to heavy metal applause. Mason crossed his fingers and toes as the guy took his time, drawing out the suspense. "Last, but certainly not least ... 'Stark Naked and the Car Thieves,'" he finally announced. Hearing that, the crowd cheered, whistled, and stomped their approval.

Chants of "Car Thieves, Car Thieves, Car Thieves" grew as the crowd got to its feet in a show of their support. Learning they were still in the running, Mason and his band breathed a collective sigh of relief.

The emcee conferred with the judges, then nodded, returned to the mike. "Okay, everyone, here are the ground rules. Each band will play one song of their choosing. Said song cannot be longer than five minutes in length. If you pass the five-minute mark, you'll immediately be disqualified. And here's the kicker, folks, *you* in the audience will choose the winner of tonight's contest! Just text your vote to 7679, battle of the bands.org. After the final song, you'll have exactly 30 seconds to cast your vote," he announced, pausing to take a breath. "At the end of 30 seconds, voting will be blocked, so choose quickly. Now, without further ado, let's get this show on the road. First up, "Jaaack and the Hell-Rippers," he bellowed into his mike. The lights dimmed as the band ripped into one of their favorite showstoppers, called "Satanic Santa."

The seductive, dark-haired, female vocalist started screeching out unintelligible lyrics to some God-awful discordant song that sounded to Mason like a cross between a cat caught in a blender and a wounded water buffalo. Death-Metal just ground on his nerves, offending his musical yearning for structure and melody in a song. As far as he was concerned, those chaotic, dissonant chords were created by a sadist. Many in the audience, though, seemed to love it. They danced to the beat of the drum, waving green glow sticks, some in the shape of a phallus. Mason was timing the band on his phone, as was April. In Mason's completely biased opinion, Jack's searing guitar solo near the end of the song was its only saving grace.

The stopwatch on his phone was counting down to the last five seconds and with two seconds from being disqualified, the song concluded. The applause from the crowd wasn't nearly as loud as before, giving Mason and his group hope.

"Up next, please give it up for "Starrrk Naaaked and the Car Thieves," the emcee roared. The crowd leaped to their feet and cheered as Mason and the band took the stage.

Davy counted off the beat, and they launched into a cover of Heart's "Crazy on You," complete with Nancy Wilson's beautifully complex guitar intro, which Mason had long ago mastered. April sang with every ounce of her being, reaching all the high notes so elegantly that Ann Wilson herself would've been proud. Many in the young crowd seemed to know at least some of the lyrics and sang along. April leaped across the stage and performed a couple of perfect cartwheels, much to the adoring crowd's delight

The song ended with Mason performing a blazing solo up and down the fretboard while April performed a series of back-flips, landing in a flawless split. The whole place erupted in applause. A gaggle of teenage girls swarmed the edge of the stage, some tossing undergarments at Mason's feet. With a group bow, they left the stage to chants of "More, More, More!"

The Emcee took the mike and said, "You have 15 seconds left to get those votes counted, please hurry and lock in your vote." Before he could put the mike down, the lights in the arena flickered, threatening to leave everyone in the dark. Mason opened the weather app on his phone to see that, rather than pushing through the area, the storm had stalled out right on top of them.

"Don't worry, folks, we have back-up generators in case the power goes out. The judges have tabulated the results and the winner of this year's battle of the bands is ..." he paused, allowing suspense to build, "Stark Naked and the Car Thieves!" he finally screeched out. The crowd was on their feet, applauding and cheering, while colorful confetti fell from the rafters, covering the band as they stepped forward to take another bow.

Bathed in the crowd's adulation, Mason and April felt ecstatic. They noticed that Adriel and Alal had left. *Fuck 'em!* Mason thought gleefully. The emcee came forward to present the trophy and the winner's check for ten thousand dollars—half of which he owed Jack Ripper for info that was worthless to them now that Officer Dipshit was dead.

Ripper caught up with them backstage. "Congrats on the big win, Rivers, y'all played some killer tunes out there. So, you ready to settle up? Where's my cut?" he smirked, with his palm extended. Mason hated like hell to pay the satanic little shit anything, but a deal was a deal.

"Yeah, about that, I'll get it to you once I've deposited this check, first thing in the morning," he replied, making a show of placing it in his wallet.

"What the fuck? You promised me half after the contest, win or lose, asshole. Now pay up, or I'll be forced to take it outta your weaseling hide!" Jack exclaimed menacingly. Jack wasn't a big guy, but both his bass player and drummer looked like they could eat their own guts and ask for more.

"Look, you'll get your money, I promise. I just can't get that kind of cash from an ATM, so you'll have to wait until my bank opens in the morning," Mason said, trying to reason with him.

Jack and the two goons lurking behind him didn't look happy. "Alright. But if that money isn't in my hand by 9:30 a.m., my boys are gonna mess up your pretty face, '*Ace*,'" Jack grumbled.

"You touch him, and I'll send your balls to visit your fucking teeth!" April hissed. Her emerald eyes flashed with anger. The asshole burst out laughing at her daring.

"Whoa, you're a real spitfire! Chill out, little mama, or Jack-daddy will have to teach you some manners," Jack said with a lascivious smile.

"Yeah? You and what army, you pretentious pencil-necked geek!" she snapped, ready to wipe the grin off his face with a sweeping roundhouse kick if he made a sudden move toward her. Mason hugged her tightly to keep her from pummeling the asshole right then.

Jack stared daggers at her, his face flushed with humiliation. He knew if he struck her, he'd go to jail, so that wasn't an option. "Just be at the 'Crooked Dick' with my money at 9:15 tomorrow morning. We'll be waiting in the alley out back. If you don't show, we'll come find you and your bitch," he growled. Turning, he strode off with the rest of his band of losers.

"You should've let me kick him in the nuts. He deserves an ass-whipping, the greedy little prick," she argued, shrugging loose from Mason's grip.

"Chill, babe. You'd only have made matters worse. I should've known he'd try to push the issue," he tried to appease her. "God, you really wowed everyone tonight. Where did you learn all those moves you performed on stage? Did you take gymnastics in school?" he asked, to change the subject.

"I learned them cheerleading in high school. That, and I also have a fourth-degree brown belt in Tae kwon do. Our satanic friend's toadies wouldn't have stood a chance against me, unless they had guns," she told him confidently.

Adriel and Alal chose that moment to appear. "I suppose congratulations are in order. There's a gentleman from Sony records who wants to speak with you about a recording deal. If I were you, I wouldn't keep him waiting. Those industry types aren't known for their patience," Adriel pointed to a curtained-off area.

"Get your scrawny asses in gear, the man won't wait forever!" Alal snapped irritably.

"You'll have to forgive Alal, she lost a large sum of money tonight. I told her not to bet against you, but alas, she never listens. Demons are notoriously bad gamblers," he disclosed coldly.

"I would've won if you hadn't given this string bean the advantage of an extra finger!" she carped, her cold eyes flashing.

"Personally, I like to think we won because we were the better band. Sorry to disappoint you, Alal," Mason said dryly. "C'mon guys, let's go see what the man has in mind," he told April and the others, leading them away.

When they were out of earshot, April stopped him. "Can you believe that evil bitch bet against us? You were right about her helping the opposition. Our lives are just a freakin' game to those monsters," she reiterated.

"Forget about them for the moment. If we can snag a deal with Sony, we'll be riding the gravy train before you know it," he said, trying to distract her.

The well-dressed Sony rep stood and extended his hand with a smile. A diminutive Asian man with large-framed glasses, he shook hands with every band member and motioned them to take seats at the judges' table.

"Excellent performance tonight, guys. My name is John Wu. I'm here to offer you a recording contract with our label if we can agree on the terms. How does that sound?" he asked, eyebrows raised.

"We appreciate you taking the time to come here tonight. We're still a little stunned," Mason told him. "I'm sorry, but the term 'contract' is rather a sore subject for us right now. Please excuse us if we don't jump up and down with joy at the opportunity, but we've been through a great deal in a brief stint of time, and we're emotionally overwhelmed," he explained, as the band took seats around the table.

"I understand completely, Mr. Rivers, but my time here is short. I need to catch the 'red eye' back to the Big Apple soon, so let me be frank. This is a one-time deal we're offering, and you should hire a lawyer to look it over before signing anything. If everything's acceptable, we'll provide a limited amount of studio time for you to record. We have top-notch engineers who will mix and master an EP of up to six songs. Once it's finished, we'll take care of all promotions and bookings. Naturally, you'd receive a percentage of royalties from any album sales," he added with a smile.

"Okay, so what's the catch? A vast company like Sony would have stipulations involved," Mason said cautiously.

The man removed his glasses and made a production out of cleaning them with an expensive silk handkerchief before answering. "You're quite right, Mr. Rivers. We would require that you and your band produce one new album a year for the next two years. If everyone is happy with the results at the end of that time, we would consider extending your contract," he replied evenly.

"And if we don't make that deadline?" Mason asked, glancing at the others.

"Well, if that occurred, I suppose we'd be forced to address that problem and reevaluate your contract. Hopefully, for everyone's sake, that won't be necessary. We have faith in you, Mr. Rivers. I like what I've heard, and I believe you and your band would be a profitable addition to our extensive catalog of artists," Wu replied, smiling.

Mason surveyed the other members of the band and shrugged. "This contract of yours, do we have time to look it over? The last contract we signed didn't turn out so well," he said pointedly.

Wu nodded, handing him a thick packet from his briefcase. Mason flipped through it, and it looked like it went on for at least fifty pages. "Please read it through carefully. If all is to your liking, we can finalize the details on Monday. Here's my card; you can reach me at that number, night or day. I strongly suggest you have a music attorney look it over before signing. If there's nothing more now, I'll look forward to seeing you again on Monday.

It's been a true pleasure meeting you and your band. Goodbye, Mr. Rivers," Wu finished. He stood, shook their hands, snatched his briefcase, and left 1.

Mason placed Wu's card in his wallet and turned to the others. "Well, looks like we'll need to contact a lawyer. This freaking contract has more pages than 'War and Peace.' It's what we all should've done before we stupidly signed Adriel's contract," he said, with a frown.

"Don't beat yourself up over it, Ace, we were all deceived by that bastard and his 'fine print,'" April said, pushing her chair back and standing. "None of that matters right now. We need to get back to the suite, Father James will wonder what kept us, if he bothered showing up at all."

"So, we're getting married tonight, eh?" Mason asked, half-joking, giving her a nudge.

"You wish, Romeo. If this thing goes south, we may not live long enough to enjoy a honeymoon," she replied grimly.

As her sobering words sunk in, the smile dropped from his face when he realized they no longer needed Father James. They'd approached him out of desperation, worried they would lose the contest tonight and incur the wrath of the smooth-talking demon.

Mason was convinced that the moment they won the contest, everything changed. Since they'd been offered a contract by the record company, they had some breathing room in which to bargain. Adriel wasn't likely to kill off a potential cash cow, he enjoyed his expensive toys and lifestyle too much. Still, while the wretched demons controlled their fate, the threat of an untimely death and eternal damnation would loom over them. Now he just had to convince April that his belief was correct.

"We don't need Father James anymore. Since we've won, I don't think Adriel will hurt us, at least not right away," he explained his logic to her.

"You really think you can *trust* a freakin' demon? That's like sticking your head in a lion's mouth, trusting he won't bite it off," she snorted cynically.

"I'm willing to bet when he sees that contract, dollar signs will fill his eyes. As long as we keep him happy, we shouldn't be in any danger of—"

"What the hell's wrong with you, Ace?" she stopped him. "These creatures are malicious to the core—they're not human. When are you going to get it through your thick head, they don't give a shit about anyone or anything but themselves! I still think an exorcism is the best option," she contended.

Mason disagreed. "I say we put it to a vote. All in favor of calling off the exorcism, raise your hands," he said, lifting his own. Jeff raised his hand, then looked expectantly at Larry and Davy.

"In for a penny, in for a pound, I guess," Larry said resignedly, raising his as well.

Davy was not so sure. "What makes you think they won't turn on us first time we say or do something that pisses one of them off, Ace? This could be our best and only chance to rid ourselves of these things, once and for all. I say let Father James do his thing. The worst that can happen is the exorcism won't work," he retorted.

By this time, April was incensed. "*No*—the *worst* that can happen is that they kill us *and* Father James for even attempting it, and we all go straight to hell."

"That's a risk I'm willing to take," Mason declared. "As long as we're valuable to them, I think we'll be safe."

"Until we're not!" April declared, aware that she and Davy had been outvoted.

"Shit, speak of the devils, here they come," Davy mumbled uneasily. Adriel and Alal approached the table as the band's divisive discussion came to an abrupt halt.

"Well, well, why all the gloomy faces? I'd have thought you'd be a little more ecstatic about your win tonight. I suggest we all head back to the suite and celebrate your triumphant victory," Adriel prompted, waiting for an answer.

"We, uh, I mean, April and I ... have decided we want to get married. We met with a priest earlier today, and he's waiting back at the hotel to perform the ceremony," Mason announced calmly.

April glared at him, then forced a smile. "That's right. Life is short and we, um, fell in love and all that," she had to agree, though seething inside. If she didn't play along, the marriage ruse might be suspect. She only hoped that Father James would catch on. There wasn't time to warn him that their original plan had been changed at the last minute.

"Well, isn't this a surprise. Congratulations to you both," Adriel remarked smoothly. "I hope it'll be a long and fruitful union. So many these days end tragically, such a pity. I see you got a contract. Alal will be happy to go over it for you, I'm sure you wouldn't want to sign anything until you've read all the fine print," he smirked, rubbing their previous mistakes in their faces.

"No offense, but we'd like to have a music attorney look it over. Someone who really knows what they're doing," Mason replied evenly.

"No offense taken ... *yet*," Alal hissed coldly. "In that case, you'll pay for it out of your own pocket." The demoness was outraged by his remark. Angering her was dangerous, but Mason gambled it was a minor detail at this point.

"We need to head back to the hotel. Father James will wonder what happened to us. I told him we'd be there by 10:30 or so, and it's already pushing 11:00," April announced, trying to move them toward the exit.

"I'm curious why you're having a priest perform the ceremony," Adriel remarked, an evil glint in his dark eyes. "The hotel has a non-denominational Chaplin on the premises. I find it difficult to believe either of you are active members of the Catholic 'faith,' all things considered," he finished, with eyes narrowed.

Mason expected his question. "We weren't aware the hotel had one. April wanted a priest, and he was the only one available at the time. It was a spur of the moment decision. Nothing duplicitous about it," he lied, as calmly as possible.

Adriel's cool gaze held his for a long moment. Mason knew the demon was suspicious, and with reason. "In that case, let's not keep the good father waiting," Adriel finally said with a crooked smile.

The other band members rose from the table, and everyone made their way out of the concert venue. The rain had finally tapered off, and the early-season cool front had swept away the stifling humidity, so they felt a chill in the air as they left the building. They loaded their instruments into the hospitality van and clambered inside. The band's ride back to the hotel was shrouded in uneasy silence. The two demons had chosen not to ride back with them ...

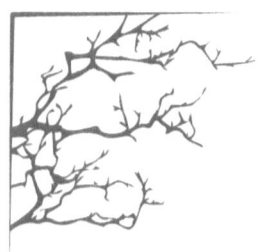

Chapter Nineteen

The Driscoll Hotel

As they arrived at the hotel and exited the van, April pulled Mason aside from the others. "I think he suspects something, Ace. We're going to have to go through with the whole marriage bit now. I just hope the minute we walk in, Father James doesn't whip out his crucifix and go full-blown 'Exorcist' on them," she hissed urgently.

"Nothing we can do about it if he does. We can't warn him with both of those demons in the room. Looking at April, he smiled and asked her, "Nervous?"

"Why would you think that? I'm getting married to a man I've known for all of four freakin' days, I have a demoness from hell as my bridesmaid, and I have less than six months to achieve stardom or I forfeit my soul. So, yeah, you could say I'm a *little* nervous," she said sarcastically, with a roll of her eyes.

The other members of the band waited for them at the elevator. Reaching their floor, they filed out into the hallway. Approaching the door to the suite, they found it open. Adriel and Alal had arrived in the room ahead of them. The two stood at the bar conversing with Father James in hushed tones as Mason and the others walked in. Neither of the demons seemed surprised by the priest's presence; in fact, the three looked downright chummy. They lifted their drinks in a toast to the bride- and groom-to-be as the band entered the room—which made Mason uneasy.

"There they are, we were just talking about you two. The father here was just telling us about your 'wedding' plans. Very enlightening, right, Father?" Adriel goaded, with a tight smile, his cold eyes betraying nothing.

Despite the air conditioning, the old priest was sweating profusely. The ice in his whiskey glass clinked in his trembling hand until he set it down on the bar top. "Uh, yes, that's right. I'm so sorry, Mr. Rivers, I told them everything. I had no choice, I—I sold my soul to Adriel many years ago. Please forgive me, I'm a wretched, spiritually weak old man. I deserve to spend an eternity in hell for my sins, I—"

With a dismissive swipe of his hand, Adriel stopped him. "Enough! I assure you, you *will*, you pathetic pedophile!" he said pointedly to the priest.

Then he addressed Mason and April. "Did you really think I wouldn't see through your little scheme to rid yourselves of Alal and myself? You foolish, treacherous humans. Had you lost the contest tonight, I would've killed you where you stood. As it is, I'm still sorely tempted," the demon growled.

Like the others, Mason was terrified, but he wouldn't admit it to this asshole. "I don't know what you're talking about? This has nothing to do with you or Alal. We only asked him to marry us tonight. What do you think we were doing there? Trying to arrange an exorcism or something?" he asked, doing his best to sound indignant at the idea.

"Are you suggesting that he was lying when he told me you wanted him to perform the ritual to banish us back to hell? Don't insult my intelligence, human!" Adriel roared, his eyes glowing like banked coals of a fire.

Mason knew he had to stick with the lie. If he caved now and told the truth, it would infuriate Adriel. It wouldn't take much to push the evil creatures over the edge.

"I'm telling you that our sole intention in meeting with him was to ask him to marry us after the contest. Why he would lie to you about that, I have no idea," he insisted, meeting his gaze with an innocent look. Mason could see the seeds of doubt he'd planted taking root in Adriel by the second. After all, lies were the foundation demons relied upon where humans were concerned.

Adriel swung back to the priest, causing him to recoil and take a frightened step backward.

"Do you swear on your miserable soul you were telling me the truth?" Adriel hissed.

Father James' heart was racing in his chest; his fear of the horrible creature was palpable. Surely the demon would take his word over this musician's. "I-I told you the truth, th-they came to me and begged me to perform the ritual of exorcism on you and Alal. The cover story was that I was here to marry them, to put you at ease and catch you off guard, then banish you back to hell. I swear I'm telling you God's own truth!" he swore, then realized his grave blunder.

Rage twisted Adriel's face into something truly abominable. "How *dare* you utter *his* name in my presence! *You*, of all humans, should know how that infuriates and insults me!" he roared in a guttural voice.

In his terror, Father James' bladder released, staining his frock. The scent of hot urine permeated the air as the shaking priest retreated from the demonic being. "I-I-I'm sorry, master, it just slipped out, it-it won't happen again," he apologized profusely.

The demon's terrifying visage curled into the semblance of a smile. "You are correct; it will not be repeated." the demon assured. With an evil grin, Alal licked her chops in anticipation.

"No, no, wait! I-I've never lied to you! Y-You promised if I served you, I'd be promoted to Bishop. I-I've done that and more. Y-You can't just—" he began to plead, as Alal grabbed him by his throat.

Before the bandmates' horrified eyes, her face transformed, as the bones in her upper and lower jaws shifted to expose rows of wickedly sharp teeth. With one impossibly quick movement, she ripped out his throat in an arterial spray of blood, catching much of it in her gaping maw, gulping it down. The priest's body shuddered and sagged in her vise-like grip.

"Housekeeping won't be pleased with the mess you've made, Alal," Adriel pointed out nonchalantly, his nostrils flaring at the scent of the dead priest's blood pooling on the floor. "Best send for some towels and cleaning supplies when you've finished your meal."

Mason and the others were shaken to their core, stunned by the violent scene that had unfolded in front of them.

"Sad to say, your *wedding* will need to be postponed. However, I've graciously decided to give you the benefit of the doubt," Adriel cheerfully announced to the stunned group. "Be advised, any more foolhardy attempts to rid yourselves of me or Alal will be dealt with in the most severe manner imaginable," the demon warned, nodding at the grisly display in front of them.

While Alal continued to feast on the dead priest's corpse, Mason and the others watched in horror. When April's trance broke, she ran to the balcony and threw up over the railing. Davy fainted, crashing noisily into his drum kit to collapse in a tangled heap. As he tried to wrap his mind around the savagery he'd witnessed, a soft, mewling sound issued from Jeff's throat. Larry sagged to the floor, weeping and babbling to himself. Mason said a silent prayer for Father James, knowing it was probably pointless. The corrupt man's soul was likely *not* in a "better place."

The sickening sight of Alal feeding on the priest's desecrated body was more than Mason could tolerate. With a roar of righteous outrage at the obscenity before him, he charged the demoness and kicked her in her head as hard as he could, knocking her off the dead clergyman's body. The powerful blow sent her flying back against the minibar.

Alarmed by this surprise aggression, Adriel moved to restrain Mason. Before Adriel could stop her, Alal leaped at the enraged musician with an unearthly growl, barreling into him, sending them both tumbling head over heels. They plowed into Jeff, slamming him into the bar, headfirst.

Alal hissed furiously to Mason. "You just made the biggest mistake of your life, you worthless excuse for a human!" With jaws spread wide, she'd lunged forward to tear out his throat, when a hand grabbed her hair from behind, yanking her off the terrified musician.

"Get off him, you satanic twat!" April screamed, shoving her stun gun into the demon's gaping maw, sending 50,000 volts of electricity surging into her. Alal convulsed, trying to bite off April's hand, but April swiftly snatched her hand back at the last second just as the demoness clamped down.

Before the hellish creature could regain her senses, April shoved the prongs of the gun against her neck and pressed the trigger again. Alal's body stiffened, then went limp as she lost consciousness. Apparently, electricity did affect the central nervous systems of demons.

Adriel snatched the stun-gun from April's grasp, backhanding her hard across the face. Stunned, but still on her feet, she spun around to deliver a vicious snap-kick to his balls. Excruciating pain exploded in the demon's testicles, driving him to his knees. As he cradled his wounded nuts, gasping for breath, the stunned look on his face was priceless.

April didn't stop there. In a flash, she scooped up her stun-gun from the floor and before he could react, shocked him long and hard until he also lost consciousness, falling forward on his face and breaking his nose. Mason watched all of this unfold in a matter of seconds.

"We've gotta—haul ass, Ace—before they recover. It's our—only chance to get out of—this nightmare alive—they'll never let us live—after what we just—did to them," she gasped breathlessly, as she helped him to his feet.

"What about Jeff and the others? If we leave 'em here, they'll kill 'em, for sure!" he exclaimed, his mind reeling at the swift turn of events.

"There's no time! They'll have to fend for themselves. Let's go. They won't remain unconscious much longer," she growled, grabbing her purse and running for the door. Mason couldn't let her leave without him—he had no choice but to leave his friends and follow her out of the room.

April bypassed the elevators, heading for the stairwell. She figured the demons would assume they'd taken the elevator. As she passed a fire alarm on the wall, she pulled the lever, sending shrieks of alarm coursing throughout the hotel. Yanking the stairwell door open, they rushed down five flights of stairs to reach the lobby. Employees and guests alike were stampeding to escape the building, as she and Mason weaved their way through the crowd of panicky people, most of whom had been in the hotel bar. Exiting the hotel, they dashed down the sidewalk until they arrived at Sixth Street, where they stopped to catch their breath. Seeing a yellow cab parked in front of the "Crooked Dick" bar, they raced toward it and clambered inside.

"WHERE TO?" THE BORED cabby asked.

"Take us to the airport. I'll pay you 500 bucks if you can get us there in under ten minutes," Mason declared, eager to to keep moving. The driver didn't bother to reply. He stepped on the gas and, with a screech of rubber, they sped off into the chilly September evening.

"It was smart not to take the Maserati, it's probably hot, and I'm sure there's a GPS tracker in it," April whispered to Mason. "I'm sorry I overreacted back there, I screwed the pooch for sure when I stunned 'em with my zapper, but I couldn't stand by and let her kill you, too," she said, shuddering at the gory image of the dead priest.

"Glad you intervened when you did, otherwise we wouldn't be having this conversation. I shouldn't have lost my damn temper, but it's all moot at this point. I love you, April, but please tell me you have a destination in mind, I'd hate to think we've made it this far, only to find those monsters waiting for us when we arrive wherever it is we're headed," he replied with a shudder.

"I love you too, Ace. *Shit*! I just thought of something. Adriel must've hidden a tracker app on my phone, otherwise, he wouldn't have known about our visit with Father James. I need to ditch it, he could be tracking us now," she anxiously exclaimed.

The cab was fast approaching the Lamar Bridge that straddled the Colorado river, separating north Austin from the south part of town. They instructed the driver to slow down for a moment. As they reached the middle of the bridge, Mason lowered his window, and she hurled the phone over the side of the bridge into the water far below.

"Well, there went all my contacts, photos, you name it," she said dejectedly.

"As long as you have everything backed up to the cloud, you should be able retrieve it with a new phone as long as you have your password," he pointed out.

"That's some consolation, I guess. Anyway, we're going to Boulder. Like I said before, I have some friends there, or rather, I used to. Hopefully, they'll still be there. If not, we'll have to come up with another plan. We can't go to my mother's house—he's been there before, and it'll be the first place he'd look. I won't put her in danger!" she replied emphatically, leaning her head against his shoulder.

The rest of the drive to the Austin-Bergstrom International Airport was uneventful. After braking in front of the entrance, the driver parked. He'd made the drive in record time with a minute to spare. Mason paid him, and they left the cab, looking over their shoulders for any sign of the demons. Inside, they went directly to an ATM, where he withdrew the maximum amount allowed of 1,000 dollars.

He was relieved his debit card still worked. He'd been afraid Adriel had already placed a freeze on the assets in his account. They would, however, be leaving a money trail to follow, and being a computer geek, the demon would surely track them here. This time of night, there was no line at the

American Airlines kiosk, so they purchased two one-way tickets to Boulder with the cash he'd withdrawn. The only problem was the plane wouldn't be disembarking for close to half an hour, giving Adriel and his toady more time to find them. They wandered around the nearly empty airport for a while.

"Maybe we should alert Airport security and tell them we're being stalked," Mason suggested.

"I don't think we should; it'll just draw unwanted attention to us and we don't need that, if we can help it. I need to use the can before we board, I hate those tiny 'johns' on planes. Keep your eyes peeled, I'll be back in a flash." She scurried off in search of the nearest restroom.

Mason wanted something to calm his nerves, but knew he'd have to wait until they boarded to buy anything alcoholic. *Shit*! He'd just remembered that April still had weed in her purse. They'd never make it through the TSA screening process without being busted. With that thought, a woman's garbled voice echoing through the concourse announced boarding had begun for their flight.

April appeared and saw the look on his face. "If you're concerned about the weed, don't be. Unless they do a body cavity search, they'll never find it," she said smugly.

"Uh, so you stashed it up your ..." he trailed off. "What about the, uh, stun-gun?"

"It looks like a phone. Hopefully, they won't examine it too closely. *Oh, Crap*! We're outta time—Adriel and his bitch just pulled up outside, they must've assumed this was where we were headed," she hissed angrily. They fast-walked over to the screening area.

They'd emptied the contents of their pockets and her purse and placed them into plastic security bins, when Adriel and Alal strolled onto the concourse searching for them. Passing through the X-ray machine to the other side, they collected their few belongings and dashed for their departure gate. Mason was *almost* certain that even if Adriel and Alal spotted them, they wouldn't be allowed to follow them past the screening area without purchasing tickets.

They finally located the gate for their flight, produced their tickets, and began boarding. All the way down the Jetway, they both kept checking over their shoulders for any sign of the demons, until they reached the plane and boarded, out of breath.

The stewardess directed them to their seats. Only a handful of people were traveling the red eye at this time of night, so empty seats were available if they chose to move. As they tried to relax, a loud disturbance occurred at the entrance of the plane. They both froze until a man came staggering through the door, stinking of liquor. Mason breathed a relieved sigh as the stewardess guided the swaying man to a seat some rows in front of them and buckled him in.

"Do you think they spotted us?" April asked apprehensively, gazing out of her window seat.

"No way to know for sure. Even if they did, they don't have time to buy tickets and board, I think we're safe for the moment," he replied, as the plane slowly backed away from the Jetway.

Five minutes later, they were taxiing down the runway. Mason disliked takeoffs more than landings. White-knuckled, he gripped the armrests on either side of him. As the plane's wheels left the runway, it slowly climbed into the night sky at a forty-five-degree angle, heading for a city he'd never been to and an uncertain future with the woman he loved. After dimming the overhead lights, they both were asleep by the time the jet reached cruising altitude ...

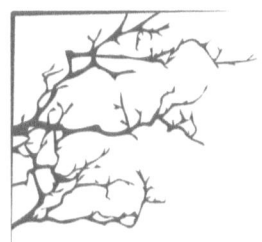

Chapter Twenty

Denver, Colorado

As the plane touched down at Denver International Airport around 2:30 a.m., the landing jolted Mason awake from an uneasy sleep. He yawned, relieving the pressure in his ears, and glanced over at April, startled to find her seat empty. He looked around the cabin, but she was nowhere in sight. *Must be in the can*, he thought, settling back in his seat. Moments later, the door to the tiny restroom opened, and she stepped out. Instead of returning to her assigned seat, she took an empty seat adjacent to the aisle. The funky aroma of weed clung to her like a second skin. Mason cringed when the stewardess openly sniffed the air as she passed April's seat, giving her the evil eye.

Once the stewardess moved back to the front of the plane, he hissed, "Couldn't you have waited a few more minutes? You're gonna get us busted before we even get off the freakin' plane!"

April merely rolled her eyes. "We're in Colorado, Ace. It's legal to buy and smoke weed in Colorado," she explained patiently.

"I'm not sure the FAA would agree with you on that. Last time I checked, it was still illegal to fire up a cigarette on a plane, let alone a freaking blunt! We'll be lucky if she doesn't report us to the Feds!"

The stewardess picked up her mic and announced, "Welcome to Denver International. Please remain in your seats until the plane has come to a complete stop. Thank you for flying American and have a pleasant stay."

As the plane taxied to a halt at the Jetway without further incident, April gave him a smug look.

When they prepared to disembark, though, the stewardess pulled her aside. "If I ever see you on my bus in the future, I'd advise you not to pull a stupid stunt like that again, Miss. We take our rules seriously. The only reason

I haven't notifed the authorities is that *technically*, we've already landed," she said sternly.

At the stern admonishment, April's face flamed red as her hair. "Yes, ma'am, sorry about that, it won't happen again," she apologized. The stewardess gave her a tight smile and ushered them out the cabin door into the Jetway.

"I don't want to hear a fucking word, okay?" April muttered to him as they strode down the long, narrow corridor into the airport proper.

Mason wasn't in the mood to gloat. "Well, at least we weren't met at the door by a phalanx of cops. I say we get something to eat, I'm starving," he said, as they walked into the nearly empty terminal. A this late hour, none of the food kiosks were open; they'd have to find nourishment elsewhere.

"As soon as a store opens, I need to purchase another phone. I'll have to retrieve all my contacts from the cloud and download them. 'Til then, we're gonna need a cheap place to crash. Speaking of cheap, how much cash do you have left after paying for our tickets?" she asked.

He pulled out his wallet to check. "Four hundred and change. *Crap*! I'd better check my bank account. I'll bet you dollars to donuts those fuckers have cleaned it out by now!" he exclaimed, opening his bank app. "*Shit*! I hate it when I'm right. The asshole even took the fifty-five dollars I had before they added the fifty grand. Now I'm really broke as a spoke," he said miserably.

"What about that 10,000-dollar check they gave us? You still have it, right?"

"Yeah, but there's no bank open to cash it. We'll have to wait 'til we get to Boulder. In the meantime, I'm calling us an Uber. There's gotta be a Jack-in-the-Crack or something like it open twenty-four hours nearby. Man, I feel terrible about leaving the guys like we did. I only hope they're still alive," he replied morosely.

"Adriel likely won't kill them, at least not right away. If anything, he'll try to use them to get to us. After what we did to him and Alal, we can't let that happen. If they catch us, we're toast!"

TEN MINUTES LATER, their ride arrived and took them to an IHOP about a mile from the airport. Mason paid him extra to wait while they went inside to order a couple of stacks of pancakes, eggs, and sausage plates. When the food arrived, they fell on it like a pack of starving wolves, devouring every bite within minutes. Their appetites sated, they gulped down half a pot of coffee to keep them alert for the thirty mile ride to Boulder.

Luckily, the Uber driver wasn't a big conversationalist. Entering the outskirts of the city, Mason spied a cheap 'no-tell motel' on the side of the road advertising "Free Wi-Fi and XXX Movies." He told their driver to pull into the parking lot and wait while he checked them in.

While he was inside, the driver gawked at April's ample bosom in his rearview mirror.

"Would you mind not staring at my tits, dude? It's really annoying me," she chided, crossing her arms over her chest.

He quickly averted his eyes, pretending he hadn't heard her. When Mason returned to pay him, she got out, slamming the door. The guy peeled out of the parking lot to disappear down the road.

"That dude gave me the creeps. 'Chester the molester' had been eyeing my boobs ever since we left the airport," she grumbled.

"Can't say that I blame him, they *are* rather magnificent," Mason said with a grin. She rolled her eyes but couldn't help grinning at his compliment.

They strolled down the sidewalk toward their room, observing only a handful of cars in the seedy motel's parking lot.

"What? No pool?" she said sarcastically as they approached their room.

"I'm pretty sure the jacuzzi is also out-of-order," he replied. Opening the door, he found the light switch and flipped it on. Half a dozen large roaches skittered off to seek refuge under the bed and a decrepit dresser.

"Ewww! I hope they don't crawl over us in the middle of the night. You picked a real winner with this joint, Ace," she grumbled, plopping down on the hard mattress.

"It's the best we could do on short notice, anything better would've drained our remaining funds. It's amazing how far we've fallen in only three hours." He walked over to check the bathroom for more six-legged occupants.

Seeing none, he left the light on; no use encouraging the little bastards. April turned back the comforter on the full-sized bed to inspect it for any creepy crawlers lurking under the sheets. Finally satisfied no tarantulas were waiting to pounce, she stripped off her clothes and lay down on her back.

"Do you think they'll find us, Mason?" she grew serious.

"I sincerely hope not, but if they do, we'll just have to deal with it. We can't run for the rest of our lives. Meanwhile, we need to figure a way out of this cluster-fuck," he replied, removing his own clothing.

"I have less than six months 'til my birthday. If they catch up to us, I won't even have that. I don't want to die, Ace. There's so much I still want to do in my life. This is all such a horrid nightmare!" she cried, tears streaming down her lovely, freckled face.

He didn't know what to say, instead, he drew her into his arms and kissed her tenderly as she wept. He reached over to a box of tissues on the nightstand and grabbed her a couple.

"You want to watch some dirty movies?" he asked, wriggling his eyebrows suggestively, in part to distract her.

"What a perv—of course, I would," she retorted, stroking his already-erect member.

He turned on the XXX Channel, where a sultry vixen on screen was being serviced by three hunky studs at once.

"That looks like fun, maybe we should've invited that driver dude to join us," she teased him.

"Not on your life, woman," he growled protectively.

"Ooh, I think someone's jealous," she purred, stroking him faster/

Crawling on top of her, he slipped inside her, causing them both to moan excitedly. Greedily, he took her mouth, kissing her, their tongues exploring, as his hands found her rock-hard nipples. She locked her legs around his waist, pumping him hard and fast.

"Faster! Harder!," she panted, between groans.

"You ... sure?" he grunted, hesitating mid-thrust.

"Yes. You're not gonna to hurt me, just do it, for fuck's sake," she said. He redoubled his efforts, pistoning his hips. "Uhhhh, that's it, harder!" she groaned, wrapping her legs around his ass.

He moaned as he felt her climax, milking him, as multiple orgasms wracked her body, bathing his swollen balls in her essence.

"Come with me!" she cried out, urging him on.

He cried out and buried himself deep inside her, releasing his seed. Collapsing on top of her, he covered her sweaty face with kisses as he tried to catch his breath.

"I love you, Ace," she whispered in his ear. Disentangled herself, she went to the bathroom to shower. He got up and followed her in. They took turns soaping each other with the tiny bar the crappy motel provided. After toweling off, they tumbled into bed and fell asleep within minutes.

The following morning, Mason's phone chimed, jolting him from a troubling sleep. Still half asleep, he reached over the side of the bed and retrieved it from his pants pocket. He'd forgotten to change the setting to "vibrate" before going to bed. He squinted to see who was calling him at 7:30 in the morning. "Unknown caller" was all it said. An icy dread wormed its way through his stomach as he debated whether to answer. The ringing finally stopped. Checking his voice mail, he saw he had three messages waiting. He opened all three and listened to nothing but dead air as no message had been left.

That may be a message in itself, he thought uneasily. As he was about to set the phone down, it rang again. On the third ring, he decided he might as well answer it.

"Hello?" he murmured softly.

After a brief silence, a familiar voice said, "Mason, this is Jeff, don't fucking hang up! Listen to me, Mason, h-he's gonna kill us all if you both don't come back! You dragged us into this fucking nightmare, at least have the balls to come back and face the outcome!"

Mason got up and took the phone into the bathroom so he wouldn't wake April. "Look, Jeff, I'm really sorry for leaving you guys in a pinch, but we had no choice, we—" he started.

"Bullshit, Ace! You always have a choice. Yours was to tuck tail and run, leaving us here at the mercy of these hellish creatures. Thanks a lot, *brother!*

If you have a shred of decency left, you'll get your ass back here ASAP! You have 'til noon to return," Jeff shakily said, voice breaking.

"Or what?"

"Or he'll torture us to death. This is all your fucking fault. If you're not back here by 12:00 p.m. today, our deaths will be on your head. They're holding us in Adriel's condo. Goodbye, Ace."

Mason stared miserably at the phone, wishing he held one of those magic eight-balls that could give him some mystical advice on what to do. *Shit*! He had no choice. They'd have to go back ...

"WELL DONE, ALAL. THAT should motivate our musical runaways to return, post haste," Adriel praised with an evil smile, as she handed Jeff's phone back to her boss. She'd always excelled at mimicry. Demons had an inherent talent for deception and hers was exceptional.

"You think he bought it?" she purred. Adriel glanced down at the trio of band members, all bound and gagged, sitting on the floor of his condo's "fun room."

"I suppose we'll find out. If not, we'll have some fun with these three, then hunt them both down," he said coldly ...

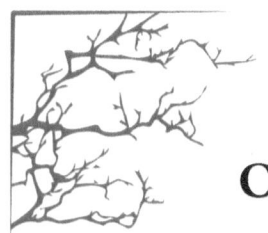

Chapter Twenty-One

Boulder, Colorado

When Mason returned to the bedroom, April was awake and sitting on the edge of the bed.

"Who was on the phone?" she asked, yawning.

"It was Jeff. Adriel and Alal threaten to kill them all if we don't return by noon today," he said tightly.

"You know we can't do that, Ace. Frankly, I'm a little surprised they haven't already tried this. It's just a ploy to get us back in their clutches," she argued. "What if we go back and he kills them anyway, just to punish us. I mean, what's to stop them from killing us next?" She argued, gathering her clothes.

"I don't know, okay? Jesus, this is all so scewed up!" he said sharply, pacing the floor.

"I know they're your friends, but are you seriously willing to risk our lives for them? You can't trust demons, Ace. I've told you, they'll lie their asses off!" she said, pleading with him to think this through.

"All I know is that it's my fault they're in this position. I can't change the fact that I dragged them into this unholy mess 'cause I was greedy and desperate to win that damn contest, no matter the cost. If anything happens to them, I—I don't think I could live with myself. Sorry, but I have to go back. If you don't wanna go, I'll understand. I'll cash this check and give you your share of the winnings, and you can go your own way. I don't know what else to do," he said quietly.

At the thought of losing him forever, tears welled in her eyes. It hurt more than anything she'd ever imagined. And without him, her prospects of attaining stardom before her twenty-first birthday and regaining her freedom were slim to none. He'd given her his answer. Now it was time for her to make one of the most important choices—or mistakes—of her young life.

After a few moments of reflection, she sighed, "Okay, Ace, you win. Just so you know, I think you're making a grave error in judgment. We'll be at their mercy, and we'll be lucky if they don't kill us the moment we walk through the door," she said resignedly.

He felt caught between the woman he loved and his closest friends. He didn't want to put her life in greater danger. But he couldn't leave his friends and bandmates to suffer horribly at the hands of those terrifying creatures, either.

"Listen, you don't have to do this. You can go stay with one of your friends, you'll be safer if I go alone," he suggested half-heartedly.

"I can't do that, Ace, I have a fucking target on my back. Eventually, they'd find me no matter where I go or hide. Now that I've thought it through, I can't involve any of *my* friends in this shitty mess either. It was wrong of me to come here. I don't want my lousy decisions to endanger anyone else's life," she said adamantly.

He didn't like it, but he didn't argue. They were both still stuck in the same leaky boat, paddling the river Styx with half an oar.

"Okay, I guess that's settled. I'll need to book us another flight back to Austin as soon as poss—*Shit*! Hold on, I don't have enough cash to pay for the return tickets, and no credit card!" he exclaimed anxiously.

"You'll have to cash that check. You need to find a bank that will cash it, or we'll be shit out of luck. I haven't had a credit card since I left college."

"What time do you think the banks open?"

"Probably at 9:00 a.m. It's a two-hour flight back, so we need to find a bank, cash the check, then get to the airport and buy the tickets. It'll be cutting it very close to their deadline, Ace."

Not enough time! Mason thought angrily. Then, in a flash, a novel idea occurred to him, resolving their current dilemma. "Maybe I could charter us a private jet here in Boulder. That would save us nearly an hour. It would take at least forty-five minutes to catch another ride back to the Denver International."

"Better get on your phone and start searching for the closest bank. Once that's done, you can try to book a flight. You won't be able to pay for anything until we have the—*Wait a sec!* I just realized, that's an out-of-town personal check; nobody's going to cash that thing, Ace," she glumly pointed outd.

Shit! She's probably right. In their mad rush to get the hell out of Austin, he'd overlooked that little detail.

"Did you even look to see who's the check made out to?" she asked, cocking a brow.

Shaking his head, he dug his wallet out, and retrieved the folded check. With a despairing groan, he saw it was made payable to "Abbadon Entertainment LLC." *Sonofabitch*!

"Well, we're screwed," he growled. Furious, he kicked the dilapidated dresser, startling three humongous roaches from their hiding place.

"I guess I'd better call Jeff back and give him the bad news. This really fucking blows!" he angrily exclaimed.

"I ... I *could* call my mom and see if she'll wire us enough cash to cover the tickets, but ... we didn't exactly part on the friendliest of terms. She might just tell me to go to hell. Kinda ironic, if you think about it," she said morosely.

"If Adriel and his toady want us back this badly, he should be the one to pay for the fucking tickets. After freezing my account, he knows we don't have any money to speak of. He's also aware we can't cash this damn check," Mason said, frustrated.

"It's all part of his game. We're not real to the likes of them. Life and death have no meaning when you're immortal. I'm going to call my mom, so hand me your phone," she impatiently held out her hand.

"What if she won't talk to you?" he asked, handing to her.

"Do you have to be such a 'negative Nelly?' Bad enough I have to call out of the blue, begging for money when I haven't even let her know my whereabouts for the past six months," she snapped.

Taking a deep breath to calm her nerves, she called her mom. It rang four times before she answered, "Lieutenant Detective Flowers. If you're a telemarketer, I'm hanging up," the no-nonsense voice stated.

"Mama, it's me," April said awkwardly. There was such a prolonged silence, she thought her mother had hung up.

"Where are you?" her mother asked tersely.

"I'm in Boulder, and I ... I need to ask a big favor of you. I-I'm in real t-trouble, Mama," April stuttered, unconsciously biting her lower lip.

Another long silence ensued before her mother finally spoke. "I haven't heard a damn word from you in six months. You drop out of college and disappear without a trace, never even bother to tell me where you're going or why, leaving me to worry my ass off. I didn't know if you were alive or dead! And now you have the gall to reach out to me to ask for a favor?" Detective Dianne Flowers asked incredulously. Relieved that her only child was alive, but still infuriated with her for being so callous, she fought for control of her emotions.

"I—I'm sorry, Mama. Things got very, uh ... complicated after Dad died. You remember that guy, Adriel, that I was dating?" April said.

"Did he hurt you? Are you okay?" her mom asked sharply.

"Um, well, no, not really. Mama, I can't get into the specifics right now. I'll just say I've made some terrible choices in the past six months and now, some of them are coming back to bite me in the ass," April disclosed vaguely. She didn't want her mother any more involved in this mess than was necessary. Besides, if she told her mother the truth, she'd never in the world believe it.

"What kind of trouble are you in, April Mae? If that bastard is abusing you, I'll cut off his—"

"No, no, listen, Mama, it's just that Adriel Abbadon is not exactly the 'nice guy' he appeared to be," she said.

"Go figure!" Dianne snorted.

"I—I, uh, owe him some money and I need to pay him back," she lied.

There was another pause. "How much are we talking about?" Dianne replied warily.

April looked at Mason, mouthing, "how much?"

He shrugged and held up eight fingers to be on the safe side.

"Uh, I need 800 dollars. I have the money to pay you back, but I can't get it until I return to Austin," she replied, mentally kicking herself for mentioning her destination.

"So, that's where you've been living. That's a lot of money, April. What do I get for this 'loan?' I need to see you! You've had me worried me to death the past six months. I've issued BOLOs, every law enforcement agency in the country has been looking for you. How you've managed to stay under the radar for so long, I don't know but, baby, it's time to come home," Dianne pleaded, trying not to weep.

Her mother's words broke April's heart. There could be no homecoming for her, now or ever. Too many bad memories, too many nightmares ... too many demons.

"I—I can't do that, Mama. You'll just have to trust me. I need the money right away and—and if you can't afford it, I'll understand. But I need to know now, we—*I* have to be back in Austin no later than 12:00 noon," she said, wincing at her faux pas.

A longer silence followed. "There's someone else there with you," Dianne stated as a fact. *Shit*! Her mother was too good a detective to miss her little slip of the tongue.

"Uh, yes, ma'am, his name is Mason. We're in a band together back in Austin," April replied, trying not to be more specific.

"I see. Are you two just friends or is it something more?" Dianne probed.

"We love each other, Mama, that's all you need to know. He's a good person, and I hope you'll get to meet him someday soon, but right now, we're very pressed for time, so I really need your answer, is it yes or no?" April said, a little curtly.

"I'll do it on one condition, I have to see you first before you and your boyfriend leave town, or no deal."

April raised both brows in a questioning look at Mason, who just shrugged and nodded his okay. What other choice did they have?

"Alright, it's a deal. We're staying at this crummy little motel off IH 36, 'Manny's Motor-Inn,' in Room 107. It shouldn't be too hard to find. I appreciate you doing this, Mama. I'm truly sorry for all the anguish I've caused you these past months," she said contritely.

"Stay where you are, I'll be there in twenty minutes," Dianne said, disconnecting.

THIRTY-FIVE-YEAR-OLD Lieutenant Detective Flowers had been searching for her missing daughter ever since she'd dropped out of college six months before, disappearing without a word or a clue as to her whereabouts. The combined stress of her job and the constant worry over her daughter's safety had caused her to develop an ulcer. April had finally made contact, but it was a mixed blessing. While she was comforted to know April was alive and well, she'd only be able to see her for a few precious moments before losing her again. It was infuriating and unacceptable. She knew in her gut April was not telling her the whole truth about the situation. She'd be damned if she let her daughter get away this time without a full explanation of why she'd had to come begging for money.

Ever since her husband had taken his life, Dianne had blamed herself for pushing him away and into the bed of his own daughter. On some level, she'd known something wasn't right once he'd stopped coming to her for sex over the last year of his life. When the truth had finally come out after his death, she'd wanted to deny the whole sordid affair. She hadn't given enough thought to how traumatized April had been before she left that last time.

In hindsight, it was little wonder that April had severed all ties with her. Her daughter had every right to be angry and hurt. If she hadn't been so blinded by her ambition to move ahead with the police, she might've recognized the warning signs of her husband's abuse. She could've stopped it before it escalated, culminating in her husband's suicide and April's subsequent withdrawal and disappearance.

Dianne called headquarters and informed her captain she'd be late getting to work. She left the house, climbed into her police cruiser, and sped toward the nearest ATM. Before withdrawing the requisite amount of cash, she hesitated, then added another two hundred dollars to the total amount. She tucked the cash in her wallet and drove down the highway, rushing to meet her wayward daughter.

AWAITING HER MOTHER'S arrival, April paced and smoked. Nothing had prepared her for this unscheduled meet. Stupidly, she'd thought to seek temporary refuge with some of her old college friends, until she realized the danger it might place them in. Their unexpected lack of funds for the return trip to Austin had forced her to make the tough decision to contact her mother for help.

Their brief conversation had felt awkward, at best. April had known her mother would be angry with her for leaving so abruptly, but at the time, it had seemed like the right thing to do. Her mother had no concept of the peril she and Mason had confronted in the past few days, and she thought it might serve her right to worry a little longer. If her mother had paid a little more attention to her husband's needs instead of her own, none of this shit would have happened.

Mason watched her pace and felt for her. It had be difficult to face someone who had screwed up your life so terribly, pretending things were hunky-dory, when the complete opposite was true.

"She loves you, babe, give her the benefit of the doubt. Nobody's perfect, she only wants you to be safe. You're gonna have to come to terms with her at some point and tell her the whole ungodly truth. If you don't deal with it, all this hate and resentment will eat you up," he pointed out, taking her in his arms to stop her anxious pacing.

"Thanks for the sage advice, *Dr. Freud*, but I don't think now is the best time to have a heart-to-heart with my mom." She pulled free from his embrace.

"Well, if not now, *when*? What better chance will you have to clear the air? For all you know, you may never see her again after today!" he said bluntly. He instantly regretted it, as fresh tears welled up and spilled down her cheeks.

"You're right. I've been imagining this moment for a long time, dreading it. But if I tell her the truth, I know how she'll react, Ace. She'll handcuff me, put me in a straight-jacket, and toss me in a rubber room,'" she said, defensively crossing her arms.

"Not if I confirm your story is true, she won't. I'll show her my new pinkie, that should be enough to convince her you're telling the truth," he wiggled the recent addition for emphasis.

"As far as she's concerned, that won't prove diddly squat. You could've been born with that extra finger."

She's right, he thought dejectedly, until he thought of a solution. Pulling out his phone, he opened the "Photo" app. Scrolling through his library, he found the picture he'd remembered. Date-stamped from a year ago, it had been taken by a friend at one of his drunken fraternity gigs. The photo showed him on stage playing his ax, with all five fingers on his left hand clearly visible. He showed April the picture and saw her face brighten as she realized it should, indeed, be the proof needed to convince her mother of the veracity of her tale.

A sharp knock on their room door announced her mother's arrival. April took a deep breath to center herself and opened the door. Dianne Flowers stood gazing at her daughter for the first time in six months.

The tall, dark-haired detective rushed to pull her daughter into her arms, crushing April to her ample bosom while scrutinizing the lanky young man standing behind her.

"I've missed you so much, baby!" she exclaimed, trying not to weep but losing the battle.

April hugged her back, then was the first to break the embrace. "I—I've missed you too, Mama. We don't have much time and there's a lot I need to tell you, please sit down," she said, trying to remain in control. The detective glanced around the room, chose the lone chair, and sat down with an expectant look.

"Mama, this is my ... boyfriend, Mason Rivers. Mason, this is my mom, Dianne Flowers," April said, in introduction.

"Pleased to meet you, Lieutenant Detective Flowers. April has told me a lot about you," Mason said, using her formal title, thinking to impress her, but it didn't.

"Okay. Let's cut through the bullshit niceties, shall we?" Dianne asserted. "I know you're in deeper trouble than you told me on the phone, April Mae. FYI, I did a background check on Mr. Rivers here, and as far as I can tell, he's clean. I also ran this Adriel Abbadon through the NCIC database and came up with nothing—zilch! He's a freaking ghost. What the hell is going on?" she demanded, ignoring Mason's surprised look.

"He's not a ghost, Mama. He's a living, breathing, dyed-in-the-wool, demon from hell," April corrected, waiting to see her mother's reaction. Dianne just stared at her. "Mama, I know it will be difficult, but I need you to keep an open mind. I swear that what I'm about to tell you is the God's honest truth, and we have proof, so please just listen and save any judgment until I've finished explaining. Do you think you can do that?" April, her hands twisting and turning in an agitated way, asked her. Dianne raised a questioning brow but nodded.

Taking a deep breath, April related what had occurred—including a graphic description of the priest's gory demise—that had led them to flee from Austin.

When she finally finished what Mason thought seemed an effective account of their ill-fated exploits, her mother's expression was unreadable.

Then she looked from April to Mason. "You actually expect me to believe you each sold your souls to this ... this ... *supernatural being*, and that you only have until your twenty-first birthday to become famous or he'll kill you and take you to hell for eternity?" Dianne asked increduosly.

"I fucking knew you wouldn't believe me. Show her the picture, Ace, it's the only proof we have that *might* convince her we're telling the truth," April said, angry and hurt that her mother couldn't or wouldn't trust her.

Mason showed her the pic on his phone, zooming it out for her close inspection. If she was shocked by the picture of him with his five-finger hand on display, she didn't show it.

"How do I know this wasn't photo-shopped or digitally altered?" she asked skeptically.

"You don't. Other than the contracts we signed, which are in Adriel's possession, I suppose there's no other way to prove to you that we're telling you the truth," he replied, exasperated by her refusal to believe. "Call the church in Austin where Father James presided and ask to speak with him. I think you'll find he's disappeared," Mason suggested grimly.

Dianne chewed her lower lip, soberly considering all the evidence they'd presented to her. If even half of what they'd told her was true, it was terrifying. She was used to dealing with the worst of the worst—the dregs of humanity, who daily made life a living hell on earth for those they preyed upon. But believing her daughter had sold her soul to some supernatural creature from hell for a shot at stardom was simply beyond her.

"If you don't mind, I think I'll make that call. What's the number for that church?" she asked tightly.

Mason looked it up and gave it to her. Dianne called, tapping her foot while waiting for someone to answer. On the sixth ring, someone did. In her official role as a police officer, Dianne demanded to speak with Father James.

There was a silence, then, "I ... I'm sorry, Father James isn't available right now, could someone else help you?" the priest's secretary said. Then she added, "He was supposed to preside over Mass today, but he never showed up, and that's not like him. He had an appointment last night, and he never returned. H-Has he done something wrong?" the secretary rambled nervously.

Dianne lied, assuring her he hadn't. After a few general questions, she thanked the woman for her help and disconnected the call. "Well, that would support what you told me. It doesn't prove he's dead, though," she stated, stubbornly refusing to admit it might be real.

"I can guarantee you he is," Mason said glumly. "We watched while Alal tore his throat out and drank his blood. His body has probably been disposed of by now. I sincerely doubt they leave any evidence behind for the cops to find," Mason said glumly.

"So, they're holding your other band members hostage until you return. Do you really think these *demons* will kill them if you don't return?" Dianne asked, frowning.

Mason glanced at April before answering. "Yes, ma'am, I do, they are evil personified."

"Well, in that case, I'm sorry, but I can't let my daughter go back with you. If you go back, there's no assurance that these ... *creatures* will let any of you live. And before you object, I should inform you that under Colorado law, she's still considered a minor. I absolutely forbid her to put her life in jeopardy again, contract or no contract!"

April looked at her, shocked. "I don't believe this, you can't force me to stay! It's *my* life, and I'll live it the way I want. You—"

Dianne interrupted, "Don't make this any harder than it already is. I don't want to handcuff you, April Mae, but I sure as hell *will* if you don't come along peacefully," Dianne warned her, resting her right hand on her cuffs for emphasis.

Mason didn't know what to do or say. The tension between April and her mom felt thick enough to be cut. April looked ready to bolt at any moment, and her mother definitely meant what she'd said. If he came to April's defense, he feared that her mother would arrest him for "coercion of a minor" or some similar bullshit charge. If he didn't say something, April would think him cowardly and hate him for not trying to talk her mom into letting her go with him. He couldn't win ... *Shit*!

He was gathering his courage to speak in April's defense, when she whipped her counterfeit phone/stun-gun out of her purse and thrust it up against her mother's neck.

"I'm *not* going with you, Mama! Please don't make me use this, I don't want to hurt you, but I'll do what I have to if you try to stop me from leaving," she growled, with hot tears coursing down her cheeks.

Shocked by her daughter's aggression, Dianne was caught off-guard and froze. She couldn't very well shoot her own daughter, and if she moved to disarm her, April would likely shock her senseless. "Okay, let's calm down and talk about this, April Mae. I'm only trying to protect you—"

April stopped her. "If you had protected me before, maybe none of this would have ever happened! It's too late now. You can't change the past, all I can do is try to change my future. If I don't go back, three innocent people are going to die, and I couldn't live with myself if that happened.

"I knew in my soul you'd never believe me, and I'm sorry we have to part like this. I was hoping you'd keep an open mind and give me the benefit of the doubt, but I should've known better. Your stubborn cop's mentality wins again," she said bitterly.

Dianne felt as if she'd been stabbed in the heart. Guilt, shame, and anger welled up inside her like a tsunami, threatening to engulf her.

"I sincerely apologize for what happened, April Mae. You're right, I can't change the past. I lost your father, then you disappeared. I can't afford to lose you again. I'm a good cop but a terrible mother. When you needed me most, I failed you, and for that, I'll be eternally sorry. Please don't do this, let me take you home where you'll be safe," she pleaded.

"*Safe*?" April scoffed at her mother's use of the word. "No place on earth is safe from Adriel and his bitch! If I can't destroy them, then I have to play by their rules. Goodbye, Mama, for what it's worth, I love you. Ace, get her car keys, cuff her hands behind her back, we're leaving," she instructed Mason.

"What about money for the flight? Without that, we're dead in the water," he pointed out.

"Did you bring it?" April asked her mother.

Dianne wanted to lie, anything to stall April's departure, but she assumed they'd search her, anyway. "Yes, it's in my wallet. You're making a big mistake, April Mae. If you let me go, I promise I won't try to stop you, but please, let me help you. If something bad happens to you, I'll never forgive myself," she begged, tears streaming from her eyes.

April looked indecisive as she pondered her mother's words. "There's nothing you can do—unless you know a good exorcist, I'm afraid I'm screwed. I have to go back and face the music, so to speak. If you tried to interfere, he'd simply kill you to hurt me," she stated sadly. Reluctantly, Mason cuffed Dianne's hands behind her.

"You know the minute I get loose, I'm coming after you. I won't let you throw your life away because some maniac has deluded you into believing he's the devil! Think about what you're doing before it's too late," Dianne snapped.

"*Shit*! It may already *be* too late," Mason said glumly after checking his phone. "The 9:30 flight to Austin was just canceled due to a maintenance problem. The next available flight out is at 10:30. We'll never make the noon deadline," he informed.

At this news, a glint of hope shimmered in Dianne's eyes. "Maybe there is a God," she whispered to herself.

As Mason's news sunk in, April shook her head. "What about charter flights, any of those available? There has to be one that'll fly us there," she asked, trying desperately to think of a solution.

"Hang on. I found one, but we can't afford it. It's two thousand dollars for a two-hour flight, Geez! That's nuts!" He shook his head in disgust while April visibly deflated.

"Listen to me, both of you. I have an acquaintance who's a pilot," Dianne offered reluctantly. "He owns a charter plane, and he owes me a large. He's here in town right now on other business. I could ask him to fly us there, but *only* if I go with you."

Mason deferred to April—it was her call. They were fast running out of time and options. April didn't like it, but it seemed to be their only way to make it back before the noon deadline.

"Alright, call him. But if he can't fly us there, do I have your promise to lend me the extra money to hire another charter flight?" she asked her mother.

Dianne agreed to that. "Take the cuffs off her, Ace, but keep them handy," April instructed, removing the stun-gun from her mother's neck.

Mason released her, stuffing the handcuffs into his back pocket. Dianne rubbed her chafed wrists to get the feeling back, then took out her phone to call the pilot. It rang four times before he answered.

"This is Hardilek, what's shakin', Lieutenant?" Scott Hardilek asked. Scott was the Fire Chief for the small town of Joseph, Oregon. He was also a licensed pilot who moonlighted frequently, flying tourists in and out of the beautiful little burg tucked away in a remote part of northeastern Oregon's scenic Wallowa Mountain Range.

"Scott, I don't have time to explain, but I need to call in a chit, it's an emergency," Dianne said.

"Of course. What can I do ya' for?" he asked.

"I need you to gas up and fly my daughter and her ... boyfriend and me to Austin, ASAP! We need to be there by noon, can you do that?" she queried.

"Well, once I'd have said no way in hell, but I recently had the fuel tank modified to hold an extra fifty gallons. We're talking almost 1300 kilometers, or 795 miles as the crow flies. We might be lucky and catch a tail wind. I can be ready to go wheels up in the next thirty minutes," he replied confidently.

Dianne saw it was pushing nine a.m. It would cut it close, but there was no other way.

"We'll see you in twenty," she said, disconnecting. "Get into my cruiser, I have to notify my captain that I'm taking some off-time," she practically ordered them.

April and Mason obeyed with alacrity, vacating the crappy motel room, leaving the key card on the nightstand. They climbed into the backseat of her cruiser while Dianne called her captain. Mason was uneasy about being in the back where criminals were normally placed. A Steel mesh cage and bulletproof plexiglass barrier separated officers from their 'guests' in the rear.

"I hate to even suggest this, but what if your mom reconsiders and locks us in here?" he muttered to April.

April hadn't thought of that. Now that he'd mentioned it, she remembered that the squad car's back doors also had no locks or handles. *Shit!* They'd left themselves at her mother's mercy. Should she change her mind at the last minute, there was nothing they could do about it.

"Damn it all, I should've gotten in the front seat! Too late now, we'll just have hope she keeps her end of the bargain. If she doesn't, and our friends die, I'll never speak to her again," she groused softly, mentally kicking herself for the oversight.

Her mother finished her call and hopped in the cruiser. "Comfy back there?" she asked, her brown eyes meeting theirs in the rearview mirror.

Mason thought that was a loaded question. "We're fine, there's no wet bar, but that's okay," he said, trying to be ease their tension.

"You're a real funny guy, Mr. Rivers. Buckle up, we're heading for the airport," Dianne stated in a no-nonsense voice. She turned the cruiser around and pulled onto the highway with a screech of tires.

"Well, I guess that answers our question," Mason whispered, relieved that they were heading for a plane and not a holding cell.

"She may be a hard-ass cop, but she's a mother first. She wouldn't do anything to harm me," April quietly observed. "But it sucks that it took the only bargaining chip I had, our friends' lives, to convince her to help us. She still doesn't believe Adriel and Alal are demons, and that scares the crap outta me," she said.

"Yeah, it worries me as well. She has no idea the shit storm that's waiting for us there. If she's not careful, she'll end up as another sacrificed pawn in their twisted little game," Mason took her hand.

April wished she could come up with some way to keep her mother from getting on that plane. If Dianne tried to interfere with their plans, Adriel and Alal would eat her for lunch. She refused to believe the terrible danger she was placing herself in by returning with them.

The ride to the airport took just over twenty minutes. Dianne parked and got out. She hesitated before unlocking the back door.

"I have to admit I was sorely tempted to keep you locked up for your own good," she grumbled, when they'd gotten out.

"I'm pretty sure I haven't broken any laws while we've been here," Mason said.

"You weren't who I was thinking of, Mr. Rivers. My only concern is for my daughter's welfare. No offense, but I don't know you from Adam," she said curtly.

"I understand," he replied, as they walked to the terminal.

Dianne was going to ask where she could find Scott and his plane, but then she spotted the attractive, lanky pilot with short, brown hair standing by a coffee vending machine.

He was shaking his hand after spilling hot coffee on it. "Miserable damn—oh, there you are, I was wondering if you'd make it in time. The plane's gassed up and the pit crew's finishing their safety inspection, so we're good to go," he said, as they approached.

"Scott, this is my daughter, April, and her boyfriend, Mason," Dianne introduced them.

"Nice to meet ya.' Let's get moving, I want to get ahead of a storm front headed this way. Probably won't escape it entirely, but it should give us a nice tailwind, cut some time off our flight," he explained, with his trademark grin that lit his face.

They followed him out on the tarmac to the hanger where his pride and joy, a Piper Cheyenne turboprop sporting twin five-bladed propellers, sat waiting for them.

"That's a really cool plane, Mr. Hardilek, but is it fast enough to get us there before noon?" Mason asked.

"She's got a 1,000 hp engine, top cruising speed of 360 knots, that's about 414 mph in optimal conditions. I figure we'll average around 350, unless there's a lot of turbulence. If we get that tailwind, we should arrive about 11:40, Austin time," he said confidently. "As they began boarding the plane, he cautioned, "Duck your heads, there's not a lot of headroom inside."

They obeyed his instructions, but Mason had to almost squat to enter the cabin. The Piper seated seven, along with a seat on the flight deck next to the pilot's.

Scott was the last one in. Glancing at the sky before boarding, he frowned when he saw storm clouds approaching from the west. "Put on your headsets if you want to chat, it'll also dampen some of the engine noise," he suggested, climbing into the cockpit to start his instrument checklist.

Once he'd finished, the pit crew outside removed the chock blocks from the wheels, and he was cleared to taxi onto the runway. As he was cleared for take-off, a sudden gust of wind from the approaching storm front shook the plane and its passengers.

They all looked out the windows while the plane gained speed and rose into the overcast sky, climbing steadily until it reached cruising altitude.

"That wasn't so bad," Mason muttered, releasing his death-grip on the arm of his seat.

"FYI, folks, we may encounter occasional turbulence until we clear the mountains, it could get a little rough. If you need 'em, the barf bags are in your seat compartment," Scott announced.

The fast-moving storm front gave them the tailwind he had hoped for, but a few minutes later, they hit the first of several air pockets that shook the plane like some giant's toy, causing Mason's face to pale. It didn't seem to bother either April or her mom.

April saw his reaction and shrugged. "I love roller coasters, so this doesn't bother me too much, but you couldn't pay get me on one of those Tilt-o-Whirls. All that spinning and twirling round and round. Makes me want to puke just thinking about it," she said with a roguish grin.

Dianne rolled her eyes at her. Her daughter had always had a wicked sense of humor.

With April's vivid description, Mason's face grew even more ashen. He grabbed the barf bag from his seat compartment and barely got it to his mouth before tossing his cookies. Thankfully, they hadn't had breakfast.

Sealing the bag, he placed it in her lap, as she covered her mouth, straining not to laugh.

"You ... are ... truly ... evil!" he sputtered, blotting his mouth with a tissue. He wished he'd thought to bring some bottled water along.

In the small, closed cabin, the smell was pervasive, hanging in the air like a greasy cloud, wiping the grin from April's face. Roller coasters didn't bother her, but the smell of puke would push her over the edge every time. Hastily, she snatched up her own bag and emptied the contents of her stomach.

It was Dianne's turn to smirk, as she watched her daughter get a dose of her own medicine. She herself had worked so many crime scenes that almost nothing bothered her now. She could calmly eat a sandwich while standing over an eviscerated corpse.

"If you need some, there's an ice chest with bottled water in the back of the cabin," Scott advised over their headsets.

Unbuckling his seat belt, Mason crouched, and made his way back to the chest. Returning, he handed a bottle to each of them. After passing over the Sangre de Cristo Mountains, the ride smoothed out, remaining calm for the rest of their flight.

"Attention, folks, we'll be landing at Austin-Bergstrom International right on time, please buckle your seatbelts, if you haven't already done so," Scott relayed over the intercom.

Ten minutes later, they touched down on the runway and taxied over to the T-hanger. The propellers slowly spun down as the pit crew guided him inside. When the wheels had been chocked, Scott climbed out of the pilot's seat, opened the door, and retracted the stairs.

"Hope you enjoyed flying Hardilek Airways," he said, with his grin. "Do you need me to hang around or is this a one-way trip?" he asked Dianne, as they stood to deplane.

"Our business here shouldn't take long. I, for one, will need a ride back when it's done. I'm not so sure about these two," Dianne replied evenly.

"Not a problem, I cleared my schedule when you called earlier, I don't need to be back until tomorrow afternoon. When you're ready to leave, just give me an hour's notice, and I'll try to have her ready to go," Scott said with a grin.

"Thanks, appreciate it, Scotty, will do," Dianne said, climbing down the steps to join Mason and April.

Mason checked the time on his phone: 11:35 p.m. They had twenty-five minutes to find a ride and make it to Adriel's condo before the noon deadline. "I've texted an Uber, they should be here in less than five minutes," he reported, as they strolled out of the hanger.

The Texas sun blazed down, the humidity thick enough to cut with a knife. The cold front they'd left behind would catch up to them soon, with storms predicted ahead of it, according to Mason's weather app.

The Uber driver arrived several minutes later, and they all piled in the back. Mason gave him directions and the driver sped off. Mason's phone rang, and checking the screen, he saw it was Jeff calling.

"Tell Adriel we're on our way, we'll be there shortly," he said curtly, and the call disconnected ...

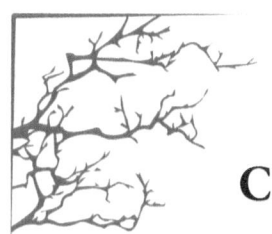

Chapter Twenty-Two

Austin, Texas

The driver arrived in front of Adriel's condo with a couple minutes to spare. Climbing out, they walked up to the front door. Reading the ominous sign attached to it, Dianne merely rolled her eyes. Ignoring the doorbell, she pounded on the door instead.

The door opened and Alal stood there smirking. "You cut it close, too bad. I was looking forward to—Who's the bitch cop? You were supposed to come alone," she bristled, as Dianne stepped right in front of her.

"This is my mother, Lieutenant Detective Dianne Flowers of the Boulder PD. I tried to keep her from coming, but she insisted. There was no other way, we wouldn't have made it back by *your* deadline if not for a private pilot she knows," April spat.

Dianne and the demoness glared at one another as Alal grudgingly ushered them inside. Before the demon could shut the door, Dianne drew her service weapon and pointed it at her.

"I'm arresting you for child endangerment, fraud, the murder of a priest, and anything else I can think of!" Dianne demanded.

The demoness stared at her like she was insane, then burst out laughing. "You stupid human, you don't know who you're dealing with. I'll be sure to take my time when it's your turn in the 'fun room,'" she sneered. Preternaturally swiftly, she snatched the gun from Dianne's stunned fingers. Holding it in both hands, she bent the gun's steel barrel and tossed it on the floor at her feet with an evil smile.

"*Holy shit*! H-How d-did—A-April was telling the truth! I-I didn't believe—" Dianne stammered, wide-eyed, backing away from the demonic creature.

"You'll believe it when I'm finished with you, bitch cop," Alal declared, ready to pounce on the badly frightened woman.

At that second, Adriel appeared behind them and commanded her to stop. "Not so fast, my pet. We haven't even been properly introduced," he purred.

At the sound of his voice, Dianne jumped, whirling around to face the creature who had brought so much misery to her family.

"It's been a while, but what a pleasure it is to see you again. Oh, before I forget, your dearly departed husband sends his regards from hell. I would've had him tell you himself, but alas, he's currently being buggered by a horde of demons," he gleefully told her, watching her face grow pale. "No doubt, your offspring has informed you by now of our true nature. Unfortunately, she tried to renege on our deal and made an enormous mess trying to elude her obligations. I don't know whether I should punish her or you or both," he added, tapping a finger against his cheek in thought.

"Let me torture her, master," Alal offered eagerly. "As long as we have the human's mother, she won't pull that little trick again."

Mason interjected, "Whoa, everybody chill out, there's no need for that. We won't try to escape, please don't hurt anyone else, we'll do whatever you say." He held up his arms in surrender.

Adriel turned his attention to him, smiling coldly. "Yes, indeed you *will*, or I'll allow Alal to take out her frustrations on her precious mother," he coldly pointed to April.

"Where are Jeff and the others? You better not have hurt them," she declared.

Adriel's dark eyes held hers. "Other than a little free dental work, they should be hunky-dory. I believe perhaps I missed my true calling. Follow me to the 'fun room,' you'll find they're all there," he responded with a crooked grin.

Leading the way, with Alal guarding the rear, he unlocked the deadbolts on a sturdy door and opened it. The three men were seated on the concrete floor, their hands duct-taped behind them and their mouths covered. Their eyes looked equally alarmed and relieved as Mason and April entered the room. Adriel reached down and ripped the tape from each of their mouths.

"Your wandering friends have returned, and lucky for you they did. What's the problem? You don't look happy. Well, I suppose having a root canal without the benefit of anesthesia might make one somewhat irritable," he said cheerfully.

All of them sported swollen jaws from the demon's stringent work with his drill. "Th-thank God you came back when you did. The monster would've tortured us to death," Jeff moaned, as he spat bloody sputum out on the concrete floor. Larry and Davy were in no better shape, both had the vacant thousand-yard stares of soldiers returning from combat. Mason was furious, but he couldn't change what had been done to them.

"You see what your little escapade cost *them*? I suggest the next time you impulsively decide to 'rabbit,' you think twice, or you'll be three members short of a band," Adriel said menacingly.

"Looks to me like we already are," Mason observed, looking at his bandmates' vacuous stares.

"Let them go, they didn't hurt you. We're back, and it won't happen again, I promise," April lied with a poker face.

"Very well, but if *any* of you thinks about deceiving us again, you'll all lose more than your pitiful, worthless lives," he warned. A switchblade appeared in his right hand. The sinister-looking, six-inch blade flicked open as he approached Davy first, then the others, slicing their bonds, freeing them. As one, they shook numb arms, trying to get the feeling back, before helping one another shakily to their feet. Davy and Larry stood, distant stares glazing their unblinking eyes. Only Jeff's still had a spark of life in them.

"C-Can we go home now? Davy wants 'a go night-night," Davy said, in a quavering, childlike voice. It was obvious to everyone that he'd completely lost it, and who could blame him? Being tortured by demons from hell was not something anyone envisaged.

While all this was occurring, Dianne had been mulling over what she'd just experienced. The way she perceived the world had tilted 360 degrees in the past fifteen minutes as the truth rolled over her like an avalanche. Reality as she'd known it had ceased to exist. If demons roamed the earth, then logically, the inverse should be true as well. And if angels were ever needed, they could use one here and now. There was only one person she'd ever met who she believed might qualify—Doctor Mia Chandler. Unfortunately, she now had no way to contact her since the female demon had confiscated all their phones. *Likely, to install tracking apps on them*, Dianne figured.

"I may've had too much fun with your drummer boy. It's a pity you'll have to find a replacement. I believe your contract with Sony states, and I quote, 'Should any current member of the band be unable to fulfill their duties as proscribed under chapter 19, subsection B, clause 3-C, etc.,' said contract shall be invalid and all monies paid in advance shall be forfeited and reimbursed immediately to Sony Music Corp.' end quote," Adriel revealed smugly.

"What *horseshit*! We haven't even signed the damn thing yet!" Mason protested.

"Oh, I beg to differ, Mr. Rivers. This is your 'John Henry,' is it not?" Adriel asked, producing the Sony contract that he and April had abandoned in their rush to escape the dreadful debacle at the hotel.

Mason snatched it from his hands to stare with disbelief at what appeared to be his usual signature on the last page of the contract. Moving closer, April also found her signature, along with those of their bandmates.

"You forged our fucking names? I don't believe this shit!" Mason exclaimed, throwing the contract at Adriel's feet in disgust.

"After that little stunt you pulled in the suite, I thought it only fair to get the ball rolling, so to speak. What Sony doesn't know won't hurt you. Consider yourselves lucky that I didn't destroy your so-called 'friends,'" Adriel hissed, scooping the contract off the floor. "From now on, you do *as* I say *when* I say. *Any* attempt at escape will be met with devastating outcome, am I quite clear? Excellent."

Adriel switched to a softer mood. "I'm afraid your suite at the Driskill had to be forfeited. For now, you'll remain here, under our watchful eyes. Alal will, ahh, see that your former drummer has a nice safe place to convalesce. Hopefully, your other bandmates haven't been too traumatized and will eventually recover. If not, they, too, will need to be replaced. Now, Alal will show the other two to their rooms, where they can recover. Help yourselves, roam around, 'mi casa, es su casa,' as the locals like to say," the demon said to the new arrivals. Opening the door, he ushered them out of the torture chamber.

Alal shoved Jeff and Larry up the stairs, leaving Davy by himself in the demon's "fun room."

Meanwhile, Adriel strolled to his minibar and made himself a drink. Dianne joined April and Mason at the far end of the living room.

"This is truly madness. I'm so sorry for not believing you about those hideous ... *creatures!*" she muttered under her breath. "As April is aware, I'm not a religious person, but as of today, I'm rethinking that. If actual demons are walking among us, it seems logical that 'God' would also provide helpers, or angels. And if true, I know of someone who might help us out of this nightmare, but she lives in Oregon," Dianne rambled nervously.

Her comments grabbed April's and Mason's immediate attention. Covertly, he motioned them into the foyer, further from Adriel's ears.

"Who is this person and how could she help us?" Mason whispered urgently. He'd piss on a spark plug if it would get them out of this unholy mess they'd created.

"Her name is Mia Chandler—well, it's *Dr.* Mia Chandler, now. To make a long story short, she was involved in a case I caught almost ten years ago. I helped to clear her of murdering her crazy grandfather and his bodyguard/lover. She then joined her half-brother who lives in Joseph, Oregon, became a doctor, and from what I've heard, she's a sort of 'miracle' healer in Oregon now." Dianne caught her breath and tried to collect her thoughts. She felt the beginning of a full-blown panic attack developing—something that hadn't happened since her husband had committed suicide.

"Kris, her adopted mother, God rest her soul, was Sheriff Pro-Tem in the neighboring town of Enterprise until she was killed. She and I were friends and she told me that Mia had this miraculous power to heal people, even bring the dead back to life. That made the newspapers when it first occurred, I think they called her the 'Angel of Oregon,'" she said hurriedly. She stopped speaking as she saw Alal come back down the stairs, eyeing them suspiciously.

Alal warned, "Remember what Adriel said, if you know what's good for you, you'll forget about any plans of escape. Personally, I'd love for you to try. I haven't fed since last night and ... I'm ravenous!" For amusement, she revealed her true demonic face to them.

Witnessing the demon's hideous visage for the first time, Dianne couldn't breathe, her sight shrank to tunnel vision, and the room spun. Her heart galloped in her chest as she collapsed in a heap on the floor, gasping for air.

"Was it something I said?" the she-demon smirked.

"She's having a fucking heart attack, you cold-blooded witch! Call 911 now!" April angrily exclaimed, kneeling anxiously at her mother's side.

Alal ignored her, waiting for Adriel's instructions. "What do you want me to do, Master? I could put her out of our misery. She shouldn't have come here; it would serve her right," she said readily.

Frowning, Adriel shook his head. "Unfortunately, we need her alive. She's leverage against any further rebellion from our rock star wannabes. For the moment, it's in our best interest to keep her alive," he replied, resignedly pulling out his phone to make the call.

"What if she informs the authorities about us? What'll we do then?" Alal asked him.

He held up his hand to silence her. Giving his name and address to the operator, he disconnected, pondering her question before he answered. "They'd never believe her, my pet. We're safe. Humans never see the forest for the trees. We've been hiding in plain sight for millennia and rarely have they discovered our true nature. If she survives until they arrive, you'll accompany her to the hospital and monitor her," he declared.

Meanwhile, April was growing frantic. Her mother's pale face was beaded in sweat, her breathing was rapid and shallow. Since Dianne had never mentioned her occasional panic attacks to April after her husband's violent death, April had no way to know that it wasn't life-threatening. The symptoms so closely mimicked one another that it could be difficult to tell them apart. April believed if she didn't get help soon, her mother could die.

"Do you know how to perform CPR?" Mason asked her, concerned.

"I took a class in college, but as long as she's still breathing, it wouldn't do any good. Damn it, where the hell is the EMS?" she asked again. As she spoke, the wail of an approaching siren reached their ears. "About fucking time!" she exclaimed, rushing to the front door.

"Just remember, if you say anything to them about *us*—"Alal began.

April cut her off. "Yeah, yeah, you'll kill us all and we go to hell forever, blah, blah. I get it, so please do me a favor, shut the hell up! You're the reason she's going to the ER in the first place, you malicious bitch!" she growled, her green eyes flashing with unbridled hatred.

Alal looked as if she'd been slapped in the face. "Why you insolent, worthless, redheaded ... I'll—" Alal snarled, coiling to attack.

Adriel stopped her with a look that would've frozen the balls off an Eskimo. "That's enough, Alal. She's trying to bait you into doing something stupid in front of the authorities. I strongly suggest you get a grip on that temper of yours," he hissed, as the EMTs arrived.

Slightly chastened, Alal clammed up as the emergency techs entered the room. "Please stand back and give us some room," a burly Hispanic tech named Enrico commanded firmly but politely.

"Are you related?" he asked April, who huddled nearby, while he was taking Dianne's vitals.

"I'm her daughter, April Flowers," she replied.

"Any history of heart problems, palpitations, arrhythmia, chest pains?" he asked, kneeling beside the hyperventilating woman.

"N-No, nothing I'm aware of, but she's a cop, and she has a lot of stress on the job," April replied, staring daggers at Alal.

"We're going to need more information. In the meantime, please fill out this Consent for Treatment form and sign it," the female tech handed her a clipboard.

"Will she be alright? We were just reunited after six months of separation, then this happened," she said, giving the form only a brief glance, before signing it.

"She's going to be fine. I've placed an aspirin under her tongue," Enrico asked, attaching EKG electrodes on Dianne's chest. "From what I've observed, though, I believe she's having a panic attack. But to be on the safe side, we'll transport her to the ER. Do you have a preferred hospital?"

"Uh, St. Michael's, I guess. Whatever's the closest. But I'm going with her," April said, staring defiantly at Adriel.

The demon didn't like it, but he couldn't very well refuse her without drawing unwanted attention.

"Your *Aunt Ally* will follow you there," the oily demon said with a fake smile. "You'll be needing a ride back once your dear mother has sufficiently recovered. We wouldn't want you to be all *alone* at such a stressful time," he slyly told her.

April rolled her eyes in disgust, before turning to Mason. "I'll be back as soon as they can stabilize her. I love you, Ace," she said, giving him a quick hug and peck on the cheek.

"Call me and let me know what's happening if you get a chance," he told her. The EMTs loaded her mother onto a gurney and rolled her out to the waiting ambulance, with April in tow.

Once they were out of earshot, Adriel turned to Alal. "Don't let her out of your sight, and text me when you have information about her mother's condition. Begone—and no more temper tantrums. We have enough problems right now without you creating more!" he hissed irritably, dismissing her with a wave of his hand.

Without a word, she turned, grabbed her purse, and strode out the front door, slamming it hard behind her, knocking Adriel's *"Welcome to Hell"* sign from its moorings to the pavement.

"She can be such a *bitch* when she doesn't get her way," Adriel growled, opening the door to replace the sign on its hook. "I suggest you make yourself comfortable, Mr. Rivers, you and your friends aren't going anywhere for the foreseeable future, so you may as well have a drink and relax," he said, pouring himself a shot of expensive single malt.

Mason would've refused, but he needed something to steady his nerves while he waited for April to update him on her mom's condition. Walking to the bar, he poured himself a shot of whiskey, tossing it back, enjoying the burn as it slid down his throat.

"Let me ask you something, why are you doing this?" he asked the demon. "I mean, surely it isn't for the money. What do you, personally, get out of torturing and killing innocent humans, aside from our souls?"

Adriel pondered a moment before answering. "You accuse me of needless torment and debauchery of you humans, but I merely mirror your own greed and selfishness. We demons entice, we cajole, but we never actually force humans to sign our contracts. Free will has always given you the illusion of choice, when in reality, your avarice and self-indulgence doom you from birth. We simply take advantage of this flaw in your DNA. We provide our clients with every decadent desire in this metaverse you call life. In return for that generosity, we take your souls when you die," he explained, while pouring them each another shot.

"To answer the second part of your question, other than the comforting knowledge that human nature has not and will never change, I receive nothing out of your self-inflicted misery. 'The grass is always greener over the septic tank,' as one of your late humorists so eloquently put it. As long as humans desire the easy road to fame and fortune, I'll gladly accommodate them. But when it's time to pay up, they all regret signing on that dotted line. They always fail to read the fine print," he chuckled darkly.

Mason was getting buzzed from the liquor. He hoped it would loosen Beelzebub's tongue as well. "So, you're saying it's our own fault for wanting a easier life, a rosier future for ourselves?" he coaxed Adriel.

"You really are quite perceptive, Mr. Rivers. You—like the legions of humans preceding you—covet the grandest things that life has to offer, but without the concurrent hard work it takes to achieve them. There are no true shortcuts in life, I'm afraid. Like the old song says, 'You can't always get what you want, you get what you need.' In your case, Mr. Rivers, you'll get what you wanted—fame and fortune—in exchange for an eternity in hell," he replied coldly, tossing back his third shot.

Mason inwardly cringed at the demon's candor. Adriel's blunt appraisal of his stupidity didn't make it any easier to acknowledge his own culpability in his current situation.

"You're right. I've made my bed with the devil, so to speak, and I take full responsibility for my actions. When April brought me to you, I was a pathetic loser, and I'm *still* a pathetic loser. I bartered my soul, and for what? A lot of money, a fancy lifestyle, and fifteen minutes of fame? All because I was too damn lazy to put in the extra effort to achieve it on my own. I see that now—hindsight sucks. But April and the others don't deserve this, you deceived all of us by waving a golden carrot in front of us. You could've at least informed us about the fucking fine print, asshole!" Mason protested.

He was attempting to provoke Adriel, but the demon didn't rise to the bait. Instead, he smiled and poured another round of the single malt, filling their respective glasses.

"If I didn't know better, I'd think you were trying to antagonize me. I see through your little ploy, but it won't work. You're thinking if you get me inebriated, I'll let you worm your way out of our contract. I'm afraid that will not happen. First, I have twice the constitution of Alal. And second, it cannot be *done*. I own you—lock, stock, and proverbial barrel. When you signed our little contract, you lost your right to an appeal. So, I suggest you deal with it. The sooner you accept your fate, the better off you'll be. Enjoy your miserable existence while you still can," the demon advised smugly.

"I just can't believe there's no possibility of my soul's redemption. If the devil and demons are real, then God and angels must be real, as well. I can only hope *He'll* take mercy on us for our stupidity and greed," Mason said defiantly.

"Never mention that name in my presence again if you want to live to see another day!" Adriel snarled, his shot glass shattering in his clenched fist.

Mason blanched, deciding to drop his little game of "Twenty Questions" at that moment. Hearing movement behind him, he turned to find Davy standing there, motionless. A thread of saliva hung from his quivering lower lip as he stared vacantly at the two of them.

"Davy go home now. Need go night-night," zombie Dave repeated in a daze.

"Your friend looks like he could use a drink," Adriel observed, pouring a shot into a fresh glass.

"I don't think that's a good idea, he's ... not in a good frame of mind, as you can see," Mason disputed warily.

"Nonsense, I insist. He'd be *crazy* to pass up a dram of fifty-five-year-old Macallan single malt. It's the least I can do for the demented lad," Adriel asserted.

He walked over to the slack-faced percussionist and shoved the glass in his hand, motioning for him to drink up. Davy stared at the expensive whiskey in his glass, looked up, and without warning, tossed it in Adriel's face.

Enraged, Adriel recoiled, and his hideous demon face appeared in all its terrible glory.

The sight of the monster in front of him was too much for Davy's already-wounded psyche—his heart gave out and he dropped to the floor, stone-cold dead before he even hit the tile.

"*Holy shit*! You actually frightened him to death, you ... you ... demonic ..." Mason cried, unable to find an apt expletive to describe the hellish creature, he kneeled by his friend's side.

"Unfortunate, but he insulted me," Adriel calmly replied. "When I'm angered, I have little control over my true face. Well, one problem solved, and another takes its place. Now you'll have to find a replacement, and quickly. Mister Wu of Sony expects to meet with you tomorrow at 2:00 p.m. to discuss recording your band. I suggest you start searching for a drummer to take his place. If you're unable find one ... well, you know what happens," Adriel said coolly.

"This is so terribly wrong. Davy had a wife and a little girl. How am I supposed to tell them that their husband and father isn't coming home?" Mason demanded, fuming.

"You'll tell them nothing. He's no longer your concern. I'd advise you to focus on the present. I'll feed him to the hell hounds, they haven't eaten since we fed them the remains of that traitorous priest," Adriel replied. Grabbing one of Davy's legs, he dragged him toward the back door.

Mason watched, revolted and sickened, as Adriel flung his former friend's corpse to the hungry canines out back and closed the door. Even with it shut, Mason could hear the crunch of poor Davy's bones, as the creatures devoured his body.

The ringing of Adriel's phone provided Mason with a welcome distraction from the carnage out back.

Adriel answered, "Yes? ... I see ... alright, when she's released, bring them back ASAP. There's been a slight ... development since you left. Nothing for you to worry about. It's taken care of—no, I didn't kill anyone. Well, not technically. No more talk on the phone, we'll discuss the matter when you return," he said curtly, disconnecting.

What a lying sack of shit! Mason thought angrily, flopping down on the couch. "I presume Dianne didn't suffer from a heart attack after all, right?" he asked.

"I'm not sure, and I could not care less. Alal didn't go into details, only that Dianne was being released. They'll be here shortly," Adriel said, pouring himself another shot of whiskey. Mason saw movement on the staircase as Jeff and Larry joined them in the living area.

They each looked around the room. "What's going on? Where's April and her mom—and Davy?" Jeff asked dully.

"We thought April's mom had suffered a heart attack and called EMS," Mason explained. "They took her to the ER, but I believe they're releasing her, so I guess it was only a panic attack. Davy ... Davy didn't make it, this was all too much for him. I—I don't think he suffered, thank Go—uh, goodness," Mason replied grimly.

"Davy's dead? What did you do to him, you fucking asshole!" Jeff growled at Adriel, his hands curling into angry fists. Mason cringed, wanting to warn him not to antagonize the demon further.

Adriel turned toward Jeff. "I'd watch who you're calling an asshole, if I were you. You're already one member short. If you'd like to make it two, keep talking. I'm sure my hell hounds would welcome another tasty treat," Adriel threatened, his eyes glowing like red hot embers.

Although still livid, Jeff yielded. He didn't want to end up as dog chow, as it seemed poor Davy had.

Larry looked stunned. "You ... you fed Davy to your dogs?" he asked incredulously.

"I assure you, he was already quite dead. What would you have me do? I can't allow corpses to pile up like cordwood. I'd be knee-deep in bodies and the smell—well, bon appetit," the demon chortled.

Larry paled, looking like he might vomit any moment. He sank onto the couch beside Mason. Placing his head in his hands, he began to slowly rock back and forth, like one of those little glass drinking birds.

Ten minutes later, Alal burst through the front door like a miniature tornado, followed closely by April and her mother. "I need a drink!" Alal growled, stomping over to the bar.

April addressed Mason and his bandmates. "Apparently, mama suffers from panic attacks—something she'd never told me." April's voice grew quieter, as she sensed the negative vibes permeating the air.

"Would've saved us a hell of a lot of trouble if she'd kicked it for real," Alal grumbled, skipping the shot glass and upending the bottle of tequila into her gaping mouth.

Dianne glared at the demoness, but wisely refrained from responding. She understood that she'd have to stay on her toes around these monsters, since apparently they wouldn't hesitate to harm or kill on a whim. She needed to get to her phone—wherever Alal had stashed them—without alerting these horrifying creatures, and call doctor Mia Chandler.

Then she had an idea. "I'm supposed to report in. I need to call my captain. They know where I am, and they know who you are. Unless you want the FBI involved, I suggest you let me make the call," she bluffed.

Adriel looked at Alal, who shrugged indifferently, continuing to chug tequila like it was water. He shook his head in disgust at her weakness for the alcoholic beverage.

"I'm afraid that's out of the question," he told Dianne. "Your presence here complicates matters in the extreme. I *was* going to use you for leverage to ensure full cooperation from your bratty offspring and Mr. Rivers, but I'm finding you more of a liability than an asset. How would you prefer to die—your choice. You're fortunate, I rarely bother to ask," Adriel said aloofly, as if discussing the weather, instead of ending someone's life.

Dianne hadn't expected this alarming response and was briefly at a loss for words. "If you kill me, the FBI and my fellow officers will hound you to hell and back. You'll never know a moment's peace," she said, her heart anxiously galloping in her chest.

"Please, stop stalling. I can make it quick and painless, no need to worry, you won't suffer," he calmly assured.

"If you kill her, you might as well kill me, too, I'm sick and tired of your power games, you demonic sack of shit!" April growled ferociously.

"Me, too, I don't want to die, but she's innocent, she doesn't deserve this," Mason chimed in.

Larry and Jeff hesitated, then crossed the metaphorical "line in the sand" as well.

"It seems we have a so-called 'Mexican standoff,'" Adriel observed coolly. "Very well, so be it. Alal, kill them all and dispose of their bodies. We'll just have to start over from scratch. Too bad, but luckily for us, there are legions of rubes in this despicable world who wish to be rich and famous," he said callously, waving his hand dismissively.

The silence in the room was deafening. Everyone, including Adriel, was staring at the demoness, waiting for her to react to his order.

Distracted, she drained the last swallow of tequila from the bottle, then turned unsteadily toward the anxious group in front of her and belched loudly.

"Ya' shurre bout thish, Abbs? I kind'a like torturin' tha' bitsshh, shame ta hafta shtop," the inebriated fiend slurred, clutching the bar top to keep her balance.

"Alal, you're disgusting, you disappoint me. In a matter of a few days, you've somehow managed to transform yourself into a raging alcoholic. Now sober your exquisite ass up and do as I command, or I'll send *you* back to hell. Which, last I checked, was devoid of intoxicating beverages of any kind," he growled, snatching the empty bottle from her hand.

Narrowing her cold, blue eyes, Alal said, "I've taken 'bout all tha' shit off you I can sshtan.' Ya' wanna kill 'em, do it yoursshelf, O, mighty mashter of tha pit!" she spat defiantly.

Mason and the other humans backed away as both demons unveiled their true hideous features, bristling with anger and ready for battle.

Chapter Twenty-Three

With mutual roars of rage, the two demons leapt for one another's throats. Mason grabbed April and Dianne and pulled them back, away from immediate harm.

"Run! This may be our only chance," Mason yelled, shoving them toward the open front door.

While Alal and Adriel were busy trying to disembowel one another, they all ran for their lives.

Once outside, they gathered on the sidewalk in front of the condo, unsure what to do next. Glancing around, Mason spied a gas can sitting in the yard next to an unused lawnmower that gave him an idea.

"Do you have your lighter with you?" he asked April.

"Wh-what? Any second now, those fuckers are gonna realize we've flown the coop. We need to get the hell outta while we still can!" she urgently replied, tossing him the lighter from her purse, which she'd grabbed on the way out.

"Trust me. If this doesn't work, run like hell and get some help," he replied grimly. Hesitating, he leaned down, and kissed her hard. "I love you, April Flowers," he said.

With the lighter in hand, he dashed over to grab the gas can. Thankfully, it was nearly full. With a twist, he removed the little cap on the end of the spout as he ran towards the front door of the condo.

Upendeding the can, he poured the gas in the open doorway and on the surrounding window frames until the can was almost empty. Using the remainder, he made a liquid fuse, trailing away from the structure and out onto the lawn. With a flick of the lighter, the gas caught. He stumbled back to watch, as flames raced toward gas-soaked porch.

As the fire reached the front porch, Alal suddenly appeared in the doorway. With an audible *whooomph,* the gas ignited, completely enveloping the wretched demoness in a wall of flame.

"Nooo, you can't stop Alal the destroyer!" she screeched.

The demon capered about as the raging inferno fully engulfed her. Fiery tongues leaped up to eat away her clothes and hair while the skin of her face and hands bubbled up and melted. Mason and the others watched in horrid fascination as she staggered off the porch like a walking bonfire.

"Argghrrfdff!" the demoness garbled through charred lips. Impossibly, she was still on her feet, advancing toward them with arms and claws extended.

Behind her, the condo burst into flames, sending thick clouds of black, oily smoke pouring from the second story. As the heat intensified, the downstairs windows cracked and exploded, causing the conflagration inside to expand rapidly.

The next-door neighbor grabbed his water hose and quickly turned on the water, dragging its fifty-foot length over to spray water on the burning abomination, only making it worse.

"Arffgogdgdd!" the burning creature bellowed angrily. Dropping to charred knees, it reached out in one last, desperate attempt to seize Mason with its blackened claws before finally succumbing to the flames.

Transfixed, they watched the horrific scene unfold in front of them. From behind him, a hand grabbed his arm, yanking him back just as the scorched monster fell forward on what remained of its face and was finally still.

"Do you think she's really dead?" Dianne anxiously asked.

"Let's hope so," April replied. "My only concern is Adriel. It's entirely possible he made it out alive. If so, we're all still in danger!" she added, checking all the upper-story windows for any sign he was still inside.

They heard the distant wail of sirens growing closer by the second.

Mason turned to Dianne, "What should we do—wait and see if he made it out, or get the hell outta dodge?"

"Normally, I'd advise staying put and waiting for the firetrucks, but that's out of the question. I think we'd better get out while the gettin's good," she replied grimly.

The five escapees turned and walked away from the burning structure as fast as they could without attracting undue attention from people gathering to watch the drama unfold.

"Unless we know for sure that he's dead, we'll be forever looking over our shoulders. *Shit*! All our phones were in there, as well as that Sony contract he forged our names on," Mason pointed out, as three fire trucks screamed past them, pulling to a halt in front of the blazing condo, now a block away.

"When they find the remains of the gas can, the cops are going to want to question us. We need to find a ride and get the hell out of town ASAP! Any suggestions on how to accomplish that fast would be welcome," Dianne said tightly as they turned the corner at the end of the street.

"No offense, Ace," Jeff interposed, "but as soon as we get to our cars, Larry and I are headed for an extended vacation in Mexico. We sure as hell don't wanna end up like poor Davy. So, I guess this is adios, dude," Jeff said, extending his palm for a handshake.

Mason couldn't blame them for trying to get as far away from him as possible. "Sorry for dragging you into this clusterfuck, y'all take care. I'll be in touch when I think it's safe for us to get back together," he offered, taking Jeff's hand.

"Don't bother, Ace, you can stick a fork in us, we're done. No more bullshit contests or risking our lives for fame and fortune," Jeff solemnly said. He and Larry turned to walk away.

"See ya,'" Mason said wistfully to their retreating backs.

"Not if I see you first," Jeff hollered, as the last two members of his old band strode off into the midday sun.

The remaining trio continued walking until they reached the intersection of Lamar and Brentwood, where they pondered their next move.

"Is there an ATM somewhere close? We're gonna need some cash to catch a ride back to the airport," Dianne pointed out.

"I think there's one in the 'Purple Iris,'" Mason said, pointing to the building on their immediate right. The nudie-bar had a large sign out front claiming to have "The hottest girls and the coldest beer in Texas" inside.

Dianne found strip-clubs distasteful, but she was pretty sure he was right. After all, the patrons had to keep those dancers' G-strings full of cash.

So, the trio wandered across the half-full parking lot and entered the darkened interior of the business, met by the bone-crushing percussion of a bass guitar. Currently, only two women were dancing, each up on a separate stage. A mixed crowd of horny businessmen and blue-collar workers lined the edge of both stages, leering up at the semi-naked women. With twenty-dollar bills clutched in their hands, each was ready to stuff their hard-earned cash into the bored dancers' tiny G-strings.

Reluctantly, Mason paid the bouncer's five-dollar cover charge. Dianne found the ATM tucked away in a corner by the entrance door and retrieved the maximum amount. Then she asked the bouncer if she could borrow his phone to call for a ride. Since she was in her police uniform, the guy didn't object, handing it to her. Her first call was to Scott instructing him to get the plane ready as soon as possible; her second was to call an Uber.

The driver said his ETA was five minutes. She thanked the bouncer, handing back his phone, and they exited the club to wait for their ride. Four minutes later, the driver pulled up and stopped by the valet stand. As they scrambled into the back, Dianne told the driver to take them to the airport.

Twenty-five minutes later, they arrived to find Scott's Cessna gassed up and ready to go. Climbing onboard, they strapped in, awaiting their turn to taxi out onto the busy runway. Once the wheels had left the tarmac with the plane safely in the air, they breathed a collective sigh of relief, leaving "Music City" behind them. In two scant hours, they'd be landing in Boulder. From there, they'd need to figure out how best to proceed.

The first thing would be to purchase new phones to replace the ones Adriel had taken. They all felt naked without them. In this digital world, losing your phone was akin to losing your entire existence. A half-hour later, they were lulled into an exhausted sleep by the comforting drone of the engines as they flew over the Texas/New Mexico border, heading for Boulder and a troubling, unknown future ...

PART TWO
Chapter Twenty-Four

Joseph, Oregon

Thirty-year-old Dr. Mia Chandler was performing a delicate endoscopic operation on a patient's brain when the head operating room nurse informed her she had an important call from some detective with the Boulder PD. The petite, curly headed Chief of Surgery acknowledged her with a slight nod of her head. That could only be Detective Dianne Flowers, so it must be urgent.

"Ava, can you take over for me? I need to take that call," she asked her Assistant Chief Surgeon.

Dr. Ava Brinkman, forty-eight years young, had been Mia's friend and mentor at the hospital in Portland where they'd met six years earlier. "Gotcha covered, boss. Go take your call," she said, shooing her away as if she were a pesky fly.

"Thanks, I won't be long," Mia said, leaving the operating theater.

Tossing her gloves and mask in the hazardous waste bin, Mia thoroughly washed and dried her hands. A nurse handed her the phone, an old landline still used by the hospital staff.

"Hello, this is Dr. Chandler, is that you, Detective. Flowers?" she asked, knowing it likely was.

"Hello, Mia, yes, it's me. First let me apologize for interrupting you at work, but I may need your help with a rather 'delicate' matter," Dianne replied cryptically.

"What's going on? Are you okay?" Mia asked, concerned for her distant friend.

"Um, that's a subjective question. I won't go into specifics at the moment, but let's just say that it involves the ... uh, supernatural and I'd hoped—" she paused. Mia finished the thought for her.

"—you'd hoped because of my so-called 'Gift,' I'd be able to help you outta some sort of supernatural jam, is that it?" she surmised, shaking her head.

"Well ... yes and no. Frankly, I'm not sure how to proceed. I've never come across anything this bizarre in my entire life. If I hadn't seen it with my own eyes, I'd never have believed it possible," Dianne replied guardedly.

"Believed *what* was possible?" Mia asked impatiently.

"Demons—actual demons from hell, I shit you not, and that's not even the worst of it. Listen, I know it sounds crazy, but it's the God's honest truth!" Dianne replied soberly.

"Um, I don't really see how I could help with something like that. Have you tried contacting, I don't know, maybe a priest or something? This really isn't my realm of expertise, I'm a healer, not an exorcist," Mia exclaimed. She lowered her voice after receiving curious stares from two nurses idling nearby.

"Unfortunately, my daughter, April—you haven't met her—and her boyfriend are the primary ones involved in this cluster-fuck, and they've already tried the priest route, with horrific results. I know you're busy, Mia, but could you please call me when you get off shift? I don't know who else to turn to, you're the only one I could think of who has any experience dealing with paranormal shit," Dianne pleaded.

Mia was silent for a moment, mystified how she could possibly help her friend with this situation. Since the detective had helped her years before when she'd really needed it, she hated to refuse her outright.

"Okay, my shift is over in an hour if nothing serious crops up in the meantime," she said, glancing at a clock on the wall. "I'll still be on call, but I'll contact you when I get home, deal?"

"That's perfect. Thank you, Mia, you don't know what a relief it is just to have someone to talk to about all this madness. I'll look forward to filling you in on all the details then. Goodbye," Dianne said, disconnecting.

That was a very weird conversation, Mia thought, as she returned to the operating theater, after first re-sanitizing and grabbing a fresh mask, gown, and gloves.

Her fourteen-hour shift went by uneventfully. Her patient was moved to recovery and from there, would be moved to ICU for further monitoring.

"Thanks for the back-up, Ava. I needed to take that call, an old friend is having some odd issues in Boulder. Frankly, I don't know what's going on, except to say it sounds extremely strange," Mia said, frowning, while they changed into their street clothes in the doctor's locker room.

"You're welcome. You wanna go have a glass of wine and talk about it?" Ava was intrigued.

"Sorry, maybe later. I need to call her back and get the skinny on the whole situation before I can discuss it, if then," Mia replied, grabbing her purse.

"Okay, we can talk later. See you at home," Ava said, pulling on a light coat to leave.

Ava had moved in with her friend and now boss five years ago after the sudden death of Kris Lacey—Mia's adopted mother—had left her the house. Kris had served as the Sheriff of both Enterprise, and Joseph. Nestled in a valley between the gorgeous Wallowa Mountains and scenic Wallowa lake to the south, it was one of the most beautiful areas Ava had ever seen. Soon after her mother's passing, Mia had been offered the job of Chief Surgeon at the Joseph Hospital, and she had, in turn, offered Ava the job as Assistant Chief of Surgery. Since they were already close friends, it seemed only natural for them to end up as roommates.

On her way home, Mia stopped at the 'R & R,' her favorite restaurant in Joseph. She was craving a burger and a basket of their famous sweet-potato tots. She eased the car up to the drive-in menu and parked, calling Ava to see if she wanted anything. Ava claimed she had to watch her 'girlish' figure; Mia did an eye roll but said nothing. She didn't normally eat much fast food, either, but there was nothing better than R & R's double cheeseburger with extra bacon to satisfy an occasional yearning for grease. Because of her high metabolism, her five-foot-two-inch body never seemed to gain an ounce of weight.

Finishing her meal and sated, she drove to her single-story frame house, where she parked her five-year-old Mercedes next to Ava's brand-new Lexus. Mia got out and walked up the sidewalk, passing a bed of red roses her mother had planted the spring before she died. An old, wooden porch swing hung suspended on chains attached to the rafters, swinging gently back and forth under the eaves of the covered porch that ran the length of the old house. The interior wasn't fancy, but it was comfortably furnished. A functional brown couch faced a small television. That, along with two recliners, a coffee table, and a small breakfast table were all the furniture she owned, except for the bed and bedside table in her bedroom, which had belonged to her mother.

Pictures of Kris in her sheriff's uniform, along with some from her earlier stint as the head detective with the Taos, New Mexico, PD, were proudly displayed on the living room wall greeting Mia as she walked in. A large ball of yellowish fur on the couch raised its head at her approach. The large bobcat stretched, looking up at her as if to say, *'Where the hell have you been? Feed me, I'm starving!'*—which was patently untrue, as was obvious from his sizeable girth. His cool, appraising stare through eyes imbued with golden amber, suggested that even though he was semi-domesticated, he was still a creature of the forest, and one to be reckoned with when pissed-off.

"Yeah, I know, you're *always* freaking hungry. C'mon, Mr. Jinx, Mama won't let you starve," she said, heading for the kitchen where she opened a large can of "Kozey Kitten" cat food. Jinx lived with her adopted aunt and uncle, Missy and Jake Anderson and their daughters, Belinda and Amanda, age eleven and three, respectively. Mia had volunteered to keep the cat while they traveled to promote Jake's latest novel.

The big feline hopped off the couch and padded over, awaiting his treat as she poured some kibble into his dish. Ava wandered out of her room in her pajamas and slippers to join her in the kitchen. Lifting a brow, she watched as the bobcat scarfed down his food.

"If I ate as often as you feed that sorry excuse for a house cat, I'd be the size of a small planet. He's had you wrapped around his paw ever since he arrived. When are they coming back for him?" she asked, getting herself a glass of water.

"Um, I think they'll be back either today or tomorrow, not sure. He is a handful, alright," Mia replied, reaching down to stroke him and eliciting a cross between a purr and a warning growl.

"That's the understatement of the century. I'm gonna rack out for a while, wake me after you talk to your detective friend. I'd love to hear all the juicy details," Ava said with a yawn. She was a good friend and a great surgeon, but her penchant for nosiness could be irritating.

"I'll fill you in if I can. Depends on what she has say," Mia said neutrally.

"Okay, okay, you don't have to go all 'Nancy Drew' on me, I can take a hint. *Oh, Crap*! I forgot tomorrow's trash day. Would you mind terribly taking it out for me? I know it's my turn, but I really need to crash for a while, I'm due back on shift in ... eight hours," Ava groaned, glancing at the clock on the wall.

"No problem. I'll do it when I let Jinx out to do his business," Mia started gathering the trash sack out of the waste can.

"Meeoooutt!" Jinx complained in his raspy cat voice.

"Hold your horses, fur-face, I'm moving as fast as I can," she told him, struggling with the front door.

As soon as it opened, the big cat raced out the door. She didn't worry about him getting lost or wandering off into the woods behind her house. There was little traffic here, and he knew which side his bread was buttered on. Mia put the trash in the can and wheeled it out to the curb, returning to find Ava curled on the couch, snoring lightly. She'd never made it back to her room. Mia shook her head, grabbed a blanket, and covered her. Then she took a much-needed shower. Dressed in her pajamas, she sat on her bed, pulled out her phone, and called her friend.

Dianne picked up on the first ring. "I didn't expect you to call back so soon, but I'm glad you did. So, let me explain this as best as I can," she said. She then described everything, starting with the unexpected call from her daughter pleading for plane fare, ending with their harrowing escape from the monsters' den and their subsequent return to Boulder earlier that day.

There was a moment of silence while Mia digested her story. "Holy crap! That sounds like something out of a freakin' Stephen King novel!" Mia exclaimed.

She was having a hard time wrapping her head around the incredible story her friend had just related. From her own experience, Mia knew there were omnipotent powers at work in the universe. Her so-called 'gift' of healing was one of them. She'd even brought patients back from clinical death, making her something of a local celebrity for a brief time. To her dismay, she'd been given the unsought title, "Angel of Oregon."

"This blows my mind, but I believe you're telling the truth. My Aunt Missy and her husband, Jake, had a harrowing experience with something similar several years ago, and they barely escaped with their lives. I'm still a little confused, though, about how I can help you?" Mia said, opening a window to let a breeze in.

"I told you earlier that we thought, or rather hoped, that Adriel had perished in the fire at the condo. No such luck. Half an hour ago, I received an email I'll read to you,

There's nowhere to hide, nowhere to run, I know where you live and where you work. Despite Alal's demise and all the trouble you've caused, I'm willing to forgive your treachery for the moment, if your brat and her six-fingered friend will fulfill their contracts with both Sony and myself. If I haven't heard from you by 6:00 p.m., I'll consider it a refusal. If the answer is no, you will all suffer the direst of consequences. Have a pleasant day! A. Abaddon.

P. S. "Don't bother to trace this email, you'll never find the IP address, it's a rather clever encryption I created and it's been bounced through routers all over the planet."

"Well, it seems obvious he survived the fire. You'll excuse me if I say he doesn't sound much like the *forgiving* type. He's also responsible for the deaths of at least two people that you know of, right?" Mia asked.

"Yes, I mean, I heard him say as much before the fire. He was going to have Alal kill us and toss our remains to his dogs, like he'd done to Father O'Hennigan and that drummer guy, Davy. There's no telling how many other innocent victims have met the same fate," Dianne surmised.

"What are you going to do? You clearly can't trust this Adriel to keep its word. Whatever else he is, he's also a raging psychopath. He's lured you all back to Austin once already and was ready to kill you. What makes you think he wouldn't try again as soon as he has you where he wants you?" Mia asked, bewildered that her friend would even think of acquiescing to the hellish creature's demands.

"I can't in good conscience allow my daughter anywhere near the bastard again, but if they don't accede to his wishes, I don't doubt he'll somehow make good on his promise and slaughter us all. We're damned if we do, and damned if we don't," Dianne replied soberly.

"We now know that fire can destroy them, or at least I think so," she continued. "We left in kind of a hurry, but I don't see how Alal could've survived. Her body was burned to a crisp when we took off. I'd even consider trying to contact another priest, but we'd have no way of knowing if one might be in league with the bastard. Even if we found one with no previous association, there's no guarantee an exorcism would rid us of this disastrous problem," she added despairingly.

"You still haven't answered my question, how do you think I might be of help. My 'gift' seems to be proprietary. So far, I've only been able to use it to heal people in extreme circumstances. Even then, it's failed me a couple times. I seriously doubt it would work on a freakin' demon," Mia explained apologetically.

"Well, it was worth a try. I'm sorry to have troubled you with this. I guess we'll have to find some other solution. Short of buying a flamethrower and getting close enough to torch his ass, I don't see any other way to rid ourselves of this hellish nightmare. Thank you for listening and believing me. Nobody else would've, they'd have laughed, tossed my ass in the loony-bin, and thrown away the key," Dianne said resignedly.

"I'm truly sorry, but I don't believe my 'gift' would be any help in this situation. If I can think of anything else, I'll certainly let you know," Mia readily offered.

"I appreciate that. I'll let you go now. I have a splitting headache and I need to take a couple of pills. Talk to you soon, Mia," Dianne said briefly, disconnecting the call.

Mia felt about as useful as a screen door on a submarine. She prided herself on her keen ability to come up with solutions to problems on the fly. But this one was beyond her realm of knowledge. *How the hell do you destroy a creature that is technically immortal?* she wondered. Short answer, you can't.

"Maybe I'm overthinking this," she said aloud. Quickly, she called Dianne back. "Listen, there might be a way to do this—" ...

Chapter Twenty-Five

"I think that's not only nuts, but dangerous as hell, Mia. You don't know if it would work, and even if it did, there's no guarantee you'd come out of it unharmed," Dianne admonished her over the phone.

Mia was aware it would be dangerous on her part. But her shrewd intellect had examined all the options, and this seemed to be the only logical choice.

"I realize it's risky, but I can't think of another scenario which doesn't end up in disaster for you guys. For it to work, I would have to be in physical contact with the creature. That's the most dangerous aspect of it I can see," Mia said calmly.

"Could you make it here in time though? I only have five hours and change to give him an answer, and the clock's ticking," Dianne asked, hating to even ask her.

"I think so. Technically, I'm on call, but I'll try to get someone to cover for me. It'll take me close to two hours to get there by plane, but it's doable."

"Thank you, Mia, you don't know how much I appreciate this. I owe you a large," Dianne said emotionally.

"No worries, I have faith things will work out," Mia said, more confidently than she felt. "Try to calm yourself, if you don't, you'll have a panic attack."

"H-How did you know I suffer from panic attacks? I've never told anyone about them. April didn't even know until I had one at that bastard's condo," Dianne asked. She'd intentionally omitted mention of her attack from her account of their trip to Austin.

Mia wasn't sure how she'd known, she just had. "Merely a lucky guess. I know how stressful your job is, it was a logical assumption on my part. I'm a doctor, remember? Look, I need to go if I'm to have any chance of making it there by his deadline. I'll text you when I'm in the air," Mia said, dodging the question.

"Alright, see you soon. I'll meet you at the airport, have a safe trip," Dianne said, not quite satisfied with Mia's explanation, but she let it go.

AFTER HANGING UP, MIA went to the living room and woke the slumbering Ava. Jolted awake, she glanced at her friend. "What's up?" she asked groggily.

"I just got off the phone with my friend in Boulder. I need to ask a huge favor," Mia replied impatiently.

"Okay, as long as it doesn't involve cleaning the freakin' cat box, the smell of that thing would knock a buzzard off a shit wagon," Ava replied with a scowl.

"You just don't like cats. Anyway, that's not what I need. Think you could cover for me for the next 24 hours? I have to fly to Boulder, my detective friend is in a serious pickle and I sort of volunteered to help," Mia asked hopefully.

"Sure. I'll be joining the ranks of 'The Walking Dead,' though, by the time you return," Ava groaned, sitting up. "Anything you can tell me about your friend's predicament?" she asked, sniffing for a hint of gossip.

"Nope. Sorry, you'll have to wait 'til I return to hear all the juicy details," Mia said, teased her, knowing it would only feed her curiosity.

"In that case, I'm going back to bed. You'd better let that little monster back in before you leave, he's had more than enough time to do his business. I wish he'd do all of it out there, the air quality in here would be vastly improved," Ava groused. Standing, she gave Mia a quick hug. "Have a safe trip, and please try not to get yourself killed," she said, knowing Mia's penchant for attracting the worst kinds of trouble.

"I'll try my best, I promise. Please don't worry. With a little luck, I should be back in time for my shift tomorrow night. Hopefully, you won't turn into a zombie before then," Mia replied, opening the front door and whistling for Jinx, a trick she'd learned from Uncle Jake. She saw a blur of fur race from the edge of the forest of Ponderosa pines surrounding the property. He shot into the room, jumped on the couch, and began licking his furry balls.

"It's no wonder you have so many hairballs," she chuckled, shaking her head. Jinx ignored her and continued his bath. With the bobcat situated, Mia called Scott Hardilek. She knew he'd returned earlier from ferrying Dianne and the others back to Boulder, and she hoped to catch him before he took another gig.

He answered on the second ring. "Well, hello, Mia. What's up?" he said cheerfully. Scott was one of the kindest people she'd ever met. She told him about her urgent need to get to Boulder ASAP.

"You're in luck, I just had my plane serviced and was just about take her up for a spin over the lake. What's your ETA?" he asked.

"I can be there in fifteen minutes. I'm hoping the weather will hold until we get there," she replied, gathering a few items for the trip.

"Shouldn't be a problem, the next front isn't due 'til tomorrow. You gonna need me to hang around after I drop you off?" he asked.

"Yes, if everything works out as I plan, I'll need a ride back," Mia replied. She hated flying anywhere, but when you lived in a remote area, it was often necessary. She patted Jinx on the head, receiving a disdainful glare. Grabbing her keys, she left the house, locking the door behind her. Minutes later, she arrived at the airstrip in the neighboring town of Enterprise to find Scott waiting in the plane. He was running through his pre-flight checklist when she boarded the aircraft, taking the co-pilot's seat.

"Right on time, buckle-up, and I'll have us airbourne in a jiffy," he said.

Starting the engines on his twin turboprop, he feathered them until they attained the proper RPMs. The wheel chocks had already been removed, so he taxied out onto the runway. Mia was regretting having eaten such a big lunch earlier—too late now. Scott eased the throttles forward, and the plane hurtled down the runway, rising into the crisp mountain air. She put on the intercom headset to block some of the engine noise as she settled in for the duration of the two-hour flight.

IN BOULDER, SCOTT WAS forced to circle the airfield because of a delay on the ground. On his landing approach, some idiot in a small jet had landed on the wrong runway and clipped the wing of another plane, causing emergency crews to scramble.

"How long 'til we can land?" Mia asked anxiously, checking the time.

"Depends. If there wasn't too much damage to the planes involved and no injuries, maybe twenty minutes," Scott replied calmly.

"That's going to be cutting it close, I need to meet Dianne no later than 5:55 p.m. Isn't there any other runway you can use to set us down?" she asked hopefully. "Technically, no, unless I request an emergency landing, but to do so, I'd need a really solid excuse. Short of catastrophic engine failure, nothing else qualifies in the eyes of the FAA," he replied.

Frustrated, Mia concentrated on the problem and had a thought. "How much fuel do you have left?" she asked.

Scott glanced at the gauge and shook his head. "Enough to keep us in the air for another hour, plus or minus a few minutes. Not to worry, we have plenty," he replied warily.

"Could you dump some fuel and declare an emergency?" she asked.

"I'm afraid that wouldn't work, you have to account for every inconsistency. The FAA is very strict. Sorry, Mia. I can't afford to lose my license," he told her. He held up a hand, while listening intently to the air traffic controller in the tower.

"We've been given the okay to land, they've cleared the runway," he said, relieved. They landed smoothly without further incident. He taxied to the hanger and killed the engines.

"Thanks for the ride, Scott, I'll call you if there's any change of plan. Hopefully, this won't take more than a couple of hours," Mia said, standing, ready to deplane.

"You're welcome. See ya' on the flip-flop," he replied, smiling. Opening the cabin door, he lowered the stairs.

She stepped onto the tarmac and spotted Dianne leaning against her police cruiser, arms crossed. Hurrying over, she gave her a big hug in greeting.

"I was wondering if I'd make it on time. Some incident on the runway delayed our landing," she said, climbing into the passenger seat of Dianne's vehicle. "Where's your daughter, April, and her friend? I was hoping to meet them," Mia asked.

Dianne put the car in Drive and sped off before answering. "At the moment, they're in a holding cell at headquarters. They're safer there," she replied tersely, weaving her way through rush hour traffic.

"*Holy Crap*! You put your own daughter in jail? I'll bet that went over like a lead balloon," Mia exclaimed, surprised at the drastic action her friend had taken to keep her daughter safe.

"Yeah, I'm a lock to win mother of the year, but it's the safest place I could think of at the time," Dianne said sarcastically.

Mia glanced at the time: five minutes before six. "Remember, when you contact him, let me do the talking, okay?" she prompted.

"I hope you know what you're getting yourself into. This evil bastard isn't someone you want to piss off, he's more than dangerous, he's as pitiless and conniving as a cobra. You sure you want to go through with this? Just so you know, if it doesn't work, we'll all be in a world of shit," Dianne replied grimly.

"Sounds like you're already in a world of shit, let's hope I can shovel us a path out of this mess," Mia replied, trying to sound assured.

Dianne pulled into her parking spot at the station and parked. They got out and rushed inside the building.

"JASON, OPEN THE CELL and let them out," Dianne instructed her sergeant. The heavy-set cop rose and did as she asked.

April and Mason stepped into the booking area, both incensed as they approached Dianne and Mia.

April cornered her mother. "I hope you're aware that Adriel will find us, no matter where you try to hide us. This is bullshit! Who's this? She your miracle healer friend?" she spat angrily.

"This is Dr. Mia Chandler, and she's risking her life to assist us with this mess you've gotten yourselves into, so please show her a little respect," Dianne asserted sternly.

"I—I'm sorry, I didn't mean to be rude, but being held in a jail cell like a criminal pisses me off," April said, glaring at her mother. Dianne ignored her, introducing Mason to Mia.

"I'm sure your mother did what she thought was best for you both under the circumstances," Mia told April. Then she said, "I think it's time to send that email now, Dianne. Is there someplace a little more private?"

Dianne nodded and led them into her office, closing the door once they were all inside. Mason and April fidgeted, as Mia took a seat at Dianne's desk. Dianne typed her password on her laptop and brought up the email Adriel had sent.

Taking a deep breath, Mia began typing out a reply to his ultimatum. The first thing she wrote as Dianne's proxy was: *'In reply to your demand that my daughter and Mr. Rivers return to Austin to fulfill their obligations to you, I regret to inform you that my answer is a firm 'no.' Instead, I have a counter proposal for your consideration...'* Being intentionally vague, Mia left it hanging, to see if he'd take the bait.

A full two minutes went by with no reply. "What if he doesn't answer?" Mason asked tensely.

"He will, give him some time. If he's truly what you say he is, his ego won't allow anyone to get the better of him," Mia replied patiently.

The laptop *dinged* with an incoming email. It was only three words: *'Explain said proposal.'*

"Here we go," Mia said to herself, typing: *'I have a dear friend who's willing to trade her soul in return for my daughter's. In return, you must agree to negate any contractual obligation due on her and Mister River's part. This is non-negotiable.'*

Mia hit "send." "Now we wait for his refusal." she said, leaning back in Dianne's office chair.

It didn't take long. The PC *dinged* a few moments later wwith his reply: *'Afraid that's unacceptable. Your daughter and Mr. Rivers signed contracts in good faith, and I fully intend to collect on their debts, with extreme prejudice if necessary. However, I would be more than happy to accommodate your friend as I'm always on the hunt for fresh souls."*

"I expected as much," Mia muttered as she prepared to type her response: *'My friend is not agreeable to those terms. She'd only be willing to trade for my daughter and Mr. Rivers.'* Mia wrote and sent.

This time his reply took longer to arrive: *'Why should I consider releasing Rivers as well? Two souls for one? In my humble opinion, that's not an equitable trade.'*

"Humble, my ass!" April opined, flipping the email off.

Mia ignored her outburst and continued typing: *'My friend would like to meet in person to convince you of her value before you make a rash decision about the equity of the trade. If not, we are at an impasse.'* She hit send and sat back to wait for his reply.

"You don't really expect him to agree to this, right?" Mason queried Mia. "He already has us, there's no incentive for him to comply. No offense, Dr. Chandler, it's incredibly noble of you to offer, but you're wasting your time trying to bargain with that asshole," Mason remarked sullenly.

"It's worth a try. I don't see another way to get you out of this mess you've created for yourselves. We have him curious, and you know what curiosity did to the cat. You ever play poker, Mason? I'm betting Adriel is overconfident and will call my hand. It's an enormous gamble, but one I'm willing to take. If he caves and agrees to a meet, I may be able to turn the tables on him," Mia replied, edgily drumming her fingers on the table. Mason didn't look convinced.

Minutes ticked by with no reply until his answer popped up on her screen. *'Very well. I'll agree to meet your* friend, *even though it's against my better judgment. I'll be flying to Boulder immediately. If she has a sudden change of heart or fails to show up, you will all die a slow and anguished death. No more deals, no more stalling. I'll contact you in an hour with further instructions.'*

"Well, looks like you were right," Mason sounded amazed. "I still don't understand how you expect to destroy him, though, what can you do? *Heal* him back to hell?" he asked, shaking his head in disgust.

"Not exactly the plan. My 'gift' has grown stronger over the past few years, and I've learned to control it better. I've never used it to harm anyone, but I'm betting it can be used either way. I guess I'll find out soon enough."

"You don't need to do this, Dr. Chandler," April told her. "Mason and I are responsible for our own mistakes. You don't know what you're getting yourself into, this asshole is the king of all liars, a veritable snake, and dangerous as hell! If he thinks you're jacking with him, he'll kill you in a heartbeat. Torture is a game to the rat bastard, he gets his freakin' jollies making humans suffer. Please, I'm begging you, don't do this!"

Mia smiled at the young woman. Rising from her chair, she hugged her. "I appreciate your concern, but I don't believe I'll need my 'gift' to defeat this creature. Evil will never conquer good, they merely balance each other out, yen and yang, etc. ... I can't destroy him, it's not in my nature to harm others, all I can do is try to right the wrong that's been done here," Mia explained patiently.

Mason stared at her. "So, you're heading into the lion's den, to what? Make him an offer he can't refuse? I'm sorry, guess I don't understand, but this sounds like a suicide mission to me!" Mason proclaimed angrily.

"Believe me, I have no intention of forfeiting my life to the likes of him. I simply plan to challenge him to a game—winner take all," Mia said calmly, with a shrug.

They all stared at her with apprehension. "Wait a damn second, you're going to risk your life and your immortal soul by challenging him to a stupid game?" Dianne erupted. "That's crazy, Mia! What the hell are you thinking?" Dianne was exasperated by her friend's logic. She was regretting having asked for her help in this debacle.

"If I didn't think I could defeat him, I would never have volunteered my help. I'm fully aware of the danger and the risk involved. What's life without risk? The hard part will be coercing him to agree to my choice of game," Mia replied soberly.

"This is insane, Dr. Chandler," Mason argued. "Please listen to me, no matter what game you choose, you'll lose. He'll find some way to cheat, and you'll be up shit's creek without a paddle. It's what he *does*! I don't know why you won't listen to us, we've seen him in action! Please don't throw your life away trying to outfox this demon. My conscience is guilty enough, without having your death on it," he implored her to change her mind.

His pleas were beginning to make Mia doubt her plan. *What if he's right? What if she was being too over-confident?*

No. She wouldn't allow the seeds of doubt he'd planted to take root in her. If that happened, she'd lose her courage, and they'd all die because she hadn't trusted her own intellect. She couldn't allow that to happen.

"I'm afraid it's too late to change the plan. He's agreed to meet me, and if I don't show, we're all screwed. It's a done deal, so stop trying to talk me out of it," she said calmly.

Mason looked at April, who shrugged in defeat. Dianne didn't like it at all. She'd only brought Mia into this mess because of her ability to heal, deluding herself that her friend's 'gift' could somehow save them from the demon's wrath. She might've imposed a death sentence on her friend and them all by doing so.

"Well, you're sure as hell not going to meet with him alone. We'll all go, we're in this mess together now, for better or worse," Dianne said adamantly.

"That sort of defeats the purpose, doesn't it? I mean, if we all go, we'll be doing exactly what he wanted in the first place," April pointed out.

"Sadly, I think she's right," Mason agreed. "There'd be nothing to keep him from killing us all should he decline to play this game you have in mind. Speaking of which, what game are you planning to challenge him with?"

"Chess," Mia replied simply.

"Chess? I'm sure he's terrible at that, he's only had, like, a gazillion years to practice? He's probably a 'Grand Pooh-bah,' or whatever you call 'em," he said sarcastically.

"I believe you're referring to a 'Grandmaster.' I know, because I am one. I've been playing competitively since grade school, I'm pretty good, or I wouldn't have chosen it as my bargaining tool in the first place," Mia replied confidently.

"That's certainly a load off my mind. At least you're not challenging him to some stupid game of Tic-Tac-Toe or Marbles—though, you *are* sorta playing for all the marbles, aren't you," Mason said grimly.

"You're right, he's had a millennia to hone his skills. The question is, *has* he? I'd think a demon would spend most of its time in pursuit of humans to torture, and souls to collect. I somehow doubt it would fritter away its free time on a board game like chess. For one thing, chess requires too much patience," Mia surmised ...

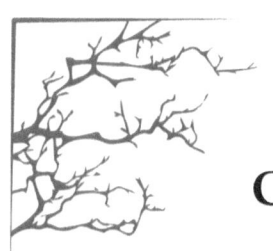

Chapter Twenty-Six

Austin, Texas

Adriel was furious with himself for having agreed to the meet with Dianne's "friend." He should have killed them all when he'd had the chance and been done with the whole mess. Nothing had worked as he'd planned with those two wretched musicians. He couldn't remember the last time he'd had so much trouble with humans. Instead, he'd let his curiosity get the best of him. Whoever this person was, Adriel was certain no one could convince him to release those two from their contracts.

Losing Alal to their treachery was a minor setback. Although they hadn't physically killed her in the fire, her essence would still require time to find another suitable human body to possess so that she could return to her gloriously evil self.

His original thought was to have this new "friend" come to his condo in West Lake hills for the meet, but after thinking it through, he'd decided against that. This one lacked the soundproofing the old one had and was not equipped with a dental chair. No, better to surprise them on their own turf. Make them sweat while they await his instructions for the meet.

He knew exactly where they were, so he needed little time to prepare. His private jet would deliver him to Boulder in less than an hour and a half. He had a place in mind for the meet. All he had to do now was let the bitch cop know the exact time.

Calling his pilot, he ordered him to have the plane gassed up and ready to leave in fifteen minutes. The pilot balked, saying he wouldn't have sufficient time to perform the necessary safety checks. Adriel told him he didn't care, to "get it done" or he'd find himself out of a job, or worse.

The pilot reported he'd do the best he could. Adriel grinned with wicked anticipation as he prepared to depart for the airport ...

Chapter Twenty-Seven

Boulder, Colorado

Dianne and the others spent the next hour waiting for Adriel's email. When an hour had come and gone with no word, it became apparent he was having second thoughts about the proposed meeting.

"What the hell is taking him so long? It's been over an hour, and we haven't heard a damn thing!" Mason groused, pacing the floor.

"Maybe he decided to forget the whole thing. I mean, what are a couple of souls to a creature like him when he has an entire planet of rubes to choose from?" Mia said, instantly regretting her choice of words.

Mason and April narrowed their eyes at her remark, but they knew she wasn't deliberately comparing them to "rubes."

"He's likely just trying to make us sweat. If so, it's working," Dianne said, wiping her sweaty palms on her uniform.

"He'd never let us go that easily. Not after what we did to Alal and his little shop of horrors. Mom's right, he's torturing us now, making us wait. I'm going out for a smoke, I can't just sit here twiddling my thumbs, it's driving me crazy!" April exclaimed, grabbing her purse and storming out of the office.

"You'll have to forgive my daughter, she's high-strung after all that's happened the past couple of days." Dianne apologized to Mia.

"I don't blame her a bit. It's not every day you have a supernatural creature from hell hunting you down for your soul."

Ten minutes later, April burst into the office with her new phone in hand and a strange look on her face. "Y'all need to check this shit out! A private jet reportedly crashed in the Chihuahua Desert in New Mexico a few minutes ago, in route from Austin to Boulder. This could be our lucky day!"

Thirty minutes earlier...

AS HIS LEARJET SOARED high above the New Mexican desert far below, Adriel was busy working a crossword puzzle on his phone, trying to come up with a five-lettered word for 'irony.' Abruptly, the aircraft shook like a rat caught in a terrier's mouth.

"Shit! We have a major problem, sir—we've lost power to the starboard engine and the other one is malfunctioning as well. I'm afraid we're going down!" his frantic pilot exclaimed.

"Well, if you wish to continue your pathetic existence in this world, I strongly suggest you rectify the problem immediately," the demon snarled over the intercom.

"Mayday! Mayday! Mayday! This is Learjet Alpha 449'er—experiencing catastrophic engine failure—will execute emergency landing protocol—30 kilometers due south of Santa Fe Regional—repeat—executing emergency landing protocol—in ... 55 seconds!" the pilot urgently called over the radio.

"Roger, Alpha 449'er, we have you on scope. At present rate of descent, radar contact will be lost in approximately 40 seconds. Be advised, emergency personnel are en route, ETA approximately 45 minutes. God speed, Alpha 449'er, over," the air traffic controller's calm, robotic voice replied. The airspeed indicator was holding at a steady 200 knots as the jet continued its glide toward the desert floor.

"Better buckle up and assume the crash position, sir. We have about three minutes 'til we run out of sky. I can glide us in, but it's going to be dicey, at best," the pilot told Adriel over the intercom.

As it glided over the craggy landscape below, an eerie quiet filled the cabin of the mortally wounded plane. The features of the surrounding desert grew clearer as the ground rushed up to meet them. Adriel cursed as he realized forcing the pilot to cut corners on the pre-flight safety check had been a grievous error. Glancing out the window, his demon blood froze at the sight of the rugged terrain strewn with massive boulders.

"Brace yourself! It's going to be a rough lan—" were the pilot's last words. At nearly 200 miles an hour, the jet's undercarriage slammed into a series of small boulders, shredding the wheels. The impact sheared away the landing gear, forcing the crippled aircraft's nose into the desert floor, flipping the plane end over end. The crash ruptured the fuel tanks as remnants of the fusilage careened into a huge pile of boulders and exploded in a hellish fireball, filling the desert air with thick black smoke that could be seen for miles. The pilot died upon impact, his mangled remains later identified through dental records. Adriel had been thrown clear of the wreckage, only to have his body set ablaze by burning jet fuel.

A lone coyote was the only creature to hear his screams as it cowered in the scrub brush a hundred yards away. It raised its mournful voice to join his until both were drowned out by the roar of the raging inferno. Adriel's essence, of course, could not be destroyed. His demonic spirit was ejected from its human shell, returning to the netherworld from which it had come.

The myths of a hell ruled by fire and brimstone were just that, fiction. As cold and black as space itself, it was an infinite void of darkness, inhabited exclusively by countless souls of the damned and their demonic overseers. Demons feared fire above all else. It destroyed their hosts, leaving them with no option but to seek another. Rituals of exorcism rarely worked in the real world.

In time, Adriel would return and exact his revenge upon hapless humans, but for now, he was powerless, caught between twin planes of existence. The distant wail of approaching emergency vehicles caused the lone coyote to flee into the surrounding scrub and disappear. Turkey buzzards circled high overhead, enticed by the carnage below, sensing a fresh meal in the making. An ambulance and firetruck made their way to the burning wreckage to extinguish the fire and begin the futile search for survivors ...

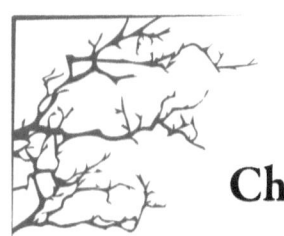

Chapter Twenty-Eight

Boulder PD

" *Holy Crap*! I think you may be right. Did the report mention any survivors?" Mason asked her, reading the newsfeed out of Santa Fe for himself on April's phone.

"They didn't elaborate. All they said was emergency crews were presently working the scene of the crash," April replied hopefully.

"I'll put in a call to Santa Fe PD and see if they can give me an update," Dianne advised, picking up her phone. "It's probably too soon, they'll have the FAA and emergency crews to deal with before they can reveal any information." Patiently, she waited while the call was transferred twice before finally reaching the captain on duty.

After a brief conversation, she hung up and turned to the rest. "As I said—too soon. She did say it was a Learjet and confirmed there were two casualties, but nothing more. She promised to keep me in the loop, that's the best we can hope for right now," she said, feeling mixed relief and unease. Until they knew for sure the demon was one of the deceased, they'd all need to keep their guards up.

Mia got up from the computer and stretched. "Well, it appears your problem may have solved itself. I can stay and wait awhile if you like, at least 'til you hear something more conclusive. Otherwise, I need to head back to Joseph. The hospital where I work is chronically short-handed," she informed the group.

"Thanks, Mia. I appreciate your coming, but I honestly don't know what to tell you. If it turns out he's one of the deceased, then no worries. If not, we'll have to deal with it. If you don't mind hanging around for a little longer, I'll make it worth your while," Dianne suggested.

"I like the sound of that. Just don't set me up with one of your girlfriends. I'm officially abstaining from the dating scene. The last one didn't work out too well," Mia said, only half-joking.

"Sorry about that. Duly noted and filed for future reference," Dianne said. "I don't know about you guys, but I'm starving. I was thinking we could grab some 'In-N-Out' burgers, my treat, if that's okay with everyone?"

They all agreed, and left the station. Dianne paused on the way out to inform the front desk sergeant she'd be back shortly. They stepped out into the cooling air, as the setting sun sank behind the majestic mountains to the west as everyone piled into Dianne's cruiser.

"If Adriel was on that plane, there's no way he could've survived, right?" April asked uncertainly.

"There's no way to know for sure. Until I hear something from Santa Fe PD, we need to presume the worst," Dianne said. "We don't know what it might take to destroy a creature like himself. If that witch, Alal, was any example, I'm guessing fire can destroy their bodies, if not the demon itself. We'll just have to keep our fingers crossed," she tried to reassure her daughter.

She pulled into the drive-thru of the popular burger joint and ordered their food. Pulling up to the window, they waited for the cashier to hand out the bags of food and drinks. Paying the cashier, she drove back to the station, where they all sat and ate inside the cruiser.

"I'm sure I ordered onion rings, did they screw us at the drive-thru?" Mason griped, searching the bag and finding none.

"Here, you can have mine, I'm not as hungry as I thought," April said, placing them on his lap.

"What's wrong, babe?" Mason asked, hungrily stuffing an onion ring in his mouth.

"Maybe I'm just stressing over this shit. It's like one huge horrible nightmare. I guess it's hard to believe it might finally be over," she replied. Handing him her untouched burger, she got out of the car to have a smoke.

Dianne's phone chimed. Answering it, she listened for a couple of beats, thanked the caller, and disconnected. "That was Captain Jenkins at Santa Fe PD. There's good news and bad. The good news is that the plane *was* registered to Adriel Abaddon. The bad news is, both bodies at the crash scene were too badly burned to be identified. We'll have to wait for forensics to do their job before we know for sure. But given it's been over two hours now with no email, I'd say it's a good bet the bastard's toast," Dianne said confidently.

Mason got out to relay the news to April, who'd missed the conversation in the car.

"It fucking figures. They'll never be able to identify his body," she snorted, tossing her smoke to the pavement in disgust.

"Doesn't matter, either way, he's out of our lives. You should be thrilled to be finally rid of him. We ought to be celebrating," he pointed out.

"I guess you're right, but my gut tells me we haven't seen the last of that asshole."

Mason felt the same but didn't reply. He hugged her to him, kissing her forehead.

"Everything will be alright, you'll see," he tried to assure her.

"I'm gonna head back to Enterprise now," Mia said. "Sorry I couldn't of more help, but it's good that things turned out better than expected. I'm glad I didn't have to face that awful creature, the thought of losing my soul to creature like that sends shivers down my spine," Mia said truthfully. In fact, she'd been truly terrified of meeting the demon face to face. "If you need me for anything else, please give me a shout. I hope this will be the end of your troubles," she said, taking out her phone to call Scott.

"I'll give you a lift to the airport, it's the least I can do after dragging you all the way out here," Dianne insisted.

"That's very kind of you, girlfriend. I'll give Scott a heads-up and tell him we're on the way.".

Mason and April climbed into the cruiser. Dianne started the engine and drove them to the airport. When they arrived, Scott was standing by his plane, chewing the fat with one of the ground crew.

"I didn't expect you back so soon. Juan here informed me a Learjet went down in New Mexico a couple hours ago. Tough break. Word is, there were no survivors," he said grimly.

"Yeah, tough break," Dianne said coolly.

Scott didn't bat an eye. "Anyway, they'll be done gassing her up shortly. I'll finish the pre-flight safety checks, and we'll be ready to go wheels up in five," he climbed back into the cockpit.

Mia gave Dianne and the others brief hugs. Mounting the stairs, she waved goodbye.

Dianne, April, and Mason watched from the car as the turboprop's engines revved up to speed. As the plane taxied onto the runway, preparing to take off, Dianne glimpsed Mia waving from the co-pilot's seat. Turning the cruiser around, she drove them back to the cop shop.

"I have some paperwork to finish before I leave for the night," Dianne explained as they entered her office. "Mason, you're welcome to stay with April and myself, at least until you can make some other living arrangements. I have a spare bedroom you can use, it's small, but functional," she offered.

"How magnanimous of you, mother," April said frostily, her voice dripping with sarcasm.

"I'm trying my best to compromise, April Mae. In the current situation, I thought he'd appreciate having a safe place to stay. If that's not agreeable, he can choose somewhere else to live, but not you together. I know I'm being a hard ass, but until you turn twenty-one, I'm still your legal guardian. If he wants to live in my house, he'll have to follow my rules. Is that clear?" Dianne said firmly, arms crossed.

"Yeah, crystal clear. What hypocritical bullshit! You and dad lived together before you got married, but it seems you've conveniently forgotten that. I suppose what's good for the goose isn't good enough for the gander," April snapped angrily.

"Are you *planning* to get married?" Dianne looked from her to Mason, cocking her brow.

At the question, Mason felt cross-examined. "Uh, w-we actually haven't discussed it. Ever since we met, things have happened so fast," he replied truthfully.

April glared at him, but she had to admit he was right—they had never discussed it. "How about it, Ace? You wanna marry me or not?" she asked, putting him on the spot.

Shit! "Look, can we at least have a little time to talk privately about it before we decide? Don't get me wrong, I love you, I really do! It-It's just ... I'm not in a great position to provide for you right now," he said, instantly regretting his words.

"*Provide* for me? Listen, bud, I can take care of myself. I don't need a fucking man to provide for me. I need someone who loves me enough to let me make my own choices and my own mistakes without judging me, not some *Daddy-Fucking-Warbucks*!"

"That's not what I meant, and you know it. C'mon, babe, I wasn't trying to be condescending, I'm just saying that—I don't know *what* I'm saying—you kinda threw me a curveball, I guess. Of course, we'll get married, if that's what you want," he replied quickly, before he could change his mind.

"The real question is, what do *you* want, Ace? Do you see us still together in six months, a year, maybe twenty? I'm not making that kind of a commitment unless we share the same vision of our future, musically and otherwise," she said soberly.

"Before we jump off the deep end here, don't you think it would be smart to wait until we know for sure that Adriel isn't still breathing air? If he's still alive, this entire conversation could be moot," Mason pointed out, artfully dodging her question.

"It doesn't matter whether he is or isn't. I've been nauseous the past few days. I—I think I may be pregnant!" she blurted, on the verge of tears.

The look on his face was priceless. "What? How the hell could that happen? You told me you were on the pill," he exclaimed sharply, making her jump. Dianne gaped at her daughter.

"Yeah, sorry, Ace, I lied. My prescription ran out, and I couldn't afford to see a doctor to get another one. In case you didn't notice, I wasn't exactly rolling in dough when we first met. It's my fault, not yours," she said, crying now.

"Babe ... that doesn't matter, it takes two to tango. But isn't it a little early to be experiencing morning sickness? Hell, it's only been—what—three days since we ..." he trailed off, mindful of her mother standing a few feet away, taking all this in.

"April Mae, it can't be morning sickness, not if you've only been having sex for a few days. It's probably just stress," Dianne said, taking a tentative step toward her, then hugging her weeping daughter.

"True, these past few days haven't exactly been a joyride," Mason added somberly.

"I'm gonna take off early tonight, the paperwork can wait, let's go home. I've missed you so much, I just want you to be happy and safe. I know I've been a terrible mother, but please give me a chance to make it up to you," Dianne pleaded softly in April's ear.

April was the first to break the embrace. "Alright, on one condition," she sniffled, wiping her nose with the back of her hand.

"What would that be?" Dianne asked cautiously.

"Mason sleeps with me, in my bed, not the spare bedroom," April said firmly.

Dianne held her tongue. If that was what it took to mend the break between them, then so be it. "Okay, you win. Just so you understand, you're going to have to earn your keep. If you expect to stay longer than a month, you're both gonna find jobs and help pay the rent. No one gets a free ride," Dianne said, trying to reassert some control.

Mason nodded, then looked at April. "I don't have a problem with that. But I need to be completely honest with you both. There's a possibility that I really am pregnant," she said dismally, avoiding eye contact.

"Why would you think that?" Mason asked uneasily.

Nervously, April paced the room. She'd been mostly truthful with Mason up to this point, but it was time to come clean. "I'd had sex with Adriel before I met you, remember?" she said, looking him in the eyes.

"Yeah, you also said that he only liked it ... you know ..." he said, trying to put it delicately.

"The old back door boogie? The *Hershey highway*? Yeah, that was his preference. But ... about a month ago, we did it the normal way. I begged him to stop before he finished, but he had me face down on the bed, and I couldn't—"

Dianne stopped her. "That's enough. We get your drift, we don't need all the sordid details," she said curtly, her face flushing.

Mason cringed at April's shocking admission, as embarrassment, anger, and jealousy all fought for possession of his emotions. "So, it's conceivable that he could have impregnated you. That's just great!" he growled angrily, wanting to punch something.

"Do I need to remind you this was before I met you, Ace? Give me a freakin' break, okay? And it only happened the one time, for cripes sake!" April shot back, defensively.

"If I remember my biology 101 correctly, that's all it takes. Jesus, what an unholy mess!" he ranted. Shaking his head, he stormed out of the room, slamming the office door.

April started to go after him, but Dianne stopped her. "You'll need to get tested to be sure, if only for your peace of mind," she said logically. "Let Mason blow off some steam, he's angry and hurt, give him time to cool off. You both need to sit down and talk this thing through," she advised.

"If I'm pregnant, there's no way to determine who the father is. You can't get a DNA sample from Adriel if he's been burned to a crisp. What if the baby turns out to be like him? This is so screwed-up!" April groaned, sobbing uncontrollably.

Dianne hugged her precious daughter and stroked her hair, trying her best to comfort her. "First thing we need to do is get a test kit. Worrying isn't going to change the outcome. Let's go find Mason, and we'll stop by the drug store on the way home," she urged, handing her a tissue.

April blew her nose and nodded. They left the building to find Mason leaning against her cruiser, smoking a cigarette. Dianne walked a few steps away to give them some privacy.

"Since when did you take up smoking, Mr. Hypocrite?" April challenged him, walking over, and taking it out of his hand for a puff.

"I quit years ago, but if it makes you feel better, I had a small relapse, okay? They still taste like crap, and now my head is swimming," he said with disgust, waving it away when she offered it back. "I could *really* go for a big, fat joint right about now. My nerves are shot to hell and back," he grumbled.

"I have just what the doctor ordered here in my purse. We'll have to wait until we get to the house, you still can't smoke it in public."

"Smoke what in public?" Dianne asked cautiously, approaching them.

"Weed. We're both jonesing bad, it's been at least a day since we've had any," April said nonchalantly.

"*A whole day*? That's terrible! I don't know how you've survived this long," Dianne exclaimed, hands flying up to her face in mock horror. "Honestly, as a cop, I don't condone its use, but personally, as long as you don't 'flagrantly advertise' and you're not driving a vehicle, I could give a rat's ass about it. If you feel the need to toke, you'll just have to do it discreetly in the backyard, not in my house," she added firmly.

Mason was visibly relieved. He'd expected her to read them the riot act. Instead, she—a cop—was basically giving them carte blanche to get lit whenever they felt like it, as long as they were careful.

"Appreciate that, Ms. Flowers. I'll certainly be prudent about it, I don't want to look a gift horse in the mouth," he said earnestly.

"This gift horse's name is Dianne. You're allowed to use it, you're not in the fifth grade anymore, for crying out loud," Dianne scolded.

They got in the cruiser once again, and Dianne headed for the local CVS.

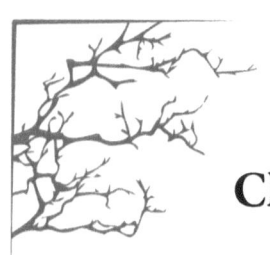

Chapter Twenty-Nine

Santa Fe City Morgue

D r. Charles Brown, Santa Fe's Chief Medical Examiner, pulled back the sheets shrouding the crispy remains of two unidentified bodies brought in from the crash site.

"*Yum*, these dudes smell like barbecued pork ribs. Reminds me, I haven't eaten dinner," his assistant, Dick Smelter, observed. Dick's macabre sense of humor was legendary among the staff.

"They're from that plane crash in the desert earlier," he reminded the doctor. "Dude must have shit a golden brick as he was goin' down. Freakin' shame. They were only a couple minutes away from a nice, smooth runway," he shook his head, crossed himself.

"Why don't you go get yourself something to eat, Dick. I'll take care of these two. I wouldn't want you to faint from hunger," Dr. Brown suggested sarcastically.

Dick's comments might annoy, but he was a valued employee. Few people could stomach the sights and smells of the "dead zone," as most of the staff called it. Charlie had gone through five assistants in the past three years—none of whom had lasted more than a few days. Dick had worked for him for over a year, and Charlie was grateful he was still there.

When Dick had gone, Charlie examined the larger of the bodies first. The flesh, muscle, and organs had been incinerated, leaving only charred skeletal remains. The teeth had been fractured by the intense heat of the inferno. It would be difficult to extract any DNA from the corpse to identify him. Even the bone marrow had been destroyed.

"Looks like you had one hell of a wienie roast, my friend," Brown muttered, working over the blackened corpse.

Wielding a surgical bone saw, he cut open the cranium and "popped the hood," so to speak, to examine the brain. As he'd expected, the brain had been liquefied, most of it cooked away. The cause of death was obvious, but Brown was meticulous about his work. Every soul that came through his door received the same attention to detail and the respect owed them. He thought of himself as a detective for the dead. He alone could divine the mysteries of who they were and how they'd met their end. Most of the time. Not so with this body. There would be no usable DNA to extract from Mr. Doe's corpse. Dental records would be useless as well. This one would end up in Potter's Field with countless other unfortunates who had defied identification over the decades.

As Charlie turned to pull up the sheet and cover the poor bastard, an indefinable sound issued from the autopsy table. He froze, turning to stare at the charred skeletal remains lying immobile on the cold steel platform.

Must be hearing things, could have sworn I heard ... he brushed the thought away. Reaching for an instrument on his tray, he fumbled and dropped it on the floor. Cursing, he stooped to retrieve it—and a blackened claw reached out and grabbed him by his throat. The doctor's eyes bulged in unmitigated terror as the cold, iron grip tightened, cutting off his airway. Frantic, he clutched at the charred, skeletal fingers clamped tightly around his neck like a bony vise, struggling to free himself from their deadly stranglehold.

Unfortunately, he only made things worse. The harder he fought, the tighter it grew. Through dimming vision, he watched as the re-animated corpse turned its blackened, grinning skull toward him. Before he died, he heard the ghastly thing hiss, "*I'mm baack!*" ...

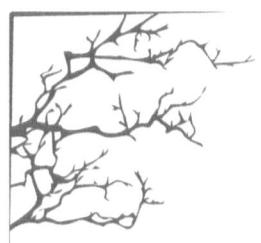

Chapter Thirty

Boulder, Colorado

Looking miserable, April stepped out of her mother's bathroom. She held out the test strip so Mason and Dianne could see the results. They leaned in, saw a tiny "+" symbol, and knew the reason for her dour expression.

"*Shit*! I'm so sorry, babe, but there's a fifty-fifty chance it could be false positive, you know," Mason suggested weakly, his gut churning like the inside of a washing machine. The thought that he might be a father sent waves of panic coursing through him.

"There's more than a fifty-fifty chance I'll bust someone's balls if they don't roll me a big, fat joint in about two minutes," she growled, flopping down on the living room sofa.

Dianne was about to admonish her when her phone chimed. She dug it out of her purse and saw that the Santa Fe PD was calling her.

"Detective Flowers? This is Captain Jenkins. I'm afraid I have some disturbing news regarding the crash victims you inquired about earlier," he said, without preamble.

Hearing this, Dianne's stomach tightened. "What have you discovered, Captain? Did you manage to get a positive ID on the victims?" she asked, gripping the phone tightly.

"Well, first things first. We knew the LearJet was registered to an initial A. Abaddon out of Texas, but we haven't located a passenger manifest for the flight. Since he filed the flight plan, we have the name of the pilot, but nothing to identify the other victim. Our Chief Medical Examiner, Dr. Brown, was supposed to perform the autopsies, but he's gone missing. No one seems to know what happened to him. His assistant stepped out for fifteen minutes to get a sandwich. When he returned, Dr. Brown had disappeared. They've tried his cell, his office, his home, nada," he explained.

"I'm not following—what does that have to do with the 'vics?'" she asked impatiently.

He paused before continuing. "His assistant found signs of a struggle in one of the autopsy bays. The most disturbing aspect was that he found several drops of blood on the floor and on two of the vic's charred fingers," he replied grimly.

Dianne felt a chill shimmy down her spine. "Any reason to suspect foul play?" she asked, knowing the answer.

"Frankly, we're baffled, but we're leaning that way. The corpse with the bloody fingers was discovered on the floor next to the autopsy table. And get this—both the corpse's middle fingers were extended, as if he were flipping everyone off."

Hearing this, the chill she'd felt earlier turned to ice. "Have you issued a BOLO (Be On Look Out) for the doctor? What about his cell, can you track it?" she asked, as her training kicked in.

"We've issued the BOLO. The GPS on his phone isn't working, either he disabled it, or his attacker may have destroyed it. It wasn't found at the scene," he said.

"What about his car?"

"The same. We're interviewing everyone who might've seen him leave the building, but so far, zilch. It's all very strange," he said soberly.

"What kind of vehicle does he drive? Make, model, tags, etc.?" she demanded.

"It's on the BOLO—he drives a gold BMW, but I doubt he's headed for your neck of the woods. He has a loving wife and three kids. It's unlikely he'd suddenly disappear without informing them of his plans—unless he was under duress, which, for the moment, is what we're assuming," he said with a sigh.

"When we interviewed him, the Assistant M. E. was quite distraught. He did say both remains were too badly burned, in his opinion, to extract any viable DNA. So, barring a miracle, the odds of positively identifying either body are slim to none," he added despondently.

"Well, thanks for the update, Captain Jenkins. If you find any leads on the doctor's whereabouts, please let me know. It could be important," she told him, ending the call.

Mason and April had been eavesdropping on the conversation between the two cops, shaken by what they'd heard.

"This doesn't sound good," Mason commented. "You think it's possible that Adriel somehow survived the crash and has taken the doctor hostage?" he asked Dianne.

"How the hell should I know? I didn't even believe demons existed until I saw them with my own eyes. They've confirmed the bodies of both 'vics' were still at the morgue, that kinda rules them out as kidnappers," she snapped sarcastically, clearly agitated by this turn of events.

"Not necessarily," April offered. "What if his spirit, or soul, whatever you call it, survived and somehow took possession of the doctor's body?" Her suggestion was too terrible to contemplate.

"If true, we have a major fucking problem." Dianne replied sternly.

"That sorta makes sense if you think about it," Mason agreed. "What other reasonable explanation could there be? We need to get the hell out of here and find someplace safe to stay until they locate that doctor. If Adriel *has* possessed him, he'll be coming for us. I don't know about you, but I'd really rather not be here when he appears at your front door," Mason declared anxiously.

Dianne had to agree. They had no way to know for sure, in which case, the logical thing to do was run. If they stayed, they'd be sitting ducks. Better to be proactive and live to fight another day.

"Okay, I'll have to call my captain and request some time off. I have a week's vacation time accrued, so it shouldn't be a problem. I'll call Mia and see if we can hole up with her for a few days in Oregon. We won't be safe until they find that doctor. Possibly, not even then," Dianne picked up her phone to call her office.

Mason breathed a relieved sigh. April stood and strolled into the backyard to smoke the blunt he'd rolled while her mother spoke with her captain. He followed her into the yard, which had six-foot cedar privacy fencing around the entire property. A thick stand of bamboo lined the fence as well, giving them some privacy.

"I knew it was too good to be true. We'll never be rid of that bastard! If fire can't destroy him, there's little chance running away will solve our problem. He's smart, he'll find us no matter where we hide," she bitterly replied, taking a couple tokes, handing it to him.

"Well, in that case, maybe we need to seriously consider soliciting another priest to perform an exorcism." He sat by her in a green, metal lawn chair.

"Yeah? Look how well that turned out. Adriel would see it coming a mile away. Besides, there's no way to be certain it would work, and we'd be putting some innocent priest in harm's way. No, we need to come up a better plan,"

"I suppose we'll have to play it by ear until then," he shrugged. He was silent for a moment before he said softly, "Are you going to keep it?"

Lifting her head, she stared at him curiously. "Keep what?" she queried, her eyes glassy from the weed.

"The baby, of course, hello? Earth calling April. I think you need to slow down on that shit, it'll turn your brain to mush," he gently admonished.

"Mind your own damn business, Sir Drinks-a-Lot! And no, I haven't made up my mind about anything yet. I just found out I'm probably pregnant and then the news that Adriel may've not only survived the crash, but has possessed another innocent's body and is likely hunting us as we speak. So, I haven't exactly had time to think about that, thanks!"

He winced at the strong rebuke, wishing he'd never brought the subject up.

Dianne picked that moment to join them outside, displaying her disapproval of their activity by sniffing and fanning the air as if she were worried about contracting a contact high.

"We're all set. I called Mia and gave her the skinny, she's sending her pilot friend, Mr. Hardilek, right away to pick us up and take us to Enterprise, where she'll meet us. In the meantime, I thought you might gather some essentials to take on the trip," she told April.

"Uh, what 'essentials' might those be? We came here with only the clothes on our backs, I think that pretty much covers it," April gave her an eye roll.

"You don't have to be snide, April, I'm fully aware of that. You still have clothes and a suitcase in your closet. Mason will have to wait until we're there to buy warmer clothes," Dianne replied, turning on her heel to march back inside the house.

"She's trying to be helpful, babe," Mason rubbed April's tense shoulders. "Give her a break, we're all stressed to the max. Biting each other's heads off doesn't help. We're in this shit sandwich together, and we're all gonna have to take a bite to find a way out of this mess."

"She's always been such a damn control freak about everything. She stuffs her emotions and expects me to do the same. I'm sorry, but that isn't the way I'm built. My opinions don't seem to matter, and it pisses me, no end. With her, it's always been 'my way or the highway,'" she growled, re-lighting the extinguished roach and burning her finger. Angrily, she tossed it on the grass at her feet and stood.

"You'll excuse me, it seems I have some packing to do," she said irritably, striding into the house and leaving him standing and scratching his head.

Women—he'd never understand how their minds worked. He shrugged with typical male ignorance and walked back inside to wait for the two of them to get their stuff together. Picking up the TV remote, he turned it on to catch some of the ten o'clock news. The anchorwoman was droning on about some Hollywood A-list celebrity caught up in a scandal that Mason didn't know or care about.

Abruptly, a large red banner that screamed "Breaking News" filled the screen, grabbing his attention. He turned up the sound. "This just in, State Police in Santa Fe, New Mexico, are searching for a missing doctor. Dr. Charles Brown, the Chief Medical Examiner, was last seen around 8:00 p.m. today and is thought to be driving a gold-colored, late model BMW sedan with the license plates DLV6969. Anyone with information about his current location is asked to call or text the number on your screen. Authorities believe the doctor may been coerced to leave. Now over to the weather," the newswoman said cheerfully. Mason muted the newscast.

He turned around to alert April and Dianne and found them standing behind him. Obviously, they'd heard it all, and wore similar expressions of dismay.

"Shit! It's Adriel, he's coming for us!" April exclaimed anxiously.

"We don't know that for sure, babe," Mason tried to calm her. "I don't think we need to rush, it's, like, a seven-hour drive from Santa Fe to Boulder.

Even if he drove at top speed, it would take him around four hours," Mason proclaimed.

"Well, regardless of that, we're not taking any chances. According to Mia, Mr. Hardelik should be here in less than two hours," Dianne said confidently.

"Yeah, but what if Adriel isn't *driving*?" April argued logically. "If he chartered a plane, he could fly here in a little under two hours. *Crap*! He could already be here. We need to get the hell out of Dodge, now! He knows where you live, Mama, he could show up on our doorstep any minute," she warned. Mason looked to Dianne to be a calming influence.

"She may be right, better safe than sorry. We can go hang out at that Waffle House by the airport until Mr. Hardilek arrives," Dianne said, making a hurried decision.

"Let's go! We're wasting time," April urged, grabbing her small suitcase and heading for the front door.

On the fly, Dianne locked up the house, tossed their suitcases haphazardly into the trunk of her cruiser, and they clambered inside. She backed out of the driveway and sped out toward the airport. In their haste to get moving, none of them noticed the black SUV parked three houses down as they passed by. Its headlights came on as it pulled away from the curb and followed them ...

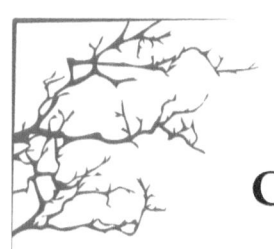

Chapter Thirty-One

Joseph, Oregon

Mia had just gotten home from the airfield when she received the distress call from Dianne. Mia told her she'd ask Scott to come get them and fly them to back to Joseph. Where she could put them all when they arrived was a question for later. Her house only had two small bedrooms and one shared bath. The small, screened porch out back was ill-suited for sleeping outdoors this time of year, as the unpredictable weather could drop six inches of snow in only a few hours.

Sitting down, she called her half-brother, Pete Chandler, who worked as a deputy sheriff for Wallowa County. Her adopted aunt, Missy Anderson, was currently the Sheriff, his boss.

"Got a huge favor to ask, Bro," she said.

"Yeah? What's up?" Pete replied.

As briefly as possible, she filled him in on the current situation in Boulder, omitting nothing important. When she finished, he was dumbfounded.

"*Holy crap*! You gotta be joking—an honest-to-God demon? How the hell do you get yourself involved in such crazy shit, Sis?" he exclaimed.

"Just lucky, I guess. Anyway, think you could put one of them up in your spare bedroom for a couple days?" she entreated. "I know it's an imposition, but my old bedroom is vacant. I'll ask Missy and Jake, as well. They still have that trailer by the side of their house, and it would be perfect."

"Good luck with that. You know how well Jake takes to having strangers dropped on his doorstep unannounced. Remember what happened a few years ago when Missy invited Gus to stay during the pandemic," he said, knowing full well that she did.

"Yes, but Gus's life was not in imminent danger at the time. Dianne's and the others' *are*, right now. I'll take the issue up with Missy when they return, but you're right. Convincing Jake may take some nut twisting, since they have their hands full now with Mandy and the book tours," she recalled with a sigh.

Amanda, or Mandy, was Missy's and Jake Anderson's three-year-old daughter, whose wild temper tantrums occurred without warning, depending on her mood. Jake cared for her during the day while Missy, as Sheriff, had to be at work. Jake worked on his novels during the evening hours. Their eldest daughter, ten-year-old Belinda, or Bella, as they lovingly called her, helped care for Mandy once she got home from school. Between his work and hers, they saw little of each other these days, and the resulting tension had strained their relationship to the breaking point.

"I suppose I could put one of them up here for couple of days, though frankly, I don't like it, Sis," Pete shifted uneasily. "If they have an actual demon after them, that'll place all of us in grave danger. I sure as hell don't want to come home from work one day to find some horrible creature lounging on my couch, waiting to kill my happy ass."

"I'll admit, there is some danger, but, hopefully, they'll resolve the issue swiftly. If the cops find that missing doctor soon, it shouldn't be a problem," she glanced at the time on her phone.

"Yeah, but what if they don't?" he asked flatly.

"Then we'll deal with it the best we can. Sometimes you need to have a little faith, brother," she said evenly.

"Faith isn't the problem. I've got plenty of faith in my nine-millimeter Glock, but that won't stop a freaking demon, for cryin' out loud!" he was growing agitated just thinking of it.

"I know you're concerned, Pete, but they don't have many options. If he does somehow locate them, they'll need our help." Mia had learned early on that her brother was a worrier and she couldn't change that about him.

"I have a bad feeling about this, Sis. I hope you know what you're doing. A lot of lives may depend on it. How the hell are we expected to protect them if he shows up? Do you even have a plan?" he asked.

"Actually, I do," she replied. "Unfortunately, I don't have the time to explain it right this minute. I need to hit the shower, grab a quick bite to eat.

Why don't you come over, you can babysit Jinx 'til Missy and Jake arrive. Ava left me a note saying they'd be by to pick him up on their way home from the book tour." Walking into her house, she locked the door, took off her clothes, and tossed them in the dirty clothes hamper on the way to the shower.

Reluctantly, he agreed, and disconnected. Running his hand nervously through his short, blond hair, he snatched his keys off the key rack by the front door and left his house, locking the door. From the moment he'd been reunited with his half-sister when she was sixteen, he'd found that, along with her miraculous ability to heal others with her "gift," she also seemed to attract trouble like a magnet. Maybe it was the universe's way of balancing the yen and yang of things. Personally, he thought it could all be blamed on bad luck. He climbed into his ancient Honda CRV and drove the four miles separating his sister's house from his own, passing a fragrant grove of tall pinons and silvery aspens that lined the highway near her house.

The residence had been built on a rocky slope sheltered on three sides by a dense copse of tall pines and assorted native shrubs. As he neared the house, he spotted a large mule deer in his headlights as it bounded off into the forest.

He pulled to a halt behind Mia's car, killed the engine, and got out. If not for the front porch light, he would've needed a flashlight to find his way to the front door. Once the sun set in these mountains, the dark was absolute. He knocked twice on the door, using his key to enter. Jinx glanced up from his nap on the sofa as Pete closed the door.

"Hey, fuzz-face, you don't look like you need babysitting to me," he addressed the big cat. Jinx blinked his yellow-green eyes in disdain, lowering his head to lick his balls. "You don't know how many times I've wished I could do that," Pete chuckled, shoving the bobcat over and taking a seat beside him.

"Wished you could do what?" His sister's voice startled him as she stepped into the room, toweling her damp, curly hair.

"Er, nothing. Just thinking out loud."

One glance at Jinx and she knew what had prompted Pete's wish. "Forget about it, you'd be coughing up hairballs all the time. Men are such pigs!" Casually, she slapped the back of his head.

His face flushed, he declined to reply, changing the subject instead. "What time do you expect them?" he asked, putting his feet up on the coffee table. Garnering a disapproving scowl from Mia, he set them back on the floor.

"If you're asking about Dianne, April, and Mason, about three hours, give or take. You want something to drink?" she replied, heading to the kitchen.

"Nah, I'm good. Actually, I was asking about the—Ouch! You sadistic fucker!" he yelped, shaking his thumb where Jinx had nipped him. He could swear the semi-feral bobcat grinned at him before jumping off the couch to join Mia in the kitchen.

Pete examined the digit for damage. Luckily, the bite hadn't broken the skin. "That's the last time I try to pet you, you malicious ball of fur!" he warned the big cat, not for the first time. Jinx didn't give a rat's ass *what* humans promised as long as he got his kibble.

"You ought to know by now not to pet him while he's cleaning himself," Mia chided with a smirk. Opening a small can of cat food, she dumped it in his bowl.

"That cat is too damn ornery. I don't know how they've put up with him all these years," he grumbled. Twin beams of halogen headlights glared off the living room windows as Jake's Ford-350 pickup pulled into the drive and parked.

"Looks like they're back," he announced, standing up to open the door. Mia joined him as Jake and Missy exited the truck, sans Belinda and Amanda, who were both asleep in the back seat of the cab.

"Sorry we're so late getting in, the plane was delayed at the airport. Some drunken dipshit on the flight got into an argument with a steward, and they had to restrain him until we landed," Jake Anderson said wearily.

The six-foot-two-inch writer's black hair was peppered with white. He appeared haggard from the whirlwind book tour that had required stops in ten cities over a period of seven days.

"It didn't help matters when Mandy threw up on that nice man in the seat behind her," Missy added. "I wouldn't have thought a man of the cloth could spout so many colorful expletives, but I don't blame him," she said wearily. The svelte, five-foot-ten-inch brunette yawned as they walked inside the house.

"Wait a second, did you say he was a priest?" Mia interjected, as Missy's story suddenly piqued her interest.

"Uh, yeah, pretty sure. He wore one of those collars, but he definitely wasn't speaking Latin when Mandy tossed her cookies all over him, though I wish he had. Why do you ask?" Jake grumbled blearily.

"Listen, something urgent cropped up while you were gone. If I can, I need to ask a huge favor," Mia replied hesitantly.

Jake groaned inwardly. When Mia asked for "a huge favor," it usually meant trouble. "If you're gonna ask me to do anything tonight, forget it. I'm so jet-lagged I can barely see straight. Plus, we need to get the girls to bed, it's way past their bedtime," he said truthfully.

"This—I'm afraid this matter won't wait. Let me catch you up to speed on what's been happening," Mia said soberly.

Sitting them down, she quickly brought them up to speed, while they both listened with growing apprehension. "So, to make a long story short, when they arrive, they'll need a place to stay for a couple days. Short of putting them up in a motel, the first place he'll look, I didn't know who else to ask," Mia finished.

Jake was shaking his head in disbelief. "I find it hard to believe they're being pursued by an actual pitchfork-carrying, soul-stealing, demon from hell. I'm sure they're frightened, but ... c'mon, *demons*? Seriously? As far as I know, they only exist in the Bible and in uneducated, superstitious minds. There's enough evil in the world without laying the blame on some mythological bogeyman," he snorted cynically—which was his first reaction to anything unusual.

"I never said he carried a pitchfork, and I'm not sure of the soul-stealing part," Mia replied. "But you, of all people, should know there are creatures and powers not of this earth that exist and are patently unexplained. I'm living proof. And, if I'm not mistaken, Missy, Pete, and you, Jake, faced just such a creature a few years back. Am I missing something here?" Mia asked, crossing her arms and lifting a brow.

He had tried hard to suppress the terrible memory of a shape-shifting monster that had tried to kill all three of them some years before. "Well, I suppose it's conceivable that an unknown entity or evil spirit could possess someone. There have been reported cases of *supposed* demonic possession throughout history and—" he began defensively.

Missy cut him off. "Don't be such an asshole, Jake. Just admit she's right," she snapped, glaring at him. Jake looked as though she'd slapped him.

Pete looked uneasily at Mia, who was at a loss for words. She knew Jake and Missy had been having marital problems for the past year. They'd both tried to hide it, but for those who knew them well, the strain in their relationship was apparent.

"As usual, *dear*, you're right. If you'll excuse me, I'm going to check on our daughters. Goodnight, Mia, Pete," he said curtly. In icy silence, he turned and stomped out of the house, slamming the door.

"Well, this is certainly awkward. If you won't be needing me any further, Sis, I'm gonna grab a little shut eye. I have a feeling I won't get much sleep tonight. Goodnight, Sis, Missy," Pete said, yawning, heading for the front door.

"I'll call you when they arrive and drive Mason over to meet you. I really appreciate it, Pete, and I know they will," Mia called out as he left the house.

Missy looked as if she were about to cry. Mia stepped over and embraced her, hugging her tightly.

"I-I'm so sorry, I didn't mean to be a bitch," Missy said bitterly, tears welling and spilling over. "It seems like lately, everything he says or does rubs me the wrong way. We—we've been having some issues for a while now, if you haven't noticed."

"No shit, Sherlock. Listen, Auntie, we've all been tiptoeing around this elephant in the room for some time now. Pete and I didn't want to say anything, but ... have you considered seeing a marriage counselor?" Mia asked.

"I've—we've danced around the issue ever since Mandy was born. I suppose we both deluded ourselves into thinking that things will get better with time. But they're not, they're getting worse. It's like we're caught in some vicious cycle, we constantly criticize each other over the stupidest fucking things," Missy despaired.

"I hate to burden you with this now," Missy told her. "If you want, I'll make other arrangements for Dianne and April when they get here. I'm sure they'll understand," Mia offered, knowing there were few other options.

"No—no, they're more than welcome to stay in the trailer. They'll be comfortable enough there for a few days. We'll just have to act normal—whatever the hell that is—while they're here," Missy said, wiping away tears with the back of her hand.

"Thanks a lot, Auntie. You go home and get some rest, it'll be a couple hours before they arrive," Mia insisted.

Missy nodded and turned to leave, when she stopped in her tracks. "Crap! I nearly forgot about Jinx. Where is he?" she asked, glancing around the room for the big cat.

"I was feeding him when you pulled in the driveway. He can't have gone far."

They stepped into the kitchen, but he wasn't there. "Jinx! Here, kitty-kitty," Missy called out, aware the feline was probably ignoring her. They searched Mia's room next, then the bathroom without finding him. That left only one possibility—Ava's room. Approaching it, they saw the door was ajar. Mia opened it, switched on the light—and found the mischievous cat sitting on Ava's bed, looking smug. The surly bobcat had left a small 'gift' on her pillow.

"Bad kitty. I'm truly sorry, Mia, you know he usually does his business outside or in the litter box. The only time he does this at home is when he's pissed at someone," Missy pointed out, grabbing tissues to remove the offending scat.

"No worries, Auntie, I'll change her pillow case. Ava just isn't a 'cat person,' and I think he sensed it right away. Cats know when someone likes them or not, right, Mr. Jinx?" she said with a chuckle, gathering the large bobcat up in her arms. Jinx didn't tolerate being picked up and held. Only Belinda and Mia could get away with it for any length of time. Missy hurried into the bathroom to flush the 'gift' down the toilet. Grabbing the oversized cat carrier—which was made for a dog—from Mia's bedroom, Missy stuffed him unceremoniously inside, and closed the gate. With some effort, she lifted the cage and staggered to the front door.

"Ugh, I need to stop feeding him so much. If he gets any heavier, I'll have to buy one on rollers," she said, struggling to keep her balance.

"I'll call you when they arrive. Oh, I almost forgot, you didn't get the name of that priest on the plane, did you?" Mia asked, helping Missy through the door.

"Nope, he wasn't exactly in a conversational mood. When we left the plane, he was still cursing in some obscure foreign language all the way down the Jetway. I don't mean to be rude, sweetie, but Jinx isn't getting any lighter. We both appreciate you looking after him this past week. See you in a bit—love you," Missy gasped, as she hurried to the pickup. Reluctantly, Jake got out and helped her load "Mr. Shits-a-Lot" into the bed of the truck without speaking.

Missy made up her mind right then to bite the bullet and call a marriage counselor as soon as possible. If they didn't address the problems soon, their marriage was in danger of sliding over the cliffs of doom.

THE SHORT DRIVE BACK to the Andersons' house was silent, save for the wee snores coming from Mandy in the back seat. Jake slowed at the turnoff to the paved road leading up to their residence. Their one-story house was situated about two hundred yards in from the highway, in the middle of a clearing that was surrounded by the Wallowa State Forest. The road had been nothing but gravel, pitted with potholes for many years. After the immense success of his latest bestselling novel, Jake had gotten it graded and paved. He parked the truck by Missy's police cruiser and got out.

"Let's go sleepy-head, we're home," he said, gently prodding Bella awake.

"Can Jinx sleep with me tonight, dad? I've missed his furry butt," she asked sleepily.

"I don't mind, you'll have to ask your mother. She may have an opinion on the matter, she seems to on every other subject," he grumbled, helping her out of the truck.

"I heard that, bud. As soon as we get the kids in bed, *we need to talk*," Missy said coolly, as she detach the sleeping Mandy from her safety seat.

Hearing that, Jake cringed. To a man, *'we need to talk'* were the four most dreaded words in the human language. *Crap!* ...

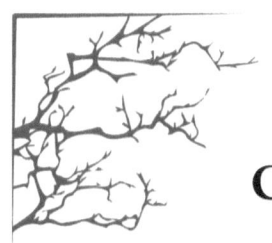

Chapter Thirty-Two

Near Boulder Regional Airport

Stealthily, the driver of the black SUV shadowed Dianne and her passengers into the parking lot of a local Waffle House, where he parked several cars away from the cop's vehicle. He watched through his tinted passenger-side window as the trio exited the car and went inside.

Adriel/Dr. Brown had wasted no time in selecting a new body to possess. In the morgue, the doctor had been too stunned to defend himself. The demon was still adjusting to his new physique. The physician had been in much better shape than Adriel's previous body, not that it mattered now. It wouldn't take much strength to kill those three. He was done playing games with these humans. Wherever they chose to hide, he'd eventually find them.

He smirked, thinking how much enjoyment he'd derive from torturing them each slowly, before dispatching them to hell for their treachery. Well, at least the souls of the six-fingered freak and his bitch would be his. Sadly, the mother had not foolishly bartered her soul—*yet*. There was always a remote chance he could snag hers, as well. If not, he would still have some fun with her before snuffing out her miserable existence.

He'd known the authorities back in Santa Fe would search for him—or rather, for the late doctor. In the morgue parking lot, he'd used the doc's gold BMW key fob to locate his car. He'd driven it to the airport and, using the doctor's platinum credit card, chartered a flight to Boulder without delay. Once he arrived, it had been relatively easy to steal a rental car. Still, he'd scarcely had time to park near the cop's house before they all scurried out the door and drove away, thwarting his plans to catch them off-guard. He'd need to be patient. He got out of the car and walked inside. By the cash register, a sign with magnetic letters read: *"Please wait, hostess will seat you."*

Feeling bored and a tad devilish, he glanced around the half-empty dining room. Seeing no one watching, he reached out, removed the "s" from the word 'seat,' and pocketed it, chortling to himself.

Moments later, a tired, middle-aged Hispanic waitress appeared from the kitchen. With a weary gaze, she led him to a seat two tables away from his quarry. Half a pencil protruded from her massive bee-hive hairdo, and he briefly wondered if the other half was embedded deep in her skull, like Excalibur, King Arthur's legendary sword. When she smoothly drew it from her hair to take his order, he was vaguely disappointed.

Her disappointment occurred when he ordered only coffee. "One moment, please," she said sweetly. Stalking away, she cursed hum under her breath, "Puto el cabron barato," which basically translated to "cheap fucking asshole" in English. Naturally, Adriel understood and spoke all human languages fluently. All demons were multilingual.

When she returned, she poured him a cup, plopping the pot down on the table. He grinned nastily at her and responded, "Gracias, la anciana. Por favor que tengas un dia de mierda."

She flushed, humiliated. Essentially, he'd called her an old woman and told her to, "Have a shitty day." She shuffled off in a huff, wanting nothing more to do with the rude gringo.

Meanwhile, Adriel pretended to browse the menu while keeping a close eye on Dianne and her companions. The same harried waitress brought out a tray with their food on it. Placing the steaming plates in front of them, she turned and walked back to the hostess station, giving him the evil eye as she passed his table.

He was on his third cup of Joe when the little redheaded bitch's mother got a call. She spoke too softly for him to hear the conversation, but her expression told him she was upset.

"Who was that?" April asked her mother as she chewed a bite of her strawberry waffle.

"That was Captain Jenkins in Santa Fe. Apparently, someone who matched the description of that missing doctor boarded a chartered plane a several hours ago." Dianne set her fork down; she'd lost her appetite.

"Did they have a physical description of the dude? Or where he might be headed?" Mason asked, a forkful of egg paused half-way to his mouth.

"I'm looking at the BOLO now. He's five-feet-eleven inches, forty-two years old, has a muscular physique, medium-length, light brown hair, a mustache, and hazel eyes. Here's the bad news—that airline only flies between Santa Fe, Denver, Colorado Springs, and Boulder. *Crap*! You were right, he's likely already here!" she exclaimed.

With that, her voice had grown loud enough that Adriel realized his cover was blown. If the cop even glanced his way, she'd recognize him in a heartbeat. Time for him to leave.

Opening the doctor's wallet, he took out a five-dollar bill and tossed it on the table as he calmly slid out of the booth, walked out of the restaurant, and climbed into the stolen SUV to await the trio's exodus. It had been foolish to follow them inside. He'd known at some point the authorities would post the doctor's physical description. He would need to be more discreet in the future, at least until he cornered them at their eventual destination. Originally, he'd planned on following them onto the plane. Now, that wasn't possible. He'd have to figure out another way or disguise himself somehow. He watched through the restaurant's large window as the trio inside stood up and headed for the exit.

ONCE OUTSIDE, THEY hopped in the cop's cruiser and sped off toward the airport, with Adriel trailing them at safe distance. He expected them to park in "short-term" parking, but the bitch drove past it without slowing. *Where the hell was she going?* Then he realized she was heading to the hangar for chartered planes.

Cursing his luck, he watched, frustrated, as she parked close to a private plane sitting on the tarmac outside the hangar. He could get no closer without arousing their suspicion, so he pulled to the curb and parked. He watched as they scrambled aboard the twin-engine Cessna Citation, raising the stairs and closing the cabin door behind them.

The aircraft taxied out on the runway and soared into the cold, black night. Thinking fast, Adriel jumped out of his rental and ran over to the hangar. Approaching a guy standing idly by a counter, he got his attention.

"Excuse me, my name is Dr. Charles Brown. I was supposed to be on that plane that just took off, but unfortunately, I was delayed. Is there any way you could provide me with its destination?" he prevaricated.

At his question, the man's eyes narrowed. He glanced down at his iPad. "Only three passengers were listed on the flight manifest, and I don't see your name there, doctor," the bald man said suspiciously.

"I was a last-minute addition. A passenger has a serious medical condition that needs my immediate attention. I was instructed to meet them but wasn't given the details of where she was headed," he lied.

The man briefly considered. "The pilot filed a flight plan to Enterprise, Oregon, and if you're wondering, there isn't another available flight until tomorrow morning," the guy said, looking at him skeptically.

Adriel had suspected as much. "I'll pay double your going rate if you can get me there tonight," he offered, with little hope.

"Sorry, doc, no can do. It isn't a matter of money. I won't have an available pilot until tomorrow. There's a nice motel down the road you can stay in for the night," he pointed back toward the highway.

"That won't be necessary. Tell me, are there any flights to a nearby town?"

The man scratched his balding head and frowned. "Well, there's the Joseph State Airport, it's the closest one. It says here it's around six miles from Enterprise. No commercial flights, though, only private charter."

"I don't suppose there are any available pilots for that destination, either?" Adriel was becoming exasperated.

"Sorry, but at this time of night, you'd be hard-pressed to find anyone who would fly you there. Even if you did, it'd cost an arm and a leg to fly a single passenger there."

Adriel was fast losing his patience; time to cut through the bullshit. "Are you, perchance, a pilot?" he asked through gritted teeth.

"Yes, I am ... but I—" the balding man started ...

"I'll pay you two thousand dollars if you'll fly me out of this shitty excuse for an airport in the next thirty minutes!"

"Uh, that's generous of you, doc, but I believe your offer is a little on the low side," the guy smirked. Adriel watched the wheels of greed spin in the man's piggy little eyes.

"Five grand, that's my final offer, take it or leave it," Adriel snapped, feeling absurdly like a game show host.

At this new offer, Baldy's eyes lit up. He could pay off his gambling debt to that cock-sucking loan shark, Jimmy Oslo, aka "The Hammer," and not because he was good at building things. The only things Jimmy ever nailed were the fingers and kneecaps of dopes who borrowed money from the fucker and didn't pay it back on time.

"It's a deal, doc. Of course, I'm gonna need the cash up front, since it's a one-way trip."

"Cash? You don't take credit cards?" Adriel asked incredulously.

"Well ... this has to be sorta kept under the table, so to speak, you understand?" Baldy said quietly, glancing around to make sure no one heard him.

Adriel understood, all right. The greedy asshole didn't want to give the company their cut of the money.

Adriel knew only one hundred dollars were left in the former Medical Examiner's wallet. If all his own credit cards hadn't been destroyed along with his previous body, he could have easily withdrawn it from his old account. That left him in somewhat of a pickle.

"Tell me, sir, what is it you desire most in the world ..." the demon asked, with a smirk of his own ...

Chapter Thirty-Three

Enterprise, Oregon

Dianne and her entourage stepped off the Cessna, greeted by a stiff north breeze that sent goosebumps racing up and down their spines. In their rush to leave, they hadn't thought to grab heavy coats from the house. April was already shivering in the frigid mountain air. The trip had been uneventful, save for some turbulence on their approach. Dianne thanked Scott again for the transport.

He smiled and gave her a wink. "You're welcome, and thanks for flying 'Hardilek Airways,'" he replied, tongue-in-cheek.

They spied Mia waiting for them by her car and rushed over with their meager luggage in tow.

"I hope you had a safe trip. Welcome to my little bit of paradise," Mia said, opening the trunk of her car. The ladies stuffed their belongings inside and climbed into the Mercedes' warm interior.

"Again, I'm sorry to impose on you like this, but I'm almost certain that Adriel is hot on our trail," Dianne said tensely. "They spotted a man who fit his description boarding a charter plane in Santa Fe with only three possible destinations, one of which was Boulder. I think we got the hell out of town just in the nick of time. I'm not positive we were followed to the airport, but if we were, and he saw us, you can be sure he'll figure out where we went, sooner than later."

"Que sera sera, not to worry. Even if he discovers your destination, no one else knows you're here. Scott certainly won't tell anyone, he's a savvy dude. If Adriel shows up and starts poking around, Scott has instructions to notify me ASAP, so try to relax," Mia said evenly as she drove. "My Aunt Missy assured me that two of you can stay in their trailer. It's fairly small, though, with only one bed, so there's not room for all three, but it should be comfortable enough for two of you," she added.

Mason wasn't happy hearing this. Logically, April and her mom would occupy the trailer. "Uh, and where will I be staying, if you don't mind my asking?" he asked tentatively.

"Well, I talked to my brother, Pete, and he's agreed to put you up in his spare bedroom for the duration of your stay. I, um, thought it would be best to put you with him. I didn't think April or her mom would be comfortable living with a male they didn't know. Don't get me wrong, Pete's a great guy, but he wanders about the house sometimes in the, um, 'Full Monty,' so to speak," Mia replied, as she reached the turnoff to Pete's house. In the headlights, the nearby forest looked foreboding and more than a little creepy to Mason. She parked in the driveway next to Pete's Honda and killed the engine.

"How far is this trailer from here?" Mason asked, as they got out of the car.

"It's about eight miles, give or take. Not that far away, really. Don't worry, April and Dianne will be fine, as long as they don't wander around in the dark and meet up with a bear," she cautioned.

April and Dianne shared looks of alarm. "You have b-bears out here?" April asked uneasily.

"Yeah, but they mostly keep to themselves. They forage at night and are easily frightened if they see a human. Except if they're with a cub. In that case, the prudent thing to do is to just slowly back away—whatever you do, don't run. Better yet, try not to go outside at night unless you have to. The trailer has a toilet, so you should be just fine," Mia advised, hoping she hadn't scared them.

Mason was beginning to think they'd made a mistake coming here. Not only would they be split up for the duration of their stay, but now he'd be worried for their safety as well. *Fucking bears*? *Seriously*? As if being chased by a demon wasn't dreadful enough, now he'd have nightmares of being devoured by voracious carnivores. He didn't know which was worse.

Pete opened the door for his guests. "You need help with luggage or anything?" he called out, stepping off his front porch.

"Um, Mason didn't bring any. They had to leave Austin rather abruptly. We'll have to go shopping tomorrow and pick him up some warmer clothes," Mia told him, introducing Mason and April.

Pete hadn't seen Dianne since the funeral for Mia's adoptive mom and his close friend, Kris Lacey, three years ago, so he gave her a big hug. He led them inside his two-bedroom home and asked if they'd like something to drink.

"I could use a shot of something alcoholic if you have anything on hand," Mason mumbled, looking about the room. April and Dianne both declined.

The first thing that caught Mason's eye was a beat-up Fender Strat perched on a guitar stand, sitting next to a small practice amp in the living room. "Do you play?" he asked Pete.

Pete looked momentarily confused, then chuckled. "I've been trying to learn a few chords, but I'm afraid I'll never be any good at it. How 'bout you?" He retrieved a half-empty pint of whiskey and a shot glass from a cabinet in the kitchen.

"Yeah, I had a rock band back in Austin, well, until everything went to shit, and I stupidly introduced them to that bastard, Adriel," he replied regretfully.

"Mia told me about all that. I still find it hard to believe, though I've had my own brushes with the supernatural, as she can readily attest." Pete poured Mason a shot of the amber liquid and handed it to him. "Her 'gift' saved not only my life, but Missy's as well. I honestly don't know how she does it, but best not to look question some things, right?" Pete added, taking a small swig from the bottle.

Mia interrupted them. "I'd better get these two out to Missy and Jake's. It's late and Missy has to get up early to feed the kids and get ready for work. My shift at the hospital is covered right now, so unless there's a dire emergency, I'll have the next few days off. Hopefully, this will all be resolved by then," Mia said.

April went over to Mason, wrapping her arms around him, and gave him a chaste kiss on the lips. "We'll be okay, for now anyway. I promise we won't go wandering around in the woods tonight. Pete, it was good to meet you, I appreciate you taking Mason in at the last minute. Hopefully, that asshole won't be able to track us here, but personally, I have my doubts."

"We'll keep an eye and ear out for anything suspicious. If Mr. Big Bad and Ugly shows up and starts trouble, he's liable to get a face full of buckshot," Pete boasted, with more bravado than he felt.

"I don't think buckshot'll take of the problem. If you could blow his head off, it might slow him down some—though he'd probably just grow another one," Mason snorted with scorn.

"If you see or hear anything suspicious, call me ASAP," Mia hoped nothing would exacerbate Pete's anxiety that night. "None of us will get much sleep tonight. The only way he can get here is by car or air. If it's the latter, Scott will notify me right away, so try to get some rest. Otherwise, we'll see you in the morning. Have a good night," Mia said, hugging her brother.

The profound trauma of losing both parents when she was only sixteen had caused Mia to create internal walls around powerful emotions like caring and loving. Kris, her adoptive mother, had helped her to lower those barriers until a bullet killed her. The support of Pete and the Andersons meant everything to her, but she was hard-pressed to articulate that, even to them. Without them, she'd have been completely lost and alone in the world.

Pete and Mason walked them out to Mia's car, waving as they drove away, until the omnipresent darkness swallowed their receding taillights from view. Mason was experiencing some spatial displacement. The sudden change from big cities to the mountain wilderness was disorienting, to say the least. The city didn't have large carnivores wandering loose that could eat you. He shivered at that last thought, following Pete back inside, as he shut and locked the door.

TEN MINUTES LATER, Mia pulled off the highway at the Andersons' turnoff and drove up the narrow lane bracketed on both sides by towering pines and poplars on the way to the house. She pulled to a stop and parked next to Jake's pickup and Missy's cruiser. Climbing out, they were greeted by the sweet, intoxicating smell of ponderosa pines permeating the chilly night air, reminding Dianne of the Christmas trees of her youth. Thoughtfully, the

Andersons had left the front porch light on for them. Without it, they'd have needed a flashlight to navigate in the near-total dark.

Mia had a key, but she tried the doorknob first and found it unlocked. They were expected. Otherwise, by this time of night, Jake would have bolted the door.

"Hello?" she called out softly, so as not to wake the children. Cautiously pushing the door open, she and the others stepped inside to find Missy and Jake sitting at their dining room table engaged in a muted but heated discussion.

Jake acknowledged their presence with a dismissive wave of his hand, stood without a word, and marched into their bedroom, closing the door quietly.

"Please, come on in," Missy said, "I'll have to apologize for Jake, he's being pig-headed, as usual. I'm Missy, and you must be April. It's good to meet you. Have a seat, can I get you anything to drink? I'm afraid we don't have any alcohol, as Jake's in recovery, but we have soda, coffee, tea, or maybe just some water?" Missy babbled, greeting her guests.

Mia could tell her adopted aunt was wound tight as a steel spring. Her tension was palpable.

"Oh, nothing for me, thanks," April replied uncomfortably, with a tight smile.

From the moment she set foot inside, Dianne knew something was amiss. Missy and Jake had obviously been arguing about something, and she believed she knew what it was.

"It's so good to see you again, Missy. I'm so sorry to impose on your family like this," she said, giving her friend a warm hug. As she released the embrace, she felt some of the stiffness in Missy's shoulders abate.

"It's good to see you, too, Dianne. You'll have to excuse my demeanor I—we've been having some problems for quite a while now. It isn't just this situation. Jake's finally agreed to see a counselor, I only hope it's not too late to salvage our marriage," Missy said, as they took seats around the kitchen table.

"I assume Mia has filled you in on our predicament. In all this insanity, I didn't know who else to turn to. She's been a godsend. I'm awfully afraid this ... *creature* knows where we went and will find us, no matter where we hide.

I don't want to endanger you or your family, but you should know up front, this demon—and that's truly what he is—will likely kill us when he finds us," Dianne said grimly.

"Then I strongly advise we figure out a way to send his demonic ass back to hell, or wherever he came from. Any suggestions on how we do that?" Missy glanced from face to face, waiting for someone to speak.

"I *was* going to challenge him to a game of chess, winner take all, meaning if I won, he'd relinquish their souls and void their contracts," Mia told her. "But that was before his plane crashed. I suspect after being burned to a crisp, he may feel a bit vindictive. Not to mention, having to go to all the trouble of finding another body to possess. I doubt he'll be in the mood to barter if he finds them."

"Do you think your 'gift' could help somehow?" Missy asked hopefully.

"I—I'm not confident it could destroy a supernatural being like him. In the past, I've only used it to heal. I'm afraid if I tried to use it to harm another—even a demon—I might risk losing it forever or make the situation worse if it didn't work. I think we need to arm ourselves with a priest and pray that he doesn't laugh in our faces when he's presented with this nightmare."

The others sat silent hearing this.

"I only know of one priest in town, and he's pushing ninety," Missy told her. "I don't think he'd be an ideal candidate to perform an exorcism. I suppose I could look on the internet and see if there's one in Enterprise, but I wouldn't get my hopes up. Even if we found one, convincing him our demon is authentic and we haven't lost our minds would be the real challenge. And we don't have a hell of a lot of time to get ready if this creature is hunting you," Missy explained.

At that moment, April felt something brush against her leg and almost jumped out of her skin at the sight of Jinx, who'd been lying, unobserved, underneath the table. "*Holy shit*! That's one big fuckin' cat!" she exclaimed, staring at him.

Jinx stared back at her until, without warning, he jumped onto her lap, all twenty-five pounds of him. Cautiously, she reached out a hand to stroke his large head, eliciting a rumbling purr of contentment from the bobcat.

"That's Jinx. He must like you. He rarely takes to strangers so quickly. A word of warning, he likes to nip—" Missy was saying, when he did just that.

"Ouch! He bit me," April hissed, shaking her hand, inspecting it for damage. Discovering no blood, she resumed petting him lightly, albeit far from the bobcat's head.

"He definitely likes you, he only does that with people he trusts," Missy just shook her head.

"Where in the world did you get him?" April asked, as the big cat curled up on her lap.

"Jake found him abandoned in the forest as a kit years ago, before I met him. He's only semi-domesticated, you can't take the wild out of a bobcat. He can surely be a handful, but he's saved our lives several times over the years, and I wouldn't trade him for a dozen rottweilers," Missy said affectionately.

Jinx yawned, and April got a glimpse of his needle-sharp fangs. "Yeah, I definitely wouldn't want to be on the receiving end of those babies," she observed, with a gulp.

"Well, let's get you both situated for what's left of the night. I need to get a little rack time, gotta be at work by 8:00 a.m. The trailer is replete with bedding and other essentials, such as toilet paper and soap. It has electricity, of course, and running water. Unfortunately, we're out of propane, so there'll be no hot water to bathe with tonight. I turned on the fridge earlier. We don't keep it on unless the trailer's occupied," Missy explained. Grabbing two flashlights from a kitchen drawer, she led them out the front door. Dianne retrieved their luggage from Mia's car and joined them on the porch.

Once outside the cone of the porch light, Missy switched on a flashlight and guided them through the pitch dark to the trailer, situated thirty feet to the side of the main house.

"Watch your step, these stairs are a little wobbly," she cautioned, opening the trailer door. Inside, she flipped a switch, causing the recessed florescent lighting to flicker and buzz to life. The ceiling inside was low, with barely enough headroom for Dianne and April to move around without crouching. April thought it was a little claustrophobic, but given the circumstances, was grateful to have it and said so.

"Well, it's not the Taj Mahal by any means, but it'll do in a pinch," Missy said with a yawn. "There's a walkie-talkie on the counter that's charged up and ready to go. If you have an emergency of any kind, use it. We keep the other one by our bed. Cell service out here is notoriously spotty."

"Thanks, Missy. Hopefully we won't need to disturb you or your family any more tonight. We really appreciate this," Dianne said gratefully.

"Oh, before I forget, the trailer door locks from the inside, but if you have reason to leave, make sure you don't lock yourself out. We lost the key years ago, and Jake hasn't gotten around to replacing it," Missy advised, with an enormous yawn.

"Gotcha. We'll be fine, don't worry. Neither of us will set foot outside 'til it's light, so go on and get some shut eye," Dianne shooed her out the door. Smiling wearily, Missy walked back to the house.

"Well, guess we'd better do the same, it's almost 2:00 a.m., and I'm exhausted," Dianne declared, switching off the lights. Using the flashlight Missy had left them, she made her way back to the bedroom area. Bleary-eyed, April followed her mother, and they sat on the edge of the queen-sized bed to remove their shoes and jackets before crawling fully clothed under the heavy blankets provided. Regrettably, the heater worked on propane as well, so it would be a chilly night.

They were sound asleep within minutes ...

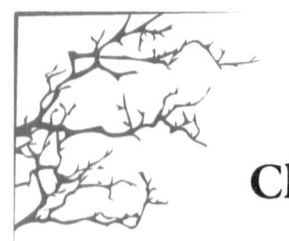

Chapter Thirty-Four

Joseph State Airport—2:00 a.m.

The plane Adriel had hired landed at Joseph's airfield and taxied over to the main hanger. As it came to a halt, the pilot from Boulder cut the engines, climbed out of his seat, and walked back to address his lone passenger.

"Well, I hope you can find a ride, this place is deader than dirt this time of the night," he told Adriel. "I presume you'll honor your part of our deal? I get a new plane, and the five grand we agreed on, right?" Baldy said greedily.

"Oh, you'll get what's coming to you, I assure you," Adriel said with an evil grin. Glancing outside and seeing no ground crew, he stood, walked over to the man, and whipped out a razor-sharp surgical scalpel he'd pocketed from the Santa Fe morgue.

Quick as a snake, the demon thrust it into the man's left eye and deep inside his brain, giving it a savage twist. He enjoyed the shocked look of surprise on the dead pilot's face as the man slumped to the cabin floor, blood spurting from his ruined eye.

"And I always keep my promises," the demon smiled, wiping the crimson blade clean on the dead man's pants. "Greedy humans, you're all the same." He turned to leave the plane, but stopped and returned to the body. Removing the pilot's wallet, he took his credit cards and what cash there was, then shoved the wallet inside the corpse's mouth. "Always put your money where your mouth is," he grinned malevolently.

Checking the hanger once more, he opened the door, lowered the stairs, and stepped out of the plane. As he'd expected, no one was around to see him raise the stairs and close the cabin door. He pulled out the deceased M. E.'s phone and scrolled through his apps until he found what he wanted and called the number ...

MASON LAY SLEEPLESS on the unfamiliar bed in a strange house, some two thousand miles from Austin, feeling vaguely homesick. He'd never traveled this far away from home, albeit "home" was a subjective term. Having slept on strangers' couches and floors for the last week or so, he'd thought he would be used to it by now. The events of the past five days swarmed his thoughts like a hive of maddened bees. He yearned for April's presence beside him, wondering if she, too, lay awake in the alien darkness, perhaps thinking of him. He felt more frightened and alone than he could ever remember feeling.

His worldview of the way the universe worked had been turned upside down and tossed on its cosmic ear in only a few days' time. Good and evil had been subjective terms to him. The words themselves were meaningless without context. All he was certain of at this moment was that Adriel was evil incarnate and would stop at nothing to find and destroy them.

Running was futile—he *would* find them. It was merely a matter of time. He was more worried for April than for himself. He only hoped that Mia and these others could come up with a way to destroy the demon before it was too late. If fire couldn't destroy the bastard, their options seemed bleak, at best. With these worrisome thoughts dancing in his head, he drifted into a fitful slumber, as exhaustion took its toll on his body.

ADRIEL HAD SCROUNGED a ride to some crappy little motel called "Terry's Travel-Inn" on the outskirts of Joseph. He'd had to pay the driver double to crawl out of his nice, warm bed in the middle of the night and pick him up from the airport. The motel's Vacancy-No Vacancy' sign was turned off, and he wasn't sure it was open. He strolled over to the garishly painted office door and loudly banged three times. Impatient, with no immediate response, he raised his fist to rap again, as the door opened a crack.

An elderly man stuck his head out to peer at the person who'd awakened him from a sound sleep. "Sorry, mister, didn't expect anyone at this time of night. Ya' caught me snoozing. I'm guessing ya' need a room?" the old man scratched his head sleepily.

"That's generally the case when one chooses an establishment such as yours, is it not?" Adriel said, trying to restrain an urge to throttle this stupid human.

The manager frowned. "Hmph, guess it *was* a stupid question. C'mon in, I'll need to get your info. Er, I didn't see a car, I need a license tag for the registration, or some kinda ID for ma' records, State law, ya' know," he moved behind a cigarette-scarred counter.

Adriel pulled out the dead doc's wallet and removed the driver's license, handing it to the old man to examine.

The proprietor mumbled something unintelligible as he recorded the information in his ledger. He turned to retrieve a room key from an array of hooks on the wall behind him.

"You live here alone?" Adriel asked nonchalantly, noticing a small cot in the corner of the small office.

The man's eyes narrowed at the question. He *did* live here alone but disliked revealing that info to a stranger. In the past year, he'd been robbed twice, as his advancing age made him an easy target for young predators. The last time it happened, the bastard had nearly shot him.

"My boy, Terry, is due here any minute, he, ah, runs the place. I'm just babysittin' 'til he gets back." The old man casually moved his hand under the counter near the sawed-off, double-barreled shotgun he kept there for emergencies. Sensing the man's disquiet, Adriel surmised he must have some sort of weapon near to hand.

"The room's forty bucks a day and there ain't no cable, been out for a month. There's free WiFi, though *it* don't work half the time, neither. Check-out is 11:00 a.m., sharp," the man finished his usual spiel, watching Adriel like a hawk.

"Fair enough. Hopefully, my business here will be concluded shortly. Is there, perhaps, a car rental agency available in this town?" Adriel handed him one of the former M. E.'s credit cards.

"Yep, but they don't open until 8:00 a.m. Johnny Six-Fingers, our *esteemed* mayor, owns it, along with the only garage in town." The old guy ran the credit card through his machine.

"You say his name is Six-Fingers? What a strange coincidence. I'm searching for a man with six fingers, but I sincerely doubt your mayor's the person I'm trying to locate," Adriel said, retrieving the card and stuffing it back in the dead doc's wallet.

"Johnny's a damn drunk, a card cheat, and a shitty mayor. That sound like the guy yer lookin' for?" the old goat asked hopefully. Like most of the town, he detested Johnny Six-Fingers and would be delighted if the asshole was in deep shit.

"Not in the least. Goodbye," Adriel said abruptly, taking the key and walking out of the office without another word.

The proprietor was glad to be shed of the stranger. Something about him gave him the heeby-jeebies. He couldn't quite put his finger on what had raised his hackles, just something about him seemed off. He hurried over and locked the front door, closed the blinds, and turned out the lights. If anyone else showed up looking for a room tonight, they'd be shit out of luck. *Fuck 'em*, he thought as he slowly made his way back to his cot in the dark.

Locating his room, Adriel opened the weather-beaten door. He felt around for the light switch and flipped it on. At the sudden disturbance, a gaggle of roaches zig-zagged across the filthy brown carpeting, searching for refuge in the shadows. The fug of a thousand cigarettes and the unmistakable funk of innumerable illicit liaisons permeated the room. An ancient TV hung bolted to the wall. That anyone would attempt to steal the piece of crap was inconceivable. He noted the full-sized bed had a large, concave indentation in the center of the mattress

Adriel snorted in total disgust at the lodgings. Hopefully, he wouldn't have to spend another night in this shithole. First, though, he'd have to find the traitorous trio, and he hadn't the first idea where to look for them. The dead pilot had said their destination had been Enterprise. The question was, where would they hide once they arrived? Would it be Enterprise or somewhere here in Joseph? He looked up the number of the Enterprise airfield and called.

He glanced at the time: 2:25 a.m. After the sixth ring, it was answered.

"Enterprise Regional Airways, how can I help you?" a man's bored voice asked.

"Yes, I need to know if you've had a recent charter arrive from Boulder in the past couple hours? It's very important, a matter of life and death," Adriel asked, his voice sounding urgent.

There was a slight pause. "Uh, hang on while I check the flight manifest," the man told him. Immediately, obnoxious elevator music filled the phone's tiny speaker, making him grimace. A minute later, the man returned, "We had a charter arrive about an hour ago. Was there something specific you needed to know?"

"I was hoping you could tell me how many passengers disembarked when it landed. Specifically, their names and most importantly, their destination. I'm a doctor and I believe one of my patients was onboard. She's very ill and would likely be traveling in the company of her mother and a long-haired young man," Adriel pressed.

The man hesitated, then cleared his throat. "No one on that flight except for the pilot; flight manifest doesn't list any passengers for that arrival. Sorry, that's all the information I have," the man said coolly.

"That's—ridiculous! There must be some mistake, I saw them board a charter flight in Boulder. I was delayed and couldn't make it to the plane before they took off. Could you please double-check the manifest? It's extremely urgent I locate my patient, her name is April Flowers." He didn't believe this guy for a second. *But why would he lie? Unless ...*

"I'm looking, but the flight manifest doesn't magically change. I'm sorry, Dr. ... what'd you say your name was?" the man now sounded wary.

"I didn't. It's Brown, Dr. Charles Brown. Listen, is there any way could you give me the name of the pilot for that charter? Perhaps *he* could be more helpful," Adriel replied tersely.

"His name's Scott Hardilek, he's also the City of Joseph's Fire Chief. You can ask him, but he's gonna tell you the same thing, Dr., uh, Brown. I'm telling you, for the last time, there were no passengers on that flight. Now if you'll excuse me, I need to get back to work," the man said, abruptly disconnecting.

Adriel was livid. He'd find this Scott Hardilek and make him talk, one way or the other ...

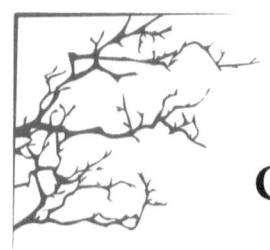

Chapter Thirty-Five

Enterprise Regional Airport

Mac McKenzie, the General Operations Manager for the Airport, looked over at Scott, who sat in the chair next to him, with raised eyebrows. "Ya' think he bought it?" he asked.

Scott took a sip of his coffee and frowned. "We'll find out soon enough. I expect 'Dr. Brown' will pay me a visit soon. I appreciate your help with this, Mac, I owe you one," he replied, clasping the older man's bony shoulder, giving it a friendly squeeze.

"No problem-o, Chief. Is this guy gonna be trouble?" Mac asked.

Scott hesitated, then said, "Can't say for sure. I've got to make a call, I'll catch you later," Scott replied, as he strode out of the control tower.

MIA WAS DREAMING HARD when her phone chimed. Groggily, she reached over to the nightstand by her bed and snagged it, squinting to see who was calling at 5:30 in the morning. "Hey, Scott, what's shakin'?" she said, after clearing the phlegm from her throat.

"Just a heads-up, Enterprise Airport received a call a few minutes ago from someone claiming to be a doctor. He was inquiring about your friends, specifically mentioned Miss Flowers by name, claiming she's ill and needed his immediate attention. Sounds like he knows they're here. Fortunately, I'd asked Mac to flag any inquiries regarding our three friends and to stonewall anyone who did. The guy then asked about me. Before I could stop him, Mac told him I was the pilot. I suspect Adriel will come looking for me next. My question is, should I be worried?" he asked her.

"Yes. *Very*! He's as dangerous as a den of rattlesnakes. You need to get somewhere safe. I suggest you go to the Sheriff's Office and hang out, you should be okay there for the time being. Did this 'doctor' mention where he was calling from?" she asked, while she dressed hurriedly.

"Don't think so, but my gut tells me he's somewhere close," Scott replied uneasily.

"Okay, I'm calling Missy and Pete to give them a heads-up. We'll meet you at the Sheriff's office ASAP," she said disconnecting. She finished dressing and called Missy. Ringing twice, the call was dropped. *Shit!* Cell service in the county was lousy even at the best of times. Putting on her shoes, she cursed the phone company. She sent a quick text to explain the situation, hoping Missy didn't have her 'notifications' turned off. Then she called Pete, and this time the call went through,

"Yo, Sis, don't you ever sleep?" Pete answered sluggishly.

Ignoring his remark, she filled him in on the developing situation. "You need to wake Mason and take him to Missy and Jake's. He's likely worried about April. We're not positive this Adriel is in town, but Scott seems to think so. I couldn't get Missy, the call was dropped. Sent her a text, but not sure she'll open it. She needs to notify State Police and put out an APB or whatever it's called on the guy," she explained rapidly.

"It's called a BOLO, they don't use the term APB much anymore," he corrected patiently.

"Whatever. The guy knows Scott was the pilot and he's likely trying to locate and question him. I told Scott to haul ass to the Sheriff's Office and wait for us there. This creature is extremely dangerous, Pete! Please be careful, I'll see you in a few," she said, disconnecting.

GROANING, PETE GOT out of bed and dressed in his deputy sheriff uniform. Stepping into the kitchen, he grabbed a couple cans of soda from the fridge and set them on the table. Walking over to Mason's bedroom, he knocked loudly, startling him awake.

"What's up, Pete?" he called out through the door.

"Got a call from Mia, she told me Adriel is here in town. Apparently, he called the airport asking about you guys. He knows Scott flew you here, and Scott thinks this dude will want to question him next, so Mia told him to head to the Sheriff's Office and wait there. Get dressed, I'm taking you to Missy and Jake's to be with Dianne and April. It'll be safer there."

Mason opened the door and stepped out, fully dressed. "I knew that asshole would find us, the sorry sack of demon shit! Let's go, the bastard could be anywhere."

Pete grabbed the trusty twelve-gauge pump he kept by his bedroom door, and they left the house and climbed into his Honda. Cranking the engine, they sped off toward the Andersons'. A few minutes later, they arrived at the turnoff. He was grateful Jake had finally paved the damn drive; his shock absorbers were about shot from traversing the previous pothole-ridden road over the years.

Pulling to a halt by Missy's cruiser, he killed the engine. As they were getting out of the car, Pete froze. Something large was moving about in the dark beyond the perimeter of light cast by the front porch light.

Shit! Must be a freakin' bear! was his first thought. Fumbling with his flashlight, he switched it on. It wasn't a bear. Mason gasped at the enormous figure of a man caught in the flashlight's beam.

Pete visibly relaxed. "Don't panic, it's just Gus Farley, he's a friend," he told Mason. Mason didn't look convinced and was inching back toward the safety of Pete's car. The enormous man looked like a Sasquatch.

"Howdy, Pete. Wha' tha' dickens are ya' a-doin' here this time o' night?'" the big man asked, squinting in the flashlight's glare.

Pete lowered the light. "I could ask you the same question. Gus, this is Mason Rivers, he's the boyfriend of Detective Dianne Flower's daughter, April. They're all here because ... well, they're being hunted by a demon posing as a human," Pete explained quickly.

The nearly seven-foot-tall, bearded giant ambled over to stare down at Mason, who looked like he might piss his pants any moment. "Well, Ah reckon thet sucks. Don' know much 'bout demons 'n' sech', but iff'n he shows up 'n' starts trouble, Ah'd be raht' happy ta' open a can o' whoop-ass on 'em, jest' say tha word," the big man said, with a friendly grin.

Mason thought the big dude could surely put a world of hurt on any normal human, but Adriel was as far from "normal" as you could get. Gus extended a hand the size of a silver-back gorilla's to Mason in greeting. Cautiously, Mason took it, expecting his hand to be crushed and surprised when Gus shook it with a moderately firm grip. The big fellow knew that his size intimidated most people.

"Ma'hty pleased ta meecha,' Mason. Ah' been a-hankerin' ta' do some fishin' at tha lake. Ah'm camped down tha road a ways, thought Ah'd mosey up an' chew tha fat wit' Missy afore' she wuz' a-headin' out fer' work," Gus said, absently scratching his crotch.

Pete knew what Gus meant by 'chewing tha fat' was trying to sweet-talk Missy into making him some of her blueberry pancakes and bacon, one of his favorite meals. Gus was always "hongry."

The mountain man lived out by Hell's Canyon Overlook, about a twenty-minute drive from the Andersons' property. His crooked elder brother, now deceased, had been governor of Oregon, and had built a luxurious cabin near the scenic Overlook, where he'd then met a grisly death three years earlier. After his demise, Gus had been granted sole ownership of the property, along with the $5.2 million dollars from their late mother's estate.

Before that, Gus had spent five years in the state prison, wrongly convicted of murder, until the true killer's deathbed confession forced his brother, the Governor, to pardon him. His long imprisonment had left Gus with claustrophobia. Subsequently, he could only tolerate being indoors for short periods of time. After his release, the Andersons had befriended him, allowing him to camp on their property any time he wished. Belinda, the Andersons' eldest girl, was especially fond of the gentle giant, treating him like a relative. Though Gus was only in his late forties, both his lengthy beard and wild mane of hair were as white as snow.

The morning sun chased away the shadows of the surrounding thicket as Gus, Pete, and Mason approached the Andersons' front porch. The front door popped open before Pete could knock. Belinda rushed past Pete and Mason to wrap her small arms around Gus' tree trunk of a waist, hugging him tightly.

"Mama, Uncle Gus is here. Pete's here, too, with some long-haired man," she belatedly called out over her shoulder.

"Nice to see you, too, cupcake," Pete grumbled, offended by her belated acknowledgment of his presence.

Gus finally managed to pry the affectionate child's arms loose. Scooping her up in his enormous arms, he carried her inside, to her delight.

As they stepped into the kitchen, the aroma of freshly brewed coffee, flapjacks, and bacon filled the air. "I received your text, Pete. I'm running late, didn't get much sleep. Mason, do me a favor, go wake Dianne and April in the trailer. Bring 'em in, we need to talk." Mason nodded and hurried out the front door. "Gus, help yourself to some breakfast, there's blueberry pancakes and bacon if you're hungry," Missy snapped out orders like a marine drill sergeant.

"Well, tha's ma'hty kine o' ya', don' mine if ah' do," Gus retorted, with a grin, patting his rotund belly. Easing his enormous girth into a wooden chair at the kitchen table, which groaned in protest. Without further ado, he forked a large stack of pancakes and a half-dozen strips of crispy bacon onto his plate.

Jake wandered out from the bedroom in time to witness Gus gobbling down their food. Glancing down at the nearly decimated plate of pancakes, he frowned in disgust. The man ate like a freaking hog. By the time Jake grabbed his cup of coffee and sat down, Gus had scarfed up the last piece of bacon on the serving platter, leaving Jake with one lone flapjack. Jake quickly speared it with his fork before "Godzilla" could snag and devour it. Gus released an enormous belch, making Jake frown more and Belinda giggle.

Dianne entered the kitchen, followed by April and Mason. At the sight of the bearded Goliath sitting across from Belinda at the table, April's eyes widened, while Missy instructed Belinda to take her morning shower.

"Well, hello there, stranger, what a surprise. Gus, this is my daughter, April. April, this is Gus Farley, we first met some years ago," Dianne announced, happy to see the big man.

Gus belched loudly again, "Howdy do, Miz' Flowers. Pleez'd ta' meet ya', Miz' April," he rose, extending his large hand.

April smiled and shook hands with the colossus, her tiny hand swallowed up by his massive paw. "Uh, nice to meet you, Mr. Farley. If you don't mind me asking, you aren't a priest, by any chance?" she asked, retrieving her hand.

"Nope, 'fraid not. Ah' ain't had much church-goin' growin' up. Ah' know'd a feller back 'n Arkansas who claim't ta be one. But ah' reckon he's daid now, he wuz' purty' old," he said, with a wistful shake of his large furry head.

"Just thought I'd ask. We *really* need to locate a priest, and fast. Pete informed Mason that Adriel tracked us down and is in the area, is that true?" she asked Missy anxiously.

"According to Mia, that's correct. He could be anywhere, as he didn't reveal his location. Apparently he talked to the Flight Controller at the Enterprise Airport and discovered Scott was the pilot who flew you here," Missy confirmed solemnly. Hearing this, April, Mason, and Dianne shared uneasy glances.

"I've notified the State Police and all local law enforcement to be on the lookout for a man fitting his description. We'll be checking all the local motels for recent arrivals, but until we locate him, I'll have to place you all into protective custody for your own safety. Scott's already at my headquarters, and we'll meet him there," Missy declared firmly.

Jake stopped eating and confronted his wife. "Let me get this straight. You're telling me that this so-called "demon" followed them to Joseph and he might come *here* looking for them?" he asked incredulously, glaring at her.

Missy rolled her eyes at him. "I'm sorry I failed to get *your* permission to allow them to stay in our trailer, but I won't apologize for giving them shelter, so get over it, *bud*," she replied glacially.

"So, I guess you didn't consider the fact that this ... this creature could also be a threat to all of us? What about Bella and Mandy? Did you even stop to think about them? Jesus, Missy ... really? What the hell were you thinking? Are you a complete idiot?" he shouted, trembling with rage.

At this outburst, Gus stood and glared down at him. Even though Jake stood six feet, two inches, the giant towered over him by a good six inches. He and Jake had had their differences in the past, though Gus tried to be cordial to him on his infrequent visits. This time, Jake was out of line.

"Ah' reckon it ain't ma' place ta say, but ah' b'lieve ya' needs ta 'pologise ta Missy, Jake. She don' deserve ta be sassed. Ah' 'spect she done had her reasons fer' not a-tellin' ya', but thar' ain't no call ta yell at 'er like ya' done," he growled, curling his ham-sized hands into fists at his side.

Jake was visibly flustered and intimidated by the big man's admonishment. Dianne and the others were uncomfortable at the potential for violence hanging between the two. After counting to ten, Jake seemed to get a grip on his temper.

"You're right, Gus, I'm sure she had her reasons. I apologize for calling you an idiot, Melissa. It was a discourtesy to you and our guests. You'll forgive me if I strongly disagree with *your* decision to endanger the lives of *our* children without consulting with me," he said coldly, seething from Gus's reprimand.

Tears welled up in Missy's eyes—not from his anemic apology—but because in all the years they'd lived together, never once had he called her a derogatory name in the heat of anger. It saddened her to her core that their marriage had eroded so much that civility between them had ceased to exist. That he'd never called her by her given name during an argument before tonight spoke volumes.

"Gus, I think perhaps you'd better leave now, and don't let the door hit you in the ass on the way out. You're no longer welcome on my property. Go. Now!" Jake commanded sternly.

Gus looked at Missy to see if she agreed with this, but she wouldn't meet his gaze. The big man sighed and shook his large, furry head. "Ah'm ra'ht sorry yer' a-feelin' this a-way, Jake. Ah' b'lieve ya' needs sum' help a-dealin' wit' tha' temper o' yorn. Iff'n y'all needs me fer anythin', ah'll be camped down yonder by tha lake. Nice ta' meet ya', folks," he said to April and Mason. "Ah'll be a-takin' ma' leave now, 'Mr. Anderson,'" he said gruffly, addressing Jake. "Thanks fer tha vittles, Missy. Ya' give me a holler if thet thar' demon feller shows up. Ah'll be tickled as a pup wit' two peckers ta tear 'im a new a-hole fer ya' iff'n he threatens ya'll or them young-un's, ya' hear me?" Gus said seriously, holding her gaze.

"Thanks, Gus. I'm sorry, this is my fault. Please don't hold it against Jake, we're ... going through some rough patches right now. I promise things will get better soon, and I'll give you a 'holler' if I need you, okay?" she replied tightly, hugging him. Gus just grunted, glared at Jake, turned and stalked out of the house, closing the door behind him.

"Let's go, we need to get to the sheriff's office. Scott and Mia will wonder what happened," Missy said curtly to Pete and the others, ignoring her pig-headed husband.

Watching her file out the door without another word, Jake felt a black hole open in the center of his heart. Belinda stepped out of her bedroom and frowned at him.

"Daddy, are you and Mama gonna get a divorce?" the solemn-faced girl asked, tears welling in her eyes.

He was taken aback by his daughter's direct question. "No, cupcake, we—we're just having some problems communicating with each other. Grown-ups sometimes argue when we don't see eye to eye. It makes us angry, and when we're angry, we might say things we don't really mean. Do you understand?" he tried to explain, taking her in his arms to hug her tightly.

She stiffened in his arms and pushed away from him. "You were mean to Uncle Gus, Daddy. He was only tryin' to help, and you sent him away!" she reproached him angrily.

"You know he's not really your 'uncle' Bella, he's—he's just a nosy, illiterate, eating machine who should mind his own business. Why am I always the bad guy? I'm only trying to protect us from—" he insisted.

Without a word, she turned and ran to her room, slamming the door.

Shit! He smacked himself on the forehead in frustration. Now everyone was pissed at him. Well, almost everyone, Mandy was still asleep. He walked to the door into Belinda's room, reached out, and opened the door.

"C'mon, Bella, I'm sorry, Daddy's under a lot of stress. I have a lot to think about, and you're going to be late to school if we don't leave soon, young lady," he said firmly.

"I don't wanna go to school. You can't make me!" she cried defiantly. With a sigh, he walked over to sit on the edge of her bed.

"What do I need to do to make you happy again?" he asked, calmly gazing at her tear-streaked face.

She sniffled, "Be nicer to Mama, and don't be mean to Uncle Gus anymore. I love him. He doesn't deserve to be treated like a hillbilly, even though he sorta talks like one," she demanded, scowling.

He knew she was right. Yet, he couldn't reconcile himself to the fact that the huge oaf had reprimanded and embarrassed him in front of everyone—and in his own damn house.

"I promise I'll try to be nicer to your mother and the big 'Wookie.' Now will you please get up and go to school?" he asked, trying to placate her.

She blew her nose on a tissue he handed her and hesitantly nodded. Standing. she snatched up her backpack. "He's *not* a 'Wookie,' he's just big. You're still being rude, Daddy," she pointed out, with a frown.

Without another word, she strolled into the kitchen, grabbed her sack lunch and her coat. He mentally kicked himself as he strolled to his bedroom and plucked Mandy from her crib. He hurried to dress her, and they left the house. Strapping Mandy in her car seat, he drove the eight miles to Bella's school in uncomfortable silence ...

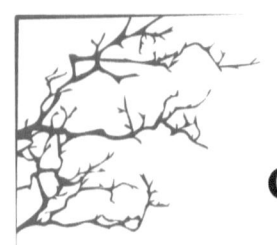

Chapter Thirty-Six

Wallowa County Sheriff's Office

As Missy and her passengers arrived at the Sheriff's office, she received a call over her police radio. "All units, be advised, we have a 10-54 at the Joseph Airport. Repeat, a 10-54 at the Joseph Airport. Proceed code two," the dispatcher calmly stated. *Shit!* A 10-54 was their code for a 'possible dead body.'

"Okay, everybody out. Stay inside the building 'til I get back, and tell Mia and Scott to stay put, too," Missy told her passengers.

"What's going on, Missy? What's a 10-54?" Mason asked, opening the door to climb out.

"It's the code for a possible dead body, even more reason for all of you to get your butts inside. This may or may not have any relevance to that demon that's after you," she replied gruffly.

Dianne paused before opening her door. "I'd like to volunteer my services. I spent five years in forensics before I made detective, and another pair of eyes couldn't hurt," she offered.

Missy thought about it and made a quick decision. "Okay. Our only forensic tech's attending a seminar in Portland, so I suppose it would be foolish to refuse. Close your door, let's roll," she said impatiently.

"Please be careful, Mom," April reached for her mother's hand. "If this has anything to do with Adriel, he might be watching and waiting. It could be a fucking trap!"

Dianne smiled, touched by her daughter's concern. "Don't worry, sweetie, I doubt he'd be stupid enough to try anything with a bunch of cops around," she replied, hoping her assessment was correct.

As Missy waited impatiently for Mason and April to get inside the Sheriff's office, Pete had taken the front passenger seat while Dianne remained in back. As they sped to the airport, Missy switched on the emergency lights. They arrived minutes later to find a small charter aircraft being observed by two of her deputies.

MISSY PULLED TO A HALT by the other cruisers, and they got out to join the deputies, who were milling around outside a Beechcraft Denali turboprop plane.

"What's the situation here, Deputy Olsen?" Missy asked, as they approached. Jenny Olsen was the newest addition to their small police force. The petite blonde had joined after an older deputy retired.

"We received a call from the Airport Manager of Operations at 0800 hours that a charter had landed unnoticed some time late last night. Apparently, the pilot neglected to file a flight plan, and when they couldn't raise him by radio, the flight controller grew concerned. One of the ground crew came out to check on the pilot and saw this," she said, pointing to the plane's cabin door. Missy, Pete, and Dianne strolled over to the plane, and upon closer inspection, discovered what appeared to be a smeared, bloody handprint on the plane's door handle.

"No one touched anything, Chief, called it in as soon as we saw the bloody print," the other deputy, Fred Firestone verified. The deputies jokingly called him "Flintstone" behind his back because of his rotund resemblance to the cartoon caveman.

"Okay, let's gear up and see what, if anything, is inside. Anyone bring a forensics kit with them?" Missy asked, looking from one to the other. Both deputies shook their heads sheepishly. "Luckily, I have one in my trunk." She walked over and popped it open.

They donned latex gloves and booties to keep from contaminating the potential crime scene. Missy and Dianne approached the plane's door, and Missy cautiously opened it while Pete joined the deputies checking the exterior of the plane. The distinctive, coppery odor of blood assaulted their nostrils. Missy lowered the collapsible stairway and climbed into the dark interior of the plane. She immediately spotted a body on the floor, a small pool of coagulated blood surrounding it.

"There's something jammed in his mouth. Looks to be a wallet," Dianne observed. She and Missy took pictures of the deceased, using their phones' cameras, as they didn't have access to the professional one used by their forensics expert. Missy noted rigor had already set in. Leaning over and, using a bit of force, she pried the billfold out of the man's clenched jaws. Opening it, she found the dead man's driver's license, as well as his pilot's license. Opening an evidence bag, she placed the wallet inside. It appeared they'd found their missing pilot.

"Firestone, Olsen, we have a confirmed DB in here. One of you call Boulder Regional and find out if this plane was reported missing; the other one call the Medical Examiner and tell him to get his butt over here," Missy directed her deputies.

While they were busy with those tasks, Dianne examined the bloody face of the deceased. "Looks like a penetrating wound to the brain was the C.O.D. possibly made by a knife or some other sharp object. There's no obvious GSR around the orbital socket and no exit wound to the back of the skull, which I'd say rules out the use of a firearm," she noted, lifting the head for a closer look. Missy agreed with her observation. There was no acrid, telltale odor of gunpowder normally present after a gun had been fired. While Dianne continued her methodical exam of the body, Missy inspected the cabin for clues to the killer's identity.

Frustrated at finding nothing out of the ordinary, a small object wedged between two seat cushions finally caught her eye. Retrieving it, she noted it was a laminated name badge with a metal clasp. *Bingo!* She recognized the name on the tag as that of the missing Santa Fe doctor. With the realization their killer was lurking somewhere close by, an icy chill ran down Missy's spine.

"You find anything?" Dianne asked, finishing her inspection of the pilot's corpse.

"Yeah, and I'm afraid it's not good," Missy replied, showing her what she'd discovered.

Pete joined them inside the plane cabin. At the sight of the dead pilot on the floor, his eyes grew wide. "*Holy Crap*! You think that missing doctor did this?" he asked, gaping at the body.

"It must've been him," Missy showed him the name badge. "He's somewhere in the area, and we need to find his ass before he locates Mason and April. Pete, I need you to go back to headquarters and place them in a holding cell for their own safety. Dianne, I strongly advise you to go with him," Missy said to both.

"That bastard's a demon, and I seriously doubt hiding in your jail will stop him from finding and killing us all," Dianne pointed out.

"I'll notify State Police we need back-up to help locate the perp," Missy stated, ignoring her friend's pessimistic remark.

"While you're at it, you'd better find us a priest. One way or the other, before this is over we're going to need one," Dianne said grimly.

"Are you Catholic?" Pete asked her.

"No, but I'm willing to convert if that's what it takes to save our lives."

Missy was wondering if she'd miscalculated by agreeing to harbor Dianne and the others. As Jake had correctly pointed out, by hiding them, she'd placed her own family in imminent danger from this vicious creature. She'd been confident the demon wouldn't be able to track her friends to Joseph—and she had been mistaken.

The Medical Examiner's arrival jerked her from her thoughts back to the present.

"Mornin', Chief," the doctor greeted her. "Looks like another beautiful day. Shame to have to spoil it with a DB. What do we have here?" he cheerfully inquired, climbing into the plane's cabin.

"Mornin', Doc. We have a deceased white male, forty-two years of age. As far as we can discern, the C.O.D. appears to be a puncture wound to the brain by a sharp implement, possibly a knife. No other visible trauma to the body," Missy replied, stepping away to give him access.

Dr. Quincy Preston was fifty-five, overweight, and losing most of his silvery white hair. He'd been the town's M. E. for as long as Missy could remember. Casually, he stepped over the body and began his examination.

While he was busy, Missy raised her eyebrows at Pete, shot him a look that said, "*Why are you still here?*"

"All right, all right, I'm leaving. You coming with me, Dianne?" he asked, pausing on the steps. Dianne locked gazes with Missy for a moment, then shook her head.

"I'm not gonna run and hide like some frightened child, Pete. It's only a matter of time before we find that monster. When we do, I'll try my damnedest to send him back to hell or wherever he came from," she snapped.

Missy wasn't convinced it would be all that easy. "When you've secured April and Mason, find us a priest, Pete. I don't care if you have to call the freaking Vatican, just make it happen," Missy ordered, scowling.

"Roger that, Chief, I'll do my best."

"Your assumption as to C.O.D. seems spot on," Dr. Preston said. "It appears the deceased's brain was penetrated by a sharp object via the orbital socket. I'll have to get him on my table to be sure, but for now, I'd place the time of death somewhere between one and three hours, give or take. I assume you've taken photos of the crime scene?" he said, packing up his medical bag.

"Yeah, we took 'em. I'll text them to your phone. Appreciate your help, as always, Doc." Missy said, as they all exited the plane.

"No problem, Chief. I should have preliminary results for you no later than lunchtime. You have any idea who might've done this?" he asked, nodding at the body.

"We believe it was done by the missing Santa Fe M. E. He ... uh, isn't exactly who or what he appears to be. I can't get into the details. Let's just say he's extremely dangerous and needs to be caught."

"Don't they all. My guys are waiting outside to transport this guy to the morgue. Unless there's something else, I'll be on my way. I presume you'll be notifying next of kin?" he asked, signaling his team.

"Yeah, if we can locate any. In the meantime, I need to find this killer. Thanks again, Doc," she said, as they walked to their cars.

Deputies Olsen and Firestone met them at Missy's cruiser. Deputy Olsen began, "Chief, I called Boulder Regional, they confirmed a Beechcraft turboprop owned by one of their employees took off around 01200 hours their time. Apparently, no flight plan was filed before takeoff, no one listed on the flight manifest, either."

"Good work, Olsen. We've now confirmed the identities of the pilot and his assassin. We have a physical description of our perp, but if you should spot him, you do not, I repeat, you do *not* under any circumstances approach or engage him. Radio me immediately. He's armed and extremely dangerous. Do I make myself clear?" Missy sternly ordered.

"Yes, Sir, Chief," they replied in unison. "One question, Sir," Firestone asked. "What do we do if he approaches *us?*" Firestone asked.

"I'd advise you to blow his brains out, but that's just my humble opinion," Dianne couldn't help adding.

Missy frowned at her. "For your own safety, if you can, pretend you don't recognize him, and notify me ASAP. But if he's aggressive and threatens you, you're allowed to use deadly force," Missy staunchly replied. *Not that it'd likely do much good,* she thought grimly.

"Olsen, I want you to check with the local motels, inns, and B&Bs in the surrounding area to see if our perp has recently checked in. Text them a picture of him, it'll save time. Firestone, cruise around town, check all the shops and restaurants, I presume this *creature* eats at some point. If he does, he'll have to get food from the grocery store or a local eatery. Give them a physical description, we could get lucky. Be extremely careful and keep your eyes open out there. That's all for now, except Dianne and I will need a lift to the station, as Pete has my car," she added.

MINUTES LATER, THEY arrived at the Sheriff's Office, where Mason and April leaned against Missy's desk, eating donuts and drinking coffee. In a corner of the room, Mia, Pete, and Scott were conversing. When Dianne and Missy walked in the door, everything stopped.

"I thought I told you to put them in the holding area, Deputy Chandler. What happened?" Missy frowned.

"They, uh, refused to be locked up, said if that Adriel dude found them in there, they'd be, like, sitting ducks. They make a valid point, Chief," Pete replied sheepishly.

Missy turned to Mason and April. "If you won't listen to reason, I can't protect you. You really think this Adriel would have the balls to storm a heavily armed cop shop to get to you? Do you?" she asked them, with arms crossed.

"I don't put anything past that fucker," April answered soberly. "We've cost him money; set his fancy condo and his toady, Alal, ablaze; killed his lucrative deal with Sony records; then fled to escape his fucking contracts we'd stupidly signed. So, yeah, I'd say he's not only capable, but motivated as hell. There really is no safe place on earth to hide from him!"

"Personally, I'd rather take my chances out here, where at least we'd have a fighting chance; and if all else fails, we can make a run for it," Mason agreed.

Missy looked to Dianne to see if she concurred with this line of reasoning. "Unfortunately, I'm forced to agree with their reasoning. This creature is totally unpredictable, and we've experienced his supernatural powers. We have no way to fathom what he could be capable of," she shrugged.

Missy sighed with frustration. "Deputy Chandler, any progress on locating a priest?"

"Uh, no, Sir. I checked with the priests in four parishes in the county. None of them were even willing to discuss an exorcism without first researching and documenting the phenomena. Apparently, there are established procedures they have to follow. Even if it's okayed on a local level, it has to be approved by higher authorities in the Church. The entire process can take forever," he explained.

"Well, we sure don't have time to cut through bullshit red tape. There has to be another way to get rid of this creature for good," Missy grumbled, absently twirling a lock of her curly hair around her index finger—her habit when she was troubled.

"I could still offer to play him a game of chess, winner take all, in exchange for their souls, but I'm afraid that horse has departed the barn," Mia stated.

"She's right, Adriel's out for blood now. He won't stop until he gets what he came for—our souls—and he'll happily kill anyone who gets in his way," April snapped.

Scott had so far stayed out of the conversation, but now he spoke up. "I still have my trusty flamethrower, if it would help," he volunteered.

"It wouldn't work, he'd simply take possession of another body like he did in Santa Fe, possibly one of *us*," Mason said, rejecting that.

"Nice, scary thought, thanks for the visual," Pete said, as a shiver ran down his spine.

"I think it's time we confront the hard truth—we cannot destroy him by any conventional means. He's an angel of darkness. To have any chance of defeating this *thing*, we need an angel of our own," Missy asserted, staring pointedly at Mia.

Everyone turned to look at her. Mia sighed and shook her head. "As I've said, I have serious doubts my 'gift' would work on such an evil entity," Mia said. "If it did, there's no guarantee I'd survive the encounter. The last time I used it, I almost died from an intracranial hemorrhage. It seems that every time I heal someone, there's a sort of psychic energy exchange that elevates my blood pressure and temperature to a dangerous level."

"Don't try it, Sis. It's too fucking dangerous!" Pete exclaimed. He realized he was being selfish, but she was his only living relative, and he'd be damned if he'd lose her to some demonic prick.

"There don't appear to be a lot of other options, Pete. If you have a better suggestion, please feel free to share. I don't want to die, but if there's the slimmest chance it could work, I have to try," Mia said softly, setting a placating hand on his arm.

"This is bullshit! You're not a freaking exorcist, for Christ's sake!" he spat, shaking off her hand angrily.

"Chill out, Deputy! I know you're worried and scared for her, Pete. We all are, but this is not the time or place to freak out. If you can't control your emotions, I'll be forced to relieve you from your duties effective immediately. No one is forcing Mia to do anything, it's strictly her choice to make. If *she* decides the risk is worth taking, you don't have to like it, but you *must* respect her decision," Missy admonished him.

Pete's face flushed bright red. Missy didn't know if it was anger or the verbal face slap she'd just administered.

"Respectfully, I disagree with you, Chief. You had a sister long ago that you lost to madness. Well, I think *this* is madness. This isn't some sick person who needs healing—it's a supernatural asshole that seemingly can't be destroyed. If fire can't do the job, what makes any of you think Mia would stand a chance against a creature like him?" he asked belligerently.

The silence in the room was deafening. He knew he'd crossed a line when he'd brought up Missy's sibling. If she fired him, so be it, but he would not sit silent with his sister's welfare at stake.

When Missy spoke again, it was with a heavy heart. "My sister was mentally ill, Pete. Mia, I am certain, is not. She's probably the most rational person in this room. I'm truly sorry, but as of now, you're suspended with pay until this is over. She may be their, and possibly our, only hope. Please place your service weapon and credentials on my desk on your way out. You're dismissed," she demanded curtly.

Peevishly, Pete removed his badge, utility belt, and sidearm, tossed them on her desk, and stormed out of the building.

"I'm sorry, Mia, but he's too emotionally involved in this. I did it for his own good, whether or not he realizes it. A deputy who's mentally distracted on the job is dangerous and could imperil the lives of other officers, or in this case, civilians," Missy explained, with a heavy sigh.

"I completely understand, Missy. I expect the same discipline from my fellow doctors and nurses at work. I do think you were a little hard on him, though. After all, you knew he was a worrier when you hired him," Mia gently rebuked her friend.

"Yes, I'm fully aware of that. Given some time, he'll calm down. Now, before I forget, I have to call Boulder Regional and give them the sad news that their pilot will come home in a body bag." She shooed everyone out of her office while she sat down to make the call. Before she could dial the number, Scott walked in to say he had an errand to run and left the building.

"I'm sorry about your brother, Mia," Dianne said apologetically. "It's our fault he got canned. I wish there was something I could say to convince Missy to reinstate him."

Mia gave her a tight smile. "It's likely for the best. Don't worry about Pete, he'll cool down soon enough. Eventually, he has to come to grips with his fear of losing me. He has deep-rooted insecurities dating back to his childhood. Our history is a bit complex; let me see if I can clarify it:

"Our father cheated on his wife, Pete's mother, with the girl who became my mom. Learning that my mom was pregnant, Pete's mom kicked Dad's ass out when Pete was very young. Pete never saw him again; he grew up without a father—and it was tough on him. Ever since he and I met and he realized he had a half-sister, he's been overly protective of me. Nothing I do or say has changed his behavior. He is what he is," Mia responded with a shrug.

Dianne was sad to hear about Pete's childhood. "My dad was killed when I was young and I have some of the same insecurities. When I was fresh out of the police academy, I thought I could change the world and make a real difference in the lives of those around me. Maybe I have in a small way over the years. But for every criminal I've taken off the streets, a hundred more seem to fill the void. At a certain point in your career, disillusionment becomes one of the many pitfalls of the job." She sipped her coffee.

"It also happens in my profession," Mia said. "I hope it never gets that bad for me, but time will tell, I suppose," Mia gave the detective a quick hug as her pager went off. Glancing at it, she said, "I gotta go, emergency at the hospital. Tell Missy to call if she needs me." She rushed out the front door.

Missy finished her call and re-joined the group. "Where's Mia?" she asked, looking around.

Dianne relayed Mia's message and Missy nodded. "My deputies are checking all the logical places this creature might be staying." She turned then to Mason and April. "Do either of you know how to handle a firearm?" she asked them.

"Uh, the last time I shot a twenty-two rifle was in summer camp in my teens, but that's a long time ago," he replied. He had an uneasy feeling he knew why she'd asked.

"What about you, April?" Missy asked her.

"I can handle a Glock semi-auto, Mom taught me how to shoot at the range when I was seventeen," she answered, nodding at Dianne.

"That's good. I'm going to deputize you both. This way, if things should go south, and you need to use deadly force, there'll be less chance of legal repercussions afterward," she said coolly.

"Do you think that's wise, Missy?" Dianne cut in. "They're civilians, for crying out loud! They don't have any law enforcement training. Just because they know how to fire a weapon doesn't mean—"

Missy stopped her. "They need to be able to defend themselves. If this Adriel *being* finds them before we can stop him, they'll need something.

Guns alone may not be enough to stop him, but they're better than the alternative. At least they'll have a fighting chance," Missy pleaded her case.

"Let's hope it doesn't come to that," Dianne said. "The larger problem is having some way to immobilize him once you do find him, if that's even possible. I doubt he'll calmly stand by while Mia laid hands on him," she pointed out.

April's eyes widened as she thought, "A stun-gun! I used one on him back at the hotel in Austin. Apparently, demons are susceptible to electric shock just as humans are, just to a lesser degree. It knocked him on his fucking ass, though I *had* already kicked him in his nuts. It slowed both him and his lackey down long enough for Mason and me to escape," she said excitedly, looking from Missy to Dianne for their reaction.

"A freakin' stun-gun? Really? I would've thought that would be like using a water pistol to put out a house fire—but whatever works, I guess," Missy shook her head in disbelief.

"It bought us some time, but not a lot. I wouldn't want to bet my life on it working again," Mason added. "Besides, you have to be up close and personal for those things to work. It isn't an experiment I'd care to repeat soon."

"I'm assuming you used the civilian equivalent of a Taser. With a Taser, you don't need to be that close. It fires two electric darts, connected by wires to the gun itself. Once the darts embed themselves into the target, then you pull the trigger on the gun, delivering the electrical current to the body," Missy explained.

"The only problem with them is they don't always work as advertised," Dianne remarked. "About fifty-five percent of the time, all it does is piss 'em off. If that happens, you'd better be prepared to use lethal force if you can't find some other means of subduing them," Dianne added.

"She has a valid point. A lot depends on the subject's body mass and other mitigating factors, such as if they're inebriated or high on drugs. In either of those cases, all bets are off," Missy said.

"I would rather carry one of those than a gun. Guns make me extremely tense," April stated.

"I can't speak for Mason, but I'd certainly be more comfortable with her being armed with a Taser than a firearm. She doesn't have the experience and training to safely handle a gun in a crisis," Dianne stated.

Mason didn't have to think about it. "I'd rather have a gun, preferably a shotgun. It doesn't require as much skill, you just point and shoot," he asserted.

"That's fine by me. Before we go any further, let me swear you both in as my deputies. Please raise your right hands and say, 'I do,' at the end."

"Do I need a ring?" Mason joked.

Missy rolled her eyes at him and proceeded. When finished, she congratulated them and lightly said he could now kiss the bride, which he promptly did, surprising April.

"Okay, now that you're deputized, I'll equip you with your weapon of choice. Mason, I'll teach you the proper way to load and unload the shotgun, and April, your mother can educate you on the use of a Taser. This will be a crash course, folks, we're short on time, so pay close attention," Missy instructed.

Opening the Station's weapon locker, she removed a twelve-gauge pump, along with a yellow-bodied Taser, handing that to Dianne. Separately, the two cops went over the basics of the safe handling of both weapons, until both Mason and April felt comfortable with them. Minutes later, Missy's radio crackled to life.

"Chief, this is Olsen. I'm at that 'No-tell' motel on Highway Fifty, I think I have a lead on our perp, he—" her voice suddenly cut out.

"Roger, say again, I lost you," Missy said uneasily. Only silence from Olsen's end. "Deputy Olsen, please report! If you need help and cannot speak, key your mike three times," Missy commanded, an edge to her voice. Still, silence. *Shit!* "Deputy Firestone, what's your 'twenty?'" she asked tightly.

There was a pause before he answered, "Uh, I'm at the 'R and R' eating a late breakfast, Chief. No sign of our perp downtown. Is there a problem?" he said, between chews.

Missy slapped her forehead in frustration, a slow burn infusing her as she struggled with her temper. "You are *supposed* to be looking for our suspect, not feeding your face, Deputy! Olsen may be in serious trouble. She reported in, but something's wrong, she won't or can't respond on her radio. Before I lost contact, she reported she might have a lead on our suspect. She's at

'Terry's Travel-Inn' out on Fifty. Drop your freaking fork and get over there ASAP! Proceed code Three, I'll meet you there, over," she snapped.

"R-Roger, Chief, I-I'm on my way, over," he stammered.

Missy and Dianne were headed for the door when Mason called out.

"What should we do while you're gone, Mis—er, Chief?" he asked.

"Stay here, don't leave the building. If we aren't back in an hour, lock the front door, load your weapons, and call the State police," she said, tossing him the key to the weapons locker ...

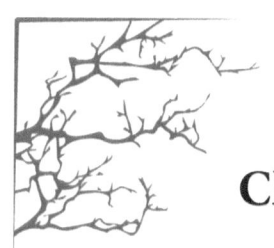

Chapter Thirty-Seven

Five minutes later, Missy's cruiser pulled into the motel's parking lot, screeching to a halt next to Deputy Olsen's squad car. The driver's door hung open, but there was no sign of Olsen. Missy and Dianne leaped out, pulling their service weapons.

Deputy Firestone arrived moments behind them. He rushed out, joining them by Olsen's empty car. "I apologize, Chief, it won't happen aga—" he began.

"That's right, it most definitely won't! If I hadn't just suspended Pete, you'd be looking for another job, deputy! Now draw your weapon, stay behind us, and keep your eyes peeled, you have our six," she snapped. Firestone scurried to obey.

Olsen's car was parked in front of Room Thirteen, with no other car nearby. The faded orange door to the room stood ajar—never a good sign. Dianne pointed to herself, then to the right side of the doorway. Missy nodded and took the left side, Firestone close behind her.

"Olsen! Are you in there? Answer me! Are you hurt?" Missy called out into the room. Despite the cool air, beads of sweat rolled down her face. When no answer came, Missy nodded at Dianne, took a deep breath, then kicked the door open wide and stepped inside. She cleared the area behind the door, scanning the room. The single bed looked like it hadn't been slept in. No sign of Olsen. *Shit!* That left only the bathroom. She noticed Dianne, right behind her, was breathing as if she'd just finished a five-mile run, and her face was ashen.

Missy couldn't check on her, she had yet to clear the bathroom. Nearing its shadowed entrance, the pungent, coppery odor of blood stopped her in her tracks. She briefly locked eyes with Dianne before reaching out to fumble the light switch on. Olsen lay in the tub, blood everywhere. Her throat had been cut, ear-to-ear. Missy realized Olsen's service weapon was missing. *Shit!* Now he had a gun.

"*Motherfucker*!" Missy hissed angrily as she took in the sight of her dead deputy.

"Chief, come quick, I think there's something wrong with your detective friend," Firestone called urgently from the front door. He hadn't seen the dreadful scene facing her, and she wanted to keep it that way. She stepped out of the blood-spattered room, pulling the door closed behind her.

Dianne had collapsed onto her knees, gasping like she couldn't get a breath, her gun on the floor beside her, forgotten. Sweat poured down her pale face.

"Dianne! What the hell? Firestone, get on the radio, call EMS. Now! Next, call Doc Preston and tell we need him and the DB wagon here, then get back to the station to protect April and Mason until we return," Missy barked, easing Dianne down on her back on the dirty, brown carpet.

"First, call dispatch, have him call the State Police and tell them we need backup ASAP. Don't stand there, deputy. Move!" she roared. The stout guy turned and hustled out of the room, keying his mike as he ran.

Missy turned her attention back to Dianne, seeing naked fear in her friend's eyes, as she struggled to catch her breath. "Hang in there, hon, EMS is on the way." Missy assured her.

"C-C-Can't—b-breathe!   T-Think—p-p-panic—t-tack!" Dianne sputtered.

"*Jesus*! It picked a hell of a time to happen. Try to breathe easy, help is coming," Missy said, trying her best to comfort her friend and colleague.

The wail of an approaching siren reached her. "About fucking time!" Missy groused. Snatching a pillow off the bed, she stuck it under Dianne's head. The ambulance screeched to a stop outside. Two techs jumped out, grabbed their gear, and raced inside.

"What's the problem?" a burly male tech asked, opening his med kit.

"I'm not sure, but she mumbled something about a panic attack. One minute she was fine, then she was on the floor," Missy said, standing to move out of their way.

First, the female tech slipped an aspirin under Dianne's tongue, while the male placed an oxygen mask over her face and told her to relax and take some deep breaths. She did as he instructed, but with difficulty.

"*Crap*! Her CO^2 levels are almost non-existent. She's in respiratory alkalosis," the woman tech barked, pulling the mask back off Dianne.

"What the hell's that mean? Is she going to be alright?" Missy asked impatiently.

"She's hyperventilating and her carbon dioxide levels are too low, most likely caused by a panic attack. It's more common than you'd imagine among law enforcement. Instead of seeking treatment, lots of cops try to hide the symptoms. If the root cause of the anxiety is not addressed, it can worsen over time," the tech explained patiently.

Slowly, as she took in slow, measured breaths, Dianne improved. "I-It's better now, I can finally b-breathe again," she announced, sitting upright.

Doc Preston appeared in the doorway. "Where's the body, Chief?" he asked as he entered the room, glancing around.

"She's in the bathtub, Doc. The asshole cut her fucking throat! He must've taken her gun, her holster's empty," Missy growled, helping Dianne unsteadily to her feet. "We need to talk about this later," she told Dianne. "I've got to notify Jenny's husband now; this is going to be tough—they were still newlyweds, damn it all to hell!" Missy exclaimed miserably.

"If you have another one of these episodes, I highly recommend you go to the hospital. They have some great doc's there who can—" the female tech began.

"Thanks, I appreciate the advice," Dianne stopped her. "Sorry I wasted your time, but as you can see, I'm fine now. Really!" Retrieving her service pistol from the floor, she holstered it. Missy wasn't so sure her friend was "fine," but she chose not to say anything.

Doc Preston, who had been examining the body in the bathroom while Dianne's minor crisis had ensued, emerged, shaking his head sadly.

"As soon as I can, I'll send you an email with the results of my postmortem, Chief. In the meantime, I'd appreciate it if you'd try not to send me anymore 'clients' right away, if you can help it," Preston said wryly.

"I'll do my best, Doc. *Shit*! I almost forgot to take photos of the crime scene. Dianne, you can go wait in the car if you'd like, this'll take a few minutes to finish," Missy suggested.

"I'm fine. Don't worry about me," Dianne said with a tight smile. "I just need a little fresh air, and I'll be okay."

She followed the EMTs outside and leaned against the fender of the deceased deputy's car. Missy watched her leave, shook her head, and started the grisly business of documenting the gory scene in the bathroom.

Dianne was debating whether she should seek help for these recurring attacks or resign from her job, perhaps both. If she didn't address the damn problem, she might put her fellow officers in danger.

If she suffered one of these attacks while in a life-or-death situation, she'd be as helpless as a two-legged hound. That was not acceptable. A solitary tear formed and trickled down her cheek to fall unnoticed. She had to snap out of it, couldn't afford the luxury of feeling sorry for herself while Missy and the others depended on her. She watched the morgue attendants wheel the gurney containing the young deputy's remains outside and load it into the waiting van.

Missy and the doctor stepped out of the depressing room into the morning sun. "It's terrifying that so much blood could come from such a petite human being," she observed, as the attendants drove away with her murdered deputy.

"Let's hope you catch this monster before he does any more damage. Good luck and stay safe, Chief," the M. E. said soberly, giving Missy's arm a quick squeeze. He climbed into his vehicle and drove away.

Missy opened her phone and found Jenny's emergency contact number. She hesitated a couple of heartbeats, then took a deep breath, and called Jenny's husband, Derek, to give him the awful news.

Dianne heard the man's heartrending cry of disbelief and denial even from where she stood, a good six feet away from Missy's phone. The man was inconsolable, screaming something unintelligible. After apologizing repeatedly, Missy finally got him to calm down a little, promising him she'd hunt down his wife's killer and make him pay if it was the last thing she did.

Missy finally ended the call, looking exhausted from the painful ordeal. "I'd rather have ten fucking root canals than have to inform someone that the person they loved and cherished is never coming home again. Sometimes I really hate this job," she declared bitterly.

She marched past Dianne to the motel office to find the front door was locked. Olsen had to have talked to the proprietor and found that their perp was in Room Thirteen. Adriel could've seen her pull up, ambushed her in her car, dragged her inside, and cut her throat. The second she found out he was registered there, Jenny should have radioed dispatch and waited for backup. Instead, she'd gotten herself killed.

Irately, Missy banged on the office door and when there was no response, she took two steps back and kicked it in, breaking the flimsy lock. Shoving the door open and stepping inside, she saw the old man. He lay crumpled on the floor in front of the registration desk, surrounded by a small pool of blood. *Shit*!

With shaky hands, she called Doc Preston and gave him the news.

"Didn't I ask you not to send me any more business?" he asked gruffly.

"Sorry, Doc. Hopefully, this the last one. This fucker is really pissing me off," Missy growled.

"I'll be there shortly. My assistants will take a little longer, they're unloading your deputy right now," Preston said, disconnecting.

Dianne had watched Missy kick in the office door, ready to back her up.

Then a voice from behind her said, "Hello, Detective Flowers, I've been searching for you, and here you are. Let's take a little ride, shall we?"

She froze in her tracks, felt a blow to the back of her head, and her world went dark.

Hearing a car squeal out of the parking lot, Missy ran from the office to see her cruiser was gone, and Dianne with it. *What the hell?* She got on her radio.

"Dianne, what's going on? Where are you, over?" There was no response. She looked around, trying to figure what to do next. Cursing, she got Deputy Firestone on the radio.

"Listen up, our perp also murdered the motel manager. Now, Dianne and my cruiser are missing, and I can't raise her on the radio. I need you to call Pete and tell him he's temporarily reinstated, we need all the manpower we still have. When you get him, bring him to the motel ASAP! You copy?" she curtly said.

"Roger that, Chief. I'm on my way. Uh, Miss Flowers is asking if her mother is okay. I told her about her mother collapsing and she's kind of frantic, over," Firestone replied.

"Tell her Dianne had a panic attack but was fine when I last saw her. When I came out of the motel office, both she and my cruiser were gone," she quickly explained. Then she had a thought, "Better bring Mason and April with you when you come."

"Mason has a shotgun. You want him to bring it?" he asked hesitantly.

After a moment's thought, she said, "He can bring it, just make sure it doesn't have a round chambered round in it. And have someone bring Pete his holster and weapon from my desk, over."

"MY MOTHER'S HAD THESE panic attacks before, but why would she take Missy's car and leave without saying anything?" April wondered, as they all hurried to Firestone's car.

"I'm not sure. Either your mother drove off voluntarily, or ..." his voice trailed off.

"Or what?"

"Or it's possible that she didn't have a choice," he finished soberly as he sped towards Pete's residence. He had called him to relay Missy's directive. Pete wasn't happy about it, but he agreed and told him he'd meet them at the curb. When the deputy pulled up in front of Pete's house, he got in the passenger seat and slammed the door shut. Mason handed him his gun and holster. When Firestone told him that Dianne was missing, and Olsen and the motel manager were dead, Pete's face paled.

"Poor Jenny. Do you think this Adriel dude is responsible?" he said, shaking his head in disbelief.

"Not sure, but the Chief had better find this sick fuck fast, or she's gonna be out of a job. Jenny was our 'esteemed' Mayor's niece," Firestone pointed out.

"Missy's doing the best she can, Fred. She's just lost one of her deputies, and she's trying her best to track down the killer of three innocent people, plus her friend who's disappeared, so cut her some slack," Pete defended her.

"Adriel must have taken Dianne," Mason remarked. "It's the only thing that makes any sense. She wouldn't just up and leave Mis—er, the Chief without telling her where she was headed."

"He'll use Mom to get to us. If we don't find him soon, he'll start torturing her," April said tersely.

Firestone pulled his cruiser to a halt at the motel. The parking lot looked like a cop convention. A State police presence had arrived, along with the coroner's van and the FBI, by the looks of it.

Missy was in the middle of bringing a state highway patrolman and the G-man up to speed when they joined them. "—when I rushed out of the office, Detective Flowers was missing, along with my cruiser. I can't raise her on the radio, and she's not answering her phone or texts. That's when I called you, Agent Norbert. I believe our perp kidnapped her," Missy asserted confidently.

"Have there been any ransom demands?" Agent Norbert asked.

"No, but I feel sure he snatched her to get to this young woman and her friend," Missy replied, introducing April and Mason.

"I see. Unfortunately, Sheriff, unless your perp makes a formal ransom demand, I don't see how the Bureau can assist you at this time," Norbert declared.

"The only ransom he's going to demand is the lives of these young people here," Missy snapped angrily, pointing to the two.

"And just how would you know that, *Sheriff*?" he asked snidely.

Now there, he had her. If she told him the truth, he'd laugh in her face and have her locked up. But she couldn't see any way around it. She'd have to be creative in her description of the details.

"So, April and Mason here, ah, signed contracts with this ... asshole in Austin, Texas. They didn't agree with some hidden clauses in their contracts, and when they attempted to renege, he tried to kill them. They escaped to Boulder, where they met with April's mother, Dianne, who's a Detective with Boulder PD, and he's been hunting all three of them ever since," she replied, as concisely as possible, given the circumstances.

Norbert mulled over his response to this story. "Still, unless he demands a ransom or has broken some Federal law that I'm unaware of, it doesn't justify the Bureau's involvement in this matter. Sorry, Sheriff, I'm afraid you're on your own with this one," Norbert said, turning to leave.

"Wait. You're refusing to help a fellow officer whose life is in imminent danger? I don't fucking believe this shit!" Missy exclaimed, furious.

"Look, I'm sorry, but rules are rules. If you can give me proof this man broke federal law, I'll be glad to assist. If not, I need to go," Agent Norbert stated firmly.

Missy glared daggers at the G-man. Then her phone chimed. It was Dianne. "Dianne! Where are you? Are you okay?" Missy implored.

"I'm afraid Detective Flowers can't talk right now, she's tied up at the moment ...," an unfamiliar voice said, with a chortle.

Shit! It had to be Adriel. Frantically, Missy waved her left arm, trying to catch the Agent's attention before he could drive off.

"Where's Dianne? I want to speak to her, *now*!" she demanded.

"You're in no position to give orders, Sheriff. If you want to see your friend again, I suggest you shut your mouth and listen to me," the demon advised.

Grudgingly, Agent Norbert got out of his car and walked back toward her.

"How do I know you haven't already killed her? If I don't hear her voice, this conversation is over," Missy stated flatly, hoping her threat would pay off.

"I have no interest in her, only her duplicitous brat and the six-fingered freak. I'll allow her to speak only to confirm she's unharmed. You've wasted the FBI's time, as no ransom demand will be forthcoming," Adriel said smugly.

After a brief pause, Dianne shouted, "Missy! It-It's me, d-don't trust him! H-He's going to ki—" her speech was cut short.

"Your friend appears to be experiencing some sort of respiratory distress. I hope she's not going to die on me, that would be most distressing and problematic for us both," Adriel sighed impatiently.

"You *know* she suffers from panic attacks, you murdering bastard! If she dies, I'll hunt you to the ends of the earth!" Missy snarled.

"My, my, perhaps your friend is in the wrong profession. It must be so stressful to chase bad guys around all the time. Enough small talk. Bring the girl and the young 'Fret Master' to me. I'll give you one hour. Only you and the two miscreants. If I see any sign of law enforcement other than you, your detective friend dies. There's an abandoned cabin on the east side of the lake, near a large cove. The driveway is roughly seven miles on the right. I suggest you make haste, you now have fifty-nine minutes," the demon instructed.

"I'll need to bring a doctor with me to attend to Dianne, she needs immediate attention. If you refuse, no deal," Missy said decisively.

Adriel hesitated before agreeing. "Just be aware, any deception on your part will have tragic consequences for your friend," Adriel growled. He either ended the call or it was dropped.

"Did you get a trace on the call for its location?" The FBI agent asked Missy.

"Didn't need to. I know where he has her. It's my old Ranger cabin by the lake. You can leave now, Agent Norbert, you're no longer needed. You heard him, I bring any backup, and he'll kill her," Missy replied dismissively.

Norbert looked like he'd been slapped. Silently, he turned on his heel and strode to his car, climbed inside, and roared out of the parking lot.

"So, what's the plan, Chief?" the burly highway patrolman asked. "You can't possibly be thinking of meeting this asshole, it'd be suicide! You said this fucker's already murdered three innocent people today. If you go there without backup, you'll be signing your own death warrant!"

"I'll have backup, just not the law enforcement kind. Now if you'll excuse me, I need to make some calls," she replied curtly.

The patrolman shrugged, muttering something that sounded like "it's your funeral," before he walked back to his cruiser and sped off toward the highway.

Missy called Mia, brought her up to speed, then told her what she had in mind.

"It'll be risky, but it might work. I don't see another viable option right now. I'll get what I need and meet you at the hospital entrance in five minutes," Mia said, hanging up.

Having listened to that phone call, Pete, Mason, and April were already waiting in the backseat of Olsen's cruiser when Missy got in. She keyed her radio and instructed Deputy Firestone to stand down and return to headquarters until further notice. He didn't like it, but he obeyed.

Next, she called Scott and told him what she needed him to do.

"Roger that, Chief, will do. See ya' shortly, everyone be careful," he said, and hung up.

Driving to the hospital, she hesitated before making one last call. Jake answered on the fourth ring. She told him she loved him and to kiss the girls for her, and without further explanation, she ended the call before he could ask questions she wasn't prepared to answer.

Pulling up to the hospital entrance where Mia stood waiting, Missy asked, "April, you have your Taser, correct?"

"Yes, ma'am, or is it 'sir?' I'm a little confused about that," she replied.

"Either one," Missy replied, as Mia climbed into the front passenger seat. "When we get there, this is what I need you each to do," Missy said, and she disclosed her plan ...

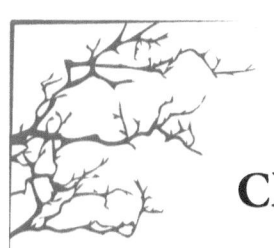

Chapter Thirty-Eight

End Game, Missy's Ranger Cabin

Regaining consciousness, Dianne found both her wrists handcuffed to the handle of an old generator. Another panic attack started the moment she awoke. Her vision swam while her head throbbed like a rotten tooth. The bastard had hit her hard. She could feel blood, warm and sticky, running down the back of her neck. Gasping from a perceived lack of oxygen, she glimpsed her surroundings and saw tall stands of pines and thick brush. The tree line ended about fifty yards from what appeared to be a large lake. A stairway led down the steep bank to a wooden pier extending out a good twenty yards from the shoreline. A small V-hulled boat was tied to a piling.

The "person" who stood in front of her was not the same one she'd met in Austin. This one looked a little older, but far more muscular than Adriel's previous avatar.

"For your sake, I hope your friend heeds my instructions," he told Dianne. "Not that it matters, I'm going to kill you all. I'll save you for last, you'll watch, up close and personal while I rape your duplicitous daughter to her death in front of you," the demon smirked, with an evil grin.

"F-Fuck—oo," Dianne wheezed, as she tried to center her mind and stop hyperventilating.

"I believe that's on the menu as well. I hope you like it in the ass, because you are going to take a beating, bitch!" Adriel snarled gleefully.

The sound of an approaching vehicle grabbed his attention. The graveled lane leading from the highway to the cabin was some four hundred yards long, winding, and cloaked by trees.

Midway down the pothole-riddled drive, out of Adriel's sight, Missy stopped to let Pete out. She released the trunk latch on the dash, and he retrieved a Remington sniper rifle from inside, chambering a round of ammunition.

Easing the trunk lid closed, Pete waved her on. Using the cover of the dense forest, he crept through the brush toward Missy's old Ranger cabin. Missy waited a minute to give him a head start, then continued driving until the cabin came into view.

"*Shit*! He has her cuffed to the fucking generator, but at least she's alive," Missy swore, braking twenty feet in front of Adriel and his prisoner. "Remember what I told you—if this plan doesn't work and things go south, you two haul ass and don't look back. No hesitation, no second guessing, you understand?" Missy told Mason and April without turning. They each said they did.

The unfamiliar man had moved closer to Dianne.

In his right hand, he held Olsen's Glock, not quite pointing it at her, but close enough to agitate Dianne. Opening their doors, the four of them stepped out of the cruiser.

"I'm unarmed, and so is the doctor. We've done as you asked, no cops, no FBI. Please allow Dr. Chandler to attend to Dianne, and then we can finish our business here," Missy said briefly. Without her gun, she felt defenseless and naked. She'd have to hope Pete could find an angle from which to take a shot, if needed.

Adriel considered her request. "Not until that redheaded bitch loses the Taser. Toss it on the ground, then the doctor may examine her, not that it will matter," the demon pointed his gun at April.

With disgust, April tossed the device on the ground at his feet. But she still had her personal stun gun and was glad she'd thought to stick it in her back pocket. To use it, however, she'd have to be in physical contact with the demon, which would prove dangerous.

Clutching her medical kit, Mia rushed to Dianne's side and kneeled to examine her. Dianne was still in the throes of the panic attack. Her face was pale, and her heart beat as fast as hummingbird wings. Spotting the blood on her neck, Mia examined Dianne's head. She found a knot the size of a golf ball just above her right ear. A one-inch gash had been opened near the center of the contusion and was bleeding, but the wound was shallow. She knew scalp wounds bled heavily, but often looked worse than they were.

"You need to slow your breathing, Dianne. Concentrate on calm breaths, that's it, inhale through the nose, exhale slowly through the mouth. I'm going to give you an injection of something to help, it should relax you and aid your breathing," Mia reassured her. Adriel watched Mia's every move, as she opened her kit and withdrew a small ampoule of Diazepam and a syringe.

After loading it, she swabbed Dianne's right arm with alcohol and injected her. The drug took effect in about a minute, and Dianne's breathing improved. Next, Mia addressed the cut on her head. Using a pair of surgical scissors, she cropped the hair around the wound as close to her scalp as possible.

"This is going to sting," she warned, swabbing the cut with a Betadine solution. Dianne winced, as Mia placed a butterfly bandage over the laceration.

"Th-Thanks, Mia, b-better now. T-Tried to warn you, he plans to kill us all," she said drowsily, trying her best to fight the drug's narcotic pull.

"Alas, she's correct. I can't afford to leave any witnesses to my existence—not that anyone would believe you. You've all taxed my patience and caused me great personal loss. No more games, the redheaded bitch will be the first to die," the demon hissed, as Dr. Brown's face transformed into the stuff of nightmares.

Mia and Missy were both stunned by the sight. Nothing could prepare them for the shock of seeing his features transform before their eyes. Dianne and the others had described it but seeing it themselves was very different. They each recoiled a step, repulsed by the creature's terrible visage and form. Missy was visibly shaken by the sight.

Mason cradled his arm around April's shoulder as she, too, shuddered at the sight of the monster facing them.

Seeing the transformation through the scope of his rifle from his position in the trees, Pete had to fight a primal urge to run away. At that moment, he was shaking so hard, he couldn't have taken a shot at the demon if his life depended on it, which it still might, before it was all over.

Adriel's guttural laugh at their reaction reached Pete's ears the same time as the steady *whop, whop, whop* sound of an approaching helicopter. *That has to be Scott*, Pete thought edgily. He searched the gaps in the tree canopy overhead for a glimpse of the chopper, but couldn't spot it through the dense foliage.

Guardedly, Adriel looked to the sky and spotted the helicopter approaching from the north over the deep blue waters of Wallowa Lake, headed straight for them.

Then, several things occurred almost at once:

With a blood-curdling yell, Mason charged the diabolical fiend.

While he was distracting the demon, Mia stealthily withdrew from her kit a syringe she'd prepared in advance, filled with a clear liquid. Making eye contact with April, she nodded.

Meanwhile, Adriel swatted Mason to the ground as he would a pesky fly, and that was April's signal to move.

Removing the hidden stun gun from her pocket, April ran toward the demonic creature. She swung her arm up to stun him—but he was faster! Grabbing her wrist, he bent it backward at an impossible angle with an audible *pop*. She dropped the stunner, screaming in agony, tumbling to the ground beside Mason, whose left arm was bleeding profusely where the monster's sharp claws had raked him.

Adriel swung his attention to the chopper, now hovering about one hundred feet above them. With a snarl, he lifted the pistol and fired six rapid shots at the craft, with a couple hitting the fuselage before Scott could pull the bird up out of pistol range.

Whipping around, Adriel pointed the gun at Missy, who had dived to the ground to grab April's discarded Taser. As she reached for it, he fired a shot into the dirt, stopping her cold.

"Time for you to die," he told her, his eyes glowing like the fires of hell. As he aimed his gun at Missy's forehead and was squeezing the trigger, something huge rammed him from behind like an out-of-control freight train.

The demon was thrown to the ground, landing with his face in the dirt, but keeping his grip on the gun. Some three hundred pounds of pissed-off mountain man landed on top of Adriel like an immense pile of bricks, knocking the wind out of the demon. Growling, he reached back, grabbed a claw-full of Gus's wild mane, and ripped it out by the roots, taking part of his scalp with it.

Gus let out a shriek of pain. Shaken, he pounded Adriel's head with his ham-sized fists—massive blows that could have killed a person—but not a demon. Adriel bent his arm with the pistol backward over his head and blindly fired point blank at the big man. With a distressed look, Gus fell next to the face-down demon, groaning and clutching his bleeding wound.

"No-o! You fucking bastard!" Missy screamed with outrage. Shaking with fury, she snatched up the Taser and squeezed the trigger.

Unfortunately, Gus chose that moment to sit up, taking the hit she'd meant for the demon. The electrodes buried themselves in Gus' back, stunning him with 50,000 volts of electricity before Missy realized what had happened. With a curse, she released the trigger. Gus's body twitched briefly like a live wire, then he lay still.

Adriel rose to his feet, pointing his gun at Gus's head, intent on ending him, when a .308 caliber bullet struck the demon like a sledgehammer, blowing him off his feet.

April caught Mia's eye and nodded. Ignoring her pain, she snatched up her discarded stun gun and leaped on top of the demon, jamming it under his chin, depressing the trigger. "Now!" she screamed at Mia, who dashed over.

Electricity coursed through Adriel's body, momentarily immobilizing him. Mia located the carotid artery in his neck and jabbed the needle in, rapidly injecting him with the entire contents of the syringe. The demon went still, his eyes glazing over as the drug took effect.

Pete came running out of the trees to join Missy and the others. "*Holy Shit*! I saw him shoot Gus, is he okay?" he asked nervously.

"He's alive, looks like the bullet went through and through, didn't hit any vitals, but he's losing a lot of blood," Mia replied grimly, examining Gus' wounds. Hastily, she dressed his wounds with gauze and tape from her med kit.

"Please don't let him die, Mia. The big guy saved my bacon," Missy said tearily. "Nice timing on your shot, bud. A millisecond later and that bastard would have blown my brains out," Missy told Pete, as her trembling hand grabbed his shoulder gratefully.

"I was shaking so damn hard, it's a miracle I didn't hit Gus."

"What the hell did you inject Adriel with, Mia?" Missy asked.

"Acetylcholine, it's a neurotransmitter. In large doses, it affects the sympathetic nervous system, causing paralysis. I gave him enough to put a small elephant down for a week," Mia said hopefully.

"Keep an eye on the fucker, if he blinks an eyelash, shoot him," Missy ordered Pete, retrieving Adriel's gun and handing it to him.

"There's no telling how long that shit will last on him, Mia. You'd better do whatever it is you *can* do, bullets alone won't stop him," Mason warned.

Mia nodded, took a deep breath, and concentrated, harnessing the mysterious energy within her, feeling it build in intensity.

Lifting Adriel's shirt, she placed her palms on either side of the paralyzed demon's chest, and a dazzling flash of brilliant blue light sparked when the two connected. Instantly, both their bodies went rigid, as the immense paranormal power coiled in her surged into the demon.

An ominous sound issued from deep within Adriel's throat, as the demon fought the intrusion of the purifying bolt of energy coursing through him. His body quivered and shook so hard Mia had difficulty keeping contact with him. Blood began to drip unnoticed from her nostrils as she focused all her energy on sending the demon back to hell.

"Exorcizmus te, omnis immunde spiritus, omni satanica potestas, in nomini et virtu te Domini nostri Jesu Christi," Mia slowly recited repeatedly, as a mantra. When they hadn't found a priest, in desperation, she'd memorized this portion of the Latin prayer of exorcism. Everyone watching was mystified, stunned by the Latin phrases coming from her.

At last, with a ghastly rending sound, Adriel's chest heaved, splitting open under Mia's hands. The malignant spirit of the demon streamed out of the wound in an amorphous cloud of ectoplasm. Hovering briefly over the body of the dead Medical Examiner, it disappeared. Adriel was gone.

Mia collapsed on the ground beside the dead doctor's body.

"*Holy Crap*! She's bleeding bad, somebody do something!" Pete exclaimed, rushing to his sister's side.

Taking out her phone, Missy hit speed dial. "Scott, I need you to land your chopper here, ASAP! We need an emergency evac to the hospital—Mia, Gus, April, Mason, and Dianne are all hurt and require medical attention STAT!" Missy hollered urgently.

"Roger, Chief, I'll set her down nearby. Is your perp still alive?" he asked, maneuvering the craft over the closest area devoid of trees and brush.

"Negative. The suspect is deceased—I believe," she replied wearily.

The sound of a rapidly approaching vehicle got the attention of everyone that was awake, as Jake's pickup slid to a halt behind Missy's cruiser. Leaping out, he ran over to the huddled group.

"What the hell! Missy ... are you alright? Is everyone okay? I heard gunshots and I—I couldn't get you on the phone and—Jesus, is that guy dead?" he stammered.

"I'll explain everything later, and yes, he's very dead. Right now, you need to help us get Mia, Gus, April, Mason, and Dianne into the chopper, they've all been injured," Missy told him.

He started to protest, then simply did as she asked. She rushed over to unlock the handcuffs on Dianne's wrists.

Still woozy from the sedative, Dianne had to be helped to her feet and half dragged to the helicopter by Missy and April, using her uninjured arm. Pete scooped up his sister and lumbered toward the chopper, while Jake and Mason struggled to get Gus up.

"Ah reckon Ah ken walk on mah own, 'tweren't mah legs that got shot," Gus said gruffly.

"Fine. Be that way," Jake snapped irritably.

He ran to the copter, instinctively ducking under the still whirling blades and approached Missy, who was about to climb inside. "I don't appreciate you leaving me hanging like you did when you called earlier. You scared the shit out of me, and I don't deserve to be treat—"

"What you 'deserve' had nothing to do with it, Jake. I saw no reason to involve you. This was police business; you're a civilian, Bud. If I had told you what was going down, you would've endangered yourself, and who would take care of our girls if something happened to both of us?" she replied. "Speaking of, where *is* Mandy?" she quickly added, moving out of the way as Gus finally made it to the chopper door.

"She's safe. When I couldn't get you to answer your phone, I went and pulled Bella out of class, she's home babysitting her now," Jake said sullenly.

Gus grunted with pain as Mason helped him into the helicopter, then climbed aboard himself.

"Jake, please just go home and stay with the kids. I'll call you later and we can talk. Right now, we've got to go. Get her in the air, Scott!" Missy barked, sliding the door closed in Jake's unhappy face.

He ducked out from under the spinning rotors, then stood to watch the craft rise into the sky and disappear over the treetops. As he walked back to his truck, the wail of approaching sirens broke the silence of the forest as two highway patrol cars and the M. E.'s van roared to a stop beside his pickup.

The cops got out, hands on weapons, looking cautiously at Jake. "Where's the body?" Doc Preston asked, getting out of the van.

"Over there, Doc," Jake pointed. "Do us all a favor and burn the motherfucker's body when you're finished with him."

"I can't make any promises. If the man had family, I expect they'll want his body returned. Where's the Chief?" Preston asked, looking around.

"Scott flew her and the others to the hospital in town. She chose to ride with them, some of them have serious injuries," Jake replied curtly.

"Sorry to hear that. I'll call her later with my report, better get to work," Preston said, and with that, he strolled over to examine the latest corpse.

Jake threw the truck in gear, turned around in the clearing, and sped off for home ...

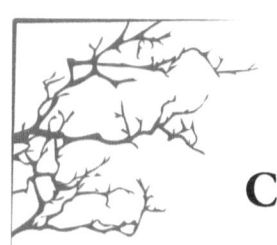

Chapter Thirty-Nine

Aftermath

S cott set the helicopter down gently on the hospital helipad. When Missy opened the door, several interns were waiting to help get the wounded out. Gus protested loudly as they helped him from the chopper and placed him on a gurney. Still unconscious, Mia was pale as a ghost, but thankfully, her bleeding had slowed. They immediately rushed her to the ER.

Missy didn't know if that was a good sign or not, but at least Mia was breathing. Dianne was waking up as the drug Mia had given her wore off. Mason was the last one out of the helicopter. An intern placed him in a wheelchair and rolled him toward the emergency room. Missy, Pete, and April followed them inside. A nurse took April back to triage to x-ray her swollen wrist.

A lady at the front desk told Missy and Pete to have a seat in the waiting room, saying she'd have a doctor speak with them as soon as they were done with their evaluations of everyone. They took seats in the hard plastic chairs, waiting impatiently for a report. An hour passed with no news.

April emerged from triage with her wrist heavily bandaged. "The doc said it's only sprained," she said, taking a seat next to Pete. "I hope your sister is okay, we owe her our lives. What she did—could do was nothing short of miraculous," April quietly said to Pete.

"Unfortunately, miracles can have a heavy price. One of these times, she won't be so lucky, and when that happens, she'll ..." Pete stopped, as emotions choked off the rest of his thought.

"Mia's stronger than she looks, bud, she'll get through this," Missy said, trying to put his mind at ease.

Then Mason entered the waiting room, his left arm bandaged from his shoulder to his wrist. Leaping up, April rushed over to hug him carefully.

"Are you alright?" she asked anxiously.

"Yeah, more stitches than I wanted to count, but I'll live," he replied.

Finally, hours later, Dr. Ava Brinkman appeared from the triage doors and walked over to talk to them all. "We did an MRI on Dr. Chandler. She appears to have suffered an ischemic episode, a minor stroke," she said soberly.

Pete felt his blood turn to ice at her words. "Is—is she gonna be okay?" he asked hopefully.

"We'll need more tests to be positive, and frankly, only time will tell. We've put her in a medically induced coma to reduce the swelling in her brain and give her the best chance of a full recovery. We won't know how extensive the damage is until she's awake. Right now, I'm hopeful. The bleeding has stopped on its own. How? I have no clue. It's possible her 'gift' is responsible. She may be healing herself; she's done it before," Ava said optimistically.

"What about Dianne and Gus?" Missy asked.

"Detective Flowers suffered a mild concussion and a lacerated scalp. I've stitched it, she'll be discharged shortly. She needs to take it easy for a day or so, but she'll be fine.

"Mr. Farley was extremely lucky, the bullet barely missed his aortic artery; a millimeter closer, and he wouldn't have made it. I had to re-attach part of his scalp, it'll be sore as hell for a few days. With some bed rest and the antibiotics I'm prescribing, he'll be back on his feet in a week or so," Ava explained. The triage doors opened again, and Dianne emerged, looking alert and spotting her daughter and friends.

April ran over and wrapped her arms around her mother, holding her tight. "I love you, Mama, I'm so sorry that bastard hurt you," April cried, hugging her even tighter.

"I love you too, hon. Hopefully, Mia sent his sorry ass back to hell, or wherever he came from. Speaking of, how is Mia?" Dianne asked, realizing she wasn't there with them.

Ava told her what had happened, to Dianne's dismay. "She saved all our lives, none of us would have survived if not for her and her special gift," Dianne said somberly.

"Don't forget about Gus," Missy said. "If he hadn't tackled the demon when he did, the bastard would have killed me, and April wouldn't have been able to stun him, giving Mia the chance to finish him. I'd say, overall, we're extremely fortunate none of us was killed," Missy added. All involved agreed wholeheartedly with that.

"I'm grateful Gus was camped nearby and heard the gunshot. It was brave of him to rush an armed demon empty-handed like he did," Mason observed.

"You were brave, too, Ace. As I recall, you charged Adriel first," April pointed out.

"Yeah, but sadly, with less effective results," he replied, glancing at his bandaged arm.

"Listen, I need to get back in the trenches," Ava said with a warm smile. "I expect Mia's lab work will be back soon. Pete, I'll call you if there's any change in her condition, but until then, there's really nothing any of you can do here but sit around and fret. Go home, get some rest, you can visit your friend Gus later. He'll be in the ICU for observation for at least one night." She turned and left the waiting room.

"Home ... that's where I want to go," Dianne said wistfully.. "It's beautiful here, but it's not home. I need some time to rethink my career ... and my life," she sighed deeply.

"I can always use a good deputy," Missy offered, smiled.

April looked at Mason, taking his left hand. "What do you say, Ace? Think you could live in Boulder, maybe start another band?" she asked.

"Boulder, you bet. Not so sure about another band. If I'm gonna be a father soon, I can't support a family on musicians' wages, I'll need to find an actual job," he said, slightly gloomy at the thought.

"Hey! What happened to your extra finger? It's gone!" April exclaimed, pointing at his hand.

Sure enough, the extra digit had disappeared. He'd never even noticed it was gone.

"*Holy Houdini*! That's just too weird," Pete exclaimed, examining the hand.

"It must have happened when Adriel left that doctor's body. Maybe a parting shot on his way back to hell. Well, I guess that settles it, my dreams of becoming a rock star are over, for sure," Mason said, with a sigh.

"Never give up on your dreams, Ace. The timing just wasn't right," April noted. "Losing that finger may have been for the best. Adriel's price for stardom was too high to pay. One thing we've learned, if you have to cheat to get it, it really isn't worth it," she said wisely.

"I'll call Scott and arrange for your trip back to Boulder," Missy said. "How soon do you need to leave?"

"As soon as possible, I guess. We'll have to retrieve our luggage from your trailer," Dianne replied wearily.

Missy nodded and called Scott. "He can have the plane ready in an hour, if that's fast enough," Missy told her, ending the call.

"That will be great," Dianne replied.

"Okay, let's go grab your belongings. Pete, I'll drop you off at your place on the w—*Damn it*! I forgot my cruiser is still parked at the old cabin," Missy said, frowning.

"No worries, I'll call and get us a ride. They can drop me off at my house, then take you to out to pick up your cruiser," Pete volunteered, pulling out his phone.

The lady driver arrived five minutes later. She drove them to Pete's house, where he paused before opening the car door.

"It was really nice to meet you two, and to see you again, Dianne. Don't be strangers, come back and visit sometime. Maybe Mason can show me some new chords next time around. Deal?" He extended his hand to Mason in the back seat.

"As long as there's no contract involved," Mason agreed, shaking hands.

Pete was about to leave, but he stopped, leaned over, and gave April a quick hug before getting out. Missy gave the driver directions to her old cabin. They arrived a few minutes later. Their M. E. had finished and taken the doctor's body away. The highway patrol had either lost interest or had another call. Everyone was gone when they pulled to a stop behind Missy's cruiser.

She thanked the driver, and they all piled out to watch the friendly lady leave, walked over, and got into her cruiser. Missy drove up to the highway and on to her house only about a mile down the highway. As she pulled into the driveway, she saw Jake's pickup was missing.

With an uneasy feeling, she opened the car door and stepped out. "Go grab your belongings and put them in the trunk, I need to check on something, be right back." Missy said tensely.

Dianne, April, and Mason went to the trailer to get the ladies' belongings, while Missy walked to the house. She approached the front door and tried the handle, which was locked. Digging out her key, she opened it and stepped inside. The house was silent except for the ticking of the clock in the kitchen. She realized Jinx wasn't even sprawled in his favorite spot on the couch.

"Hello? Is anybody here?" she called out. Quickly, she searched the house, finding it empty. An uneasy feeling in her stomach grew as she spotted a small envelope on the kitchen table propped up against the saltshaker. She knew it was from Jake.

She picked it up and almost opened it; then she shoved it in her back pocket, deciding that whatever he'd said, it could wait. Whatever Jake's frame of mind was, she knew he would never harm the kids. As she turned to leave their home, Missy felt a giant hand squeezing her heart. Tears stung her eyes as she stepped back outside, locking the door once more.

Dianne was closing the trunk as Missy approached the cruiser. She saw the tears in Missy's eyes. "Is everything alright?" she asked, concerned.

"Oh, everything's fine, I think my husband may have left me, and took the kids and the cat, but other than that, it's ..." her voice faltered, as she got in the car.

"I'm so sorry, Missy. I—I had no idea things were that—I mean, *Shit*!" Dianne said, flustered.

"I've known for a while this could be coming. It's just that I always thought I'd be the one doing the leaving. Ironic, right?" Missy revealed bitterly.

None of them knew how to reply to that, so they stayed quiet. She turned the cruiser around and, in an uncomfortable silence, drove them to the Enterprise airport.

When they arrived, Scott was speaking to one of the ground crew. He waved and came over to take the ladies' bags as they got out of the car.

"She's gassed up and ready to fly, we should get moving. There's a front coming, and I'd like to take advantage of the tail wind," he said with his usual roguish grin.

"Well, I guess this is goodbye, for now, Missy. Please thank Mia for us all when you see her. We can never repay her and all of you for saving our lives. I hope you and Jake can work things out. Please call and let me know if there's anything I can do to help," Dianne said tearfully, giving her friend a bear hug.

"I could still use a good deputy, if you change your mind," Missy murmured in her ear, releasing her from their tearful embrace.

"I'll keep that in mind. I'm not sure what'll happen when we get back, but I'll talk to you soon," Dianne replied with a tearful smile.

Scott loaded their luggage on the plane. Mindful of their injuries, Missy carefully hugged April and Mason, watching while they boarded the aircraft. As the engine roared to life, Dianne waved through the cabin window. Missy waved back as the plane began its taxi onto the runway.

When the plane took off, she trudged back to her cruiser, got in, and sat staring out the windshield at the distant snow-capped mountains. She took a deep breath, let it out, and retrieved the crumpled envelope from her back pocket. Gathering her courage, she tore it open, and began to read ...

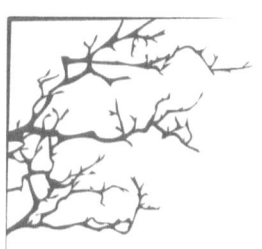

Chapter Forty

Epilogue - Nine Months Later

April and Mason Rivers had gotten married and were now the proud parents of a baby girl they named Misty Dawn. Mason managed a local music store in Boulder, and to help make ends meet, in his free time he taught guitar. April was a part-time vocal coach at the University of Colorado. She'd re-enrolled and began taking night classes at home, working toward a Bachelor of Music Arts degree. They were happy together and content with their lives together and their new roles as parents.

SOON AFTER HER RETURN to Boulder, Dianne had dealt with her panic attacks. She'd found an excellent psychologist and had identified and addressed most of the psychological triggers causing them. After much thought and consideration, she had retired from the Boulder PD and accepted Missy's offer to work as her deputy.

She took a sizeable pay cut, but on the upside, she didn't have to deal with the stress and headaches that went with being a large city cop. She sold her Boulder home, giving April and Mason enough money for a down payment on a small house in the suburbs, and placing some in a trust fund for her granddaughter Misty.

The move had been poignant, as she would not be there to help care for Misty, and it tore at

her heart to be so far away from her family. April assured her they would visit as often as they could, but that was little consolation. To stay in touch in the meantime, she and April used FaceTime often, so Dianne could see how

Misty Dawn was changing. Until she could find a suitable home to purchase in Joseph, she was renting a small house.

FOLLOWING LONG MONTHS spent recovering from the minor stroke that had paralyzed the right side of her face, Dr. Mia Chandler eventually made a full recovery. She'd worked with a speech therapist for six months before she could once more speak normally. As soon as she could communicate well, she'd gone back to work at the hospital. Fortunately, the stroke had not affected her motor skills, so her work as a skilled surgeon continued.

MISSY'S FEAR OF OPENING Jake's letter only confirmed her love for him and concern for the state of their marriage. Instead of the "Dear Jane" letter she'd feared, Jake's note only told her that to let off steam, he had taken the girls to the "R and R" for burgers and ice cream.

They'd started seeing a marriage counselor the very next week and were now reaping the therapy's benefits. Among other things, tests had revealed that Missy had been suffering from postpartum depression after Mandy's birth. Jake had his own issues to deal with—deeply rooted insecurity from growing up without a mother and an inferiority complex he hadn't known he had. Relieved to have her parents on good terms again, Belinda's grades improved, and she was a contented girl.

GUS FARLEY HAD RECEIVED a certificate declaring him an Honorary Deputy Sheriff from Missy, on behalf of herself and the department. He had healed well from his wounds and was soon fishing in Wallowa Lake and enjoying Missy's blueberry pancakes again.

PETE HAD BEEN REINSTATED and had recently been promoted to Sargeant. To celebrate, he'd invited everyone over for a barbecue at his house.

Mia arrived early to help by preparing some side dishes. Missy and Jake cautiously accepted, knowing Pete's penchant for grilling up peculiar "mystery meats." Dianne arrived with some of her scrumptious fruit salad for dessert. Knowing Gus's voracious appetite, she'd doubled the recipe. Scott brought along some chips and dips. Gus was last to arrive, his hands and his stomach empty.

Learning that Gus had saved Missy's life, Jake's attitude toward him improved significantly, with help from his therapy. When Gus appeared at Pete's, Jake smiled and handed him his favorite, a can of grape soda ice cold from the fridge. They all sat down around Pete's expanded kitchen table, as their host brought in a large, steaming plate of meat and some sausage links from the grill out front.

"Mmm, that smells delicious, Pete," Missy said. "What are we having today? Chicken? Or something more exotic?" She started questioning him tactfully.

"The main meat is a surprise," Pete said with an evil grin. Gus was already salivating at the delicious aroma.

Missy rolled her eyes. "Enough with the cloak and dagger, bud, just tell us what it is," she encouraged.

"You'll have to taste it, first. But before we eat, we need a blessing. Mia, will you do the honors?" Pete volunteered her.

Mia narrowed her eyes at him for putting her on the spot, but she complied with a brief, but thoughtful prayer of thanks for their family and good friends. Everyone murmured amen at the end.

Gus didn't waste a moment afterwards, piling his plate high with everything.

Missy took a tentative bite of Pete's surprise, nodding her approval. "It's delicious, now will you please tell me what it is I'm eating?" she asked, between bites.

"It's alligator meat, flown in special for the occasion," he announced, mischievously.

For a moment, Missy looked as if she was about to spit her mouthful into her napkin, but she decided she wouldn't give him the satisfaction of getting her goat. "Okay, you've had your fun, now give it up, what is it really?" Tired of his game, she demanded to know.

"They're rattlesnake fillets, courtesy of our esteemed Mayor, Johnny Six-Fingers. Pretty tasty, right?" he said, taking another big bite.

"And just where did Johnny get them?" she asked suspiciously.

"Said he found 'em on the highway, they were already dead. It's not like I *killed* them," Pete replied defensively.

Everyone but Gus stopped chewing, staring down at their plates.

"You mean to tell me ... we're eating ... fucking roadkill?" Now, she did spit her bite into her napkin, revolted. Excusing himself, Jake rushed to the bathroom.

"Mama said a bad word," Belinda giggled, getting a smile from Gus.

"Ah reckon Ah've say'd worser," he told her, taking the last serving of fruit salad.

"Johnny said it was fresh, for crying out loud. If you don't like it, don't eat it," Pete grumbled, frowning.

"If'n ya' ain't a-gonna eat thet las' piece, Ah'll take it, don' seem ra'ht ta let 'er go ta waste," Gus offered, eyeing the remaining morsel hungrily. No one objected, so he eagerly speared the remaining piece onto his plate, to the others' surprise.

Mia began a mass exodus. "Well, I hate to eat and run, but my shift at the hospital starts in fifteen minutes. Thanks for the company and the, um, 'food,' Pete. Bye all, love you," Mia announced, pushing back from the table. Finding her purse, she rushed out the front door.

Jake returned to his seat in time to watch Gus scarf down the last of the tasty fruit salad. "Say, look at the time, we should go as well. It's a school night, and I know a young lady who needs to finish her homework before she goes to bed," he said, receiving a frown from Belinda.

"Ya' know, I've got a charter flight to California tonight, better go prep the plane. That was some good barbecue for roadkill, Pete." Scott clapped him on the shoulder good-naturedly, standing to leave.

"The trouble with you guys is that you have no sense of adventure. Who wants to eat the same boring stuff all the time?" Pete grumbled, sulking.

"Next time you get the urge to barbecue something, *I'll* pick the meat. No more surprises, bud," Missy declared emphatically, with a shake of her head. Giving her deputy a quick hug, she gathered Mandy from her playpen, they said their goodbyes, and left.

The only guests left at the table with Pete were Dianne and Gus.

"Ah reckon Ah bes' be a-moseyin' on, too. Them wuz good vittles, Pete, ma'hty good. See ya' later, gator," Gus said, with a wink. Lifting his large frame out of his chair, he shook Pete's hand and said goodbye to Dianne. On his way out the front door, he released a huge fart, making them laugh.

"I believe that was his way of giving his compliments to the chef," Dianne observed, with a chuckle.

"Well, I guess it's better than nothing. At least there aren't any leftovers to deal with when he's around. The dude will eat *anything*," Pete said, shaking his head.

"Well, guess I'll see you in the morning. Thank you for the dinner, it was an ... 'interesting' evening," Dianne said, giving him a brief, awkward hug.

He walked her to her car and opened the door for her, with a smile. "Thanks for coming, drive careful, goodnight," he said. The smile eased from his face as he watched her drive away.

ONCE THEY WERE BACK at home, Missy gave Mandy a bath, then got her ready for bed. Belinda did her homework and was in bed by 10:00 p.m.

With the girls down for the night, Missy grabbed her jacket and joined Jake in the backyard. It was a chilly, clear evening, and she shivered as she sat down beside him, snuggling up against him for warmth. They stared up at the star-filled sky overhead, marveling at how the starlight they were observing had been traveling for billions of years and saddened by the knowledge that most of those distant galaxies no longer existed.

"Beautiful, isn't it," Missy sighed, gazing up at the heavens.

"Yes, and so are you," he replied, leaning over to kiss her gently.

"My, aren't we frisky?" She shivered and broke the kiss.

"Let's go inside and you can see for yourself," he said suggestively, nuzzling her ear.

Something large and furry leaped from the dark onto his lap, disrupting their romantic interlude. Missy chuckled as Jake eased Jinx up from his aching balls, shoving him off on the ground. The big cat gave him an indignant glare before turning and disappearing into the night.

Together, the two Andersons stood, arm-in-arm, and walked back inside, closing the door on another chapter of their mundane, but rarely boring, lives in the scenic Wallowa Mountains ...

A Final Message From the Author:

I HOPE YOU ENJOYED "The Fret Master," the Fourth of my *Wallowa Lake Thrillers*. The previous three novels in this series, also available in eBook and Print on Demand formats, include: "Angel of Oregon," "The Wood Sprite," and "The Wailing," the first of the eight.

After reading one of my books, your personal review of it—good or bad—could alter how I write the next one. Be assured your comments will be read and listened to. Reviews are the only way any author has to gauge what readers think of his writing. Reviews don't have to be long or fancy, just what you liked or disliked about the novel.

Please send your review to my personal email:
bullwinkledobie@gmail.com

Don't miss out!

Visit the website below and you can sign up to receive emails whenever James Dobie publishes a new book. There's no charge and no obligation.

https://books2read.com/r/B-A-TZLV-RZCCG

BOOKS 2 READ

Connecting independent readers to independent writers.

About the Author

James Dobie published his first thriller/mystery novel in 2022, although by then he had already written six more. He has now finished drafts of all eight standalone sequels in his Wallowa Lake Thrillers series, only half of which have been published. *The Fret Master*, is James' fourth *Wallowa Lake Thriller*, a standalone sequel to the first three, *The Wailing*, *The Wood Sprite*, and *Angel of Oregon*.

A native Texan, James lives in Austin, where he creates gripping new psychological/paranormal novels at a fast pace and enjoys playing his guitar when he isn't writing. He stays busy scheming ever more dire ways to hurl his characters, at unexpected moments, into shocking danger. Many of his heroes are spirited, defiantly different females caught up in situations rife with danger.

Readers' reviews of James' novels are greatly appreciated and may be sent to his email, .

Read more at www.jamesdobiethrillers.com.

www.ingramcontent.com/pod-product-compliance
Lightning Source LLC
Chambersburg PA
CBHW031157020726
47499CB00002B/396